I0762034

# HOUSE OF WOLVES

CASEY L. BOND

hunt the shadow
guard the flame

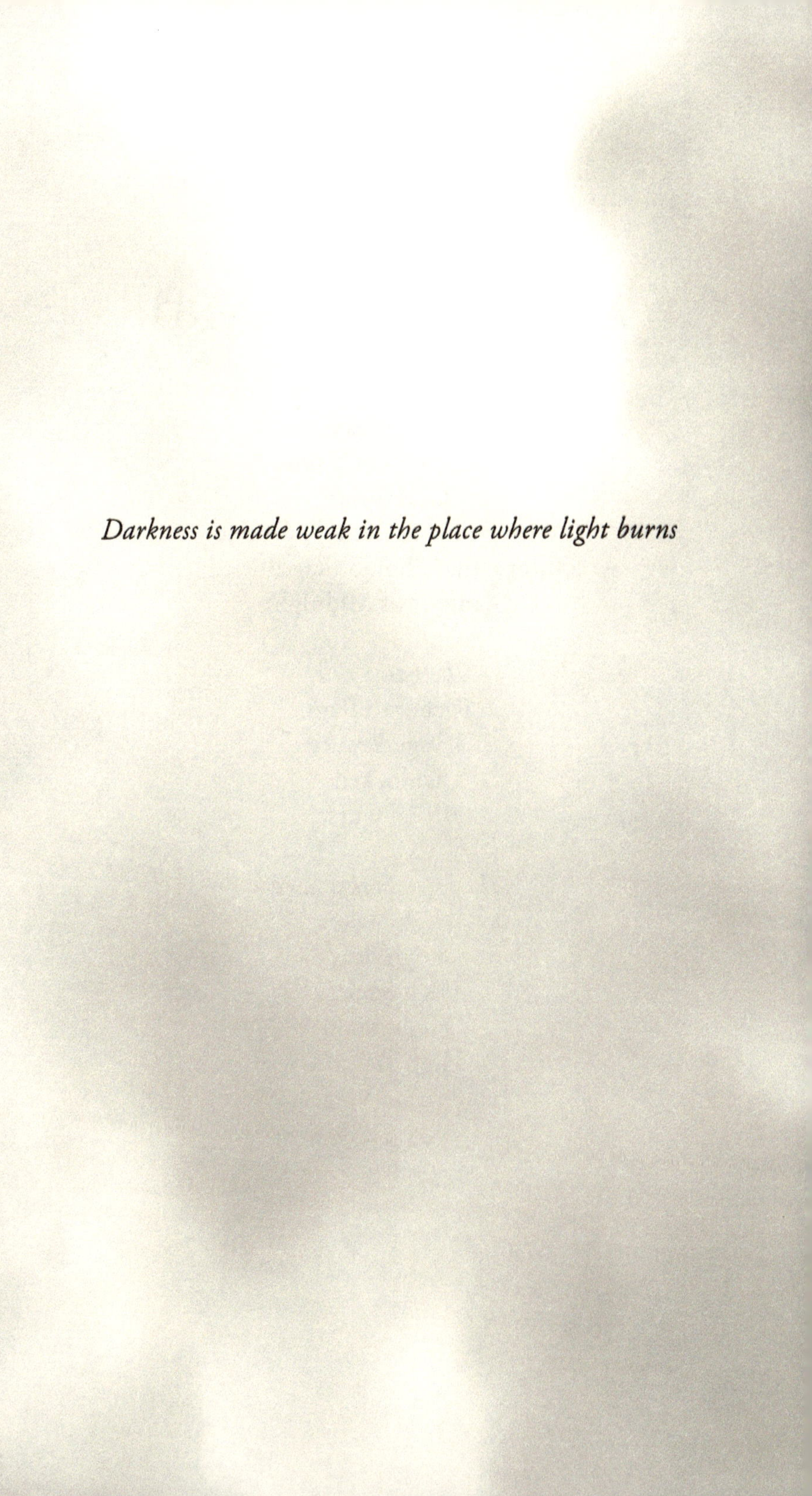

*Darkness is made weak in the place where light burns*

# ALSO BY CASEY L. BOND

House of Eclipses
When Wishes Bleed
The Omen of Stones
Gravebriar
With Shield and Ink and Bone
Things That Should Stay Buried
Glamour of Midnight

*The Fairy Tales*
Riches to Rags
Savage Beauty
Unlocked
Brutal Curse

*The High Stakes Saga*
High Stakes
High Seas
High Society
High Noon
High Treason

*The Harvest Saga*
Reap
Resist
Reclaim

*The Keeper of Crows Duology*
Keeper of Crows
Keeper of Souls

*The Frenzy Series*
Frenzy
Frantic
Frequency
Friction
Fraud
Forever Frenzy

House of Wolves
Copyright 2021 Casey L. Bond

ISBN: 978-1-0879-1453-4



Book Cover, Trailer, and Interior Formatting designed by **The Illustrated Author Design Services**

Edited by **The Girl with the Red Pen**

Dunes & Wolves Character Scene by **Art by Steffani / Steffani Christensen**

Close-up Character Portrait by **@Nessiarts**

Once upon a time, there lived a grandmother who loved her grandchildren more than any words could describe. When they were little, she would tell them stories before they fell asleep to nap. She would weave beautiful tales of whimsy, and whisper tales of warning, which children often preferred, their minds intrigued by a danger from which she would keep them safe.

One of her granddaughters loved the story she told of a she-wolf that lurked in the woods, waiting to devour children who strayed too far from home, or too close to her den. With fur as dark as night, eyes of fire, and teeth dripping with blood, she painted a vivid and fearsome picture of this wolf. Perhaps she thought to warn her granddaughter of becoming the girl who strayed too far from home, but her granddaughter didn't care anything about the silly girl or the story's warning.

She preferred to imagine herself the wolf.

That granddaughter was me. And this book is dedicated to Betty Setliff, my grandmother – a brilliant woman who weaved stories so vividly, I believed they were real. And who encouraged me to pen stories of my own. This is the story of my she-wolf.

# 1

Like a strong perfume too liberally applied, Zarina's bitterness wafted into my rooms before her. I'd never seen my eldest sister look anything but harsh and poised, a façade she'd honed to perfection and one I had always envied. But as she approached, that careful mask chipped away and by the time she drew near, my stony sister was nearly molten.

The slapping soles of her sandals against the stone floor was the only sound in the House of the Sun, which otherwise lay eerily empty. All the servants had abandoned their positions to watch Noor claim her rightful place atop her mother's temple.

Zarina's pleated gold dress had been tailored to match Father's ceremonial kilt. Her hair was sleek, tied at the nape of her neck. Around it lay an ornate red collar necklace that draped to the swells of her breasts, its colors alternating in shades of dried and fresh blood.

The affronted look she wore made me wonder if she felt as if she'd been stabbed in the back, or that Noor had taken a dagger straight to her heart.

Either way, I didn't have time for her anger. I was leaving before Noor could command someone to make me stay. Someone… or some mutt. I refused to be locked in any room again. I'd be gone before they knew it, and this time I wouldn't leave a trail for Beron to scent.

I ignored my oldest sister and continued to rummage through my things, plucking out what I needed and what I might be able to sell. I piled some gold jewelry on the bed, then turned to gather more from my chest of drawers, which had been built specifically to hold my garish baubles. The stand on top for my aureole lay empty. I'd abandoned it and my past in Lumina, and though it was frightening changing my trajectory, it was the right decision.

I'd trusted my youngest sister – who frankly should never have given me the opportunity to do so – and stood with her against our tyrannical father. Finally, though not fearlessly.

Now, he lay dead. I wondered if the priests had dragged him into the sand where every inch of him would rot. Where he would never reach the hereafter and the desert and scavengers would share his corpse until nothing but bone remained. I smiled. Eventually, the sand would claim even them.

"You traitor," Zarina gritted as she stopped an arm's length away, the ragged edges of her tone pausing my hands. She clenched her fists at her sides.

I narrowed my eyes. Did she come there to fight? Slowly, carefully, I informed her, "I am no such thing."

"Noor is *not* the heir of Sol," she said so resolutely, I wondered if she might actually believe it.

"You saw her. You know that she is." From atop the temple, Sol's light poured from Noor. There was no doubt that she had descended directly from the sun goddess. None of the prior Atens' skin, or very soul, had ever glowed, yet Noor had a golden, sunny corona outlining her shape long after she killed our father. I could see it from afar as I slipped away.

That aura emerged as she came into her powers, sometimes leaking into her eyes, making them glow warm and golden. But Zarina hadn't journeyed to the Dusk Lands, or Lumina with us. She hadn't seen the progression of Noor becoming exactly what she'd been born for.

However, Zarina had seen some things long before Noor transformed. She was endowed with a trove of sun diamonds, so hot only she could bear to wear them – again, because of her lineage. Because of her mother: Sol.

Zarina had been groomed by our father since birth to trust only him. Perhaps she doubted her own mind because of his poisonous teachings. He'd promised her more times than I could count that she would succeed him as Aten. He told her Sol would listen when he recommended his eldest daughter. That he would pass me and Noor over.

He lied.

He knew who and what Noor was. He always had.

And like every other lie he spat, his false promises led to hurt and pain. This time they were Zarina's, and she was unaccustomed to such feelings. He hadn't coddled her, but he had made it clear who she must become if he was to recommend her as the next Aten. As a result she'd fought, stretched, and crammed herself to fit the mold he described. She cut away the pieces of herself he found invaluable to earn his favor, his praise, his occasional manipulative kindness.

Hadn't all of us, his daughters, done the same a thousand times over?

Zarina pointed a trembling, accusatory finger at me. "Father told me what she, and you, have done. I cannot allow it. I cannot let her become Aten and steal this kingdom away."

I tilted my head to the side. "This kingdom was never yours." It was never even Father's, truth be told. He only held it in trust for a time until Noor came of age and her body matured enough to contain the power her mother bestowed upon her. "Father was a liar. A divider. I'm not sure what he told you, but you can be assured it was untrue."

She seemed to weigh my words, standing quiet for a long moment. "He said that in Lumina, you not only convinced Lumos to help you, but that the two of you made a darker bargain. One with Anubis." She hissed the 's' of his name, drawing out the sound to a whisper. She took a step closer as if we were confiding in one another. So close, she bent to place her mouth at my ear. "He said you released him from his earthen prison. It was *he* on the temple steps, wasn't it? You can tell me the truth, Citali. You don't have to fear her, or Anubis."

My bones went hollow. I pushed her, her shoulder giving way. "Don't speak his name in this House. Don't even speak it in this kingdom!"

No one uttered the name of the banished god of the dead without consequences. When the Sculptor sealed him into the fire in the middle of the earth to punish him for trying to kill Lumos and Sol, even uttering his name was forbidden. His history served as a warning to us all; to be on guard against any dark magic that might escape the depths and spew like lava onto the land, so that if anyone dared dabble, they knew what fate and consequences lay ahead of them.

Anyone who dealt with the banished god invited a curse on herself and her family.

"The dark one can make *anything* appear real with his magic. He could make Noor *look* like Sol poured through her. He spins illusions like twisting storms of sand," Zarina scoffed.

She must stop talking about him. I took a steadying breath, hoping she might see reason, and if she refused, at least to shift the conversation into safer territory. "Father was desperate to cling to power, Zarina, and he would have cut off his own limbs to keep Noor from ascending to the role of Aten. He lied to you in a final attempt to turn you against everything he hated – Sol *and* Noor."

She threw a hand in the direction of the temple. "Explain the jackal on the temple roof, then."

This conversation was becoming exasperating. "That was no jackal, sister. It was a wolf. The Wolven is the Luminan equivalent of our great Sphinx."

She shook her head. "Father told me that in the darkness of the moon's kingdom, you sought another way to usurp him. He warned you would come back changed. It is obvious the dark one has twisted your mind."

"Have you forgotten how Father twisted you to shield *himself*? Or how he tried to run away, leaving you standing atop the temple alone?" I spat. "Father was a coward until his dying breath. A liar. A murderer. You *know* that. How can you possibly trust his word after all that's happened?"

Zarina held a calculating gleam in her eye. "What did Noor do in Lumina to provoke such a strange change in her when we had no indication of it here in Helios – *her home* – land of the sun and Sol herself?"

"Noor did nothing but come of age," I explained tiredly. "And there were signs long before, if you'll stop to think. Think of the sun diamonds, Zarina."

My sister merely shook her head and gave a mirthless laugh. She raked her hair back, holding the strands tighter to her scalp. She did that when she wasn't listening.

"The Sphinx even *told* Father that Sol would reveal her heir when Noor came of age. Zarina, the goddess was waiting for Noor. She did nothing in Lumina but attempt to find the crown, but instead found she didn't need it because of who she is. She is Sol's heir."

Zarina's elegant frame straightened. "I once thought you would stand with me no matter what."

"I'm not standing against you now, but I know the truth and won't stand against Sol. Not anymore."

Her eyes caught on the small pile amassed on my bed. "You're leaving? If Noor is so wonderful and judicious, why do you feel the need to flee your home?"

"I have no reason to stay."

A slow, vicious smile spread over her lips. My fists curled at the sight, as she looked just like Father in that moment when he was about to do something malicious. "I know where you're going. Father told me of *your* great secret, too."

As if he'd sliced me from the grave, her words cut across my chest, directly over my heart. No… No more. Never again would someone threaten him.

"I should pay him a visit. Introduce myself," she threatened with a saccharine sweet smile.

"I'll kill you if you go near him," I quietly vowed.

She slid her hand into her pocket. Instinctively, I took a step back. When she withdrew her hand, she brought something with it: an obsidian dagger with some sort of engraving along its edge. I had no time to decipher it before she vaulted into action.

Zarina bared her teeth. "You say you will kill me, Citali? What if I kill you first?" With those words she lunged, slashing at my side.

I sucked in my stomach and jumped back, narrowly missing her blade. "You're insane!"

"You have been corrupted." She carefully punctuated each word with another jab, stab, slash. "Anubis has his claws in you. Father warned me that you and Noor had set him free. I can feel him writhing within you. I smell his burn on your skin."

Wild but fluid, she cut the air between us. Fever turned her eyes to glass, her skin ashen.

"The only one possessed is you – by the dark one and our wretched father!" I blocked a slice with my forearm, sucking in a breath when her blade zipped through my skin. A guttural cry clawed from my throat. "You cut me!"

I didn't have time to evaluate the wound, because Zarina kept jabbing, stabbing, and slicing. Positioning myself behind a small table along the wall, I slid it out between us. Zarina gave a push and it teetered, then toppled, crashing onto the floor and breaking apart. I grabbed a spindly leg and used it to fend her off, bludgeoning as much as I could.

I bloodied her knuckles, cracked her brow, and split the tender skin there so that blood pooled in her eye. She blinked and wiped furiously to stanch the flow and clear her vision as I prepared for her next attack… or to see if she was finished and her anger quenched.

Lunging again, Zarina's feet slipped over the blood she'd spilled from me; now hers mixed with it. "This is madness, Zarina!"

She answered with a roar and another slash, and her knife caught in the wood of my table leg. She ripped it out, splinters and dust falling to the bloody floor.

I took a risk and snatched her wrist, stopping the dagger. She tugged and pulled to free herself, gritting her teeth and growling. Her sandals slipped as she tried to use her weight to her advantage.

"Where did you get this? What sort of blade is this, Zarina?"

She snapped her teeth at me, then slipped in the sticky blood and lost her footing, sliding to the stone. I kept hold of her to stop her blade and keep her close, all the while striking her with the wooden table leg. She covered her head and face, screaming for me to stop. Her forehead was bruising, her lip swelling and bleeding. With one blow to her chest, the red beads layered around her neck, now soaked with my blood, broke and scattered over the floor, some landing in the crimson smears and puddles underfoot.

"Stop, Citali. Please!" she cried, panting, her teeth coated in blood. Her free hand braced in the air between us to block my next strike

I pointed the spindly table leg at her throat. "Threaten him again and I will end you. I took it from Father for years. I will not take it from you!" I roared. I brushed errant strands of hair from my eyes. "I will never endure such threats again and will eliminate the source of them without hesitation. This is your *only* warning. Blade or no blade, I will best you. I swear..." I squeezed her wrist for good measure. "I'll kill you and drag you into the dunes and lay you to rot beside him."

Suddenly, she relaxed. Her breathing slowed and she looked spent. "Please. I'll leave you alone. I'll leave the palace," she vowed.

"I don't care what you do or where you go now. Just stay far, far away from me and mine. And if I free you and you try to cut me again, I won't stop the next time I raise this stick. I'll beat you into the stone itself," I panted, my chest heaving as I gasped for breath.

I couldn't let on, but my vision was swimming. I'd lost a lot of blood. It continued to splatter onto the floor at our feet, constant as a fountain.

How could an arm bleed so much?

I released her wrist, jabbing a finger toward the door. "Get out," I gritted.

She nodded. Her feet slipped as she shakily stood. I raised my arm to see how bad the cut was when I felt a sharp prick on my left side. Zarina's fist was against my skin. No... not her fist. The handle of her dagger was pressed against my stomach. The blade had sunken in as far as it could. A wave of warmth crashed over me.

Zarina's face was contorted in rage when she pushed the knife in further, then twisted the blade with hateful glee.

I weakly pushed her away as hot saliva flooded my mouth. A cold sweat beaded on my brow and my knees shook uncontrollably. "What did you do?"

She jerked the dagger out of my body, sending a white-hot, searing pain through my stomach.

I couldn't hiss.

Was afraid to move.

Could barely breathe.

Blood suddenly oozed from the wound. At first, it didn't seem that bad. Just a little seeped from the wound. *It must not be deep*, I thought.

I was wrong.

A moment later, it flowed, pouring like the river running south from Helios into Lumina. If I thought my arm bled a lot, it was nothing compared to this wound.

Zarina's dark eyes were now wide and tears welled in the corners. Her chest heaved and her hands trembled, her fist opening to reveal the glass-like dagger as it clattered to the floor. She pressed blood-coated fingers to her mouth as if surprised by her actions. The obsidian turned to gold from blade tip to pommel when my blood swelled over it. Along the blade's edge, the sun goddess's name was now inscribed.

"Sol claims your blade. Touch it now, Zarina. Please," I gritted. "See what punishment the goddess will mete out. She saw… *everything*."

"Sol isn't here," she asserted, her voice quivering. "This is a House, not her temple."

"Sol is everywhere, as is Lumos. And beyond the sun and moon gods, the Sculptor watches."

I kept my breaths shallow, but deep hatred welled in my chest, mixed with disbelief and fear, and most potently of all, agony. I'd come so close to leaving this place and finally going to him, finally able to be what he needed me to be.

I looked at my eldest sister, who watched to see if I would lash out or keel over. Despite my weakening voice and the fact that every word felt like she'd stabbed me all over again, I promised her one thing. "Until my last breath, in this life or in the hereafter, I will not rest…until you are dead, body and spirit."

Zarina hesitated only for a moment. She did not apologize or cry for help as she sloppily fled the room, a trail of sticky, crimson footprints evidence of her retreat.

I didn't know what to do.

There wasn't much I *could* do now. My hands shook and my arms felt like leaden weights, but my legs felt like the spindly table legs, too weak and frail to hold me up any longer.

A cold sweat beaded on my forehead and spread down my neck and arms.

I fell to my knees with a million thoughts racing through my scattered mind. I thought of him. How to save myself. How I couldn't bear to leave this world without seeing him one more time. I wasn't ready to die. Didn't want to leave him.

*Noor…*

Noor would help me, but she wasn't there.

Frantic, desperate thoughts rushed through my mind. There was only *one* who might hear me, and with the commotion outside, I wasn't sure even *his* senses would be able to cut through to find me.

Still, I had to try.

I pressed my wound tighter, hot crimson bubbling around my fingers despite my efforts, then took a deep breath and screamed his name as loud as I could. "Beron!"

My voice tore at my wound.

Sliding onto my side, I braced my weight on my elbow, holding myself up as long as I could. Then my elbow buckled, slipping outward. My temple cracked against the stones.

Suddenly he was standing at the doorway. *He heard me.*

"Citali?" his worried voice cried.

A slow blink.

He was on his knees, cradling my head. My hair was wet and cold now, but his hands were hot and strong.

I didn't feel strong anymore. Feeling bled from my fingers and feet, leaching from my arms and legs like water evaporating from a sponge.

"Look at me. Stay with me," he begged. "Caelum!" he growled.

My vision swam, focusing on his sharp cheekbones and jaw. I thought of Beron's usual smirk. His teasing laugh. Even his frustrated growls. The way he chased me and told me I was a nuisance, a spoiled, ridiculous, petulant girl.

He hated me. But he was here now. He came when I needed him most.

Tears pricked at my eyes. I couldn't hold them, and they slipped onto the floor and his skin and mixed with my blood. I began to tremble, growing colder until my toes and fingers seemed frozen and the frost spread up my arms and legs.

I wouldn't survive this but needed Noor to know… so she could protect my greatest secret, my greatest weakness. My greatest love. My lips and mouth were as dry as the desert. They were numb and didn't feel like mine, but tingled when I whispered, "Tell Noor…"

He stopped and brought his face closer. "I'm here, Citali. Noor is on the way."

A tear fell from my eyes, pushing down my cheeks. We both knew there was nothing to do for me now. "Tell Noor to take care of him," I pushed out weakly, wincing when a sharp stab of pain rushed through my wound.

"*You* can tell her. Caelum heard me. She'll be here in a second."

"Tell her to take care of him," I slurred.

A loud buzzing filled my ears, but the pain began to release its grip on me.

"Who?"

A shake.

"Who, Citali? Who should Noor take care of? Talk to me."

A vision came to mind of a tiny hand curled around my finger, with dark hair and skin that matched mine, so, so soft. Perfect little bowed lips. Toddling steps… he had grown so tall since the last time I'd seen him. "He's so smart," I tried to say, but my words came out garbled and unclear.

He called me Cit-i. If things had been as they should, he would have called me mother.

"My son," I finally managed. My voice sounded distant, drowned in a deep, dark sea that threatened to pull me under with each rhythmic pull.

Strong fingers stiffened on the back of my neck. "You have a son?"

"Beron?" I breathed, finally focusing on him. We locked eyes. "Protect him."

"I will. I swear it. But you have to stay with me so you can protect him, too. Who did this, Citali?"

"Zarina..."

Could he hear me through the roar?

Could he see me through the bright white light that appeared as nothing more than a glimmer, but grew and blossomed in its intensity as it approached? Did he feel her heat? It thawed my frozen skin.

Sol was here for me. My spirit cried. I'd done such wretched things to her daughter, but still, she was here.

And then suddenly, Sol retreated.

Did Beron see the darkness stretch over her face, stripping me of her warmth before it slithered into my veins, cold as ice?

A terrible howl resonated through me, rattling my bones with enough force that the sand itself trembled. But it couldn't extinguish the fire Sol had kindled within me.

# 2

I woke in a strange room to unsettling darkness and chilled air, wondering whether I'd dreamed the altercation with Zarina, and the goddess had never come to carry me to the hereafter. Or that Sol had come, only to abandon me in the end. Was that how it felt to be found so horribly unacceptable?

My mouth was uncomfortably dry. I pushed up onto my elbows and they sank into a plush mattress. Taking in the familiar stone walls, pale wood furnishings, and the smell of sand and home, I knew I was in the House of the Sun. But this was not my room. Lumos – the moon god – was in Helios. His pale, cool light slid in from the balcony and leaked across the floor.

That meant Noor *had* become Aten. That much I hadn't dreamt.

I pressed a hand to my side, surprised when I found no bandage. No wound. There was no pain or soreness beneath the skin. I gingerly sat up, throwing the blankets off and sliding my legs so that they dangled off the bedside for a moment, still trying to wrack my memories for something true. My feet hit the floor and Lumos's silvery light kissed my skin with a sigh.

I tugged at the fabric of the dress I wore. The gauzy gown was clean, but it wasn't mine and I couldn't remember putting it on, or even coming in here. I felt the back of my neck where I'd dreamed Beron's hands had been. Where he'd tensed when I told him of my son.

In my dream, my hands, hair, body, and clothes were soaked with blood.

It flowed like the great river and then claimed the blade that had cut me down – Sol herself had turned it to gold.

Shaking my head, I tried to push the image away. It was only a dream, after all. A dream that felt so real I couldn't help but call it back to me.

There was no blood on or even near me. The stones beneath the bed and beyond were pristine. If I had moved or been moved, there would have been a bloody trail at the very least, yet not a single dark stain marred the porous stone. Blood would not have been so easily washed away.

I padded to the balcony where silver light shimmered over the eddying river water and stars glittered in every inch of dark sky. From here, I couldn't see the temple at all.

"Citali?" a male voice called out from inside.

I turned as Kiran, the priest who had favored my sister before she was Aten, stepped out of the room and joined me. A pale curtain fluttered in the cool night breeze, gently striking his leg as he assessed me. "Are you well?"

"Why wouldn't I be?" I croaked. He wore a simple white kilt, his olive chest left bare, but not sculpted like Caelum or Beron's.

His hands reached out for me. "Aten Noor said you shouldn't be out of bed." I hissed as his fingers hovered near my shoulder. Kiran swallowed. "I'll find her and tell her you're awake."

My brows drew in. "Why would the Aten concern herself with such trivial matters?"

His lips parted. He licked them, struggling to search for the right words. Why was he being so benevolent all of a sudden? Why had she asked *him*, of all people, to watch over me as I slept? And why did she not want me out of bed?

His gentleness made my heart roar.

"Listen, priest—" I started, no longer caring who he served.

Just then, Beron strode past him and the night itself seemed to ripple around him like heat on the horizon. It recognized and celebrated its Wolven. "Would you please let the Aten know that Citali has awoken, Kiran?" he asked Noor's little friend, flashing a kind smile. The meek, placid fool inclined his head respectfully, then ran along to do as he was told. "Thank you," Beron added, raising his voice so it reached Kiran's ear.

The Wolven stood with me on the balcony for several long moments. His hair was the color of night and his skin the pale silver of Lumos himself. I once thought he looked like he could only ever belong in Lumina, but in that moment, he looked like he belonged here in Helios now that Lumos had returned to bring soothing, cool night to our land. The thought enraged me. I was certain the Luminans did not feel that Helioans belonged in their precious pale jewel of a kingdom.

"How do you feel?"

His gruff tone calmed me. Beron wasn't one to handle me gently or try to ease me into something. He was blunt, which was how I preferred to speak and be spoken to. Despite the fact I had come to hate him before Noor claimed her rightful place as Aten, I knew he was honest. He wouldn't spread sugar where salt was needed.

"Confused," I admitted, standing straighter and crossing my arms over my chest against the night's chill.

"Not weak?" he asked. His legs were slightly parted, as if he would chase me if I gave him a reason to – and I knew he would. That was all he'd done during the latter part of my forced stay in Lumina, I thought with a grimace.

"Not at all." Any residual feelings of weakness fled when my father lay still and dead on the temple's highest platform. "Have I been ill?" It was the only thing that truly made sense. Fevers could cause one to become so lost in their own mind, they sometimes couldn't find the way back to themselves.

"Ill?" he asked, the dark slashes of his brows slanted. "You have no memory of what happened?"

I had fleeting memories, but they made no sense. Would Beron make sense of them for me? I decided to test my dreams and measure them against reality.

"With Zarina?" I rasped. I needed water.

He gave a single nod, watching me carefully. Too carefully.

My heart suddenly felt too large and uncomfortable in my chest.

"Did you think you'd dreamt it?" he asked quietly.

I pressed a hand to the place where she'd wounded me, holding it there and remembering the sharpness, the vitality leaking through my fingers, the hope draining away, and the feeling of utter helplessness… until Beron heard my scream and came to my aid.

Where was the wound she'd dealt?

"How long have I been sleeping?" It must have been weeks, maybe months for me to be completely healed. I hadn't inspected my skin but didn't feel the raised sliver of a scar on my flesh. Still, if I'd lain for so long, why didn't I feel as weak as a newborn lamb? How could I feel like nothing had happened? Did Sol heal me somehow? Had Noor? "Beron?" I pressed.

His lips parted as he glided a hand through his hair.

Just then, my younger sister stepped into the moonlight, her dark hand wrapped in Caelum's pale one. "Kiran said you had woken," Noor led.

"I'm sure Beron sent word to Caelum before Kiran even left my sight," I gritted.

She didn't deny it, but instead nodded. Caelum watched me carefully, as one might watch a vital fire as it began to sputter and flicker.

I wasn't sure how, but Beron and Caelum could speak to one another in their minds. Caelum was the Lumin, vessel of the moon god himself and ruler of Lumina. If Noor had simply been chosen to be the next Aten, she and Caelum would be equals. But nothing about Noor was ever simple. And the fact that she was the only daughter of a living god elevated her above all other statuses, even that of Caelum.

I wasn't sure he knew it, or even cared. He was smitten with her and she with him.

I studied their cuffs, given as a promise of eternal love. His cool, moonlit cuff glowed on her bicep, and her cuff of fire and gold burned on his.

Noor looked me over. "Citali…"

"I'd like a moment alone with you," I interrupted. Our conversation might not be held in confidence, but I would prefer to speak only to her.

She extricated her hand and nodded to Caelum, who waited until Beron peeled himself off the balcony. I wasn't sure what that was all about. He hated me, and the feeling was certainly mutual.

Except that if everything I thought I'd dreamed was true as he insinuated, he came when I yelled for him. Beron saved me.

That was a bitter pill to swallow. I knew better than most that it required less effort to hate an enemy than to forgive them.

Noor peered into the room to be sure we were alone. "They're gone." She came to stand beside me. I wondered if she was nervous, considering our last encounter on a balcony…

"If Beron managed to hear my cry from the temple, through the roaring crowd, then he's still listening and feeding Caelum every word I say. I might as well have let them stay," I groused.

"Do you want me to call them back?" she asked, a teasing smile playing at the corner of her lip.

"Zarina said that Father told her we freed Anubis. She said we were corrupted."

Her lips parted and for a second, she considered it. "We would know if he'd been freed."

She was right. If Anubis was present on the earth, everyone would know. But then, how did I explain the feeling deep inside my gut that said he had been liberated and was coming for me? "Noor –"

My sister waited for me to find the words.

"We didn't release the dark one, but I think someone else did."

Her head tilted to the side. "What makes you think that?"

"I can feel it," I told her, pressing a hand to my stomach where the unease lay.

Noor swallowed. "Let's hope you're wrong."

"I'm not," I told her. "It's like I can feel him or sense him somehow. I couldn't before Zarina…"

"Could it be that you feel him because you brushed death's hand?" she asked.

I shook my head. "I don't think so…"

The two of us were quiet for a long moment. Noor seemed to wade through my admission and all it might imply. I had no doubt that she wondered whether what I said could even be true, but it was. I had no proof to offer her, only a feeling, but it was as strong as the bond I could see stretching between her and Caelum.

"Did you save me?" I asked.

Noor opened her mouth, then shut it. Finally, she answered. "You don't remember what happened?"

"I know Zarina came to my room. I know she stabbed me, and I know... I know I was going to die. I yelled for Beron. I remember him being there and then, I saw this blinding white light. I thought it was Sol, but was it you? Did you heal me?"

Tears welled in her eyes, but she didn't let them fall. A skill she'd honed from years of abuse. A skill she still hadn't extinguished. "I couldn't," she finally admitted. "So, rather than let you die, Beron did."

I tilted my head to the side. "The Wolven can heal? You mean he's good for something *other* than tracking women who sneak out of their rooms?"

Noor did not smile. Her reticence made my heart race again. What did this mean? "Citali, do you remember *how* he did it?" she carefully asked, watching for my reaction.

"I don't remember very much, but for what it's worth, I'm glad he did."

"You might not be glad of it for long," she hinted.

I froze. "Why?"

She looked to the stone at our feet, then to the sky where Lumos's bright face shone above us. "Lumos spoke to him and allowed him to heal you, but the only way for him to do that was to bite you." She paused, meeting my eyes. "His bite will make you like him."

I blinked, processing what she'd just said. "Exactly how will I become like him?" My breath thinned and became ragged. My blood and bones heated.

Noor's eyes turned from brown to incandescent gold. She put her hands out to calm me. "Citali, don't lose control of your emotions. It might cause you to shift."

"Shift?" I tried to steady my breaths and slow my heart to maintain control like she said. "You can't be serious. Are you telling me I'm going to turn into a *beast*?"

"Beron is no beast," she sharply reminded. "He saved your life when it would have been far easier to let you die."

*Perhaps he should have*, I thought bitterly. What did this mean for my son? Was I a danger to him now? Would I live out the rest of my life and never safely fit into his?

Noor leaned on the rail, resting her weight on her forearms, then gave me a sideways glance. "Not going to try to toss me over, are you?"

So, that ugly memory had surfaced for her, too.

"Tempting," I tried to joke. "But I think I've had enough excitement for… Wait. How long has it been since she stabbed me?"

"A few hours."

My mouth gaped and my lashes fluttered in surprise. "Hours?"

She nodded. "I cleaned your skin and hair and changed your gown, then Beron carried you into one of our unused rooms so you could rest. He stayed outside your door in case you shifted unexpectedly, but insisted Kiran watch you. He wanted Sol's priest there in case you needed her when you awakened."

My eyes widened. "He knew the exact moment when I woke…"

She nodded. "He sent Kiran in first because he didn't want to startle you. He wasn't sure what you would recall."

I gnawed at the corner of my mouth, wondering where *he'd* bitten me. How hard did he have to drive the canines into my flesh for this transformative healing to take place?

"Citali…" Noor drew my name out softly. "You have a son?"

I did. My greatest secret and proudest achievement, yet the one I was forbidden to reveal. I cleared my parched throat. "Do you remember when I was confined to my rooms for a few months…?" A heavy silence settled between us. One full of moments that now slid into place and made sense when they didn't quite fit before.

"We were told you were ill," she admitted quietly.

I shook my head, my chest feeling lighter after telling my deepest secret. Something in me screamed that it was okay to trust Noor with this, with him. When I lay dying, I knew if I asked her to care for my son, to raise him and protect him, she would.

"He's two," I told her. "He lives with his father's parents."

She stared at the river flowing by as if it didn't have a care in the world. "Where is his father?"

"Dead."

"Courtesy of our father?" she asked, though she knew the answer.

"Yes." Father had him killed.

She turned to face me. "Who was he?"

"A guard." Disappointment shone on her face. "I loved him," I defended. "We loved each other. I don't sleep with all the guards I speak to, though I know that's what you think. I can see it on your face when you see me with them. The ones I speak to regularly knew Merik and respected him. Those closest to him know of our son because he told them before he died. He was so proud. Merik's friends watch out for our child and vowed to keep him safe. Even against Father, even unto their deaths, they pledged to try to keep him from harm."

"I remember Merik." Noor picked at her cuticles. "He was kind."

I sighed. He was kinder than any other man I'd met. And funny. His smile could melt gold faster than Noor's heated hands.

More pieces of the puzzle of our lives slid into place.

"I wish things had been different," she said.

I wished the same. I wished our father hadn't killed the man I loved. I wished he hadn't sent my son away or threatened him every time he wanted to manipulate me. I wished so many things had been different, but they weren't, so there was no point lamenting the fact. We couldn't change the past, but the future changed every second; every decision shifted the sandy path beneath our feet.

Noor looked to Lumos. “Father used him against you, didn’t he?” I nodded, and she caught the movement. “Is that why you tried to kill me?”

It was hard to admit. I wasn’t proud of it. Shame flooded my face, heating it until it burned. “He said he would kill my son if I didn’t kill you in Lumina. He didn’t want you to survive the trip or return to Helios. Now I know why.”

“And now I know why taking those steps to the top of the temple by my side were the most difficult you had walked.”

Noor had already forgiven me. Empathy shone from her expression as bright, sunny rays. But I wasn’t sure I could forgive myself, or if I even wanted to. I didn’t deserve forgiveness because at the end of the day, part of me regretted not carrying out Father’s orders. Not because I wanted Noor dead. I didn’t.

I hated myself for not being strong enough to do it for my son. I was never strong enough to protect my child from Father. And I knew when I took that step up the temple side and faced him with Noor at my side, I’d damned my own child. The look Father gave me was one of promise. He would keep his word because I had not kept mine.

I failed. He wouldn’t.

He would take the one joy in my life and crush it.

I pressed my eyes closed, wishing the roaring in my ears would stop.

A delicate hand landed on my shoulder. “He’s gone now. He can’t hurt you or your son.”

“Father told Zarina about him.”

Noor stiffened. “Let me send Beron and a few trusted guardsmen to collect him. Your son can stay here, under guard.”

“It was here where she struck. The House of the Sun isn’t safe.”

Noor shook her head. "You were alone. The House was empty. She was emboldened because she found a rare opportunity, one we will not make the mistake of affording her again. Let me send Beron. He will not let anyone hurt your child, Citali. I wouldn't suggest him for the task if I didn't completely trust him."

"I want to go with him."

She went still again. "Citali, Beron said that until you shift for the first time, you're vulnerable. Until you can control yourself, you might put *others* in danger, even though you wouldn't mean to."

My heart raced. "I am no danger to my son. I love him more than anything in this world. I would never hurt him."

"Just… let Beron and his pack bring your child and his grandparents here safely. Please." Her eyes pleaded for me to agree.

While everything inside me screamed to run from this place, straight to my baby, I wanted to protect him – even if it meant protecting him from me.

"I'll allow it on two conditions: one is that they leave now before I change my mind, and two, once they deliver them safely here, they'll hunt Zarina down. But it is *I* who will end her life. I promised her that when she took mine."

I expected Noor to argue, perhaps to balk at the thought of more bloodshed in her House, but she simply straightened her back and called for Beron. We walked from the balcony into the room and waited for the Wolven to arrive.

More than a head taller than me, he strode into the room with purpose. "I want you to go and get my son and his grandparents. Bring them here and appoint only those you trust with your own life to keep them safe while they are in this House. They are not to be left unguarded for even a second."

A simple blink. A slight bow. "Thank you for trusting me with this task," he replied.

"If *I* am a threat to him and the Sphinx refuses to intervene, I want the next strongest creature to ensure his safety," I told him. "For now, that's you." I couldn't help the venom that slid from my mouth. If he thought I would be a docile pup, he was wrong and needed to know it now.

When Beron's toothy, daring grin flared, I felt like clawing it from his face. But I needed him. I needed him not to hate me for a little while longer. Until I shifted, all that mattered was my son and keeping him safe, once again. Then he could return to his customary role of aggravator.

Beron was a threat in Wolven form. Even Father recognized that atop Sol's temple. He'd tried to skitter down the steps like a beetle in hot sunlight chased the comfort of a sliver of shadow, and found gnashing teeth set in a powerful jaw, ready to devour him. I smiled at the memory of him turning from Beron and running.

As would my cowardly sister. I had underestimated Zarina, but that was a mistake I would never repeat. If she would kill me, she wouldn't hesitate to harm my son.

Beron craned his neck to the side, the vertebrae popping in succession. "Tell me where to find him."

"His name is Reyan. He is two, with dark hair and brown eyes several shades lighter than mine." I told Beron where to find Merik's parents' house, then asked him to see them to safety and have someone he trusted watch their home until we could bring their belongings to the House of the Sun.

He listened intently as I described their dwelling and how to find it, then nodded to Noor before striding away. He passed his brother in the doorway. "I'll be back soon," he promised, speaking louder as if assuring me and not only his Lumin and brother.

My heart lodged in my throat as I waited…for what, I did not know. The minutes lengthened and stretched and wrapped tightly around my ribs until even the act of breathing became difficult.

Beron's Wolven howl echoed through the night, followed by three different howls echoing his from various directions.

"How many more of *them* are there?" I asked Noor.

"A small number that Beron commands, all chosen by Lumos, though none are endowed with Beron's...unique gifts." Her glowing, golden eyes cut to me. "I suppose in a way you are also Lumos-chosen, Citali."

"Not exactly," Caelum interjected, clearing his throat as he joined Noor once again. "No offense, Citali, but Lumos did not choose you for this fate. He gave Beron the choice – to save you, or not. A choice that didn't come without consequences for both of you."

I narrowed my eyes. Noor had explained my consequence: turning into one of the beasts and becoming a danger to everything and everyone I loved. But what consequence did Beron bear?

Did my transition into one of his guards require him to give up a piece of himself or his power? Now that I was one of his kind, would he expect me to join him and the others? Did he think he could order me about?

I didn't feel different, other than the miraculous healing of my mortal wound.

Noor gave Caelum a pointed look. "Beron will explain everything later."

I didn't like the warning in her tone, or the wary gaze Caelum aimed in my direction.

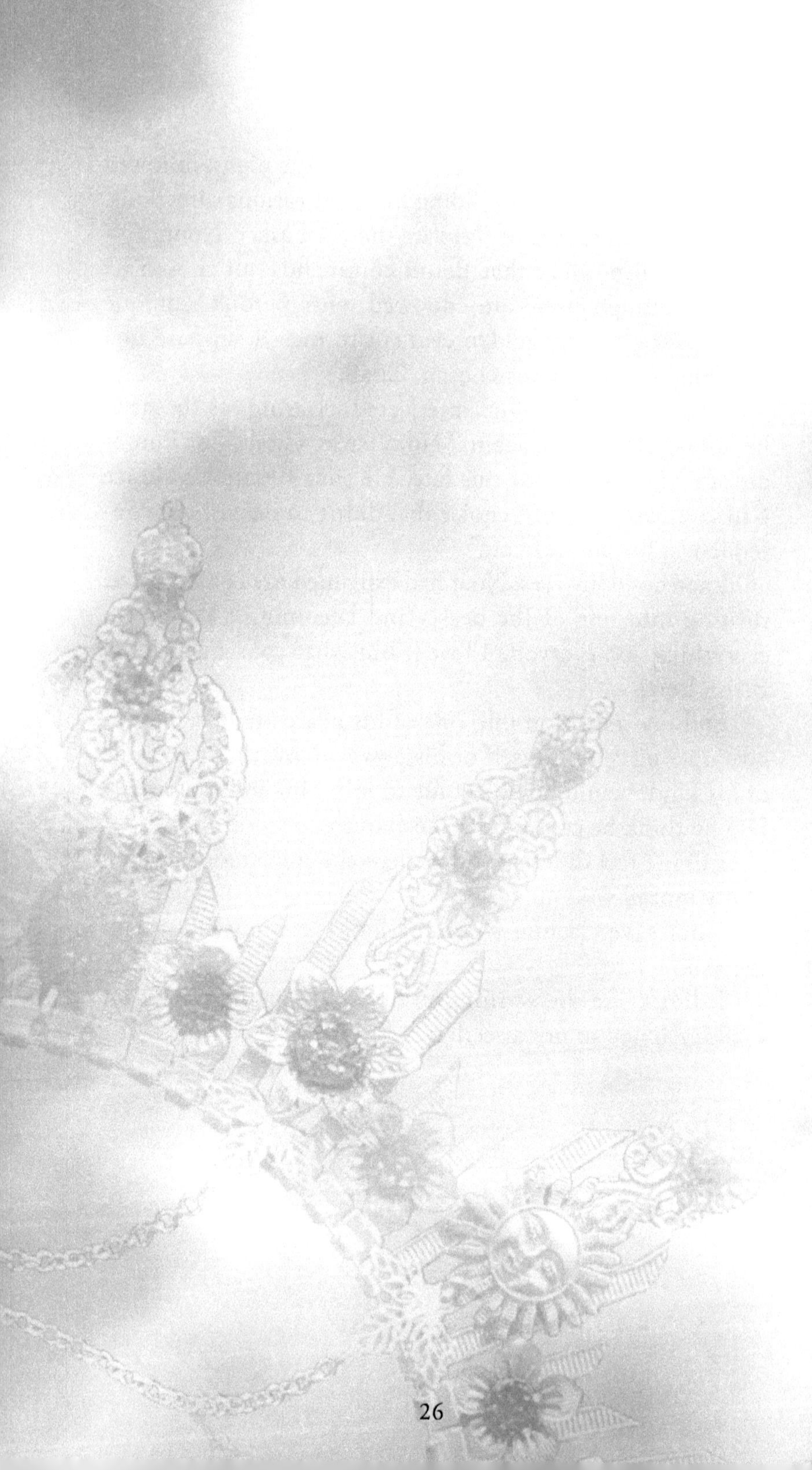

# 3

I strode from the room, finding my bearings and setting off toward my rooms. Caelum caught up with me as I approached the familiar arched doorway. "Citali, perhaps you should avoid your rooms for now..."

Ignoring him, I pushed ahead, stopping short only a few steps into my bedroom.

A hush fell over the space.

The stone had been scrubbed, but the blood left a ridiculously large stain on the floor. The door to my armoire was still open, as were the drawers of my jewel chest. The pile of gold and few garments I'd piled on the bed lay undisturbed.

"You were going to leave last night," the Lumin said from the doorway. I didn't dignify his observation with an answer. "Are you still contemplating it?"

I squared my shoulders, walked to the bed, and ran a hand over the silken blanket. If Zarina hadn't come into my rooms, I'd already be gone.

*Perhaps the safest place for Reyan and me is where no one knows to look for us.*

Zarina could come back here. This was her home. She knew every nook and cranny in which to hide, every passage meant for servants – not Atenas, as we'd been told a thousand times – and every place weapons were stored. "I don't feel safe here," I rasped. "I don't think he'll be safe here, either."

He clasped his hands behind his head and let out a long breath.

"What do *you* think, Caelum?"

He let out a frustrated sigh. "I don't know."

"Why didn't Noor follow you?"

His pretty blue eyes met mine. It would've been so easy to love him if I thought he could reciprocate, but Caelum had only ever seen Noor. I suspected they met the night we went to spy on him but had no proof. If I had been the first to catch his eye, would it have mattered? Her fiery cuff burned brighter on his bicep now as if answering me, announcing he was Noor's and always had been.

"I wanted to speak to you alone," he finally answered.

"Why?" I asked. "To distract me from the agony tearing through my chest? Sorry, Caelum. Even *you* aren't powerful enough to do that."

"I have a request." He released the back of his head and let his arms fall to his sides.

"What's that?"

"Tell one of us if you decide to leave. Tell Noor if you'd like, or tell me. I'd like to think we became friends in the Dusk Lands...." He didn't mention how I'd thoroughly shredded that friendship in Lumina. "Or you could confide in Beron," he offered separately.

"Why should I?" It wasn't an unreasonable request, and I knew his motive was as pure as his heart, but this was their chance to wash their hands of me. I'd done nothing but cause them grief. I'd tried to lure him away at every opportunity, kissed him when I knew he wasn't seeking it and Noor would see. I hurt them both, time and again.

"Because we care about you," he said softly.

I scoffed, "I tried to kill Noor, Caelum. I tried to do to her what Zarina managed to do to me. How could either of you possibly care about what happens to me now?"

"You are letting those things overshadow the agreement you and Noor forged on the steps of Sol's temple. That covenant, the step you took forward, erased all past grievances."

"In her mind, maybe," I said softly. *But it did not erase my guilty conscience.*

"And in mine," he added. "If you hadn't faced off against your father with her, I'd feel differently."

"Would it be you I'd have to fight in order to flee this place if I choose to run away? I wouldn't fare any better against you, I'm afraid. I was never taught to wield weapons."

"Your father was too afraid of you to sharpen you further," he said. He walked a little further into the room, avoiding the stain of my blood. He braced a hip against my bed. "Beron is nearly there…" He stared through me, his eyes unfocused.

"Can you see what he sees?" I whispered.

He shook his head. "I can hear his thoughts, but I can't see through his eyes."

"Is he upset? Does he sense danger?" My heart beat erratically, thrumming in my ears.

"No, he's being cautious."

I bit my thumbnail to keep quiet and planted my feet to keep me rooted in one place.

"He's shifted into human form… He stole some clothes from a line and slipped into the house. It's dark. Quiet. He thinks they're sleeping."

I steepled my hands over my mouth and pleaded to Sol and Lumos, begging them to let my son be alive and unharmed. A howl tore through the night. I rushed to the balcony. Caelum followed. "What is it?" he asked.

"Did you not hear the howl?"

He shook his head.

Another came from the same direction, but this was a deeper tone. There were two wolves to the west. Caelum's eyes unfocused as he spoke into Beron's mind. "They're chasing Zarina. They caught her scent from her rooms here and are pursuing her. She's running from them."

I clutched my chest, tears welling. Grateful but still terrified.

Until I saw Reyan and held him in my arms, I would not rest.

Caelum raked fingers through his dark hair. "Your son is well. Beron is holding him as his grandparents gather what they need. They're all safe."

"Why doesn't that seem true?" I asked him.

His gaze focused on me shrewdly. "He'll be far safer here with us than he is at their home, vulnerable as they are."

"I want to take him somewhere else, someplace Zarina does not know."

There was a feeling in my gut, something visceral and urgent, pleading with me to take Reyan and run away. Maybe it was the fear that someone else would try to part us again, perhaps permanently this time. Maybe the feeling came from Sol. Perhaps it came from Lumos. Wherever it originated, I could not ignore the instinct rearing in the pit of my stomach.

A rush of emotion swept over me. Urgency. Relief. Worry. They churned together in a plume of smoke that choked my lungs. I gripped the balcony's rail, barely registering Caelum's concerned voice. "Citali? What's the matter?"

"I'm not sure," I exhaled, pressing a shaking fist against my chest.

The sensation was strange. I was experiencing so many emotions, but the feelings weren't mine. Caelum stood nearby, his hands ready to steady me if needed. "Beron is hurrying back with them."

"Is he alone?"

Caelum shook his head. "Two are with him, remaining in their wolf forms to guard him. The others are still stalking Zarina."

"She'll evade them," I predicted.

"Why would you think that?"

My eyes snapped to his. "I need to speak to Noor."

"Why? What is it?"

"I just remembered something Zarina said." I breathlessly pushed past him, skirting the blood stain on the floor and rushing into the hallway, shouting for my sister. I'd been so focused on surviving and making sure Reyan was safe, I'd forgotten.

She appeared in front of me, startling me. "What's the matter?"

I leaned in with trembling hands. "Zarina doesn't believe you are Sol's daughter. Father told her that you made a pact with… the dark one."

Her lips parted in surprise. "Me?"

"She thinks he made an illusion to cast you as Sol's heir. That you, with his help, stole the position of Aten from her."

She fumed silently for a long moment. "He simply will not die," she finally whispered. "Not even when I block the breath from his lungs and toss him into the sand does his vile nature wither away. No, he corrupted unto his dying minute and his malice survived even death. It lives and lingers in Zarina now."

"She believes him," I told Noor. "It was righteous anger blazing in her eyes when she fatally wounded me." That anger hadn't lasted long. My blood washed over it, dousing the flames. She let the dagger clatter to the floor with a shocked expression, then cried out.

"Where is the knife?" I asked. "Where is the dagger she used on me?"

Noor's eyes flicked to Caelum. "We never found it. We assumed she took it with her."

She didn't. And if she had returned for it before Beron reached me, she would have finished me off.

"Are they almost here?" I asked him.

He searched for his brother's thoughts and nodded. "Very close."

"I need a moment to change," I told them.

"Do you need help?" Noor asked.

I shook my head. "I can manage."

She and Caelum stepped into the hall, lingering just outside. As they spoke in hushed tones and whispered words, I couldn't stop the flare of jealousy at their intimacy. I rummaged for something better than the gown I wore, but all my fingers found were similar gowns, fit for an Atena.

I wasn't that person anymore. I outgrew that title when I stepped forward with Noor to face our father.

A thundercloud gray, fitted linen dress appeared between grander garments. I tugged it on, wondering again where Zarina's golden dagger had disappeared. It used to lay on the floor, my blood washed over it. It couldn't have moved on its own unless in the commotion, Beron had sent it skittering over the floor. I checked under the bed, but the space was clear. Muttering a curse, I promised myself that when I did find the blade, I would carry it on my hip until it stung Zarina's flesh as it had mine.

Would her beloved Anubis spare her from death's cruel kiss the way Beron had?

"Citali?" Noor said from just outside the doorway. "They're here."

I rushed from the room and into the hall. "Where?" I asked breathlessly, hope blossoming in my chest.

"Downstairs," she replied, running at my side to the staircase. At the bottom stood Beron with my son cradled in his arms.

His round, caramel eyes lit when he saw me. "Cit-li?"

Tears crushed from my eyes. With great difficulty, I blinked through them and rushed to my son. "Reyan." I held my arms out and he reached for me. I brought him to me and held on tight, one arm holding his weight, the other pressing his head to my shoulder, feeling his soft, dark hair. He smelled so sweet and innocent. Though he'd grown from an infant into a toddling child, he still smelled how I remembered.

Padren and Malia stood a few steps behind the Wolven, winded but grateful. Merik's parents were wonderful. They had taken our son in without a second thought and took care of his every need. I sent gold to them through Merik's friends and made sure they wanted for nothing. It was the least I could do for what they'd done for me – for us – and for the price they paid because Merik had dared to love me.

Tears welled in Malia's eyes. She nodded to me once, her lips pursed tightly. Padren hugged her to his side.

Reyan pulled away and his hands found my cheeks. He pushed them together and excitedly said my name again. "Cit-li!"

I smiled. "Rey-an."

He grinned.

I looked into his eyes and told him the truth that fluttered in my heart. "I missed you, Reyan. I missed you so much."

I'd missed him every moment we were kept apart. Every second. Every step he'd taken that I wasn't there to see. Every bite of new food. Every squeal and cry and giggle. I would miss him, and his childhood, no more.

He laid his head back on my shoulder as if to say he felt the same way.

I patted his back and swayed.

Beron's blue eyes never left us. Without looking in his direction, I felt his gaze. I finally mustered the strength to meet his unwavering stare. "Thank you, Beron," I told him.

He inclined his head once, remaining quiet, then his eyes flicked to Caelum and something passed between the brothers. I wondered what it was like to have conversations the way they did. Was it possible to block thoughts from one another? I hoped for their sakes it was. Some things were best kept private.

"There are rooms prepared for you," Noor told them, coming to stand beside me. She studied her nephew with kind, sparkling eyes.

"Thank you, Aten. You are too kind," Padren told her. The dark hair he'd given his son was almost drowned in gray now. Malia's, though she was younger than he, had turned a shimmering silver. When I looked at them, I saw Merik, though he lived on most vividly in the features of our son.

Reyan's breathing slowly evened out and his small hand went limp on my chest. I glanced at Malia. She gave a motherly smile I wasn't sure I'd ever possess, filled with kindness and understanding as she ran a hand over his soft hair. "He is like Merik in that he enjoys his sleep. I'm surprised he didn't sleep through the whole ordeal."

"Ordeal?" I questioned, my eyes darting to Beron.

"Just being awakened unexpectedly and hustling to pack and come to the House safely," she hastily expanded.

I relaxed again. "How did you know to go with Beron? I didn't think to send a note with him."

Malia smiled. "I have a sense about these things, and I could tell that Beron has a good heart. He was very concerned for our safety and promised to take us directly to you. His friends guarded us as we fled our home, and they've given their words to protect it and see that our things are brought over. Though… I must say, I'm not sure we are worthy to reside in the House of the Sun," she added modestly.

"You are more worthy than I," I croaked. "You always have been."

I still wasn't sure this was the safest place for Reyan or for them. I needed to discuss this further with Noor. But if the Sphinx would guide us, I would follow her instructions. As long as she didn't blather another riddle to unravel.

"Perhaps we should settle in. It's been a very long and unfortunately eventful night," Noor offered, waving a hand toward the staircase.

Padren bowed to her and took hold of Malia's hand. With slow, aged movements, they followed their Aten up the steps. Malia paused, looking back at me and Reyan with a question in her eyes.

"Can I hold him for a little while?" I asked quietly.

"Of course you can, Citali," she said. Sadness soaked her voice.

I had dreamed about the day I would be free of my father and could come to reclaim my son. I never dreamed when I woke this morning that it would be this day. And while I knew it would be hard for his grandmother to part with him after being the mother to him I was unable to be, I didn't expect to feel so guilty about doing what I knew in my marrow was right.

She and Padren turned and continued up the steps after Noor. Caelum and Beron stood nearby, engaged in a silent conversation that seemed intense. Panic claimed me.

"Is she near?" I held Reyan a little tighter.

Beron shook his head. "She has fled. The others cannot find her, but her scent is nowhere near the House of the Sun."

I looked to Caelum. He swallowed thickly, as if recalling our earlier conversation about leaving this place.

His cool eyes flicked to the Wolven's. He took in a sharp breath, then his dark lashes fluttered and I grew frustrated. "It's rude to converse about me in my presence. Especially when I can't hear it."

I turned and carried my son up the steps. Beron and Caelum caught up to me outside my rooms, where I hesitated to enter. The scent of blood seemed sharper than it had been only moments ago, though I wasn't sure how or why. The same stains lingered, but nothing fresh remained. Nothing that should leave such a stench.

"Don't go in there," Beron said with a grit to his voice that almost made my knees buckle. "Please." He looked to my boy, then to me. "Stay in another room. Anywhere but in there. It isn't safe. Beyond that, it's not good for you."

"You have no idea what's good for me," I quietly snapped.

Lumos's Wolven bristled. He bared his teeth.

I bared mine.

I was not his concern.

He'd saved me and I had thanked him, a paltry offering for allowing me time to hold and know my own child, but I was not beholden to him. I wouldn't be controlled by man *or* beast now that I was free.

Reyan gave a soft sigh and Beron calmed himself. The tension bled from my shoulders with a whisper.

"Perhaps it *would* be best, Citali, if you did not stay in your rooms. Zarina might look there first if she dares return," Caelum gently suggested.

How was Caelum able to soothe me while the same words uttered by his brother made my very blood boil?

I hated this. Hated that he was with my sister even though they belonged together. Though I hadn't truly wanted to be his wife when Father assigned us the dark task of stealing the crown of moonlight from him, it was nice to have a real friend. I wasn't sure Noor would appreciate us maintaining such closeness now that he'd made his choice and Lumos had more than accepted Noor.

And Beron… well, he caged me and chased me every time I made it past his defenses, nipping at my heels and snapping at my face. On more than one occasion I'd threatened to run him through and take his pelt to wear as a trophy or keep as a rug. To say we weren't friends would be an understatement. Which made the fact that he saved me even more confusing.

"I'll find another room," I finally agreed. They were right. I didn't want to take Reyan around the remnant of such carnage. Nor did I need to be reminded of the events of that horrid spectacle.

Caelum walked beside me down the hall toward where Noor was showing Padren and Malia to their room. He lingered, waiting in the hallway as she made sure they were comfortable. The room was likely finer than they'd ever slept in, which meant they weren't comfortable and wouldn't relax while they were in Noor's presence. She was the Aten. They never imagined the Aten would deign to speak to them, let alone tuck them in. I nearly snorted at the absurdity of it all.

Noor was fussing so much and they were thanking her so profusely, quickly spiraling into an awkward, cringe-worthy, yet funny scene I couldn't tear my eyes away from.

Caelum nudged my arm, not hard enough to move me, but just enough to share that he also thought it was funny. Beron looked between me and his brother, disgust curling his upper lip. My smile faded.

*What was his problem?*

"Citali," Caelum began, "I want you to know that I'm still your friend."

*Perhaps the Lumin can read my mind now, too,* I thought to myself with a smirk playing at my lips. A smirk that fell away when I considered that maybe he could. "Noor would not appreciate us being friends, Caelum."

"Then allies," he offered.

I nodded, speaking around the knot in my throat. "Allies."

"Allies protect one another. I will not let harm come to you, to these people," he gestured toward Padren and Malia, "or Reyan."

"I'm wary of promises and vows, Lumin. People often break them and when they do, it's irreparable."

I walked to the end of the hall and took the empty room on the left, settling onto a chaise lounge upholstered in a vibrant shade of green velvet, perfectly content to hold Reyan in my arms and never again sleep. To smell his scent and feel his breath and know he was alive and safe, secure that nothing and no one could keep us apart now that we were together. Mother and son.

Caelum and Noor spoke in the hall before she entered the room. She perched on the end of the chaise, the glow in her eyes dimmer now. She looked like my sister, but not. She looked like the Aten, but more. Because she was all those things.

"He looks like you," she said softly.

I gave a small smile. "I see Merik in him, too."

She nodded, silently agreeing. She was quiet for several long moments and it set my nerves on edge. "You're considering taking Reyan and leaving the House of the Sun."

I fought against rolling my eyes. Of course Caelum would tell her. No matter the bonds that held, allies never usurped lovers.

"I don't know what I'm going to do yet, but I will take him away if it means keeping him safe from Zarina – or anything else that might threaten him."

"I would never threaten him, just so you know. I realize this new sisterly bond is tentative and new, but I hope you know you can trust me with that, and with him." She tipped her chin toward my sleeping son.

I *did* know that. Noor didn't have it in her to harm a child. She defended herself when I lashed out, but she was never the one who started the fights. She only ever ended them.

Unlike Zarina.

"You've been through a lot in a very short time," she said.

"We both have."

She gave a small, sad smile. "Sol will appear soon. I'll ask her to burn away what remains of your blood."

"Thank you."

"Citali – if you want to leave, you have my blessing and my full support. Whatever you need, I will provide. No matter what."

My chest tightened. "Why?" I croaked.

"Because you are my sister."

Truthfully, I didn't deserve her. I would not – could not – be as gracious to her as she was to me if our positions were reversed.

"So, if you go and you wish to tell me, I will hold your secret. And if you choose to go and not tell me where you'll be, I will respect and honor your decision. Though, I certainly wouldn't complain if you managed to let me know in some way that you're safe and well."

*Safe and well.* Would we ever be those things as long as Zarina breathed and the dark one was freed? Would we ever be able to relax and feel joy?

"What about you? She *will* come for you," I warned.

Noor's mood and countenance darkened, my familiar sister resurfacing. "Let her come."

The Aten stood and walked toward the door. Poised with her hand on the frame, she paused. In that moment and with that simple movement, she looked like her mother – like Sol. I dimly remembered her from my early years. Not well, but well enough to regret every cruel word and deed I'd committed against Noor.

"Citali?"

My eyes raised to hers in answer.

"The Sphinx wants to see you at Sol's first light. She will meet you atop the temple."

Though I expected her words, it still made butterflies erupt in my midsection. At least I wouldn't have to wait and worry for long. The dark sky had already brightened into a deep azure; a color not unlike Beron's eyes, I realized when I encountered him lurking in the shadows just outside the door.

Noor joined Caelum in the hall; the wake of footsteps echoed behind them. Beron did not follow. He did not leave. He sat, and waited, and watched, guarding me. Guarding Reyan.

He did not look tired, but alert and aware.

His presence and attentiveness were the only reasons I managed to close my eyes, relax, and drift off to a deep, dreamless sleep.

# 4

A ghost of a touch moved a strand of hair out of my eyes. I blinked to find Beron crouching in front of me. "It's time," he said softly.

I looked at the window and sure enough, Sol's rays were beginning to brush the sky. I sat up and Reyan blinked awake. "Cit-li?"

I held him tighter for a moment. "Reyan, I have to visit someone. Would you like to go and see Malia?"

He nodded, still drowsy, and rubbed the sleep from his eyes with his little fist.

"I can take him, if you'd like," Beron volunteered, standing when I stood.

"I'm not sure," I told him haltingly. Would Reyan be afraid? He only met Beron last night. In the next moment, the sky seemed to lighten significantly. The Sphinx was likely growing impatient. I would let my son decide. "Reyan, can Beron take you to grandmother?"

Surprising both of us, Reyan leaned toward the Wolven and let him take hold of him. The muscles in Beron's arms rippled when he lifted him, the veins under his skin rolling.

"Thank you," I said, looking down and wondering how many more times I'd have to say those words to him, knowing they would never be enough.

He glanced outside. "You should hurry."

Sol shone brightly over the land, revealing an unmistakable winged shadow swooping over the balcony. If I didn't start moving now, the Sphinx would come to me. I wasn't sure how Reyan would react to her. She was terrible and beautiful and all the things I wished I was and could one day be. If I had an ounce of her intimidating strength, Zarina wouldn't have dared come close enough to stab me. If I had an inkling of her wisdom and knew Zarina's planned treachery, it would have been *her* blood soaking my sandals and not the other way around.

I took a final look at Beron holding my son and strode from the room.

The Sphinx was not atop the temple when I emerged at the top. I shielded my eyes against Sol's bright rays and looked past her enormous statue, where my gaze caught on Noor. She was walking far into the dunes, along the crest of a particularly large swell before disappearing on its other side.

"She's speaking to her mother," the Sphinx suddenly said from behind me in the tinkling, childlike voice that made the hair on my neck and arms rise. I hadn't even heard her claws rake against the stone or the beating of her great, translucent wings.

I turned to face her, wary. Angry. Still hurt.

She stared at me, neither of us speaking, until I grew tired of whatever game she was playing. "Did you summon me only to study my face, or was there a greater purpose?"

She gave a feral grin. "*There* is the tongue sharper than shards of broken glass. You don't want another riddle?"

"Your riddles are useless."

She scoffed, "Not if you are smart enough to solve them."

"I'm not, so I won't waste another moment trying," I grumbled. "If that's what you wanted, I think we're done here." The moment I turned my back to her, a deep rumble of a growl rattled the stone under my feet.

My pulse quickened, not out of fright, but out of something more primal than simple fear. If she was a beast, then so was I. Never again would I cower – not even to her. I turned back to face her, a keen awareness shining in the depths of her solid black eyes. With her great paw, she clawed at something on her back. A familiar glinting, golden dagger clattered to the stone.

I moved without warning, without thinking. That dagger was mine.

Before I could take hold of it, her giant paw crushed my palm flat against the stones. She brought her face close to my ear. "You are welcome, Queen of Wolves."

"I am no queen," I gritted. Nor was I wolf… *yet.*

She smiled and eased her paw off my hand. I grabbed the dagger and took a slow step backward, then another.

"I told you that you would be queen one day; I just didn't say what you would become queen of," the Sphinx purred. "It was *you* who assumed it would be Lumina, or that you might somehow wrest Helios from your father's punishing grip."

While Noor and I were sequestered in Caelum's homeland Lumina, the Sphinx visited us both and presented us each with a riddle. She told me I would be a queen, and in the same breath told me that the crown of moonlight was always within sight, within reach. She distracted me, which was her intention all along. I wasted precious time searching for a crown I could never hold. Her riddle kept me preoccupied and out of Noor's way.

What the Lioness didn't reveal was that the crown was a permanent feature inlaid into Caelum's fair brow, one only visible by the light of Lumos.

"It was her destiny," she growled, as if she'd heard me. She shook her mane contemptuously. "You foolish girl, I can hear every word cutting through your mind. I thought nothing was as sharp as your tongue, but find that when it comes to you, even *I* am sometimes mistaken."

I bared my teeth at her, a small voice inside trying to rein in my fury. "Noor did not have a son to protect. *I* did. You championed her, but left me to –"

"To the wolves," she interrupted, a savage smile spread on her red lips. "To your destiny."

The Sphinx began to circle me, but I would not be intimidated. Not by her. I moved as she did, breath quickening, every sound pricking in my ear. The click of each of her claws, the tuft of fur on the end of her tail swaying through the air, the wind ruffling every soft piece of her mane. She stopped suddenly.

"I did not like the Wolven when I first met him," the Sphinx admitted. "He thought himself my equal. I like you even less. You… you think you are my better…"

*I am.*

She laughed. "I shall enjoy watching your first transition, little wolf queen. I hear it's excruciating. Sickening, how your bones snap and pop and rearrange themselves to turn you into something you never wanted to be."

I narrowed my eyes at her and tightened my fingers on the handle of the golden dagger.

There was nothing that could compare to the pain a mother would feel if harm came to her child.

She shook her mane and body and from her waist fell a golden belt, with a loop just large enough through which to thread the dagger. "You are not, and never will be, stronger than I, Citali. But you are a force all your own. I must respect that. Mother. Queen. Hunter. Claws and teeth with a sharp tongue and an even sharper wit."

I snatched the belt from her, buckled it onto my waist, and shoved the dagger into the golden loop. "I'm glad you finally see me for what I am."

She grinned. "And for what you *will* be. Bloody your teeth on your murderous sister for me, will you?"

"After I run her through," I promised.

"Lucky you sent your Wolven after the boy child when you did. Zarina had just found their home."

With her words, every muscle in my body went rigid. "What did you say?"

The blackness of the Sphinx's eyes softened a fraction. "The wolves didn't want to upset you, lest you shift while you were still weak. You want to be at your strongest when you transition. The first form you take will be the one you shift into unto death."

Hot fury slid through my veins and my bones seemed to burn from the inside out. They had claimed Zarina was nowhere near Padren and Malia's dwelling…

"When the Wolven appeared, she fled. She fears *him*. And now that she knows there are more, she will alter the plans she devised. But be warned – she's garnering an impressive following. Make sure you are clever when you lay your trap for her."

"Why aren't you protecting *her*?" I asked shrewdly. "She is the daughter of Sol's former Aten, too."

The sky seemed to darken with the Sphinx's thunderous countenance. "She is a daughter of Sol no more. She has been disowned, disinherited. She whispers to Anubisssss now," she hissed softly. "As you are fully aware, there are lines that once crossed, cannot be uncrossed; things that once done, cannot be forgiven. You are intimately familiar with that territory because you came perilously close to crossing into darkness, but you chose a different path than Zarina now has."

She looked to the dunes where Noor had disappeared. "Sol is apprising Noor of the treachery threatening her kingdom's newfound peace. Your sister may be Sol's daughter and the rightful Aten, but her heart is very much human. Zarina mistakes her mercy, and mistook yours, for weakness."

The night I was attacked, I thought the fight was over. I was going to let Zarina go, even after she slashed at and fought me. I thought she just needed to vent her anger, that she would never truly hurt me.

Underestimating her was my mistake.

One I would not repeat.

One that almost cost me my son.

A ripple of fury slid through me at the thought of Zarina slinking through the shadows, close to his home as he peacefully slept in the small bed Padren had crafted for him just before he was born.

I remembered the instant bond and love that formed when I looked at his face, and he took hold of one of my fingers and cried until his face turned red. I knew in my heart that I would do anything for him.

I would die for him.

I would kill to keep him safe.

My finger sung down the sharp, warm metal of the dagger I still clenched.

The next time Zarina and I met, she would taste my blade.

The Sphinx flexed her formidable muscles and stretched tall, moving to the statue of Sol at the temple's corner. She grinned at me as she stretched her wings. "Goodbye, Queen of Claws and Teeth."

She flapped her great wings, pushed with her muscled legs, and launched herself into the sky. She circled the temple top a few times, her broad shadow sliding beneath her, then glided into the sand in the direction Noor had walked.

I jogged back down the temple steps. After I saw Reyan, Beron and I needed to talk.

Padren and Malia were sitting in the Aten's private dining room. Seated on Padren's lap, Reyan chewed a piece of soft fruit. His eyes lit up when he saw me. "Cit-li!"

"Rey-an," I greeted with a wink, settling into the seat beside Malia.

I ignored the curious stares from Noor, Caelum, and Beron at the other end of the short table, obviously curious about my early morning meeting with the enigmatic Sphinx. It was too intimate and small a space for my tastes, but at least there were two Helioan guards standing sentry outside the doors.

Reyan happily chomped on his food when he wasn't smashing it on the table. I laughed to myself, thinking that this table now belonged to Noor. An awkward silence descended. Malia was tense as she looked between me and my sister.

"We need to talk, Citali," Noor finally said. "And what we need to discuss affects Padren and Malia, so I think they should be included in the conversation."

She did, did she? There was certainly no sending them away now, not that I necessarily would've proposed it, but I would have appreciated the choice that she'd just taken away. Aten or not, that wasn't her call.

I narrowed my eyes at her. "Very well. Tell us what you learned in the dunes, Aten." I sat back in my seat and crossed my arms. When Reyan reached for me and began to whine, I moved to take him from Padren and settled back in my seat. I bounced Reyan on my knee and he giggled happily. His laughter could chase away any storm, and the sound deescalated the tension that had been building in the room.

"What did you learn atop Sol's temple?" she challenged first.

"Many things. I'm sure you know that Zarina is collecting a number of acolytes to follow her unto their deaths."

She nodded. "Did the Sphinx reveal to you the number our sister has amassed?"

"She did not inform me of that detail."

"She has hundreds," Noor said, tearing off a chunk of bread and smearing it with sweet berry jam.

Hundreds? How had she swayed so many? I expected twenty or less of the witless to follow her ravings. "We have far more in the guard," I brushed off her concern.

Noor gave a slight shake of her head. "We can't trust all the guards. Some have been compromised. Some spy on us for them."

Then we needed to find a way to determine who was disloyal.

I couldn't fathom any guard of Sol and Helios listening to such mad ravings as Zarina was surely spouting. I needed to find Merik's friends and ask them to look out for us once more. But what if some of them had turned against us? Who could we trust now? "If we can't trust the Helioan guard to uphold you as Aten, where does that leave us?" I asked.

Beron answered, "Treading water in the middle of the river, surrounded by hungry crocodiles."

I slid my attention to him. "So, we're all in danger and no better than we were last night when my sister drew near their home?" I gestured to Padren and Malia.

Padren's fork paused just shy of his mouth. "We were in danger?" he gasped.

I wouldn't have sent Beron for them if I didn't feel in my gut that the danger was imminent. "My murderous eldest sister was chased away, but she came very close. Isn't that right, Beron?" I asked, watching his reaction.

If he felt flustered, his features didn't betray his thoughts. "I didn't think it was *wise* to frighten anyone," he answered pointedly.

"Well, I think the *wisest* thing you can do in a situation like this is to inform the ones directly impacted and let the individuals make a personal decision regarding their safety and the safety of those they love," I answered sweetly.

He bristled. "What if you knew their decision would be rash and potentially detrimental to them?"

"You have no right to dictate their decision-making process, detrimental or not!" My voice rose a little. I calmed myself when Reyan stopped chewing to look at my face.

"Stop pretending you're talking about them when we are clearly discussing you, Citali," he said in a dangerous, low tone. "Your emotions will run high until…" He glanced at Padren and Malia, unwilling to say the words.

My brows rose. "Don't stop now. They should know the price you and I both paid when Lumos allowed you the choice to spare me."

"And do you regret it?" he asked sharply.

"Not even a little," I bit back.

Malia wiped her mouth and quietly rose, taking Reyan from my arms. She bounced him on her hip and walked away from the table toward the balcony. She spoke in sweet tones to him, made silly faces, and kept him entertained.

I refocused on Beron. "I don't regret it for one second, no matter the price."

"What price?" Padren finally interjected.

I answered him but held Beron's sharp as ice gaze. "I am to turn into a beast, like him."

Padren's voice cut through the intense battle waging between me and the Wolven. His eyes widened. "Citali…" his voice wavered.

"Don't," I gritted. "Don't pity me. Don't fear for me. The change will come regardless, and worry is a waste of time."

"Will Reyan also be changed?" he asked, leaning forward.

"No," Beron answered him.

"Will he be in danger from Citali?" Padren pointedly asked the Wolven as if I wasn't sitting at the table at all. My mouth gaped and hurt drummed through my chest.

Beron rapped his knuckles on the table. "I don't believe so, but she has to learn to control her emotions until the first transition occurs."

"When will that be?" Padren queried.

"That is between Lumos and Citali, I'm afraid." Beron crossed his arms. His cool eyes slid over me. "But I don't think it will be long."

Fear eased into my bones. I'd told Padren there was no need to worry and nothing would change, but I was afraid and worried about what was to come. I didn't want to come so close to having my son back only to become a threat to him myself.

Beron's eyes softened a fraction and he relaxed in his seat.

Noor cleared her throat. "Until we know more and can hunt Zarina and find those she's managed to sway to her side, and until you transition, I think you would be safer elsewhere," she said to me before looking around the room. "All of you."

"Lumina?" I asked, my muscles tensing. "Do you think we'd be safe in the House of the Moon?"

Caelum shook his head. "That is too obvious a choice. There's another place that only a select few know exists. I won't speak of it here." He and Beron shared a glance.

I sighed, exasperated. "I wish the two of you would stop talking amongst yourselves. This conversation was supposed to be open and honest, including *all* those in attendance."

Noor sat up straight and gripped the chair arms so tightly, I wondered if she might melt them as she'd done at the House of Dusk. "Until you transform, we are all left vulnerable. We cannot watch over you, them, and Reyan, *and* focus on

Zarina and whatever trouble she's brewing. It would stretch our resources too thin."

I opened my mouth to protest but shut it without saying a word. I didn't feel any different. When would this great change come? Perhaps it wouldn't.

Beron leaned forward, looking more wolf than man, despite his form. "After you are altered, not even the three of us together could stop you from finding Zarina and ensuring your safety and that of your son. I've seen it."

I swallowed thickly. *What has he seen?*

# 5

Beron's attention flicked toward the door a second before the knock came. The legs of his chair scooted across the floor and he was at the door, opening it quicker than any of us could have moved.

He offered to help the two men as they carried in two large trunks. I recognized the large chests from my time in Lumina… a place of unpleasant memories. "This is the most vital of your belongings. The rest is being packed and will be brought here for safekeeping," Beron told Padren and Malia.

"I guess we're already packed, then," Padren said, trying to add levity to a heavy situation.

"The rest of us should prepare," Noor said.

"Are you going with us – for a time, at least?" I asked my Aten sister.

She shook her head. "My place is here now. Beron will see you to safety, but I will visit when I can."

I glanced to Caelum and he gave a nod. With that small gesture, I could see he believed we would be okay, that Beron would take care of us, that in time, all would be well.

I just had to be patient, remain vigilant, and grow as strong as I could until Lumos was ready for me to become woman and wolf.

The two men who'd carried in my trunks stood with Beron, another silent conversation taking place between them. Caelum had even tuned in.

Noor shrugged when I quirked a brow. I moved to Malia, playing peek-a-boo with Reyan for a few moments, even as I studied the strangers from the corner of my eye.

Both the men were tall, muscled, and clad in tunics the cool hue of Luminan silver. Black trousers and boots sharpened the look and set them apart from the normal guardsmen of Lumina. These were Beron's men.

Not only was the familiar silhouette of a howling wolf embroidered over their chests, there was an anticipatory, almost feral gleam to their eyes.

The one with dark hair was named Holt, if I recalled correctly. Beron trusted him to guard me once in the House of the Moon. He, too, had failed to confine me in my rooms.

Malia saw the moment his eyes turned upon me. "Perhaps I should take Reyan to our room so you will have time to pack and… handle matters." Her brow slowly rose as she nodded to the behemoths gathered across the room.

My chest tightened with worry. I still didn't feel safe here. Noor had just voiced the same.

"Would you mind if I walked with you?" Caelum asked with a charming smile that set Merik's mother at ease. She gave me a wink and carried Reyan across the room to where Caelum and Padren were waiting. Caelum squished his cheeks and made a silly noise. Reyan giggled at Caelum's surprising array of silly faces.

He would make a good father one day. Not only because he loved my sister, but because he would pour as much energy into his children as he did his kingdom. He would parent the way his father once had, and his children would turn out like him.

Kind. Fair. Steady.

Noor glided toward me, her eyes fixed on him. She gently cupped my elbow, her heat warming my skin, and leaned in to whisper. "I think Beron wants to introduce you to his men."

Her touch faded as she disappeared from sight, eliciting a short gasp from the least familiar of Beron's men. He tried to cover his surprise with a cough to save face, but his blue-green eyes sparked against mine. "Does she do that often?"

Since he hadn't spoken the question into their minds, I presumed he wanted me to hear it or perhaps answer. Beron deferred to me with a nod. Holt's counterpart was taller than Beron by a few inches, his chin pointed, making him appear more fox than wolf. Especially with his red hair.

"Sometimes it's helpful, but it's always somewhat startling," I told him honestly.

Beron smirked as the fox-faced man curiously and unabashedly studied me. Holt, who boasted dark hair and skin a few shades lighter than Helioan and darker than Luminan quietly watched us all. His pale brown eyes held no fleck in them, but were solid and strange.

"This is Red," Beron introduced, gesturing to the fox-faced man. "And I assume you remember Holt."

I nodded once. *Oh, I certainly remembered Holt's frustrated growls*, I thought to myself with a small smirk.

"Where are the others?" I asked Beron.

Red grinned. "Does she already know everything?"

"Not… everything," Beron hedged. "But she did hear our howls last night."

Red nodded appreciatively. "Could you differentiate the tones? It's good that you can already tell us apart."

"If you're insinuating it's a wolfish feature emerging, I can assure you it's not. I could have distinguished the different tones before. It's like walking into a room with different people speaking in their unique voices."

Beron quirked a brow as if he would argue the point further, but Red cut in.

"So, are you in denial about what's changing within your body?" Red asked with a grin, his eyes raking over me. Not lasciviously, just… curiously.

"Not at all," I bristled. "I just know my body and it has not yet changed."

Red's brows slowly rose. He nudged Beron and the two exchanged a silent glance I would stake was very loud within their minds.

I watched Holt, who stood so still, his chest barely rose and fell. "I'm sure you're happy to see me again."

He didn't reply, just stood like a statue watching us all. He'd had no better manners at the House of the Moon under Vada's watchful eye.

"Citali needs to finish packing," Beron told the men. I suppose I had begun the task the night I tried to leave, although I hadn't known at the time that the path to safety would lead straight to the Wolven. "Holt, would you stay here and watch over Padren, Malia, and Reyan's things?" The silent guard gave a decisive nod.

"Red, would you go to their room and stand guard outside?"

"Of course," Red answered. He tipped his chin up. "I look forward to getting to know you better, Citali."

I narrowed my eyes at him. Who said I wanted to get to know any of them?

Red just laughed as if he knew exactly what I thought.

Beron walked with me to my rooms. The halls were silent as death and the quiet put me on edge. That was how it was just last night before Zarina came… I wished I could remember more. I pressed a hand to my left shoulder.

Beron stopped. "Does it still hurt?" My brows furrowed as I peeled my hand away, suddenly uncertain why I felt pain in my shoulder. "That's where I bit you," he admitted.

My lips parted in surprise. My body remembered, even if my mind didn't.

"You shifted into the Wolven, *then* bit my shoulder?" When he nodded, I decided to ask another question that had bothered me since I'd awakened. "Was Sol there when you arrived? I saw a light and felt heat, but Noor said it wasn't her."

"I did not see light or heat, but Noor was at your side."

I wanted to ask why he had chosen to save me when I wasn't worthy of saving, but wasn't sure I was ready to hear his answer. He likely did it for Noor's sake, or out of devotion to his brother and his new chosen mate. Or perhaps his Wolven instinct demanded he bite me. I vaguely recalled him shaking me to keep me lucid. Maybe he thought his teeth would be a stronger incentive.

Imagining myself as a wolf wasn't easy. I had seen Beron in his Wolven form. He was a large man, more than a head taller than me as we stood beside one another, and his wolf was ridiculously large. I was much more petite. Would my wolf be no more than a pup beside him? What would it feel like to be the same as Beron?

I continued walking to my room, refusing to think about the bite or the change it might elicit any longer. Those thoughts would only slow me down, and something deep within was urging me away from this House.

"Where are we going, Beron?"

His blue gaze fastened onto mine. "You'll see."

"Is it far from here?"

He nodded. "Very."

"Good."

When we arrived at my rooms, three large trunks were waiting with their lids open, ready to be filled. I bit my thumbnail, unsure where to start. I had no idea where we were going or what I would need there. Surely I wouldn't need gowns and gold. *What on earth should I bring?*

"Bring it all, if you like. Or bring nothing," Beron answered intuitively.

"What would I wear if I brought nothing?" I asked, cocking my head to the side.

A sly grin tugged at his lips and he quirked a brow.

*Wolf, indeed. How about insufferable pig?*

I turned to my wardrobe. I would pack every gown I owned just to spite him.

Tossing garment after garment into the trunks, Beron just chuckled and watched me. My eyes drifted to his every so often. When his playful demeanor hardened just a touch, I paused.

"Citali," he began, "I want you to know I'm not your enemy."

I swallowed thickly, strangling the orange fabric of the skirt in my hands. "Neither are you my friend."

"I want to change *that* much, at least," he said. "If memory serves me right, we got along *very well* at times."

There were times he was so incredibly charming. His sweet words and what I thought was genuine interest had erased his brother and the crown from my mind when I needed to focus on them most. I thought part of me hated him for that, but in truth, I was to blame for losing sight of my goals.

Not to mention that when we fought, we battled like lions, complete with lethal claws, flying fur, and sharp, snapping teeth.

I tossed another skirt into the trunk.

I couldn't worry about Beron now. Not his feelings or hopes or worries. Not his smirk or smile or lame attempts to make amends. Not even his guilt, which I saw weighing heavily on his broad shoulders. He still wasn't sure saving me was the right decision. I was grateful, but I wasn't sure in the end he would be.

He claimed he wasn't my enemy, but would I turn out to be his? Or would we manage to work together to eradicate the threat to my son, my sister, and my kingdom? We only had to be civil until I became like him and could hunt Zarina myself. He said himself that I would be unstoppable.

I crossed to the armoire and began tossing gold atop the shimmering fabrics. If I was leaving Helios, I was taking part of my kingdom, and Sol, with me. Even more importantly, I was taking my most precious things. When this was over, I knew I wasn't coming back.

I crouched in front of the drawer closest to the floor, then worked the inlaid wood until the false bottom gave way, one corner popping up. Beron watched as I withdrew a worn blanket that once carried Reyan's newborn scent, a small tuft of his hair held tight by a tiny blue string, and a folded letter that held Merik's heart. These were his last *written* words. Words filled with hope…just like the last words he'd uttered before dying.

Slamming the trunks closed, I looked to Beron. "I'm ready."

He nodded once and looked to the door. Red and Holt entered just as Caelum and Noor escorted Padren, Malia, and Reyan down the hall. "Cit-li!" my son happily shouted as they passed. I hurried to catch up with them, taking Reyan when he held his arms out for me.

Beron's men carried my things into the room where we'd left the other trunks. Noor drew close, drawing a hand over Reyan's soft hair. "Are you ready to take a special trip, Reyan?"

His eyes glittered as he smiled at Noor and reached out for her. She took him, pleasantly surprised. She cooed at him and glanced to Caelum with joy alighting her eyes. "You're such a big boy, Reyan."

He giggled and tried to stretch his trunk even longer, giggling and ultimately falling over onto her shoulder. He'd warmed to her quickly. Noor's smile glowed like her eyes.

Reyan noticed their eerie radiance and went still, then he poked at them and it was my sister's turn to laugh and catch his curious fingers.

Caelum and Beron helped with the trunks as Noor leaned closer to me. "Beron can communicate with Caelum, and he with me. Please let me know if you feel like you're in danger in this new place you're going."

"What could you do if I was?"

"I could come and open a portal to another place."

"You would have me run?" I asked, gritting my teeth at the thought.

"For now," she agreed. "For now, I would. But when you change, it will be Zarina and her devotees who will be scattered to the wind by your mighty teeth." She smiled. "I warned Beron once at the House of Dusk that you would shred his heart if he got too close. I've never misjudged your ferocity, sister, only your reasons for being so savage."

"And what do you think of your savage sister now?"

Noor looked from Reyan to me. "I'm proud."

A fist formed around my heart, then squeezed tight. "I'm proud, as well," I told her. "And I'm glad you convinced me to take that step."

I didn't tell her how afraid I was about what that step might mean for my future, and for my son's. I wasn't good at admitting my feelings, but if something happened to me during the transition from human to beast, I wanted her to know. "Noor," I said, pausing to collect the right words from my mind. "If something happens, please see that Reyan –"

She adjusted her hold on Reyan as he pretended to fly like the Lioness.

"You don't even have to ask, Citali."

Yes, I did. I looked at my feet as a great knot formed and tightened in my throat. I nodded my thanks, unable to speak it.

"Focus on your strength and listen to Beron – he'll help you if you let him," she added shrewdly, "and stay focused. This will be over before you know it."

The golden glow in Noor's eyes intensified as if even she didn't truly believe our ordeal would end quickly or without a fight. The dark one was hard at work. Zarina, we were sure, was his vessel on earth now – something he hadn't had for a very long time. He wouldn't squander this chance to wreak havoc and wreck peace. He may not get another.

I only wondered why the Sculptor allowed it at all. Why had he preserved Anubis, though banished, in the fiery center of our world? Why not tear him from existence?

"Do you know of anyone who didn't survive this… change?" I asked, fear overwhelming me.

"I asked Beron and Caelum the same thing while you slept, after what happened. They both agreed that you're different because Lumos chose the others, while he let Beron choose you. But I don't think he would have given Beron the option if he didn't intend for you to conquer it."

Conquer it. Not just survive it. Not get through it well enough. Noor believed I would conquer it.

"If anyone can overcome this hurdle, it is my savage sister," she added.

Reyan began to squirm. Padren came close to comfort him, but it wasn't Padren he wanted. Nor was it Malia or I. "Beron!" he yelled, flinging his arms out and grasping at the air toward the Wolven.

Beron smiled and walked to my son. "Reyan."

"Up," Reyan said, raising his hands to the ceiling.

Beron glanced sheepishly at me. "Not sure your mother will approve, little one."

"Up?" Reyan again pleaded.

"What does 'up' entail?" I asked the Wolven.

"A ride on my shoulders. I won't let go of him, I promise," he rushed to say. "It's safe; he just likes the perspective."

I nodded my permission. "Very well."

Beron grinned and Reyan squealed as the Wolven took him in his arms and lifted him over his head. Reyan straddled the back of Beron's neck and fisted his dark hair, making Beron wince. "Up!" he giggled.

Caelum smiled at his brother with my son atop his shoulders, then slid a meaningful look my way. I ignored him. I'd told him Noor wouldn't appreciate us remaining friends, and yet there he was, acting as if that was exactly what we still were. Like he didn't remember any of the awful things I'd done to separate him and Noor; like I hadn't tried my best to make him want me instead. Like he might be okay with me wanting his brother. It would require too much energy to consider the number of things his look might have implied.

"Are we ready?" Noor stood beside me and waved a graceful hand, opening a portal. Darkness leaked from the other side, colliding with Sol's warmth. Red went first, just to make sure all was well. He met with another man I would bet was also a beast, and a moment later, they stepped back into Helios to help heft the trunks.

I offered to take Reyan from Beron, but my son clamped onto Beron's forehead possessively. He did not want to get down just yet. "Stay up!" he demanded.

"Come with me," Beron said, holding onto Reyan's legs as they hung over his shoulders.

I wanted to ask where we were going. Why I felt nervous and excited, yet terrified and alive. While some of those feelings were mine, I knew some weren't. How, then, could I feel them? Clutching my chest, I tried to breathe and untangle the strange coil of emotions in my chest.

Beron handed a protesting Reyan to Padren, who hovered nearby. The Wolven stepped in front of me. "Citali?" he said carefully, craning his neck to lower himself to meet my eye. His hands fell on my shoulders, steadying me. "What's the matter?"

"I… I don't know."

"Do you feel strange? Are you hot? Dizzy?"

I shook my head, my mind feeling like it was submerged in the river with currents rushing all around me. "No, nothing like that. It's hard to explain." I met his concerned blue eyes and felt an overwhelming amount of worry. "It's you," I breathed.

His dark brows kissed. "What's me?"

"I can *feel* you."

He removed his hands. "Sorry."

"No, not like that." I pressed a hand to his heart. "I think I can feel… your emotions."

Or maybe it wasn't Beron's. Maybe it was someone else's, or everyone's all at once.

Beron swallowed, then glanced meaningfully at Red, Holt, and the third wolf standing with them. "I'm going to take her inside," he directed at the wolves before turning to Merik's parents. "You should give her space for a moment, and if all seems well, follow," he told Padren and Malia.

If I had felt like myself, I would have told him I was fine and insist again that I'd never hurt my son or his grandparents. But I still felt…more…strange…*off.* Beron might be right. But even if he was wrong, no harm would come to anyone. We had to be careful.

His wolves muttered their approval and promised Beron they'd bring our belongings through. Noor stayed to keep the portal open and Caelum remained with her. He pressed his lips together and nodded to the portal, his eyes flicking from mine to it in silent invitation.

Beron's hand found the small of my back and I met Noor's wary stare as Beron and I stepped through her portal. I didn't know what was happening to me, but if this was the first sign that I would soon change, I wasn't sure I would conquer this after all.

# 6

I stepped away from the Wolven's touch and left the warmth of Helios for the shadowed, cold night. Instinctively I knew we were in the kingdom of Lumos, but nowhere near the House of the Moon.

There was no powder-soft sand, only rocky earth and scant tufts of dried grass. The rock rose and fell in great, water-hewn dunes. The sounds of cricket song, small animals scampering nearby, and a distant whooo from somewhere overhead greeted us among trees that leaked green, spindly needles and stood as tall as Sol's statue above her temple.

Warm candlelight glowed from the windows of an enormous house built with logs the size of barges, broken only by walls of windows.

With careful, hesitant steps, Padren walked through carrying Reyan. Malia kept to his side. They were taken aback by the structure in front of us.

"I've never seen such a home," Padren muttered, studying the sheer bulk of it.

Malia agreed, "It's beautiful and sturdy." She looked around. "It looks like it's part of the landscape."

It was an ingenious camouflage, I had to admit. Concealed in the forest, a house of wood for a den of wolves.

Reyan whipped his head this way and that, listening and looking. "Lu-mos," he said, pointing to the sky over Padren's shoulder.

Through the slender trees, a familiar silver face shone. I smiled at my son. "That's right. Lumos is here. And in the morning, Sol will come."

Reyan smiled, then saw Beron at my side. "Woof-en."

A laugh escaped my throat as Beron offered my son a wide smile. "You are a little parrot. You repeat everything you hear, huh?"

Reyan threw his head back and giggled. "Woof-en."

Red and Holt and the wolf I hadn't yet met worked with Caelum to carry the trunks through the portal.

A familiar warmth caressed my back.

"Citali." Beron spoke from behind me in a low, sultry tone that made my attention snap to him. I was met with a smirk and a dimple, and my heart clapped against bone and breast as he continued. "Padren, Malia, and of course, Reyan…" My son glowed under Beron's attention. "Welcome to the House of Wolves."

My lips parted. I had never deluded myself to believing Noor or I knew all the Luminan brother's secrets, but this was a rather impressive one they'd kept close to their chest. And from the guarded way they spoke of it while in Helios, we weren't the only ones who didn't know this House existed.

The less who knew, the better.

The safer we would be here.

Padren and Malia thanked Beron, then bowed to his guardsmen and thanked them for carrying their things through. Noor and Caelum joined us, and the portal disappeared behind them. Noor slid over to Beron and placed a hand on his bicep. "May I have a few moments alone with my sister?"

Beron quickly stepped away. "Of course. I'll be just inside." His blue eyes flicked to Caelum's and the brothers each took a handle of a chest and hoisted it up, walking it into the House of Wolves. Beron's House.

This was his world, his home. These were his mountains, rocks, and trees. The animals who roamed the forest surrounding us belonged to the Wolven, too.

Here, he was King.

My rib cage tightened as I recalled the Sphinx's words. She called me Queen of Wolves, Queen of Claws and Teeth.

Panic coursed like lightning through my veins. As if the terrified forks had called it to life, the sky began to cloud. In the distance came a rumble of rolling thunder.

Noor waited until everyone was inside before speaking. "Citali, place your hand where the portal was." I glanced in the direction it had been, but nothing was there. "You trust me with your son but not in this?" Her dark brow rose in challenge.

I would meet it. I walked to the place where the portal had been and felt lingering warmth. Noor nodded and gestured for me to reach out to it. When I did, the portal reopened. "How?"

"Through Sol," she revealed. "You and I will fight this battle together. She made it so that you can open this portal. *Only* this portal. And it can only be opened by you."

"What about Beron?" I looked to the grand wooden House, suddenly uneasy. "Does he know of it?"

Noor took a deep breath. "I trust Caelum implicitly. I love him with my whole heart, though I admit we have much to learn about one another. I trust Beron as well. But this isn't about how I feel. I want this portal to be for you. If you think for a second you are in danger, I want you to escape immediately and without anyone questioning your reasoning."

"Why?" I asked. It was a simple, one-word question loaded with many longer ones. Why was she doing this? Why concern herself with me at all? Why did she go to Sol for me? Why would the sun goddess make an exception for me?

"Citali, I have forgiven you. I understand the reason behind your actions. I see it in Reyan's eyes and hear it in his laughter, and I would've done the same, if not worse if our situations were reversed. On this, my mother agrees. So, the only forgiveness you need to seek to truly move forward is yours."

I hated it when she spoke so wisely and sensibly, though it made my terrible conscience sigh with relief. "I'm not ready yet," I told her honestly.

"I know," she said. Her gaze slid to me. "What happened to you a moment ago? You looked ill."

"It sounds insane, but I think I can feel Beron's feelings sometimes. I felt a rush of feelings flood over me at the House before coming here, but when he stood in front of me just now, I nearly drowned from them." I turned to her. "I'm not sure he wants us here or appreciates us in his space."

"Did you *feel* that from him?"

I shook my head. "I felt… intense worry."

Noor took in a long breath and blew it out. "Both of you have things to work through, but I believe that if Beron is worried, it's because he cares. And not about only himself or his space." She paused and seemed to choose her next words carefully. "Citali, in this cause against Zarina, you and I have to be united, and not only for the sake of Helios or revenge. The Sphinx revealed two futures to me that involve Reyan. We must protect him."

My eyes widened. "Two possible futures for my son? What did she show you?"

"The most probable future is that we are protecting the next Aten," she said proudly. My spine stiffened. Why wouldn't Noor's children succeed her? She looked to her feet, then back up at me. "You will raise him to be honorable and strong and good, Citali."

"What is his alternate future?" She'd only mentioned one, and while it was expected or could have been imagined, it was only one fork in the pathway of my son's life. Noor and I both knew that only one path would be taken, while the other would be eaten by the sand.

"That if he chooses not to walk the path of Aten, we are protecting the future Wolven."

Aten or Wolven? My brows furrowed. I couldn't be more pleased with either option, though clearly, I preferred he choose Sol.

"The only thing that might sever these paths is Anubis, who would use him to fulfill a darker purpose."

Another flood of emotion hit me, this time not Beron's but my own. My heart tried to tear through my chest. Sweat beaded on my forehead, neck, and the small of my back.

"Citali?" Noor said cautiously, noticing the change.

I couldn't quiet my thoughts or rein in my body's sudden response. I gritted my teeth. The thought that Zarina had almost taken me from him and was now trying to trample either of these beautiful pathways made my skin boil. Noor eased her hands out as if to catch me, or perhaps to protect herself. "It's okay."

"It is certainly *not* okay." Even my voice was hysterical. I was not okay. Nothing was okay.

Beron pushed the door open and stepped onto the porch, the door hanging on its hinge as his broad stride ate the distance between us. "Calm down," he said. His voice was soothing but stern.

I hated the sound. I hated how my body and mind responded to him until I managed to tear my emotions out of his grasp. "Do not order me about, Wolven. Have you so quickly forgotten our past?"

He slowly stalked toward me. "I haven't forgotten even a second." His voice was like the gravel under my sole. Rough.

Sharp in places. Smooth in others. "Nor would I want to. Our history is uniquely ours."

Noor's brows rose.

Caelum hurried to our small group, quickly followed by Padren stepping out onto the porch, his brow wrinkled in concern. Red and Holt flanked him, anticipation thrumming through their veins and making their feet and fingers uneasy.

But I wasn't beholden to any of them now.

Beron had saved me, but only because Lumos gave him the means and the choice.

The moon god sparked in the sky, climbing higher so I could better see him. I stumbled through the wood, away from everyone and everything until there was only me and the moon god, surrounded by a sea of trees and valleys, rock and ridges. My ears rang and my vision hollowed, darkness swallowing everything around me until only Lumos's silver face remained.

"Citali!" Beron shouted sharply. "Stop." My feet obeyed. Again, I tore my will from his grasp with great difficulty. "It isn't your time yet." He reached me in the wood and we faced off directly beneath Lumos's cool light.

I whipped around to face Beron.

Wolven.

Menace.

He said it wasn't my time, but what did he know? Did he sense what I felt?

The thought stilled my lungs for a moment. Did he hear my thoughts even if I could not hear his?

He eased toward me with his hands out. "Don't go to him yet."

"He calls me," I rasped. It felt like Lumos was gripping my heart and dragging me toward him with it.

"His call is always there. It's how we can shift at will. But you need to strengthen yourself before you answer him, remember? For Reyan, if for no one or nothing else. Your son needs you to be at your strongest."

*Reyan*. I glanced toward the large log house and a shadow crossed the window, one of Malia holding my son. The strength bled from my muscles in an instant and I held a trembling hand to my brow. I was a horrible mother to him. I'd never been strong enough and still wasn't. Perhaps I never would be.

My breaths shuddered and my head swam as the earth tilted precariously.

Beron swooped in and scooped me up before I fell. He carried me to the House, his footsteps jarring me, but I saw none of it. Even behind my lids, I could only see Lumos. His silver face was emblazoned on the darkness like Sol's name was etched upon Anubis's.

I woke to Sol's light, thankful that Lumos had moved on and wondering if coming to the kingdom of the moon was a mistake. My mood lightened considerably when I heard Reyan's laughter from someplace deep inside the House of Wolves. I threw off the soft blankets and walked barefooted down a long wooden hall, jogging down a grand wooden staircase. A hearth dominated the room, built with natural stone that stretched to the hollowed ceiling and allowed the smoke to pour outside. A fire, content and warm, crackled in its bowels.

Around the fireplace, chairs and chaises in comfortable shades of tree bark were arranged in a semi-circle. A young man with curly pale, Luminan-sand hair sat sprawled in one. He looked up when my feet hit the landing, then he tracked me down the stairs. He sat up straighter, leaned his meaty forearms on his thighs, and smiled. "I take it you're Citali."

"Your parents must be very proud of your deductive skills," I snipped.

He laughed and leaned back in his seat again. "The others said you were a bit testy last night."

"Testy?" I stopped, crossed my arms, and leaned against the trunk-like banister.

"Yeah, you know. Agitated. Irritable. Moody… testy."

I gave him a false smile. "Who told you this?"

He swallowed uneasily as I sauntered over. "Uh… just the guys, Red and Holt. Plus, I saw some of it."

"You were here?" I asked, raising a brow.

"Yeah, I was here. You don't remember me?" He grinned as if he didn't believe I could possibly forget him. He was muscled and handsome enough. Apparently, those features were wolfish requirements. It was apparent he certainly wasn't used to being forgotten by women.

I pressed a finger over my lips and looked at the ceiling. "Nothing comes to mind."

A swish of fabric.

Beron stood in the doorway with his arms crossed, making his shirt pull tightly over his chest. He wore comfortable trousers and was barefoot. His dark hair was wet, his jaw freshly shaven. "Citali, I see you've met Chase."

Chase stood and glanced between me and Beron. Beron's cool gaze slid over me. "Feeling better?"

I narrowed my eyes. "Better than what?"

Beron's dimple popped with his smirking smile. Instead of answering, he wisely replied, "There's breakfast in the dining room."

I smelled fresh bread and heard the sizzling of meat, the boiling of eggs. My mouth began to water and I forgot Chase once again as I pushed past Beron. I was starving.

"Citali?" Beron called after me, but I didn't have time to stop as I followed the scents to a vast room with a table that had been hewn from a massive tree. It gleamed in the sunlight streaming in from the window, some sort of heavy resin protecting the wood and enshrining the orange red striations among the darker rings. The edges had not been sawed away, but lay as the Sculptor had made it. On the table were several small platters of food.

Beron caught up with me. "Eat before holding Reyan," he warned.

Anger coursed through my flesh. How dare he insinuate I would hurt my son!

"It's the hunger. It has to be sated," he gently explained. "I know you won't hurt him, but you need to eat. The food will settle your agitation."

"I am *not* agitated," I hissed.

Red coughed to cover his laugh, and even the stony Holt sitting beside him smiled.

Padren stood and pulled a chair out for me. "Here. Sit with us, Citali." His head swiveled.

I crossed the room to Padren, who pushed my chair in as I lowered myself. Beron appeared with an empty plate and started to fill it with bread, but I snatched the porcelain dish from his hand. Oh, no… I was not Noor. I knew what the action of filling another's plate meant in Lumina. "You're not feeding me, Beron. And my room better not be anywhere near yours."

He raised his hands in surrender and backed slowly away, his infuriating dimple deepening. Behind him, Chase sauntered into the room. As I filled my plate, he mouthed the word, *Testy*.

I held his gaze as I stabbed a sausage with my fork. He cringed as the tines screeched over the platter. I held it up in warning and Chase's dark blue eyes widened. Beron laughed out loud and I moved the sausage to my plate, crudely sawing it apart.

Chase didn't laugh for long, and he didn't mouth any more words.

"Where are Malia and Reyan?" I asked.

Padren smiled. "She took him to the back porch for a few moments. Beron has squirrel and bird feeders situated all around the house. He's enamored with the wildlife right now."

"And safe, far away from me, his own mother," I hotly added.

Padren leaned in and despite the lines in his skin and the dark circles beneath his eyes, I saw Merik. The familiar pang of guilt slid through my chest. "Eat, Citali. Trust Beron on this," he advised.

I relented and chewed a bit of sausage. My eyes narrowed at the Wolven. I was irritated by how trustworthy and good and perfect he was when I felt worn too thin, bore a treacherous heart, and had never been described as good – or even decent.

Padren gestured to the rolls. "They are quite good. The cinnamon butter is delicious."

Noor liked jam. She would be slathering her bread with far too much if she were here. There were five different kinds on the table – none made from nightthorn berries, thankfully…

I took a roll and smeared the cinnamon butter on top, taking a bite fueled by anger. The butter melted in my mouth and the delicious flavors exploded on my tongue. Padren was right. The more I ate, the more I realized that Beron was, too. As the hunger abated, my muscles and mood relaxed.

Red filled his plate and moved to sit in the chair across from me. Chase slid into the seat beside him. Holt stood with Beron behind the two younger wolves, but all the men's attention was focused on me. Padren wiped his mouth before excusing himself. "I believe Malia is calling for me."

"I didn't hear her," I told him, silently imploring him to stay.

He hooked a thumb over his shoulder. "Yes. There it was again. I know my wife's voice and her insistence. I'll be just outside if you need me, Citali."

I needed him now, but he, too, was leaving me… to the wolves.

The men waited until Padren closed the door behind him, sealing Reyan's happy squeals out with him. I turned to Beron, still chewing my bread, though slowly now. I wasn't sure what he was scheming.

"We run together every day we can," Red finally said. "We want you to join us today."

He looked at Chase and elbowed him in the arm. What had he said to earn such a blow? I scanned Chase's chiseled face, then Red's more pointed one.

"When will I be able to speak into your minds?" I asked politely.

The pack deferred to the Wolven. "That comes with the first shift."

"Are you sure you want this?" I asked him pointedly. His brows furrowed. "Are you sure you want my unbridled thoughts running through your head?"

Red chuckled and shook his head.

"What?" I snapped.

He grinned as he confessed, "I was just thinking that you were a born wolf. This transition will be easy for you."

*Queen of Wolves*, the Sphinx had dubbed me.

"So, will you run with us?" Holt surprised me by asking. His voice was as deep as the woods that unfurled outside the window. "I have no doubt you can keep up."

To that, I raised a glass. I'd given him chase more than once when I was running from the rooms they tried to lock me inside in the House of the Moon. "I will."

Chase grinned. "I don't know; she's so tiny. I bet she takes four steps to our one."

"Are we running for pleasure or to race?" I asked.

He shrugged. "Which do you prefer?"

I rose from my chair. "I'll need to change clothes. If I'm racing, I don't want to be encumbered."

"Citali," Beron laughed, "do you intend to run in one of your gowns?"

I shot him a feral grin, full of the teeth he kept saying I had. Perhaps he envied them. "Oh, Wolven. Believe me when I say that I fully intend to. I have one that will allow that and much more."

Red bit his lips to hold his laughter, the grin still peeking out.

"And Chase…?" His dark blue eyes snapped to mine. "Racing isn't about who is fastest, but who is more ruthless and willing to cut down her opponents to win."

When I looked away from the pup, I was met with Beron's look of approval, then his nod.

I left them to ready myself.

# 7

I had nothing to wear for running. There were only dresses, gowns, and gold stuffed into my trunks, and I was wearing one of the plainest garments I owned. Kevi and her dancing girls came to mind, along with what they'd altered and worn to swim.

I didn't need anything *that* skimpy, but I did need to be able to move. I had no false illusions that I would beat, let alone keep up with the tall, muscled men waiting downstairs, but I had to try. That sincere effort alone could earn their respect. In time, maybe I could garner their loyalty. Maybe comradery would bind this small Wolven army to me, and we could work together to hunt the same prey: Zarina.

Something in the back of my mind whispered that she was not the only one we needed to hunt. The dark one's name hissed through my thoughts. The fact that she grew up trusting Father and had made some nefarious pact with Anubis did not excuse her actions. She did so willingly. Soberly. Her mind was clear when she stabbed me. There was anger on her face when she twisted the blade. But then something shifted and for a moment, she looked shocked.

I didn't care what excuse she would offer for what she'd done: whether it was Anubis, fear, or desperation. What she did wasn't an accident, but perhaps the most damning thought that roared inside my chest was that Zarina knew about Reyan. She knew I had a son and still thrust her blade into me. She knew he was small and innocent and vulnerable, yet she still went to Padren and Malia's to hunt him.

She would live to regret it, I vowed, sliding the golden dagger from the ring on my belt and slicing through the material of one of my dresses. It was gauzy and easy to separate and knot. I worked it into a short, sleeveless dress, then bent and stretched to make sure it was loose enough that I could move well. When I was satisfied, I slid the dagger back into its loop and hurried to meet the wolf pack.

Beron stepped onto the landing just as I reached the top of the staircase. Strangely, he didn't say a thing, just raked claw-like eyes over my skin. I could almost feel tugs on my dress's fabric.

Narrowing my eyes, I started to go around him when he stepped in front of me. "You can't wear that, Citali."

"What do you care what I wear?"

He scrubbed a hand down his face, then straightened his back, working the muscle in his jaw, the dimple flickering like angry fire made into flesh. "I don't."

"Good. Then if you will excuse me, I need to tell Padren and Malia that I'm going on a run." I started around him on the other side but he shifted, positioning himself in front of me again.

Beron's blue eyes that held the dark and light hues of the sea itself, flickered. "I told them. They said good luck."

I smiled sweetly and placed a hand on his chest. "Then let me pass, Wolven. I have a race to win." Beron sighed. "Are you regretting your decision to save me yet?" I teased, hoping he wasn't as I jogged down the steps. Red, Holt, and Chase were standing on the porch. They'd rolled their trouser legs up and taken their shirts off, and combined, they had more muscles than I could count. Without their shirts, they looked even larger than they had before, though I wasn't sure how.

Each was barefoot.

Holt gave me a quick once-over before turning to look at the forest. Red grinned and pointed at my feet. "You'll regret not wearing anything on your feet. The rocks are sharp."

"I can't run well in sandals. Where is the finish line?" I asked, ignoring the Wolven's proximity and the way his warmth radiated to me despite the cold air.

"You'll need to stay with us," Beron said.

"Do you need me to define the word 'race' for you, Wolven?" I teased.

"You don't know the terrain, Citali. Do you need me to define the word 'lost' for you?"

I narrowed my eyes. "Are you saying you aren't powerful enough to find me if I go off the beaten path?"

Beron stepped closer, then leaned down so his warm breath fanned the shell of my ear. "I could find you anywhere."

Goosebumps skittered over my neck and spread down my arms. I tilted my head so that my lips hovered near the corner of his mouth. "Prove. It."

Chase cleared his throat and when we looked toward him, he wiggled his fingers. "Hi. We're still here."

"As if we could forget," Beron barked, straightening to his full height and taking his warmth away.

Chase's wild curls twined in the biting wind.

Beron's eyes caught on the skin of my arms, still pebbled, though not by the chill in the air. "Sure you don't want to wear something warmer?"

I glared at him.

"Please don't change," Chase begged, watching Beron for a reaction.

Red joined him, donning a cheeky grin. "Why should she? It gets hot when you're racing. Right, Citali?"

Both stopped laughing immediately and I wondered what he'd said to quiet them so quickly…

"I'm comfortable, Beron, but thank you for your concern." With that dismissal, I walked off the porch. I expected the rocky fragments underfoot, but not the frigid temperature of the ground. It was colder than anything I'd felt before.

Holt came to stand beside me, his dark hair hanging in his eyes. He gave a sideways glance, then looked at my feet. "I know *you* aren't worried about my feet," I told him, only half-teasing.

"You think because I followed orders concerning you that you know my thoughts? You're going to regret this. I did. Chase and Red did, too. We all learned the hard way."

"Then, perhaps it's a lesson I have to learn for myself, too."

He nodded once.

Red and Chase shoved each other as they joined us. They were like young children in Helios. Always picking at one another, albeit lovingly, dragging one another into mischief.

In the distance, the cap of a mountain sharply rose, draped in pristine white lace. I took a step toward it. "What is that? On the mountaintop?"

"Snow," Holt explained.

"It's only five ridges away. Think you can make it that far, Citali?" Red asked, jutting his pointed fox chin at the snow-capped mountain.

I rolled my eyes. Of course I could.

Chase winked at me. "There's a reason I have this nickname, you know."

"You'd rather *chase* behind those who win?" I asked with a grin.

He grinned, flexed his shoulders, and bent his neck side to side. "You're about to find out."

Beron was quiet behind me as Holt called out the location where we would meet once more for my benefit, as they all knew this land as well as they knew Lumos's face.

"Do you need a head start?" Chase asked.

"Do you?" I asked

He chuckled in reply. "This is going to be fun."

"Ready yourselves," Red warned a moment before shouting, "GO!"

I pushed forward, my legs burning as they took three strides to the wolves' one. I pumped my arms, managed my breaths, and ran like I'd never run. I pictured Zarina in front of me and soon I ran toward her, my teeth bared, a wake of flying, frozen earth and rock behind me.

Together, we pushed toward the bottom of the first valley where Chase and Red pulled ahead, leaping a small stream I had no choice but to splash through. Holt was there. "You're faster than I thought," he said, his voice holding a tiny hint of strain.

As I started up the next ridge, a strange feeling washed over me. I glanced to the side and saw Beron behind me. He tilted his head. Did he not sense anything? This time, it wasn't his emotions. It was something I couldn't name, other than wrong. Out of place. Disturbed.

I sought out Sol and saw her flaring above. She was here, watching over me.

The portal was here if I needed to run.

"Is that the fastest you can run, Wolven?" I panted. "Your pups are in better shape than you!"

A growl rumbled from his chest just before he revealed his true speed, his stride devouring the space between he, Red, and Chase. Holt stayed with me until I began to tire as we climbed the next hill. I had the rush of a sprinter, but no endurance. Worse than that, the strangeness within the pit of my stomach continued to grow. I searched the forest for the source. "Go ahead," I panted. "I'm right behind."

He hesitated, but something was wrong, and I didn't want him near in case I was right.

This dreadful wave was no symptom of becoming a wolf. This was dark and dire. Vicious and vital. It felt familiar and foreign all at once.

I stopped atop the next hill to see the sky briskly darken, clouds thickening overhead and blocking my view of the sun goddess, though her light still shone beyond the dome of dark billows. Suddenly, the ground shook. I crouched and watched for lightning as thunder echoed over the sky and white tufts rained down all around me. I caught one in my palm and felt its icy temperature, watching as my skin melted it into a small droplet of water.

It was snowing.

Like the decorations Vada had arranged and hung for the ball in the Dusk Lands.

In a blink, the frigid wind turned hot and the frosty snow and the very mountain I stood upon disappeared. I appeared among a different range, one comprised of tall waves of burnt orange dunes. In the sand, it was dark. Lumos was nowhere to be found and Sol was missing from the sky. The only light came from the horizon, bright like freshly kindled fire. In the distance, I saw someone climbing along the crest of the dune, to its peak. Swathed in a dark, tattered cloak, my breath caught when he raised his head.

*Father.*

Fear tore at my heart and clawed up my throat.

*This can't be real.*

"You disappointed me, Citali," he said, drawing close, too close. The flesh of his neck had weathered into dried ribbons of flesh that rattled as he spoke. "We made a bargain."

A sweet, heady smell like incense filled the air between us before it slowly turned fetid. My feet sank into the sand as I backed away, my eyes wide and disbelieving. "You're dead. I watched you die by Noor's hand."

"But you did not see Anubis raise me. Zarina witnessed it. My only *faithful* daughter. The only worthy one among you," he spat.

I lifted my chin defiantly, refusing to let him see how his image rattled me. "Noor is Sol's daughter, but her heart makes her more than worthy. She loves the people of Helios. She immediately sought to feed and care for them, as you had refused to do for many long years."

He laughed, the skin around his eyes sagging grotesquely. "Sol made Noor Aten, but what will Anubis make Zarina?"

My heart thundered along with the sky. The fire on the horizon slowly spread through the clouds so that ash and fire rained down upon the sand.

Sol chose her Aten to represent her on earth, endowing them with a certain amount of her magic. Lumos did the same with his Lumin. But how could Anubis work while bound within the world's dark center? If he could, would he grant my sister the power to unearth him?

If he somehow rose, he would unleash his fury on us all.

I heard a familiar voice and glanced over Father's shoulder to see Malia there, slowly walking in the sand with Reyan in her arms. When he stretched and reached toward the earth, she sat him down. He fell onto his bottom and raked his fingers through the warm grains. "Sand!" he said with delight.

I started toward them, gesturing wildly. "Malia, no! Take him away from here."

She gave me a confused look. "I can't. You brought us here with you."

My eyes flickered to Father's before he turned with an evil smile and stalked toward my son.

No matter how hard I tried to struggle forward, my legs were leaden weights, mired in the sand. The dune was achingly long, but Father would still reach Reyan before I could get to him. I had no doubt that when he did, he would kill him. I had to stop him. I ground my teeth as I dragged my feet, step by step. Angry tears fell with the effort.

"Father, no!" I shouted, clawing out as if it would do any good.

And then, whatever it was that had been holding me back, finally broke. I stumbled at first and then raced like Sol's hot breath over the sand. My hand reached out to grab the back of his cloak when something hard caught my stomach. The breath exploded from my lungs as my back hit the ground with a thud.

Blinking back tears, I stared at the clear sky overhead where Sol once again shone down on me. Beron loomed, a look of sheer rage etched on his face.

"What were you thinking?" he shouted. "If you want to end your life, do it in Helios. Not on my watch and not near my home!" Beron panted, out of breath, sitting on his knees with his hands braced on his thighs.

More tears. I couldn't breathe and sucked in as much air as I could. Pushing up onto my elbows, I became aware of the other wolves surrounding me. "Where is he?" I wheezed, shakily pushing onto my hands and knees. I scrambled over frigid rocks hidden among the needled trees, cutting my palms and slicing the skin over my legs before I fell to my side, spent. "Where… where did he go?"

"Who?" Beron bit out.

"My father… I was just with him in the dunes."

"No, Citali," Beron shouted, "you weren't! Your father is dead, and you almost joined him in the same hereafter you threatened to send me to more times than I can count. You almost ran off the face of a cliff!" He stabbed a hand toward a sheer drop-off, just feet away.

I shook my head, thoroughly confused. "I didn't see it. I-I saw the sand, and him. He was going after Reyan and I…"

Beron stood abruptly, gave a firm glare to his wolves, and then shifted, morphing into the raven black coated Wolven, looming and angry. His gums pulled back to show gnashing teeth and for a few seconds his blue eyes focused on me. Then he was gone, running in the direction of the House.

Holt was beside me in an instant, helping me up. Blood slid down my shins and dripped from my hands. Everything stung. My muscles, the cuts and gashes, my pride. I stared at the trail of angry tracks Beron left behind.

"He's just upset," Holt gently explained.

My entire body shook. My legs were weak. The feeling of wrongness and that putrid smell lingered. "I don't understand what happened."

Red sighed and scrubbed at the red scruff forming on his chin. "From our perspective, we were waiting for you and you were taking longer than Holt thought it should have, so we started heading back to look for you when we heard you scream. Beron took off faster than I've ever seen him run. We couldn't come close to keeping up with him. He reached you just as you were about to run off the cliff. He tackled you so you wouldn't kill yourself. You were so close, I was afraid you'd both go over."

I stared at the ledge again, bewildered as to why I never saw the drop off. I wasn't sure the wolves believed me, but it was true. The cliff wasn't a cliff to me. It was a dune full of harmless, orange sand.

A fall from a dune might mean a tumble, along with sand in your eyes and mouth and plenty in your clothes. But it wouldn't mean a broken body the way a fall off the rock cliff would. I understood why Beron was afraid and upset, but his hasty departure… hurt.

Pressing a hand against my stomach, I tried to steady my thundering emotions as if pressing against the memory of my knife wound, staving the bleeding as long as I could. I wondered if I would always feel its phantom presence as real as the dunes I'd just seen.

Chase swallowed thickly when a deep howl tore through the trees. He tried to smile, but it looked more like a wince. "Noor and Caelum are waiting for us at the House."

"He called them?"

Chase nodded.

Holt looked sheepishly in my direction. "I can carry you if you can't walk. Your feet..." He pointed to the rock and dirt where bloody prints remained. Running barefoot had shredded them, just as they warned. As usual, I hadn't listened to those who knew better.

If I wanted to strengthen myself before transitioning, this was *not* the way to do it.

"I can walk," I rasped stubbornly, my eyes still tracking Beron's path.

"Please?" Holt asked. "I don't want to see you hurt any more than you already are."

My brows furrowed and my shoulders sagged under the weight left in the wake of my vision. "Why? I haven't been the least bit kind to you, Holt."

He shrugged.

"He'd carry me if I were hurt. Wouldn't you, Holt?" Chase said with a tight smile, hooking an arm over Holt's broad shoulders.

I took a step, ignoring them, then hissed when rocks re-opened the wounds on my feet. I quickly realized I *needed* help, even if I didn't want it. Glancing at Holt over my shoulder, I winced. "Are you sure you don't mind?"

Without another word, he nodded and scooped me up. He didn't speak the entire way back to the House of Wolves. And surprisingly, neither did Red or Chase.

All three wolves studied the forest as though it might shift and change in an instant for them, as it had for me. The pack believed me, even if the Wolven did not.

Noor and Caelum were waiting in front of the House when Holt and the wolves returned me to it. My sister grimaced when she saw my bloodied skin and her face turned to ash.

She pressed a hand over her stomach. "Beron warned us, but... after what happened, I could go a lifetime without seeing you bleed."

As could I. "I just learned a valuable lesson, sister," I told her.

"What's that?"

"That I can't yet run with the wolves."

Red attempted a chuckle, but it came out forced.

A great shadow soared overhead. The Sphinx was here. My eyes snapped to Noor.

"I need you to come with me to Helios for a short time," she said. "The Sphinx will guard us. She'll join us on the ground when you're ready. I can clean your wounds and help you dress, if you'd like," she offered graciously.

"I can manage." She quirked a brow at my bloody legs and feet. I sighed. "I guess I could use some help."

"Wait, wait, wait – did you say the *Sphinx* is going to land here?" Chase asked, excitement blazing in his dark blue eyes.

Caelum laughed. "She doesn't like Beron, so she might make a meal out of you, Chase."

Red tracked her movement across the dimming sky. Sol was moving away from Lumina, toward Helios. She would meet us there, and the goddess of the sun would watch over me and Noor.

"Beron's inside," Noor said, nodding toward the House's door.

"I know." My response came before I thought about him at all. Somehow, I knew Beron was inside, still angry at me despite the fact I didn't mean to scare him. Maybe he didn't believe me when I told him what I saw. "I want to see Reyan before we go," I told her.

Noor held the door open for Holt, who carried me over the threshold, careful not to knock any part of me against the door frame. Reyan was asleep on one of the lounges near the blazing hearth, his head on Padren's lap. Padren's lips parted at the sight of me.

"I'm okay," I whispered. "I fell."

Uneasy, he nodded.

Across the room, Malia's head was tilted back. She, too, was napping.

Holt carried me upstairs and gently eased me onto a chair. Red came in with clean rags and a large basin of water. He nodded at me as he and Holt left the room, closing the door behind them. I scooted forward on the upholstered seat, trying to touch as little of it as possible so I wouldn't stain it with my blood.

"I'm not sure where to start," Noor admitted. She knelt in front of me and dipped a cloth into the warm water. She took my hand, turned my palm up, and began to clean the rocky grit out of my shredded flesh.

"The Aten should kneel to no one," I told her, hoping to lighten the mood, but meaning every word.

"The Aten is appointed to serve her people. She kneels when she deems it necessary." When she was satisfied that my right palm was clean, she took great care with my left. "Beron said that you almost ran off a cliff."

I shifted, uncomfortable even remembering it. "Did he tell you what I saw?"

She shook her head. "He was too upset to say more than that. I know it wasn't on purpose, though. Sol was blocked so she did not see it, but she could sense darkness. And I know that you wouldn't do anything to part yourself from Reyan."

My shoulders sagged in relief that my sister believed me.

I explained to her what I saw and felt. When she moved to take up a fresh cloth and towel to clean my knees and shins, her hand trembled against my wounds – not from fear, but anger. It showed itself in the tightness around her eyes and shoulders, in the thinning of her lips. "Do you believe he's been raised from the dead?" she asked.

"I'm not sure. The rest was a vision. Maybe he was, too." With a new rag, she cleaned my knees, then my shins. "Where are we going, Noor?"

"The Sphinx demands we go into the sand to rid the world of Father's body. This cannot be coincidence." The Lioness was a foreteller, but I wondered if even this had caught her off guard. She hadn't warned me. Or perhaps she would be all too happy to let me dive from a clifftop.

"Sol is here," I argued. "We can't go to Helios."

She shook her head. "She will join us for this."

I hoped Sol reduced every inch of him to ash and bone and then scattered him in the wind, never again to be collected.

"Citali," she said, dragging the cool cloth down my shins and wiping the trails of blood away. "When we return, I think you should find Beron and talk to him. He's very shaken."

I shook my head. Now that I'd had time to think about it, my hurt was quickly turning to irritation. "I told him what I saw and tried to convince him I wasn't trying to kill myself. I know that's what he thinks, but I wasn't."

She tied strips of fabric around my feet, knotting them at the tops the way the priests did when they ventured into the sand, until every inch of my soles were bandaged. I doubted even a single grain would manage to push its way through her neat handiwork.

"He knows that, deep down. But right now, he needs reassurance that you're okay. The Sphinx is going to help us. I've spoken to her and my mother. There is a way to ensure that the dark one cannot corner you again, and to protect Padren, Malia, and Reyan."

"What about the wolves?" I added. They needed protection, too. She nodded. "Even Beron? Does the Wolven need this protection, too?"

She smiled knowingly. "He is very powerful, but yes. Sol would see him guarded as well. As would you, I take it."

"He saved my life," I offered in explanation with a slight shrug. I owed him any protection she, Sol, the Sphinx, and I could muster.

"Then I must have only imagined the lingering glances you aimed at him at the House of Dusk, as well as those he returned in kind?"

I sat up straighter. "Then you must also recall the way we fought at the House of the Moon, not to mention the fact that I pursued his brother for a time. Do you think those lingering looks somehow erase the fact that he hates me?"

"If he hated you, he wouldn't have saved you, Citali."

I shook my head. I knew why he saved me: for Reyan. Because despite how I acted, he wanted my son to have his mother.

Because Beron was good.

Noor stood and crossed the room, then rifled through my trunks. "Do you have a preference?"

"Something light." If Sol would burn fiercely enough to scorch our father's remnants away, I wouldn't be spared from her heat, only the damage it inflicted. Noor brought a thin, dark blue dress with tiny straps and fabric that would breathe as much as anything could in Sol's presence.

"Will Beron stay here? I want Reyan to be guarded," I said, exchanging my ruined dress with the new one.

She nodded. "I'll ask, if you want."

"Please." No matter what my sister said, I was sure I was the last person he wanted to see right now.

"I'll go talk to him and meet you out front."

"Do you think the Sphinx would frighten Reyan?" I asked curiously.

Noor tipped her head to the side and considered. "I don't think so, but I don't know Reyan well enough to be sure."

Neither did I, unfortunately. Not enough to say for certain whether he would respond to her with fear or delight. The feeling of failure struck me in the chest again.

Noor quietly lingered near the door. "You will come to know him better with time. It isn't your fault or his that you've been kept apart. Give yourself some grace, Citali. You're on the right path now, even if there were ruts and bumps along the way."

I nodded, my throat twisting into a knot.

She was right. Reyan and I were finally on the right path, as were me and Noor. Maybe in time it would smooth and become easier.

"My emotions have been high and low and everyplace in between," I tried to explain. "I'm never sure if I'm overreacting or underreacting, and sometimes things that seem real aren't and things that are real seem like they're not. My mind is a tangled mess of golden string."

Noor smiled. "Well, luckily, you have plenty of friends to watch over you as you unravel it. I'll go speak to Beron."

She strode out the door while I stood, letting my shredded feet adjust to the feeling of holding my weight. I left no bloodied prints on the wooden floor, so I went to find my son. If he might one day be Aten, the Sphinx would not harm him. And if she was willing to land among the wolves, she wouldn't harm them, either.

Malia and Reyan were awake when I descended the staircase. I lifted Reyan from his chair and brushed his soft hair out of his face. "Reyan, would you like to meet someone very special?"

He nodded profusely.

"She is not like you and me. She looks like a lioness. Do you know what a lioness looks like?"

Reyan shrugged his shoulders.

"Like a very big cat. But she has a woman's face. She is our Sphinx and she watches over us. She is good." *Mostly. When she wants to be.*

Malia and Padren froze. "The Sphinx is coming here?"

I nodded. "She will escort Noor and I to Helios for a short time."

"You're going back to Helios?" Padren asked. I looked at him, pressing my lips into an apologetic line. "Does the Sphinx require it?"

I nodded. "As does Sol. I'll be back as quickly as possible. In the meantime, I need you to do me a favor. Stay in the House and stay near Beron."

"What happened to you out there?" Padren asked, gesturing to the woods. "And don't insult my intelligence by telling me you fell."

"I will tell you everything when I return, I swear it. But for now..." A shadow fell over the lawn outside. "She's here."

A pair of translucent wings flapped before the window. "Bird!" Reyan squealed.

I smiled and kissed his head. "She does have wings, yes, but you will see that she is not a bird. She is the Sphinx, a lioness." I looked at Padren and Malia. "Come and meet her, but mind her teeth."

They shared a wary glance, but soon joined hands and trailed behind me. Reyan twisted this way and that as we walked through the house in his eagerness to see her. Red, Holt, and Chase stood just off the porch with Beron nearby, Caelum and Noor at his side.

Beron's gaze collided with mine. He was still furious, judging by the intensity of his glare. His dimple had evaporated like a droplet of cool water in the dunes.

The Lioness sat proudly, taking up much of the clearing in front of the house.

Reyan went quiet, staring at her in awe.

And when she smiled at him, somehow it was soft and not the feral, toothy, terrifying grin she was fond of showing me. "Hello, sweet Reyan," she cooed as I walked down the steps.

He regarded her wings, her muscled, furry body, and her mane, finally settling on her face. "Pretty," he decided.

The Sphinx inclined her head graciously.

*Who is this creature and where has she hidden her claws?*

He reached for her.

"Bring him near, Citali," she instructed. When I hesitated, she added, "I will not hurt him. I give you my word."

Walking past the gathered wolves and leaving Padren and Malia behind, I brought Reyan forward. He squirmed in my arms. "Would you like to walk?" I asked him quietly.

"Walk!" he parroted.

I sat him down and held his hand. He paused in front of the Sphinx and reached a pudgy hand toward her face. She shrank down so that she could stare him directly in the eye, then inclined her head. His tiny hand inched toward her face. "It is okay, Citali," she reassured again, her tinkling voice calm and steady. "He may touch my face."

He stroked her mane and then stepped backward. "Pretty kitty."

The Sphinx smiled at my son. "You will be quite powerful one day, Reyan. And no matter your choice, I pledge to watch over you."

Reyan watched the Sphinx as she rose to meet me again. "We must leave now."

I crouched in front of Reyan. "I need you to go with Padren and Malia for a little while."

He shook his head, his lower lip trembling. He threw his arms around my neck and hugged me tight, crying. I couldn't stop the answering tears that welled in my eyes. The tangled golden cord inside my stomach rose into my throat. "I will be back very soon," I promised.

And soon, I would change and be strong enough to protect him. Soon I would be with him always.

*Soon...*

My heart was the earth and his hiccupping cries shook and fractured it.

"Reyan, I need to go with the Sphinx and Noor. I promise to come straight back to you when I return."

He clung tighter.

My tear-filled eyes flicked to Beron, who moved forward. "Reyan," he softly said, placing a comforting hand on my son's back. Reyan eased his grip and looked up at the Wolven. "Would you like to go inside and play while she's gone?"

My son's sad eyes met mine. "Cit-li."

I hugged him again. "Rey-an. I won't be long, I promise you. All is well," I croaked.

He looked at the Sphinx and then back again. "Okay."

He hugged me once more and then held his hand out for Beron to take. I mouthed 'thank you' to the Wolven and he nodded forcefully. He'd already spoken to Noor. He would stay with my son and his grandparents. He would protect them.

The Sphinx stretched to her normal size, towering over us, as Noor opened a large portal. I'd barely walked through before glancing over my shoulder and watching my son, Beron, and the House of Wolves disappear, leaving only the sand in every direction I looked.

Sol sparked the orange sand as she raced toward us, but still, there were shadows. I wasn't afraid of the night, but now that Anubis's name had been invoked and I felt his dark power surround me… filling me with sight and smell and fear, I was afraid of what lurked in the shadowed places. Even among the sand of our dunes, where life for Helioans both began and ended.

Noor called to Sol, reaching for her mother's bright face and drawing her fast over the sky. The dunes undulated bright and dark until Sol chased all shadows away. Finally in her presence, I felt safe. Noor relaxed as well, until she turned and began to walk the swells.

A figure appeared atop one crest. The priest, Kiran, waited for Noor. His eyes flicked to me, but quickly rebounded upon my sister. His feet were wrapped like mine, though the sand wasn't as hot. Lumos had provided the desert with his soothing coolness that still lingered in the grains.

His kilt rapped in the wind. "Aten," he greeted. "Citali."

"Thank you, Kiran," my sister graciously answered.

I could only muster a derisive, "Priest."

"He lays in the next valley, undisturbed," the priest reported, waving toward the spot where Father lay.

Noor gestured for him to guide us to the man's corpse.

I followed Noor into the dunes, my dress flapping with hers as the wind roared, somehow not upsetting even a grain of sand. At the valley's bottom, just as Kiran had indicated, Father lay. His eyes had been eaten away. His skin had withered. But it was the sight of his neck that made me grasp mine. Already desiccated. The left side wasn't whole. Fleshy, stretched, too thin ribbons rattled and revealed the white bone within.

Sol had wasted no time allowing the elements and creatures to feast on him.

Noor crouched beside him. I stood opposite her. Kiran knelt at Father's head, his eyes closed and his face turned to Sol.

Father's tongue had shriveled and turned the color of tar to match the pits of his eyes where flesh still covered the bony sockets. The skin of his bald head peeled in layers. His lashes listed in the wind. Even his fingernails had receded from the skin. His legs were drawn in.

"Is this how you left him?" Noor asked Kiran.

He cleared his throat. "This is where he was placed, but his legs were not in this position. He lay limp, his arms and legs spread wide apart when we left him. Perhaps an animal moved his extremities, or the wind," he offered in a failed attempt to comfort us.

There was never comfort to be found with regard to our father.

I looked at Noor. "When he came to me in the vision, his throat was like this."

"You think it was him?"

"If it wasn't truly him, then whomever used his likeness against me knew exactly what he looked like." *And that I would see him and know…*

This seemed to upset my steady sister. Upset, then infuriate. Her face took on the look of calculating consideration. "Then we destroy the source so that if the dark one tries to use him again, you will know that what you are seeing is false."

I nodded, more than willing to see him burn away to nothing. To never have to look upon his evil face again, or question whether Anubis had brought him back to torment us.

"You should step back," Noor warned.

Kiran and I both moved away. She didn't have to ask her mother to come. Sol descended of her own volition and poured her flames over him. He was consumed almost instantly, her rage so intense that when she was through, not even chips of bone remained.

He was nothing.

He couldn't hurt anyone now.

Noor stood and waited while Sol eased higher into the sky. Kiran began to shift his weight uncomfortably. The sand all around was scorching hot again.

I wondered if the sands would shrink now that the night would cool them, or if they would always be like this. Never growing, but never changing. Once a scar was made, the skin was forever altered. Some damage could never be undone.

I stared at the spot where Father had lain, staring to make sure there was nothing left for the dark one to piece together or use against me again.

Noor's voice pulled me out of my thoughts. "Would you walk with me, Citali? I want to show you something."

I nodded. "I will."

She glanced at Kiran's feet. "You should go back before it worsens."

He bowed to her and she dismissed him as if they'd never been friends, or more.

Noor walked farther into the dunes, far away from the place Father had been thrown, then burned away. When he was out of earshot, she glanced at me. "Do you wonder about my closeness with Kiran?"

"I saw him touch your hand outside the House of Dusk," I admitted.

She tilted her head. "Why didn't you tell Father?"

"I considered it. He should never have touched you. But in the end, I decided not to. Father would have killed the priest, which would have angered Sol. I didn't think he deserved the chance to sever another spirit from their body."

The spirits of Sol's people fueled her fire, but death had given Father a sense of unbridled power. It was that power, and fear, that he fed upon and which fueled *him*.

"Kiran and I were always friends," she began. "He walked me into the dunes with Joba and I often allowed my thoughts to stray. I shouldn't have. I knew it was wrong, but I wondered if we could have been more if Sol hadn't called him to the priesthood. Now, I know why she called him. I was supposed to find Caelum. Kiran is supposed to guide me spiritually."

We continued in silence, in careful regard of one another. This strange peace between us was tentative and loamy underfoot. We had taken the step forward together, but the old wounds lingered even if Noor didn't want to acknowledge them or admit she was still as wary of me as I was of her.

We walked over and down the dunes until we came to the crest of a tall one that overlooked its grand twin. The wind was at our backs, tearing our dresses forward, but across the divide between the dunes, the wind died and the sand did not shift. A single line of footprints led to the top of the crest where a curved line of piled clumps of bone clung to the crest of the tallest dune in sight.

I knew immediately that the footsteps were Noor's. She gestured to the furthermost pile and sat in the sand. When she patted the sand beside her, I sat down beside my sister.

"That is what's left of Mother's flesh and bone," she said, gesturing to the bones at her side. Then she counted off the wives and lives Father had taken in the years after Sol's death, pointing to a different pile of bones for Mina. Liraen. Eirlet. Nikka. Joba.

*She carried her mother's remains all the way out here?* She was so young, only seven, when Sol left the earth for the sky again. I wondered how the goddess had done it. How had she peeled herself away from Noor? I could not bring myself to forget Reyan. Even when I could not be present, I compelled others to check on him and report back to me. Of course, the goddess could see her daughter from afar and was still able to protect her. I'd witnessed it more than once. But the distance and threats from Father tempered Sol's ability to shield Noor.

"Why did you bring me here?" I croaked.

"Because it's a sacred and safe place. Not even the dark one's magic could linger beneath the sands here."

"What do you want to talk about?" I asked, trying not to fidget. I wanted to go back to my son, but there was something holding me still. Was it Noor? Or could it be Sol?

"I want you to see something, but it will be hard for you."

"Whatever it is, I've survived worse," I told her.

"Barely," she whispered.

Noor waved her hand in front of us and the forest of dunes disappeared, replaced by the House of the Sun, in my room. I was seeing from Noor's eyes. Feeling through her skin. Sol's fire burned within her heart and hands. It had poured from her face and eyes.

This was the night she claimed her place as Aten. She should've been elated. Instead, fear coursed through her veins, fueling her harried steps and thoughts. Those became mine, too, until the two of us blended and became one. Until no longer did I sit in the sand beside the living and the many dead, but instead raced through space and time until my feet struck cold stone, sticky with my sister's blood.

My heart beat feverishly.

I stumbled toward the blossoming blood stain on the floor. My feet waded and slipped. Beron knelt over her, his broad form blocking my view of Citali.

Her arm was lifeless at his side; a twig among the spindly legs of her splintered table. Her feet were splayed, motionless.

"Lumos, no," Caelum breathed just behind me.

"Beron?" my voice shredded as I rushed around him to see her.

He pressed his weight onto a wound on the side of Citali's stomach. He looked up at his brother, terror and blood streaked over his face. His breathing was as frantic as mine. Panic rushed through the blue of his eyes. "Noor… help. She's dying. She's slipping away. She won't answer me now. And her eyes…" his voice broke. "The fire in them is gone."

Citali's blood streaked his cheeks, brow, neck, and arms with finger marks that were small and dainty. They were hers.

"Who did this?" I grasped her hand, leaned over to hold her eyelids open, and then patted her face. "Citali? Citali!" I shouted. "No."

Darkness had fallen. If Sol was here, maybe she could help, but I didn't have the power. I had no control over life and death. "SOL!" I screamed, demanding that she come to right this wrong. But in my gut, I felt her refusal. The dark one was near.

Lumos's light bent through the window, bathing Beron in blue. His eyes flicked upward and he went very still.

A familiar scent lingered in the air. Did he smell it? That putrid, sickening scent?

"Beron?" Noor's voice asked.

The Wolven wasn't breathing.

Caelum rushed to me, stilled my hand that was reaching for his brother. "Don't touch him," he warned, falling to his knees beside me, pushing me – Noor – behind him. "He's going to…" Caelum shielded me with his body as Beron shifted into the Wolven, full of bristling black fur and long teeth. He focused on Caelum for a long moment, then with his fangs, tore into Citali's shoulder, slinging his head back and forth. Her skin tore; a horrible ripping sound only drowned by his growl.

I scrambled toward Beron, but Caelum clamped his arms around my waist. Pushing to get free, I screamed, "Stop it, Beron!"

With my fire and fury, and with the sun in my hands, I burned Caelum to free myself, burning through Beron's fur to get him off my sister. "Stop!" I roared.

Beron collapsed onto the floor, turning human in a blink. A hand-shaped burn bubbled the skin on the side of his neck. He fumed, but the blistered, red wound quickly healed.

"Stay away from her and from me," I warned the brothers as I gathered Citali to me, her shoulders in my lap, my arms guarding her torso and the shoulder Beron had bitten. It bled now, too, but only barely. I looked all around at the blood-soaked floor. At the two men I had foolishly trusted with my life, and with Citali's.

Beron panted as Caelum slowly stood, trying to calmly explain, "It was the only way to save her, Noor." I hated his collectedness, that he thought he had a right to even speak to me, to stand in my House now.

"He saved *nothing*. He merely finished her off!" I cried. Tears filled my eyes and I clutched Citali's lifeless body closer, holding her head against my chest. My fingers drifted over her soft, dark hair. "I'm so sorry I failed you," I told her.

"She's not dead," Beron rasped. "Lumos… Lumos let me save her. But for her to live, I had to change her, Noor. I'm sorry."

"Change her?" I studied her chest. "She's not breathing, Beron. You bit her and now she's dead," I said woodenly.

He shook his head. "She is alive. I can feel every piece and part of her."

Citali suddenly gasped, her body twitching against mine, but she did not open her eyes. Her chest began to rise and fall. Her first breath was frigid, like death. But those that came after warmed my skin.

My eyes snapped to Caelum, then Beron. "Explain. *Now*. Before I incinerate both of you." I was already barely able to contain the fire writhing for release.

"Zarina," Beron stuttered. "Zarina stabbed Citali and left her for dead."

My mouth hung open.

"I heard her scream my name and ran here as fast as I could, but she lay dying. She'd already lost so much blood…" He shook his head. "She gave me a message for you, Noor." Beron sat up, crossing his legs to cover his nakedness as best he could. "She told me to tell you to protect her son. She made *me* vow it as well."

My heart stopped. Then pounded. My lashes fluttered. "Her son?" I looked at Citali's slack face, easing a sticky palm down her cheek. "You have a son?" I asked her. Tears clogged my throat and pricked my eyes and nose.

She had a son. And Father had known.

My heart cried for her. As teardrops fell, sun diamonds plinked against the bloodied stone.

I let them fall, allowing her blood to catch and coat them all, holding Citali tight and with my heart, telling her I understood now. I understood everything.

Caelum moved to sit at my side, rubbing my back and shoulder, silver tears filling his eyes. But it was Beron who broke my heart. His breaths turned shallow. He rocked back and forth, scrubbing a harried, bloodied hand down his face, through his hair.

"I begged Lumos to save her. He told me that only I could do it, and that to spare her life, I had to bite her knowing that if I bit her, she would become a wolf. She would become mine."

The scene vanished and air caught in my chest. I was back on the dunes, sitting on the sand beside my sister.

*Become his…*

"Why did you show this to me?" I asked.

"So you would know exactly what happened."

And I did now. I knew what she had felt when Zarina stabbed me, including that she was ready and willing to disintegrate Caelum and Beron, as Sol had Father only moments ago, to avenge me. And that was before she knew of Reyan and realized Father knew about him and was using that knowledge against me…

Another thought struck me. Beron hadn't hesitated, either. He'd spoken to Lumos, but when given the option, Beron shifted and saved me. He acted instinctually, instantly. He came to me when I yelled. He tried to save me himself and when he couldn't, went straight to Lumos for help.

Then he shifted and bit me, knowing that we would forever be bound in a way that only few were: his pack.

"Why do I feel like you made the scene vanish before I heard everything pertinent?" I asked her shrewdly.

She frowned. "You should learn to be grateful for the gifts you receive." With that, Noor stood and walked away from the sacred place.

The wind blew over our faces, caught sand and swirled it through the air as she waved her hand and made a portal that led to darkness and needled trees, the only warmth flickering from the windows of the House of Wolves. Helioan sand sprinkled over the land of the moon in swirls that smelled of home as the portal closed behind us.

# 8

Malia was waiting on the porch in a wide, wooden chair when we returned. She started to stand when she saw the Aten reappear, bracing her hands at the edges of the armrests, but Noor stopped her. "Sit and rest. That's not necessary. We're family now."

I knew Malia well enough to know she would never be comfortable being so casual with her Aten, no matter who bore the title or what the Aten was to me. If the Sphinx, Sol, and Noor were right and Reyan chose the path of Aten, and Malia lived long enough to see him flourish, she would still bow to him. A boy she had raised as her own.

Noor quietly let herself into the House, allowing us privacy.

The woods sang all around us with night song that felt alive. It breathed, screamed, and lumbered. If I listened closely and for long enough, I could almost hear Lumos's light creep over the land.

"Reyan is asleep on the chest of the Wolven." Her tone wasn't sharp, but it bore many questions. I fought a smile, knowing Beron was likely not sleeping and would hear every word. "He hasn't let Reyan out of his sight since you left."

"I asked Beron to watch over him while I was gone. I know you and Padren have raised him, but there is strange magic at work here and Beron is the strongest in this land."

She was quiet for a moment, the moonlight catching on the silver streaked through her dark hair. She sat up and leaned in. "I thought you wanted to marry his brother?" she said quietly, watching me.

I shook my head. "I wanted his brother's crown." *I wanted power.* "Not the man who wore it."

With Malia's "Ahh," came a single nod. She settled back in her seat and folded her hands over her stomach. "And now, have you found the man you want in Beron?"

"Must I want anyone but myself and my son?" I retorted.

"No," she said breezily before her glance flicked to the window. "But you can't expect me to believe there's nothing between the two of you."

My lips parted. A sigh crested in my chest, then broke, escaping and becoming another of the night's sounds. "Beron and I… have a complicated history."

"The best matches do," she advised with a smile. "My marriage to Padren was arranged. I hated him before I ever met him. I thought, if it wasn't for him, I could live a longer, independent life, but that wasn't true. My mother would simply have found another groom for me to wed. It took months for us to become civil, and over a year and a season of heartache for us to become friends. That friendship, over time, became love. I never would've believed it when we first exchanged cuffs, but it is a love I would fight for. A love worth dying for. Merik felt the same for you."

I wasn't sure what to say. I had loved Merik, but it was my love that led to his death. That his mother still cared enough for me to speak of a future with anyone else made my heart feel heavier.

"You loved my son, Citali. He chose you, despite our warnings – we didn't know you at the time, but knew of your father."

"I was the wrong choice."

She shook her head. "It was the right one for him. I won't lie and say that in my grief, after… I didn't blame you. But his death was not your fault. He looked the threat of death squarely in the face just for another moment with you. He was smitten, Citali. And it wasn't simply a boyish crush. He was making plans and had already told us how when Zarina became Aten, he would steal you and Reyan away. He had sketched the floorplan of a modest home he planned to build for the three of you."

Her words surprised me. Merik mentioned running away, but he'd never told me of his plans to build. The thought made almost-forgotten memories brim to the surface. We had our plans for escape all worked out. His friends would cover for us as we bribed a riverfarer to take us to the divide. I would gather all the gold I could carry to trade for what we needed later. It would be a perfect life with just the three of us. I'd asked the practical questions of how we would feed ourselves and where we would live, but Merik would tell me not to worry and say that Sol would see us through. He was so sure of it, so entranced by the dream of our future. I wondered sometimes if that dream didn't blind him to the present and the threats that lurked within it.

"I just wanted to let you know that it's okay to move on. You've grieved for Merik far longer than custom requires."

I wrinkled my nose at the thought of the mourning period. At custom and tradition and what others deemed appropriate.

What was a year but a slow twist of the sun? Like Zarina had turned her blade within my flesh. Maybe time *didn't* numb loss, but slowly inflicted a wound that when uncorked, would make a person bleed out.

It wasn't as though a predetermined, socially acceptable number of days could erase a feeling as great as love or the sacrifice it demanded. Nor could the sands of time erode the residue guilt left in its wake.

Still, her telling me this meant so, so much to me.

"Malia, I haven't thanked you enough for what you've done for me and our son."

She waved me off. "He is our blood. We only did what is right. No thanks are necessary, Citali. Besides, you've been more than generous to us."

Fighting tears, I huffed a laugh. "There's not enough gold in Helios to show you how grateful I am." A knot formed in my throat. "I just hope that you know… I want to be the mother I've always dreamed of being for Reyan, but I want you to be part of that journey, too. I won't take him away."

Tears splashed onto her cheeks. "I know that, my girl," she said, waving me over. She wrapped her arms around me and held tight, kissing my cheek. "I know the heart that lives behind the shield you've forged to protect it."

"Until this change is made in me, I still need you to guard Reyan…" I didn't tell her that she might even have to protect my son from me, but the implication hung heavily between us. After what happened this afternoon, I felt more vulnerable than I ever had. How easy it was for the dark one to fool me. My every sense had curled to his demand.

She patted the back of my hand, then took hold of it. "I will always be here for whatever you need."

I wondered if she meant it. If she'd kill me if it meant keeping Reyan alive. If the wolf I turned into became a monster, out of touch with reality, would she slay it?

Malia loosened her grip when the door opened and Caelum stepped outside. Noor's fiery cuff licked at his bicep. "Noor just left. She wanted me to tell you she was going to see Kiran about a book."

"Another book?" I lamented.

"The more we know about the true foe we face, the better prepared we can be," he wisely said.

"We won't find what we need in faded ink and whisper thin papyrus!" I argued. "We need to find my sister Zarina, learn the names and faces of those who follow her, learn their plans, and then make our own."

He shook his head. "Not until you've transformed."

"They'll attack us first if we remain stagnant," I insisted.

"We are not stagnant," the Lumin argued.

My irritation continued to rise. "Waiting is foolish! While *we* wait, *they* build. We need to strike while they're still fledgling, still stumbling after this birth with weak legs and an unsteady gait. If we wait for them to strengthen, the battle will be far bloodier. Did Lumos tell you to wait? Have you asked him for advice? Does he know where they are gathering? How they are preparing?"

His eyes darted to the window. Beron was likely telling him to drop the matter, but this was a matter worth pressing forward. Besides, they all treated me like I was fragile. Like Zarina had shattered me and my pieces were barely stitched together.

Malia stretched and faked a yawn. "I should go inside. The hour is late."

She knew I didn't want Caelum the way she once thought, but Malia was intuitive and knew Caelum wanted more than just to tell me Noor had gone home and to argue about our frustrating passiveness.

What infuriated me the most was that he hadn't answered my questions about the moon god and how he might help us.

Malia closed the door and her shadow moved across the wide window on the way to her room.

There was a tension around Caelum's eyes, tightening the skin. Was he concerned about Noor spending time with Kiran?

"You're worried." I blurted, standing at once from the chair's arm.

"No I'm not," he argued.

"Your eyes sort of… squint when you're nervous about something."

"No they don't," he hedged.

"Liar."

"Fine. Something's bothering me." He let out a long breath. "I hate it when she and I have to part," he said, staring at Lumos through the trees.

"Is it the priest?"

"No," he drawled, his brows drawn. "*Should* I be concerned about him?"

"Not at all. My sister is oblivious to all others as long as you breathe. It's just… some people get jealous."

"It's not jealousy. I just… I have a terrible feeling in my chest that won't go away. Lumos put it there." His eyes flashed. "Even *he* doesn't know where Zarina and her acolytes are hidden. He can't see them."

Finally. The truth, though I didn't want to dwell on it yet. There was plenty of time for that. But not enough to settle Caelum's heart. "You should go to her."

He glanced at me. "She's with Sol's priests. I always feel like I'm intruding when I'm with them."

"What if you're only listening to your head and not your heart, and what she truly wants is you beside her to face whatever this is together? If you're unsure of how she feels, you should ask her. My guess is that she hates being parted from you, too. Besides, Sol's priests and Lumos's need to work together, along with Noor and you and anyone else who might be able to fight the dark one."

"Why does everything have to be so complicated?"

I shrugged. "Because it is."

Perhaps that was what the Sculptor had truly chiseled: chaos. An unending cycle of triumph and heartache.

"Our mother's inside," he said quietly. "Noor formed a portal before she left and brought her through it. I told her about the attack, and after… but she needs to know about what happened today. Beron's telling her now."

I inwardly groaned. Vada had hated me from the moment she met me at the House of Dusk, and my stay at the House of the Moon made things infinitely worse. I was bone tired from emotion and exertion. Facing Vada was the last thing I wanted to do. I might sooner face Zarina.

At the thought of my murderous sister, the golden dagger warmed against my side.

Caelum smiled. "Don't act so excited."

"She hates me," I told him.

He gave me a sideways glance that didn't deny my claim. "Beron said to tell you she loves Reyan, though."

"Thank Sol," I teased.

He chuckled as he turned back toward the door, then paused with his fingers on the handle. "Your father's gone now, Citali. Don't forget that. No matter what you see."

I nodded. "I know."

"You knew earlier, too."

But I'd forgotten. It seemed so real.

"I don't want to see you hurt… or worse."

"Thank you, Caelum," I rasped.

"Just remember to be wary of mirages. If it looks too good to be true, it likely is."

"Spoken from experience?"

"Becoming Lumin was not a gentle transition." He opened the door and held it for me.

I'd never considered how he became Lumin, or how Beron became the Wolven. I'd heard a few funny stories about their childhood, but nothing about the change from young men to something… more.

Vada sat primly in a plush chair near the fireplace.

Caelum settled on the arm, nearest the flames. *He truly did miss my sister...*

Holt reclined quietly on Vada's other side, thrumming nervous fingers on his chair's armrest. Beron sat across from them in a cooler, darker spot with Reyan's head on his chest, like Malia had said. A little spot of drool darkened the fabric of Beron's shirt where the corner of Reyan's mouth met it.

Beron's cool eyes met mine and held.

Where had Malia and Padren gone? And where was Chase?

My eyes trailed up the steps, then rebounded to Beron again.

His gaze slid over me, as if he was making sure I'd returned whole and unharmed. I walked toward him and reached out for my son, but the Wolven waved me off. "He's sleeping."

"He'll fall asleep again. You can't hold him all night."

Beron quirked a brow in challenge.

"You should visit with your family."

He never looked away. "I am. Sit," he said, patting the padded cushion next to his. "For just a little while."

I took in a slow breath and settled beside him.

Vada's icy gaze was sharp like the moon diamonds she was so fond of wearing, but they softened when they slid to her son and mine. She wore a gown in the deep green color of the needles in the trees just steps from the House. Her hair was twisted and pinned neatly.

"Citali," she greeted coolly.

"Vada."

Holt glanced between the two of us warily before excusing himself. "I'm going to join Chase. We'll keep an eye out for Amaris."

"Red is nearing the Dusk Lands."

*Dusk Lands?* "Where is Red going? And who is Amaris?"

Holt quietly slinked away without answering.

"Amaris stayed behind to guard Padren and Malia's house. Now, Noor has stationed guards around it. She rotates them daily so they don't get complacent and so she knows at least some of them are loyal," Beron explained in a low, soft voice so he didn't wake Reyan. "Noor wants one of us to stay and be present in Helios for now. Our sense of smell is keen. If Zarina reappears within the city, we'll know it," he said. "We agreed to take turns. Amaris needs a break, so Red is going now to relieve her. Chase will take his place next."

*Amaris? I haven't heard the others speak of her yet.*

"Do you want one of us to watch over things from Lumina?" Beron asked Caelum and Vada.

Caelum shook his head. "The guard is informed. The only threat comes from Helios at this time."

Beron inclined his head, though it appeared that he and Caelum continued the conversation in their minds.

I pictured Red, a sly wolf with rust fur, racing through the Dusk Lands toward the sand. When Noor and I left our home for that place, I thought it was the most dismal land in existence. It likely still was. Dead and gray and desolate. Sol and Lumos would have to dance over the sky for a thousand years to coax life into that soil. Maybe longer.

In my mind, among the drab, gray weeds and reeds, Red was passing another figure, trading places with a wolf I hadn't met.

Was Amaris as large as the rest of them? I wondered if she was as quiet and pensive as Holt, bolder than Chase, or slyer than Red.

"I brought a few things for you," Vada said to me. "They're in your room."

"Thank you." I wasn't sure what she'd brought for me… maybe fresh-baked bread and nightthorn jam? Or perhaps she'd slipped a few glowing sand scorpions into my room.

"I understand why you behaved as you did, Citali. I, too, am a mother," she said suddenly. A warning growl rumbled in Beron's chest. She ignored him, just as I expected. Just as I would have. "I will be Beron's mother until I leave this world to glisten in the night sky, and I will continue to be his mother as I watch from the sky above."

I narrowed my eyes at her. Why the warning?

"Don't threaten her," Beron warned, keeping his tone low. "You don't owe her this… any of it. You saved her. That should be enough."

I turned to him.

He stood, keeping hold of Reyan while leveling a glare at his mother. "This discussion is over."

Her eyes cut into him and though I didn't think she could speak into his mind, he knew her shrewd thoughts.

I moved to take my son. This time, Beron didn't dare object when I took him into my arms. He babbled a little, but settled back to sleep almost instantly. I left Beron and his mother to their argument and walked up the steps to the room I'd been given. Gently, I laid him in the bed beside me, covering us both against the night's chill. Then, I watched him for the longest time. Just watched him breathe. Watched his eyes flinch beneath their lids as he dreamed. I hoped his dreams were bright and wonderful.

Because somehow, I knew mine wouldn't be.

Time had altered his face so drastically. He was growing up too quickly. I'd missed so much, only glimpsing from time to time, pretending to be a friend when I was so much more, just so it was easier for him.

Until Sol came, I didn't shut my eyes. I watched over him until she could.

And I savored every moment with him I had been gifted.

It felt like I'd only slept a few moments before Malia came into my room, smiling tenderly at me and Reyan as we stirred awake. "The others are going running, but they decided you should rest. I decided you should choose what was best for you."

I gritted my teeth, fuming. "Thank you." I eased from the bed, careful not to wake Reyan.

Malia held a pile of dark clothing out to me. "This is what Vada brought for you. Did she tell you about them?"

I shook my head. "We didn't get that far."

Malia's nose scrunched in confusion, but she didn't pry. "Well, these are delicate leathers stitched with special thread."

"How is the thread unique?"

"It's built to be strong while you are in this body and break neatly when you enter the next, so you can retrieve and mend the garments later. It seems Vada's sister is sick of constantly making new clothes for the Wolven's folk," she added with a grin.

I took them from her and quickly changed out of my dress. She held my belt and dagger until I could slide them back on. My feet were still tightly wrapped, even if some of the fabric strips were charred at the edges.

"She sent boots for you as well."

A dark pair sat near the door, small enough for my feet and tall enough to skim the bottom of my knee. They were perfect. I tore at the wrappings, unraveling my bandages to reveal the skin of my soles – so recently shredded and sore – now healed.

I plaited my long hair and tied a scrap of fabric around the end, throwing the rope of hair behind me when I was finished. "Vada threatened me last night."

Malia straightened, her usually content face twisting into a scowl. "Whatever for?"

"She's worried about her son."

Malia scoffed. "Which son? The Wolven or the Lumin?

"Beron," I confirmed, taking the boots from her waiting hands.

"She thinks *you're* a threat?" She gave an indignant look.

"Maybe she thinks I'm too weak, and that I'll hurt the pack by being the weakest among them."

"Well," she said, crossing her arms. "Sitting in the House today wouldn't remedy that, now would it?"

I quickly tugged on each boot, tightened the laces, and tied a knot that would not work its way loose.

"I'll see to Reyan," she promised. "We'll stay inside until you return."

A weight lifted from my shoulders. "Thank you."

She shooed me out the door. "Hurry. And this time, if you see your wretched father, use your knife first and then let the Wolven devour him."

I rushed down the steps where I saw Holt and Chase standing with Beron and… a female. A female whose upper lip curled when she saw me. If she was wolf and not a woman, her every hackle would have raised.

She was beautiful, with burnished red hair that fell to her shoulders. Big doe eyes glanced over me dismissively as she brushed her delicately freckled skin. She stood awfully close to Beron. Close enough to whisper. Close enough to touch.

She smirked and craned her neck to look at the Wolven, and I could almost feel my fingernails lengthen.

I remembered her from the House of the Moon. From the ball. She'd danced with Beron once, then disappeared.

I jogged down the steps, decided. The new boots and clothes fit perfectly, and I wouldn't let Beron and his little friend spoil my morning. "Good thing you weren't planning to leave without me," I said easily.

"You could use some rest after yesterday," Beron answered, his muscles tense as he raked his eyes over my new look.

I attempted a smile and extended my arms. "I'm fully rested."

"You haven't eaten," he volleyed, crossing his arms.

My upper lip flinched. "I'm. Not. Hungry."

A wide smile blossomed on Chase's lips. "Obviously," he muttered. Holt smacked his arm.

Beron ticked his chin toward the woman standing before him. "Citali, this is Amaris, who we spoke about last night."

She rudely stared instead of uttering a pleasantry, so I greeted her in kind. If the girl thought I didn't already have teeth and claws, she was sorely mistaken.

"Who's running with Citali?" Beron asked his pack, slicing the tension so it could build anew.

Holt's level gaze met mine. "I will."

"You got to spend time with her yesterday," Chase complained.

The female blinked at their silly spat. "You've *got* to be joking..." she muttered loud enough for all to hear.

"The choice is yours, Citali," Beron said.

"Good. Then I'll run alone."

"Not after what happened during the last run," he growled.

I passed by him and Amaris. "I don't need a watchdog, Wolven."

"And if you encounter the ghost of your father?" Beron's deep voice slid toward me.

"It won't be a problem today," I answered, not looking back as I stepped into the trees. "Sol made sure nothing was left of him for the dark one to use."

I took off running, but the wolves easily caught up. Chase slowed his pace to match mine, as did Holt, though I wasn't sure where Beron and his pretty friend had gone. "Let me guess – he gave you a silent order?" I surmised as we took the first hill.

Chase snorted. "It was anything but silent. You seem to be very skilled at burrowing under his skin."

"The feeling is mutual," I gritted, pushing faster up the steep incline. It was so much easier to run in these clothes. The light-as-air trousers were like softened butter, while the tunic was fitted so my arms could move freely. We crested the peak and began our trek toward the valley below.

"Amaris isn't so bad when you get to know her," Chase said. "She's just not friendly to strangers."

"And she's used to being the only female," Holt added.

I dodged a boulder, side-stepped a jumble of tree roots, and somehow managed not to turn an ankle. "I don't care."

When the ground leveled, Chase jogged ahead. He turned and ran backward faster than I could push to keep up with him. "Will I be able to run like you when I change?" I shouted to him.

He slowed again. "Like me?" he asked with a laugh, pointing to his chest. "No one can run like me."

"Except Beron, who easily outruns you," Holt playfully reminded him.

Not the slightest bit winded, Chase waved off Holt's comment. "He doesn't count. He's not what we are. He's the Wolven. We're his wolves."

A sudden stitch formed in my side. I winced and pressed a hand to it, a feeling colder than the frosty wind cutting through the leathers. A cold sweat burst over my skin and darkness buzzed through my vision, a graceful swarm.

"Citali?"

Suddenly, Holt was there. He hooked my arm over his shoulder.

Chase swam in and out of view. "Beron's coming," he promised.

"I don't need him. It's just a muscle cramp," I told them both. Lying, knowing this was something else entirely. Something sharp. Wincing, I took my arm from Holt and folded my body, seeking relief.

That strange feeling of wrongness slithered around me, constricting until it tugged, like a rope around my wrist. I stumbled toward it and caught its heady incense aroma… and that sweet, rotten spice. The fetid, putrid scent lingered where the more alluring one had been, as if magic had tucked death itself into a bouquet of flowers and spice.

*Father?*

My lips parted. That scent was present yesterday when I thought he had been resurrected. It lingered in my rooms after Zarina left me for dead, and not even the metallic smell of my blood could smother it. Noor hadn't noticed the stench, but when she fit me into her skin, I caught its scent…

The Sphinx's large shadow fell over the three of us for a second before she moved and began to circle overhead like a vulture over carrion. Did she smell it, too?

"She's back," Chase marveled, a tinge of fear in his voice.

The scent was on the wind. It slid between the needles all around us, rattling them in their perches. Then it withdrew, and when I searched for the feeling that heralded the tug, I met resistance. As if something didn't want me to give chase. Something pushed back instead of pulling forward.

"This way," I gritted, running along the base of a hill in the direction from whence the smell originated.

"Citali, no!" Holt shouted, quickly catching up to me. His hand found my bicep.

Desperate, I wrenched my arm from his grip. "Come with me. I'm not hallucinating, I swear it. I smell something familiar."

"I'm at your side," he shouted. "If you see anyone or anything, you tell me."

"I promise."

Chase ran to my right, searching the sky for the Sphinx. "Beron and Amaris are almost here."

We raced until the land sloped, then ended, and we came to a place where a great, wide river split the earth. The water was blue green, crashing over pale gray rocks, frothing and angry. Its clean scent erased the heady smell I'd been tracking.

I flung my braid off my shoulder and paced the rocks in frustration. I almost had it. Whatever *it* was. The scent got bolder, just before it disappeared.

Holt's feet raked the gravel as he abruptly turned to face Beron and Amaris when they burst from the trees.

"You're late," I teased, still feeling uneasy.

The Wolven's blue eyes held mine as he rushed toward me. His hands clamped onto my biceps, gently despite the fierce look in his eyes. "Are you okay?" I nodded, speechless. "What did you see?"

"I didn't see anything, but rather caught a scent."

Beron sniffed me. Leaned in and inhaled, his eyes closing. When he opened them, his pupils were dilated. He drifted toward me again, as if I were that indescribable thing tugging at him.

"What are you doing, Wolven?"

Beron didn't shrink away. He stepped closer. I didn't know there was any space left between us, but he erased it in a single, slick movement.

"Describe the scent, Citali," he breathed against my lips.

I put my hand on his chest and pushed, placing distance between us. It was only inches, but I could breathe easier.

"I smelled something familiar and remembered that when Father appeared to me yesterday, the same scent was in the air. So, I followed it here, but the river erased it. At least, I think it did. Do you smell it?"

He smirked. "There are a million scents swirling around me, but right now, I smell nothing but you."

"Then get your nostrils out of my hair," I snapped, backing away from him.

Amaris let out an inhuman growl despite being in human form. She stalked into the woods, leaving the rest of us behind.

A shadow passed over us and the Sphinx let out a ferocious roar that rattled both river and rock. She flew in the direction of the House of Wolves. Her translucent wings caught Sol's rays and scattered shimmering light over the earth.

Chase grinned at her, completely entranced. He didn't care that she could shred him without even baring her claws. Maybe that was what struck him with awe. His head whipped toward me. "Is she landing at the House?" he asked me.

"Probably," I grumbled just before my stomach growled.

Beron smirked in my direction.

"I'm still not hungry," I lied.

His dimple popped and his eyes glittered like moon diamonds now that his pupils had retracted. I started toward the House. We hadn't gone far into our run before I smelled the sickly-sweet rot and left the run to seek what had been hidden from me, so the return trip was short. Chase walked at my side. Holt and Beron trailed behind, having a quiet conversation that Chase sometimes ignored me to join.

"This is a sign – maybe from Sol," Chase suddenly chirped. His curly, sand-colored hair wasn't even damp, yet the back of my head was soaked with sweat.

"What is?"

"Two days, two runs – both interrupted by evil. Perhaps you should stop running, Citali."

"And be weak when I shift into your form?"

Chase laughed with his whole body. "Weak is not at all how I'd describe you."

"What word would you choose?"

He shrugged playfully. "You can't properly be summed up in one singular word, Citali."

"You barely know me. I'm sure you could manage."

He grinned. "Let's put it this way. There is only one thing in Helios I fear more than you, and her roar just sent shivers up my spine. Shivers!"

"Speaking of the Sphinx, were you expecting her?" Holt asked from behind.

"No."

"I wonder what news she brings, then," he replied.

"I'm not sure, but I pray it's not in riddle form. She was gracious enough to speak plainly yesterday, but my prior experiences with her haven't always been so pleasant, or clear," I admitted as we crested a hill.

Chase stopped suddenly, looking from me to Beron and Holt behind us with wide eyes.

"What?" I glanced around the woods, seeing no threat.

"Citali, you just answered him…" Chase said.

"Yeah…?"

Holt's usually serious lips tugged at the corners. "I didn't speak my final thought aloud."

My lips parted. "Are you sure?"

A "yes" came from all three men.

I let out a whoop. "Think something else, one of you."

They were quiet. Beron's smile fell and he glared at Chase, who ignored him entirely to focus on me.

"Did you hear what I just said?" Chase asked with a hopeful grin.

My shoulders sank a little. "No."

"It'll come," he promised, mouthing something to Beron over my head. As if he even needed to.

"I can't wait until I can hear everything all the time. Have fun trying to keep your secrets then."

"Just remember that we'll be privy to yours as well," Beron reminded me.

I shrugged. "My greatest secrets are ones you already know."

I felt the absence of them in the lightness of my shoulders and heart and their heaviness in my mind. My secrets knew Sol's light, but that meant Reyan was known to those who sought to destroy him.

Taking off in a jog toward the house, the others fell into step. "How else can I get stronger?" I asked them. I couldn't help but feel I was running out of time.

"Your sister attacked you with a blade." Chase's curls bounced with every stride. "Which means you should learn to use one to at least defend yourself. Ultimately, you should sharpen your senses and hone your body until you're the weapon and that blade on your hip is nothing but another pretty accessory," he advised.

He was right. "Can you show me later?"

He swiveled his head back to look at the others. "Of course. You're one of us and we take care of our own."

I didn't tell him I didn't feel like I was a wolf yet.

I wasn't an Atena, either, and I would never be Aten.

But those titles didn't matter because I knew where I fit perfectly, no matter where I was or who surrounded me.

I was Reyan's mother.

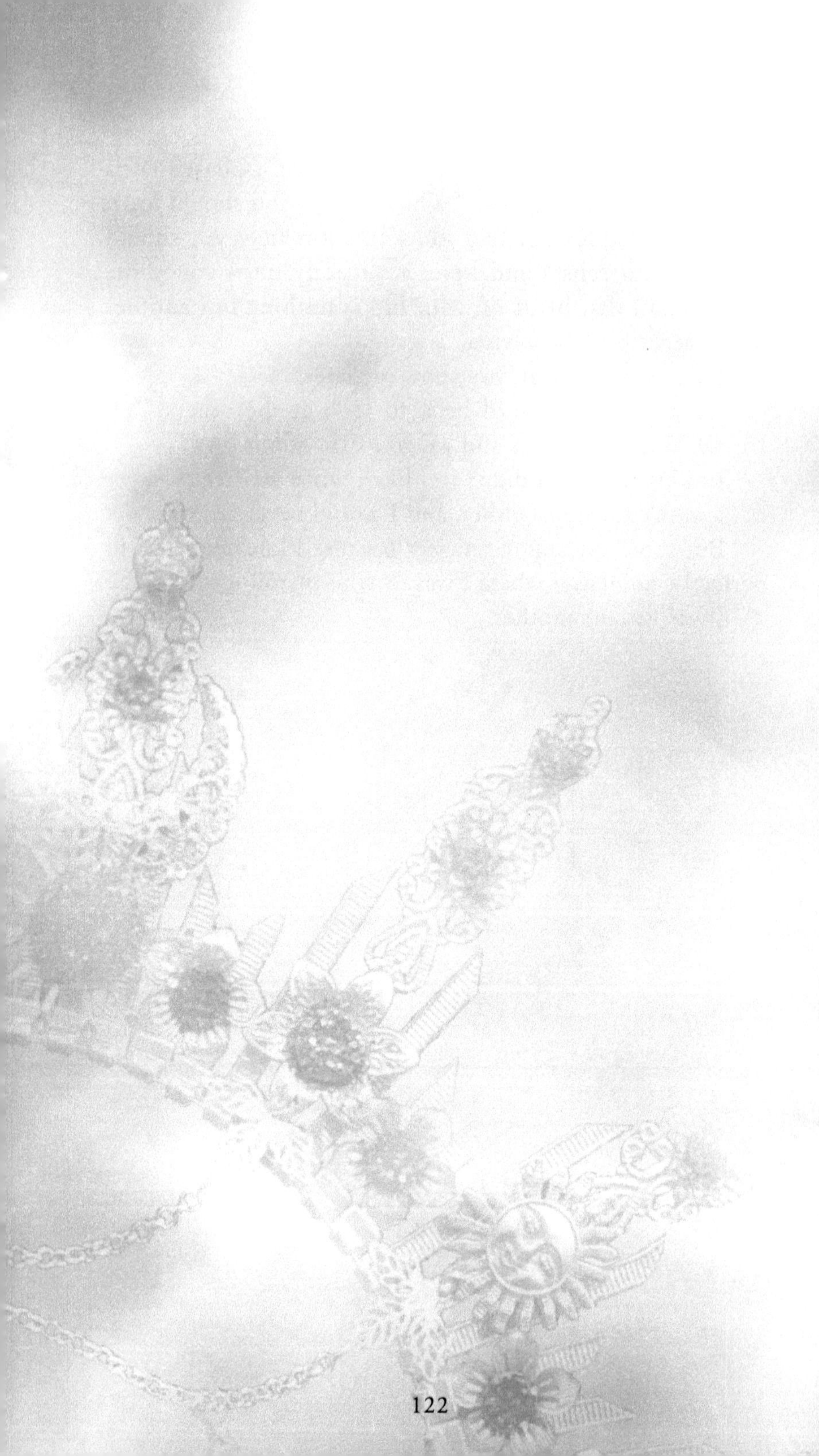

# 9

My son's laughter filled the air as we left the trees and entered the clearing in front of the House of Wolves. The Sphinx had landed and had shrunk herself so that she was little larger than a winged house cat. Reyan, on all fours, chased after her. With calm grace, she let my son pet her mane, her back. He even poked at her wings.

She adored him.

That adoration faded from her majestic face when she saw me. "We must talk."

"It's lovely to see you again, too," I smarted.

The Sphinx bowed to Reyan. "I'll see you very soon, little one."

He took her mane in his chubby fingers and drew her face close, then kissed her forehead. Her black eyes were glistening when she pulled away. She bowed to him a second time. The cool wind warmed and tousled Reyan's soft, dark hair. He grinned up at me. "Cit-li."

"Rey-an."

"Look at the pretty kitty!" he squealed.

I crouched beside my son. "I need to speak with the Lioness, okay? I'll be back soon."

This time, the phrase he'd become used to no longer phased him. Reyan ran to Padren and threw his arms around his grandfather's legs. My heart longed for the day he didn't have to part with him. And my tongue hoped for a time the Sphinx didn't have to speak words that might not prove true.

How close Zarina had come to parting us for good.

Standing, I glanced at Beron as she and I walked away. In his eyes was a similar promise: *I'll be here. I'll guard him.*

As the Lioness bowed to Reyan, I inclined my head to the Wolven.

I followed the Sphinx as she wended trails that led away from the House and climbed to the top of a high ridge where a wide swath of sky shone among the trees. "The Wolven can't hear us this far away," the Sphinx explained. Her fathomless eyes locked onto mine.

"What can't he hear?" If she revealed a new secret, Beron might soon know it anyway. I heard Holt's thoughts in my mind today. If they couldn't already, the wolves would soon hear mine.

"He will know it when you return, but you should hear it first, Citali. It's only right." Cold fear slithered up my spine. "Sol gave me the honor and responsibility of hunting the dark one and severing the power he has over the people he's deceived – her people. Today, I tracked his scent into this forest where it crept over the land like grasping fingers searching for something they've let loose of and need again."

My heart stuttered. "It was *his* scent I caught?"

She gave a regal nod. "Tell me Queen, did your wolves sense it at all?"

I sifted through my memory. Holt and Chase ran beside me, to guard me as they were instructed, but they didn't smell anything out of the ordinary.

My lips parted. If the wolves couldn't smell Anubis, how could I?

"I know what Anubis seeks," she said, her voice turning deep. "Sol claimed his blade, but not until after Zarina cut *you* with it."

"She turned it into gold." I took the dagger from the loop on my belt and held it out for her to see. The sun goddess had carved her name into the metal, infusing it with her heat and radiant light.

"Sol believes that when he made the blade, Anubis infused it with his essence. When it cut into your body, some of his dark power crept into your flesh…or perhaps your fury caught hold of it and won't let it go. It's why Sol wouldn't heal your wound and wouldn't allow Noor to even try. But when the Wolven asked Lumos to intercede and save you, and Lumos allowed him to bite and change you… that small amount of Anubis was sealed inside you."

My ribs felt too tight, like my throat. "Get it out."

The Sphinx balked. "I cannot."

"Get it out!" I shouted.

She stretched into her giant, true form and shook out her mane, her claws gouging the earth near my feet as she lowered her head. "I. Cannot."

"He'll find me."

She roared in my face.

I returned her fury. "I didn't steal his essence; he almost killed me with it!"

She began to pace, her chest still rumbling with anger. "Almost, Queen of Wolves. But part of the dark one is in you. Whether he made the mistake of leaving it behind or you stole it doesn't matter. He never meant for *you* to have it, and he wants it back."

I pressed my eyes closed, but they snapped open when a thought crossed my mind. "He pulled away when I sensed him… That means I can hunt him."

The Lioness smiled. "Yes, Wolf Queen, you can. And Sol wants you to find him."

"She thinks I'll find him before you?" I tried to tease, still reeling from the news and wishing Anubis's blade had never touched me.

She answered with a wicked grin. "I'll help you shred him. You can't take *all* the fun." She shrank again until we were the same height. Her obsidian eyes shone. "Until this ends, Anubis and you will hunt one another. That means that anyone near you is in danger."

Which meant that my son was.

Padren and Malia were.

Noor and Caelum.

Beron and his wolves.

"Am I to go with you, then?"

The Sphinx cackled, suddenly sounding less young and more wizened. "Not at all. As you are, you're no hunter. You cannot face the dark one without becoming what you're meant to be. As you are, you stand *no* chance against him. You're weak and quite pathetic."

I bristled, my skin heating like Sol was trying to make me depart this world again.

"Calm yourself," the Sphinx chided. "What I say is truth. Your body is a house of sand and inconstant flesh. Your sister proved that much to you when she cut into you. But soon, you will be clad in claws and teeth. Your body will finally match the fierce spirit trapped within your heart. You still won't be my equal, though, Citali. Don't forget…I know the thoughts inside your mind."

I wasn't trying to hide them. And frankly, she was right. Currently, I was not her equal. Clad in flesh, I was nothing more than easy prey. Soon, though… Soon, I would become wolf. Hunter. I wondered if even the Sphinx would be brave or bold enough to call me weak or pathetic then. Would she say anything about me was inconstant when I was a wolf?

She tilted her head, assessing me, almost as if she could see the wolf that grew within my bones and didn't appreciate what she saw.

If Anubis pulled back from me now, where would he dare hide once my senses were keen and my bloodthirst was unsated?

"How long until I change?" I gritted.

She tipped up her chin. "Only Lumos decides. Sol does not know."

I was sick of waiting for someone else to tell me what was best for me.

"There is no way to force such a change. The god of the moon will choose for you, and you will listen."

I narrowed my eyes at her.

"I want to take Reyan and his grandparents away," the Sphinx said matter-of-factly, as if the decision had already been made.

My breath caught. "Where?"

"Away from you. The dark one knows of them because of your fool of a sister. He will seek them out. He'll destroy them, and you, with them."

"I have to know they're safe. I have to know where to find them."

She straightened her back. "You cannot know."

"Are you saying the dark one can also hear my thoughts?"

The Lioness sighed. "Sol is not sure, but it is possible. Just as it is possible for her to speak into my mind, and for the Wolven to commune with his Lumin and pack. This is the only way your son will truly be safe."

"How will I know they won't be hunted down while they're away from me? Who will protect them?" I asked, anxiety and fear clawing up my throat.

"I will guard them," she offered. "In time, you will trust my words. I mean no harm to your son."

In time, maybe. But not now. Not after the riddles and distractions and bait she used to sway me from my goals…

A rumble tore from her great chest in response to my traitorous thoughts. Her fur stood on end, as did the hair on my arms and neck.

"How will you manage to hunt Anubis *and* guard my family at the same time?"

"The ways of the Sphinx are not your concern, but know that I am far more capable than you at present. I will protect the future Aten with my life, Queen of Wolves, even if I must shred the skies and earth to do it. And not because Sol, Noor, and you demand it, but because the future depends on it." She sniffed the air haughtily. "And… because I like the child."

I would have laughed if I wasn't panicking at the thought of what lay inside my flesh, part of Anubis's malevolent essence. Worse than that, to keep my son safe, I would again have to send him away, trusting only the Sphinx herself to protect him.

Zarina thrust a blade into my stomach, but this felt like a knife to the heart.

Padren and Malia would understand. They would take Reyan and go with the Sphinx with no questions asked. But I wouldn't know where to find them.

"When you become wolf and rid yourself of this darkness, you will find him. Even I could not stand in your way then," she said, her voice gentler.

"How do I rid myself of the darkness? If *you* can't get it out of me, and Sol and Lumos can't, what can?"

The Sphinx's solid black eyes fastened onto mine. "The pathway is unclear, but remember this: darkness seeks darkness. Light seeks light. The answer will be revealed to you in time."

I wasn't sure it was an answer I would like.

"I need to take them now," she said suddenly, sniffing the air. I strained my senses but didn't smell Anubis on the wind. "Sol demands it."

I looked to the sun goddess's bright face, scarred by the tree branches that lay between us. "Take care of my son," I whispered. "I'm trusting you." The wind turned warm, tousling strands of my hair and calming me just enough to take the first step back toward the House of Wolves.

I had to once again say goodbye to my child, promising to see him soon.

To lie and tell him all was well and put on a smile when all I felt like doing was crumbling into a million tiny fragments. When I wasn't sure that even clad in teeth, it would be enough to rid myself of Anubis's dark pulse.

I had to ask Malia and Padren for their help one more time. Perhaps for the last time.

Then I had to tell Beron I was putting his home and his pack in danger just by being there. He would probably ask me to leave, but I didn't know where to go. Until I changed, I couldn't hunt beyond the occasional scent trail.

What did the future hold?

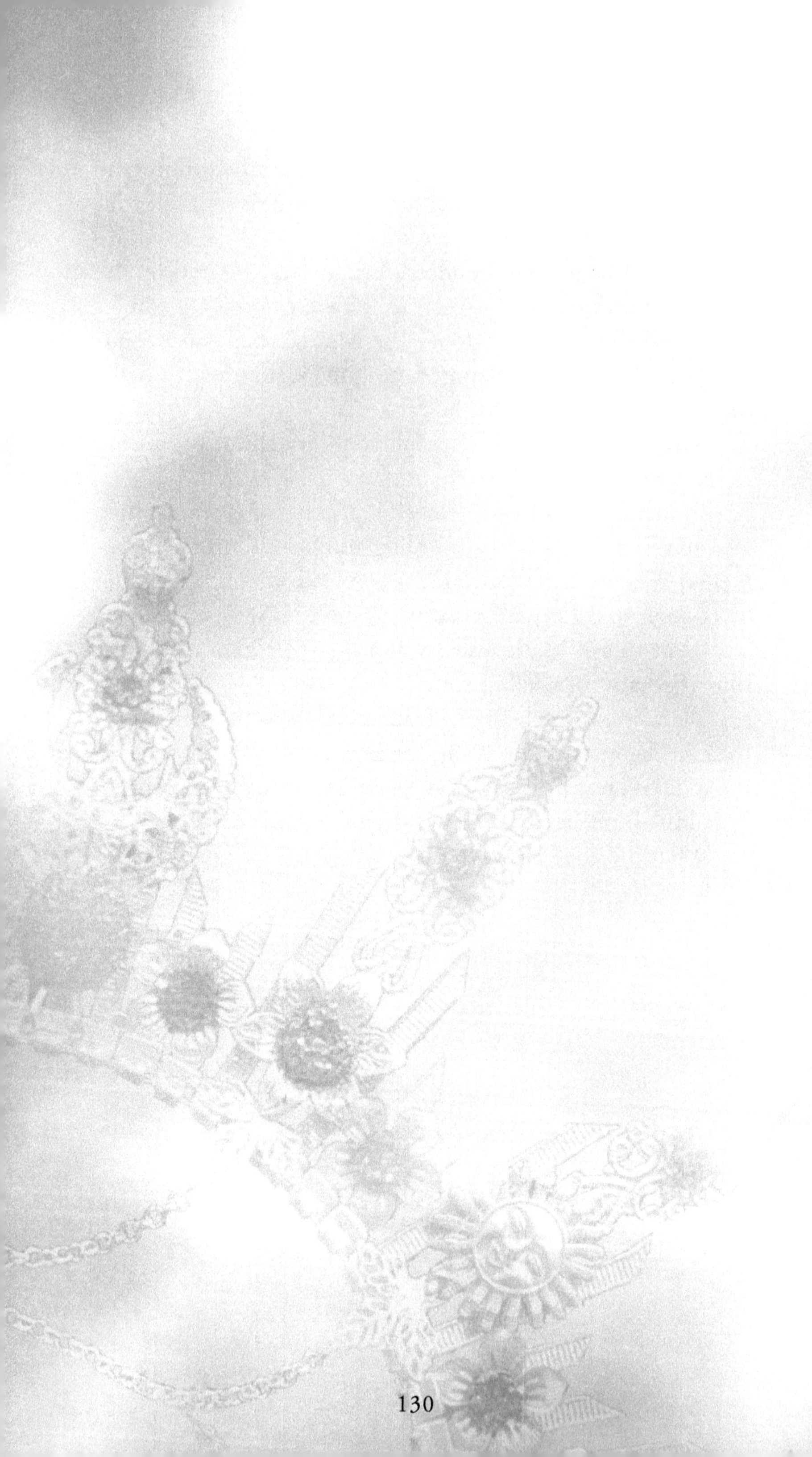

# 10

Backtracking took much less time than I anticipated and before I wished, the Sphinx was standing before my loved ones and Beron's pack. The Lioness told me that Beron would *know* when I returned. Could he feel my emotions the way his sometimes swept over me, or was I too weak to keep the despair off my face? The utter agony of having to – once again – send my son away for his own safety broke my heart.

Whatever the Wolven saw or felt in me, he took a step toward me.

Noor cut him off, wrapping me in a hug. Her warmth comforted me. "This is for the best, but I can't imagine how hard it is for you."

"Do they all know?" I whispered.

She shook her head, pulling away. "I can tell them if you'd like."

"No," I rasped, tears filling my eyes. I swiped them away as Noor hid me from sight, collecting myself as best I could. I didn't want to frighten or upset Reyan.

Malia and Padren each had one of his tiny hands. "Cit-li sad," he said, running to me. I crouched and caught him in a hug. I ran my hands through his soft hair, smelled his baby smell, and wished for another way to keep him safe, with me.

His grandparents approached. "Citali?" Malia asked cautiously.

"The Sphinx has invited you to go with her for a time, the two of you and Reyan."

Padren ticked his head back in surprise. "Whatever for?"

"She can keep you safe right now. I can't. I'm putting you in danger by being near you." My eyes flicked to Beron. "*All* of you."

"But, how?" Malia asked, confused.

I smiled at my son, swallowed my tears, and as calmly as I could, explained. "When Zarina stabbed me with the dark one's blade, part of his essence and power seeped into me. When Beron healed me, it sealed that darkness inside. That means that now, he can sense me and I can sense him. That is how I know he's coming for me."

Beron's blue eyes turned to ice; ice, layered with both guilt and defiance. He would do it all over again to save me. I knew that. But like Lumos warned, we would both face consequences far beyond those on the surface for allowing Beron to heal me. Now, not only would I turn into a beast, but I was also harboring part of Anubis within my body, however unwittingly.

I was already part monster.

The apple in Beron's throat bobbed.

His chest rose and fell, faster with each passing breath.

The horror in Malia and Padren's eyes was something I would never forget. As much as Anubis had seared himself inside me, so did this defining moment.

I held my child and kissed his head. He hugged me, oblivious to the truth of my turmoil, his tiny hand patting my shoulder and stroking my braid. "Cit-li."

"I will miss you, Reyan," I told him. "I love you so much." He pulled away, his eyes wide. Merik's light brown eyes. "I want you to know that… here." I touched the skin over my heart and he placed a hand over his own, mirroring the motion. "No matter what comes. Know that I love you."

He hugged my neck and pressed a kiss on my cheek.

Padren cleared his throat and raked a hand through his graying hair. "When are we to depart?"

"Now," the Sphinx insisted. "We must leave right now."

"Why the urgency?" Noor asked.

"Because Sol demands it," the Lioness replied cryptically.

I rose and picked Reyan up. "Be good for Padren and Malia, and for the Sphinx. Don't spoil her too much."

He grinned. "Okay."

"Careful of her teeth," I told him.

The Lioness scoffed indignantly.

When Padren and Malia came toward us, Padren gave me an awkward, fatherly pat on the back that almost broke me. He was the father every child should have but didn't. Malia leaned in and kissed my cheek. "Don't worry for us. We will be fine and we'll take care of your little one. We'll wait for you," she promised as she tucked an errant strand of hair behind my ear.

In a blink, the Sphinx shrank so Padren and Malia could climb onto her back. I held Reyan up for them to take. "Is this safe?" Malia said nervously.

The Sphinx grinned. "Of course it is. To me, flying is as natural as walking on land. Perhaps as easy as breathing."

"Just don't forget you're carrying them," I told her.

In an instant, her grin fell away and she puffed out her chest. "I never forget." She grew into her gigantic form once more and with a great flap of her wings, they lifted into the sky. Surprisingly, the Sphinx was gentle in her flight as she took them away.

I numbly watched until the trees obscured them, then raced to a clearing where the sky was clear, hoping to catch one last glimpse, but she was gone. My son was gone.

My legs weakened and I fell to the ground, curling my knees to my chest and wailing, certain the Sphinx could hear my cries. I clawed my fingers through my hair as I rocked back and forth and sobbed. Dark clouds of anxiety filled my chest with so much force and pressure that I couldn't breathe.

Had I done the right thing? Would she truly keep him safe?

"Citali…" Noor was nearby, sitting with me. "When we left the Dusk Lands, I felt the moment Sol was no longer within reach as a hollowness in my chest. I imagine from a mother's point of view, it's a thousand times worse."

A sound of frustrated desperation slid from between my teeth. "You need to stay away from me, Noor. It's not safe for you as long as…" I couldn't bring myself to say it out loud, though my brain screamed, "*some piece of the dark one is writhing in me!*"

"It's okay," she said. "I'm not afraid of you."

Nothing was okay, and I had a horrible feeling it never would be. "You should be. You're the Aten now. Our people need you."

She shook her head.

"If he's using Zarina, what's to say he won't use me?"

She squared her shoulders. "Because you are the sharpest of the three of us. You won't allow it."

"Sharp, yes. But un-whole. I'm nothing but shards. Broken." My throat hurt. My eyes burned. I couldn't seem to compose myself or stop shaking. Crying. Panicking. Rocking.

"Shards still cut," Beron said softly as he crouched beside me. His words made me cry harder. "Citali, look at me."

I couldn't.

"Please?"

I finally managed to raise my quivering chin to meet his blue gaze. There was a steadiness in them I hadn't seen in Lumina, or in anyone's eyes but Caelum's when he looked at Noor.

"You trusted me with your son," he said.

The wolves stayed near him. Resolute and loyal. They were friends. Family. Yet more, sharing a bond no others did.

"I did," I croaked. I did so because I knew his heart. I'd learned it despite the games he and I played in the Dusk Lands; he in an attempt to protect his brother, and I in an attempt to take the crown. I learned it in Lumina under the moon that rose above the sea. As he swayed and moved me and we danced beneath a thousand fake snowflakes. As he watched and waited outside my door… frustrated because I couldn't be what he wanted or needed.

He reached out a hand and waited for me to decide to take it. I stared at the lines carved into his palm. Some deep, others shallow, filled with slashes and creases that made up his story. Each one as human as those on my own hand. I slid my palm into his. He felt it trembling, felt me crumbling, but tenderly folded his large fingers around my tiny ones.

"Trust me with you. I promise I won't let this consume you. I won't let you falter or fail. I swear it. You will be reunited with Reyan as soon as this is over, and it will end in our favor."

I shook my head, dejected. "You don't know that."

"Yes, I do." He leaned in closer. "I *do*, Citali."

"Have you received a vision from Lumos?" I asked, the tears finally stopping.

He shook his head. "I don't need a vision to know this. We must succeed. If we fail, both kingdoms – the world itself – suffers. And we cannot let that happen. Not for those we love. You…" his voice choked. "You *will* stop him, for Reyan's future, and yours with him."

My stomach growled loudly.

Beron cracked a smile and squeezed my hand. "How about we start with breakfast? Then we can make plans." I opened my mouth to protest, guilt crawling up my throat, but his cool eyes filled with blue flame. "Don't. We are your pack now. You're one of us, and we take care of our own… Okay?"

The knot in my chest didn't unfurl, but it did loosen a little. I nodded. "Okay."

With the Wolven beside me, I trudged back to the House of Wolves feeling nothing like a queen, completely distraught over my son's forced absence, and, to add insult to a grievous emotional injury, completely starving.

But it was a first step.

# 11

I watched Noor over my shoulder as we reached the porch steps. Near the tree line, she waved her hand to make a portal, then clasped hands with Caelum. Together, they walked through, her head craned toward me as she left, her brows drawn and troubled.

Holt opened the front door, offering a sympathetic smile as he waved me inside. Beron's hand ghosted down my skin, hovering at the small of my back as we made our way to the kitchen.

Merik used to touch me like that. A touch that wasn't true contact, but could be felt. For weeks, then months, he and I danced around one another without touching at all.

The restraint we both showed brimmed with want.

I knew Beron didn't want me the way Merik had, but there were moments I thought he might. While Noor and I were vying for his brother's heart, there were times I thought Beron might want me to seek his instead. To leave the thought of Caelum and his precious crown behind and turn my focus on Beron – not the Wolven. Just Beron…

"Citali?" his smooth voice came from behind me.

I'd stopped and hadn't realized it, too caught up in memory to move. When my senses returned, I didn't have to be prodded again. My feet rushed toward the overwhelmingly delicious scent of food. My mouth watered as I pushed my way to the dining room. On the table lay small, fresh loaves of bread alongside a small jar of the sweet cinnamon butter Padren had suggested. A mountain of eggs, cheese, and smoky smelling meats were arrayed in bowls that ran the length of the table. I filled a plate and sat to eat, unable to stifle the moan that erupted when the flavors first hit my tongue.

Across the room, Beron poured water into a glass, then brought it to me. Amaris stayed near the door with her arms crossed and one leg propped against the wall where she leaned. Holt and Chase settled across from me. Chase watched me almost as carefully as Holt, scratching the scruff appearing on his chin and upper lip.

Beron settled beside me. He took a roll and bit into it, slowly chewing. His control infuriated me. I couldn't chew and swallow nearly as fast as I needed to, and he was content to take his time. Savoring every bite. Mentally, I bared my teeth at him, squirming in my seat, unable to fill the dark pit in my stomach.

Why did wolves need to constantly feed?

Quickly, the food on my plate disappeared and the frantic pangs began to fade away. With the hunger gone, my mind cleared and the tension in my middle eased. I felt more like me again.

With my hunger abated, my thoughts returned to Reyan. I wondered where the Sphinx had taken them, if he'd enjoyed the flight, if Padren and Malia were comfortable or wished Merik had never been assigned to guard me.

I gasped as a feeling of overwhelming worry struck me. My eyes snapped to Beron when I realized it emanated from him. He straightened his back and tension formed at the corners of his eyes. "Are you trying to stop me from sensing you?" I asked.

He sat the roll he'd been snacking on down on his plate and stared back without speaking.

"Can you sense *any* of us?" Chase asked. I stared at him, then at Holt, followed by Amaris. While I could plainly *see* her disdain, could I feel it? Could I feel any of them?

"No," I answered, then turned to Beron again. "Only you."

Chase tugged at his collar.

"Have you calmed down enough where we can talk about this situation rationally?" Amaris pushed off the wall. "Or do you need more coddling?"

My muscles tensed and my fingers curled around the handle of my fork. *Coddling?* I sensed the flutter of a pulse at her neck, watched her skin stretch and settle with each beat. That was where to strike...

Before I could stand and attack, Beron's stern, deep voice cut through the air. "Run the perimeter, Amaris."

She snarled, "But we need to –"

Beron leveled her with a glare. "What did I say?"

She scowled but left. If she'd been in wolf skin, her tail would've been tucked between her legs. At least the bitch could follow directions.

"Set the fork down," Beron softly said.

I flung it behind me hard enough that it clattered off the wall.

Chase grinned wolfishly and surveyed the table, possibly inventorying the other utensils available to me.

Holt leaned in and braced his forearms on the table. "The way I see it, our plan remains the same, with one notable exception." He gave me a pointed look.

Beron nodded. "Agreed."

"What's the plan?" I asked, finally relaxing against the back of my chair.

Beron deferred to Holt, who rapped on the table twice. "You get strong. You shift. Then, instead of waiting for the dark one to move, you hunt him – with us at your side, of course."

What he said made sense, but I wondered how much time would pass before Lumos allowed the change, and if the dark one would wait until then before attacking. I needed to be ready now.

Beron's lips parted and a breath huffed between them. "I heard you, Citali. I just heard your thoughts."

I looked at Chase and Holt, but they shook their heads in unison. "We didn't."

"I'll need you to teach me how to block them when necessary," I told Beron.

He gave a sly smile. "I'm not sure I can."

"Liar. I don't feel your emotions anymore."

His dimple popped. "Perhaps I'm learning to block them." He leaned back in his seat. "My mother is hosting a little get-together tonight, one that's been planned for some time. I don't think we should let Anubis ruin our plans."

Chase clapped loudly. "Yes!"

Even the corners of Holt's lips tugged upward.

Though I wanted to join in the celebration, fear clawed inside my chest. I didn't want the dark one to be drawn to Lumina in his search for me. I shook my head. "You guys go ahead. I'll stay here."

"That's not an option. You either go with us or we stay here with you," Beron said.

"That's not fair!" I pointed out. "You should go. All of you should."

"You're part of this pack now, Citali. We stay together," Beron dared, leaning in close enough that I could see the ice chips in his eyes.

I gripped my arm rests; thankful I didn't have Noor's heat. It would've incinerated the wooden grips. It may have burnt the whole House down around us. "What if *he* senses me there?"

"*He* won't."

I rolled my eyes. How could Beron be so confident when I was so frightened?

"I've seen us there," he said. "Lumos sent a vision. We need to be there. And I can promise you *he* won't show up..."

"What sort of get-together is this?" I asked, my voice sharpening.

"Just a small one. It's not a big deal," he said.

I took in a deep breath. "I need a bath."

Chase barked a laugh. "If we're going to the House of the Moon, all of us do." He clapped Holt on the back. "We'll go find Amaris and head to the river to wash up."

He and Holt left the room. Then the House. The room flooded with silence after their departure. For several moments, Beron and I drowned in the stillness.

"There's a spring just down the hill behind the House," he finally said. "The water that bubbles in it is warm. If you're not comfortable bathing in the spring, I can bring in water and fill the bath in your bathing room."

"The spring is fine."

He stood abruptly, the chair legs raking loudly over the wooden floor. "I'll bring soap and towels for you."

I thanked him and slogged outside. I wasn't sure how a warm spring could bubble amid the cool mountains, but hoped he was right. There was a bitter, frosty bite to the air that breathed and blew through the needled trees. A narrow, worn trail led from the back of the House and meandered down the steep hillside.

I didn't have to descend far before I saw it; a small pool of gently bubbling water so oddly blue it didn't look real. Steam wafted from its crystalline surface.

Unlacing my boots, I stepped out of them and waited for Beron before I undressed further. I heard his footsteps crunching on the trail and a moment later he emerged, carrying towels and a bar of floral-scented soap. His eyes fixed on my naked feet until my toes curled. He held out the small bundle.

"Thank you."

Instead of leaving, he lingered, like the steam skirting the water's surface. His eyes trailed down the braid laying over my shoulder. I could almost feel his fingers appreciating each plait. My pulse quickened. He stepped forward and inhaled deeply.

I tightened my grip on the bundle in my arms. "Beron?"

He pressed his eyes closed. "I need to stay near enough to hear if you have any trouble. I won't intrude… or peek." That damned dimple flared, curling my toes again. He turned on his heel and retraced the trail. I couldn't hear or see him but I knew he was near, just as he'd promised. I sat my soap and towels near the rocky edge of the small pool.

The cold air kissed my skin as I tugged the soft tunic over my head and shrugged out of my fitted trousers. I didn't care if the water was warm or hot, but in my eagerness to get out of the frigid wind, I clambered into the water and made an ungraceful splash.

"You okay?" Beron's voice came.

The water was deliciously and surprisingly hot. It comforted my aching muscles and heart. I needed to believe Reyan was fine, safe with Padren, Malia, and the Sphinx. No harm would come to him.

*No harm will come to him.*

In my mind, I quickly repeated the phrase several times until the panic gripping my chest loosened its grip. Until I thought I might believe it.

"Citali?" he repeated, his tone sharper.

I blinked rapidly, clearing my mind and saying the first benign thing I could think of. "How do you stand this… frost?"

He seemed to relax and the tension bled from his tone. "Because I was born to it, I suppose. It's a fair question, though. I'm not sure how you survive Sol's sweltering heat."

I remembered him in Helios in his Wolven form. Even with his fur coated in sweat, he guarded us until Noor became Aten. Suddenly a flash of memory surfaced of Beron hovering over me, holding my head up because I couldn't. My bloody handprint marred his cheek.

A different memory emerged; one of delicate toes dancing through soft, pale sand. Of bronze skin shining beneath the moon, of the bearer of that skin wading into dazzling waters. It was my smile that flashed over my shoulder. My hair in the salty breeze. It was my skin he marveled at, my shape he memorized.

But this was not my memory. It was Beron's.

"Wolven?" I called out. Rocks tumbled as he stood. "I'm fine," I quickly added. "I just have a question."

"What's that?" he asked. Rocks skidded down the slope from the area where he sat as he settled back down.

"Were you just thinking of swimming with me on the Luminan shore?"

Silence was his first answer. His second was a long groan. "You saw?"

I laughed. "You might need more practice keeping your thoughts from me." I dragged the aromatic soap across my skin. "Unless… you meant for me to see it."

I might have imagined it, but it sounded like he raked his hands over his face, through his dark hair.

Satisfaction purred in my stomach until Amaris's sultry voice clashed with Beron's. "Not. Here," he snapped. "Not now."

"Fine. But we *will* discuss this later," she hissed before stomping away.

When the back door of the House slammed atop the hill, Beron softly cursed, then apologized for her behavior.

"Is she your lover?" I asked, hoping it wasn't the case, but knowing it likely was.

"No," he said. "She isn't, has never been, and never will be. That's a line I won't cross with her."

"Because she's part of your pack?" I guessed.

"Partly."

I couldn't tell if Beron reciprocated her feelings. Since the moment she'd arrived, they'd seemed to possess a level of intimate familiarity and comfort. They stood closer than I would expect friends to and spoke to each other in quiet whispers. Maybe he cared for her but didn't realize it yet. Sometimes, our bodies subconsciously translated the words of our heart.

Merik had been assigned as my guard. After a time we threw caution to the wind and for a blissful, dangerous few months, it worked. Until I learned I was with child, and then Father… Well, if things had been different and we'd broken things off before any of that happened, it would've been awkward to see him all the time. He might not have been as effectual in his duties, and I might've been more apt to drift away from him, potentially putting myself in danger.

"She says she'd be happy with only a physical relationship, but I know she'd eventually want more," he confided. A quiet pause. "What do you think?"

"I don't know Amaris well enough to know how she might feel or react."

He was quiet for a moment, then… "Would you be able to separate the two – physical and emotional intimacy?"

I ran the bar of soap over my skin, savoring its sweet floral smell. "Me? No. I couldn't separate them and wouldn't want to. Nor would I want to lie to myself and settle on what scraps were thrown to me. I want more than meaningless intimacy could ever provide," I answered honestly. "When Sol walked the earth, I was very small, but I remember her as Noor's mother. Every night, she would read to Noor, Zarina, and I. One of her stories always stuck with me. It was a story about a queen whose heart caught fire and burned when she met the one she was meant to find. The flames did not hurt her heart; it only kept the flame of their love alive. She told me never to accept less than someone who sets – and keeps – your heart ablaze, and I don't intend to."

I sank down, letting my hair go soft in the blue water, before emerging and scrubbing it clean. Beron and I didn't speak after that, until I was ready to leave the spring.

The wind howled through the trees, bending their branches sideways as if they were clawing to get away. I lamented the distance to the House. My wet hair was freezing.

I quickly wrapped a towel around it before grabbing the second towel. "Beron, I'm going to make a run for it."

"What do you mean?"

Without pausing to explain, I just shrieked as I climbed out and threw the towel around myself, grasping the ends and running like I was trying to win another race. "Get my clothes!" I yelled back at him. Scrambling up the hill, the back of the House was in sight. I flung the door open and rushed inside, shivering, my teeth chattering so hard I thought they might break. A very surprised Holt stood from his chair in a small kitchen alcove.

I checked to make sure I was covered, and thankfully, nothing had slipped during my frantic flight. "It's ridiculously cold," I explained.

His dark hair was wet. He gave me a teasing grin. "We wolves bathe in the river, even when it crusts with ice."

I shook my head. "I will *never* be able to do that."

He cleared his throat. "Many things will change when you do. Even your body temperature will rise."

Beron stepped inside, saw Holt, and froze. "What's going on?" he quietly asked.

"I just need a second to thaw before I can move again," I explained, smiling back at him.

"It's been a second."

"And I'm leaving puddles on the floor. I'll dress and come back down to clean them up." I walked away from the wolves.

Beron called after me, "Holt will see to the floor. Take your time."

I didn't want to dissect whatever silent conversation the two were having, so I hurried upstairs. Noor was waiting in my room, sitting on my bed. She sat up straighter when I closed the door behind me.

"I wanted to let you know that Reyan, Padren, and Malia are all doing well."

"You know where they are?" I asked with chattering teeth.

Noor waved her hand and a blissful warmth filled the air, instantly thawing me and chasing every shiver away. "I don't, but the Sphinx showed me a brief glimpse of them. She knew you would want to know." She let her hand graze the air and showed me the briefest image of Reyan, playing in soft, warm sand like he was built to tame it.

"Thank you for coming to tell me."

She stood. "I'll see you again later tonight. I need to see Kiran before I dress."

Of course the priest was still clinging to the hem of her ceremonial dress.

"Did you find the book you seek?"

She craned her head back and sighed. "Kiran's still searching. He remembers Saric mentioning a book written about the dark one. He hasn't found it, but Saric wouldn't have destroyed it. He was wise. He believed that only the vain or foolish chose to forget their past. That's why he was always reading and preserved every book and scroll he could find."

I wondered if Zarina had known where to look for it and stole it so we wouldn't have the knowledge. Had Noor considered that possibility?

When she stood, I could see unseen weight pressing heavily on her sister's shoulders. If the aureole of an Atena was heavy, I couldn't imagine bearing the title of Aten. Still, she bore it gracefully, naturally, as though she could carry Sol herself if she had to.

In fact, she already had, in carrying her mother's bones into the sand when she was far too young and weak to heft them. There was nothing I could imagine her being incapable of now.

"Caelum is checking with Lumos's priests, as well. They, too, have kept careful records of their history."

I blew out a tense breath, looking at her attire. "Is that what you're wearing tonight?"

Her mouth popped open slightly. "No..."

"Well, what exactly is this little event we're to attend?"

Noor coughed out a laugh. "Beron didn't tell you?"

I stiffened. "He said it wasn't a big deal."

One of her delicate brows lifted with one side of her mouth. "Today is Beron's birthday."

My lips peeled apart in irritation. *He never said!* Now I felt like a fool.

"Vada's been planning this ball for months. She's invited most of Lumina." *I know one person she wishes would not attend...* "Vada wants you there, Citali. I can see your feelings paint your face, but she does want you to come. She told me so."

I tightened my grip on the towel's edge. "She certainly doesn't. She hates me. She must have another scathing warning to issue."

My sister walked to the window and blankly stared out into the trees. "You are uniquely connected to the dark one and those who align with him. If trouble comes, she said you'd scent it and warn everyone so they could all be kept safe."

Fair enough, I supposed. Beron deserved a grand party for his birthday, uninterrupted by evil. And though I couldn't stop it, Anubis's stench was one I couldn't mistake. "Aren't you afraid the event will draw Zarina and her acolytes like moths to a flame?"

She shook her head. "I think the flame Zarina seeks is you, and the last place you were sensed was in her mountains, not in the heart of Lumina."

"Anubis doesn't need to search for me. He only has to reach out for the part of himself he left behind. It doesn't matter where I am, he can find me," I said bitterly.

There was no place to run, nowhere to hide.

Noor bit at her cheek. "When he comes, you don't have to fight him alone. Sol's ire burns hotter by the day. She seeks him constantly, as does Lumos. Caelum has prepared the Luminan guard and warned them to be ready. The guard of Helios has their instructions, as do both orders of priests. And, of course, the Wolven and his pack are with you. All will be on alert tonight. If you smell him, all you need to do is say the word and everyone and everything will converge to find Anubis."

I shook my head and laughed. "So, I'm to be the bait."

She shrugged. "You're a unique temptation for the dark one, but I hope you aren't bait tonight."

The thought spoiled in my stomach and damning thoughts echoed through my bones. *What happens when we find Anubis? Will Sol burn and Lumos seal him in darkness? Will the Sculptor intervene – again?*

This plan was forged hastily – necessarily so, but it was incomplete – and when you failed to see the larger picture, you couldn't possibly prepare for every scenario. They said I needed to be strong so I could shift and then hunt. But that plan depended on me alone and had no contingencies upon what Anubis might do to destroy it – and me. He'd almost succeeded with the vision he spun on the cliff's edge.

Beron's assurance that Lumos had seen us at the party tonight, and that the dark one hadn't permeated the celebration flitted through my mind.

"Will you wear your moon diamond gown?" I asked, glancing toward my trunks.

"I honestly haven't given much thought to what I'll wear, but I brought something for you… if you'd like to wear it, of course."

My brows kissed as she moved to the bathing room, her words echoing out to me.

"Beron said something in Lumina that stuck with me. He said that while my eyes burn gold, yours are a dark flame that burn just as hotly. He said yours were a flame sealed in shadow." She brought out a fitted, glittering black gown that made my mouth gape open, stunned and speechless. Her thumb raked over the inky material that dripped in her hands like it was a living, breathing creation. "This is the closest dress I could find to match that description."

The sequins flashed black to gold. Shadowfire, indeed. It had small straps that would cross my back, holding the fabric tight against my torso. "It's beautiful."

"He's right, Citali. Remember that. Your flames, shadowed or not, burn just as hot. Whatever piece of Anubis is in your skin… make him regret ever dragging you into this fight."

"I fully intend to," I told her.

She handed me the gown. "I should go, but I'll see you tonight." She glanced from the gown to me and smiled knowingly. "I wish I could be here to see Beron when you come downstairs in that…"

"Why?"

My sister tilted her head to the side. Both her brows rose. "He was paying awfully careful attention to you to make such an observation, Citali. He pays careful attention to you always."

With a wave of her hand, Noor was gone.

I recalled the image Beron had painted of me in his mind on the shores of his home. I'd bribed Kevi for information, and then I bribed her again for the loan of swimming garments, determined to enter the sea in case I wouldn't get another chance. I managed to slip past Holt that night, who'd been distracted with a pretty Luminan girl who came to see if he needed something to drink. Beron found me on the shore. He was fuming when he realized it was me, but then he calmed. He watched and kept his distance quietly as I took my first steps into the waves.

Since I couldn't swim, I didn't go in far. Beron had mentioned sirens being among her waters. A feeble attempt to scare me from the deep, I was sure. But he didn't know that the sea *was* the siren and those who drew near were undoubtedly subject to her song.

Even the mighty Wolven…

The ocean concealed the depth of her secrets like a sly woman's skirts might conceal the dagger strapped to her thigh; her sweet song lilted over the crashing, ebbing tide. The lyrics claimed she lured the weak and proved the strength of those who dared listen long enough.

He didn't know that I recognized the huntress in her because I felt that same hypnotic power resonating in my bones. Noor once said that we were all sharpened knives in Father's arsenal, but that wasn't true. We were sharp, yes. But we were blades, not because of him, but despite him. We honed ourselves as a means of self-protection.

We Atenas were sirens, too. Sirens of the sands. Sirens of circumstance. Deadlier than the deepest water and the creatures that made their home in it. As overwhelming as a turbulent current. Fathoms more complicated than the salty beast that filled the yawning crevices of the earth and held both life and death within her briny heart.

Lying on my blankets beside where Noor had been sitting were two small wooden chests. I gently spread the dress Noor had brought for me out on the bed. The nearest chest held perfumes, powders and lip stain, combs and brushes.

The second was a chest bursting with silver and gold. Bangles, necklaces, a broad collar of silver links and a matching golden one. There was also a chained harness of strong alternating links of silver and gold, built with a ring like the one I wore around my waist now, the perfect size to fit my now-golden dagger. To hide it, yet keep it with me.

Noor had tucked a note into the trove. "To honor Lumina and her Wolven, but worthy of a queen in her own right."

I studied her swooping words and wondered if Sol had revealed to her, as she had the Sphinx, that I was to become the Queen of Wolves. Wondered if I was doing the very thing I'd once accused her of – forsaking Sol and Helios for a different life.

Now I realized Noor hadn't done that. She wouldn't have even if she wasn't Sol's heir, even if she wasn't destined to become Aten. Deep down, I think I knew the truth, but my mind was so singularly focused and desperate to beat her to the crown, I let myself become cruel. I hurt her the same way our father hurt everyone he touched.

I became a poison, just as potent as him.

I became his hand.

I'm just glad I didn't become the embodiment of his will.

Zarina had become exactly that.

A chill elicited shivers again. Now that Noor was gone, her heat slowly seeped out of the room. I needed warmth, but I didn't know how to make a fire.

Padding to the door, I paused at the frame, battling with myself about whether I should bother one of the wolves when footsteps creaked down the hall. At once, the decision was made for me. I gripped the handle, twisted, and peeked outside. Beron stopped in the center of the hallway. His eyes collided with mine, then dipped, skimming my flesh in a deliberate caress.

I clenched the top of my towel a little tighter and tipped my chin up.

"Citali?"

My skin pebbled at the sound of his voice.

My voice wavered when I began to ask, "Can you make a fire in my room?" so I cleared my throat and began again. "Or show me how to do it so I can make it myself?"

The air was filled with unseen crackles of lightning, courtesy of the storm brewing between us. One that promised carnage if it was unleashed. I withstood the feeling of tiny forked lightning while he moved past me and entered my room to build the fire for which I'd asked.

He arranged a pile of wood and promised to return in a moment, disappearing down the hall again. Only then did I fully exhale.

Those precious deep breaths shallowed again when Beron returned cradling a small bundle of kindling in his palms. Within it, a tiny ember pulsed. He pursed his bowed lips and blew, igniting that dark ember until it flared hot, orange lace dancing around its edges. A flame caught as he gently tucked the kindling beneath the stacked logs. He stayed, blew, and made sure it was burning solidly. Together, we watched the flames spread. Grow. Dance. Thrive. The heat built and chased the chill bumps from my skin.

Beron braced his hands on his thighs and sat so still that the only movement I could discern was the slight shrug of skin and shoulder when he inhaled and exhaled again.

"Thank you," I told him, then added, "I wish you a happy birthday."

"Did Noor tell you?" he asked.

"Yes."

Quietly, he stood. His eyes crashed into mine for only a second before his brows furrowed and he let himself out of the room. I wasn't sure what I'd done wrong… For many long moments, I considered the short, quiet exchange as I combed my hair in front of the fire the Wolven built for me.

Maybe Beron didn't enjoy celebrating his birth.

He was nineteen today. He and Caelum were born eleven rotations, not even a full year, apart. In only a few rotations, my age would align with his and Caelum would see twenty rotations.

My thoughts flitted to Noor. Barely seventeen. The age at which I bore Reyan and the age at which I watched Merik die. Father not only killed *him*, he slaughtered everyone he even suspected might possibly have known of the two of us and our son. Only a trusted few knew. Far fewer than the number of bodies that burned atop Sol's temple the next day.

The only three who escaped his murderous temper were Padren, Malia, and Reyan, and only because he had need of them. He used my son as a whet stone to keep me sharp and pointed at the hearts of anyone he deemed a threat – namely, Noor.

Bathed in the crackling fire's heat, I dragged the comb through my long hair, smoothing tangles and taming waves into straight lines. The dress Noor brought lay on the bed where she left it. It glittered in the firelight. My thoughts strayed to Beron and what she'd insinuated. Of the strange, tense few moments we spent quietly as he built my fire, a thousand unspoken words filling the air between us while I was woefully unable to weave them into meaningful sentences.

What would it be like if he *did* appreciate me in the dress, as Noor suggested? To lay on the bed with him hovering over me, his weight pressing me into the billowy down, his bowed lips red and raw from kissing, his chest gleaming with a sheen of sweat upon which the fire danced, wildfire in his cool eyes, balancing fitfully on the cord that separated control and finally throwing caution to the wind…

My heart crashed against my chest, but I pushed that vision into the crackling fire where it belonged. Beron had made it clear this afternoon that he would never involve himself with someone in his pack. Such hot-burning relationships, once ended, would only cause strife and animosity. Those feelings would certainly weaken the most tightly knit pack, if not cleave it.

Rising from the stones in front of the hearth, I tossed the comb into the small box Noor had provided and slipped into the black gown, amazed at how well it fit. I realized that Noor had likely visited the seamstress and noticed it hanging among the dresses the woman had ready and waiting to be claimed by whichever Atena became Aten.

No one thought it would be me, and my sisters were both taller than I. Noor was curvier. Zarina the slenderest of us three. But she'd had the hem taken up for me and I couldn't be happier.

The satin straps were delicate, but sturdy. It was a dress crafted for provocation and movement. For dancing. And while I knew I shouldn't crave that mind-numbing release that the rhythm and motion of dance provided, I couldn't help it. At the very least, tonight could be my last chance to dance as… *me*. And at worst, it might be my last.

In the bathing room framed in silver, a large mirror hung on the wall. In its reflection stood a girl who looked the same as she had only days ago, though her skin felt confining, like she'd quickly outgrown it. Or maybe what she'd outgrown was her past and she was ready to accept her future, assuming she had one.

What I *didn't* see in her was Anubis. Thanks to Beron, not even a scar remained where Zarina had cut me with the obsidian blade. There were no marks beneath my flesh branding me as his. No ichor filled my veins. But dark flame burnt in my eyes, just as Beron had described it to Noor, and her to me. He'd seen it before I was stabbed. Had it always been there?

Most would describe their color as a deep, warm brown, but by candlelight my eyes assumed the orange-black of burning cinders. I could only imagine them shimmering with rage, the flames intensifying as they seared.

I knew what to expect tonight: Dinner. Conversation. Music. Dancing. Wine. Mingling with strangers who were as curious about me as they were about Helios. Who would whisper as though we were friends and ask why Caelum had passed me over for Noor, and whether I was seeking Beron's company because I truly liked him or had been hurt by rejection and was merely seeking out the next best option.

Gossips were as predictable as Sol's path across the sky.

When Noor and I first came to the House of the Moon, Caelum arranged to celebrate Noor's birth just before she came of age and claimed her heritage. Helioans did not make grand gestures for the occasion the way Luminans did, but his effort to honor her life meant a great deal to Noor. I could see it in the way she looked at him.

Something shifted between them when we left the Dusk Lands for Lumina, and that spark caught and burned brightly by the time she became Aten in a foreign land, destined to return home and take back what was rightfully hers from our father.

I dipped my pinky into the vat of lip stain. It wasn't red and it wasn't quite violet, but a strange shade in between that was just as gloriously rich.

Decadent.

Tempting, like a ripe pomegranate.

I brushed it on, then washed and dried my hands, wondering why my palms felt hot and why I was so hungry – again. Famished, actually. I wondered why I suddenly felt everything and nothing and far too much and too little to be comfortable. Why I wanted to hurry to the party and get the night over with, especially since I dreaded looking Vada and any of those from the House of the Moon who remembered me in the eye, yet wanted to linger in my room so I didn't have to go. Maybe the pack would forget me and leave me behind.

"Hurry up, Citali!" Chase yelled from the hallway as he passed my door, banging on it twice for good measure. "It's time to go. Noor and Caelum are here."

I took a deep breath, telling myself I could do this. I could hold my head high and stand with Beron and his pack of friends. At his party, I could sate my thirst and insatiable hunger and this fire in my palms and chest and cheeks would die down.

Because if ever there was someone to celebrate, it was Beron.

The evening of Noor's celebration, Caelum had thanked Lumos for her life. For her presence in his. The Lumin thanked Sol.

Tonight, Beron's family would thank both gods for him, too, as would I. He saved me. He begged Lumos for a way to let me live. For Reyan. And if I managed to live a thousand more years, even if he wasn't part of them, I would thank the goddess of the sun and god of the moon for Beron.

# 12

I laced a pair of black sandals up my calves and slid on some of the silver and gold jewelry. Bangles – my favorite, followed by an anklet from which varying Luminan coins dangled, then a single moon diamond strung on a delicate strand of barely-visible silver corded my neck. The pale blue stone settled in the hollow at the base of my throat, framed by my collar bones.

The rock was cool against my heated skin, providing the barest hint of relief. Enough to allow me to leave the room and make my way downstairs.

Holt and Chase were near the door, donning their guard uniforms. Each wore dark trousers tucked into polished black boots, topped by silver tunics embroidered with a single, howling wolf. Chase had somehow tamed his wild hair and tonight his curls lay in neat coils close to his scalp. It made him look different. Older. Chase was handsome, which meant the young women would certainly take note of him tonight. He gave a wide grin when he saw me. "If you were battling the night sky for supremacy, you've won, Citali."

I tried to smile. "Thank you, Chase."

Holt had combed his dark hair, too, but it still fell into his eyes. He tugged uncomfortably at his collar, his eyes flicking across the yard to where Amaris stood with Beron, talking with Noor and Caelum. Caelum laughed heartily at something one of them said and clapped his younger brother on the shoulder.

I pressed a hand to my forehead. "It's so hot in this House. I need air."

Pushing through the behemoths, I stepped onto the porch and was relieved when the cold wind slid over my overheated skin. I pressed my eyes closed for a moment and reveled in the cool breeze. When I opened them, Sol was leaving the sky in dramatic ribbons of citrine and gold, azure and violet. Between the blazing colors, Lumos painted the night sky in darker swaths studded with the brightest stars. As night fell, their number would only grow.

I marveled at the violent clashing of vibrance and darkness until I felt someone's stare: Beron's. His throat shifted as he took in the dress.

Noor, wearing her moon diamond gown, gave a smug smile, punctuated her feelings with a wink, and ticked her head to the Wolven. Caelum's hand was on his shoulder. It squeezed and Beron snapped out of whatever daze he'd lost himself in.

Amaris was dressed in a simple but elegant silver dress that fell to the ground and trailed a few steps behind her. Her hair fell in deep red waves down her back and diamonds winked from her wrists, ears, and throat. She turned to Beron, latched an arm around his, and tugged him toward Noor. "We'll be late to your own party, thanks to *her*."

I bared my teeth. Holt and Chase flanked me. "Easy..." Chase said in a low tone.

Noor waved a palm across the air and it rippled, revealing the awaiting darkness. She held the portal open as Beron and

Amaris stepped through. Holt and Chase were next, peeling away from me to follow their Wolven.

Caelum gave me an apologetic smile and offered a forearm, which I accepted. He had two arms, after all. Noor took hold of the one he'd reserved for her and let loose a throaty chuckle. "This is going to be interesting," she murmured.

The portal closed behind us and Caelum straightened, standing taller when Beron turned to find me standing with him and my sister. The Wolven growled something to Amaris and Holt as the three strode toward the House of the Moon.

The instant my feet touched the Luminian shore, the waves sang and the sea called to me. I'd forgotten her voice. For a moment, I imagined dragging every inch of silver from my body, unlacing my sandals, and running to her, splashing and wading until she took me under.

"Citali?" Noor said. I raised my head and she pointed to the House. "Are you ready?"

"As ready as I'm going to be," I muttered.

The House of the Moon was packed with people. As we walked through the foyer and the crowd parted for our entrance, varying scents assaulted me, though none were necrotic. Caelum's people greeted him like a friend. They welcomed Noor just as warmly and graciously included me in their greetings as we passed through to the grand room where the ball was well underway.

Musicians played in the far corner and tables were stretched along the walls, filled with foods of every variety. I unlatched my hand from Caelum's arm and took off toward them, unable to focus on anything but my hunger. Chase and Holt intercepted me. "You look like you're famished," Chase cooed. "Perhaps even a little testy."

Holt playfully dared the youngest wolf, "Test her and see who wins the fight between you."

"She hasn't even shifted yet," Chase scoffed, puffing out his chest.

"Do you think I require a wolf body to shred you, Chase?"

He grinned. "Personally, I would *love* to find out."

Holt smacked the back of his head.

The three of us filled our plates and I wended through the crowd to find an empty and somewhat secluded table near the musicians, tucked in the shadows. I focused on chewing the food on my plate and drinking my wine, unable to appreciate my surroundings until my hunger was curbed. Once it was, I finally looked around the room, mesmerized by the exquisite decorations.

Silver and black glass spirals hung from the ceiling, twisting back and forth and making the ceiling look alive. The tables were draped to match. An immense ice sculpture sat in the center of a fountain where the Wolven was engraved in a stunning likeness. From his sharp eyes to the proud set of his chest, down to the paws that though still, were ready to claw ground and foe to protect Lumina from anyone who would harm her, the Wolven was a fearsome beast.

I noticed Amaris and Beron standing together by one of the food tables, filling their plates and seeking a seat. Holt noticed them searching and waved them over. Before Beron saw his gesticulations, I almost kicked the young wolf under the table and told him not to tell them where we were, but it was too late. The two started toward our table.

"Shouldn't the Wolven sit with his mother and Caelum?" I asked, shifting uncomfortably as the two drew near.

"Vada wishes he would, but he sits with the pack. Always."

Beron's dark hair was combed back. Though he wore an outfit that matched Holt's and Chase's, he commanded attention. Like Caelum, the people of Lumina loved their Wolven. He waded through well-wishers, graciously thanking them as he made his way over to where we sat.

Amaris settled on Holt's side of the table and sipped her wine without acknowledging my presence.

It was clear the wolves were conversing mentally when Holt's posture stiffened and he flicked an irritated glance at Amaris.

Chase chuckled under his breath and shook his head. "You're going to have to get used to it," he finally told her.

"Get used to what?" I asked as Beron extricated himself from his guests to take the chair between Amaris and Holt.

Chase stabbed his fork in my direction. "To *you*."

I spread my palms flat on the table. "I'm not competing with you; nor am I impeding your relationship with Beron," I told her matter-of-factly. I wanted to scream that if he wanted her, not even the dark one would be able to drag him away, but something made me choke on the words.

Amaris looked stricken. She froze before her chest started heaving.

Both men at my sides growled and I wondered what it was she'd spoken into their minds.

"Care to say that aloud?" I dared her.

Beron had gone completely still, his crystal wine glass paused halfway between the table and his lips. A splintering ping sound came just before the glass he held exploded. He turned to Amaris, fuming, panting, angry enough to shift into his Wolven form.

I stood up abruptly. "You know what? Suddenly I'm full." Glancing at Holt and Chase, I asked, "Which one of you wants to dance?"

Both looked at each other, then at me, like I'd lost my mind. I knew they expected me to wolf out on Amaris, but this was Beron's birthday and I had no intention of causing a scene. The day had been beyond trying already, so salvaging the peace this evening was important. Tomorrow, Amaris could wage a war if she chose, but not here and not now.

"Don't both volunteer at once," I muttered awkwardly, flinging my napkin onto the table.

Holt slowly stood as if he still wasn't sure he should, seeming surprised that his legs had lifted him, almost as if he was considering sitting back down and backing out of that which he'd spontaneously agreed. I wasn't sure which of us was more surprised.

Chase coughed a chuckle and warned me, "He has two left feet."

I glanced at Holt's feet. They were perfectly normal. "Liar."

"It's a figure of speech," Holt explained, smiling. "It means I'm not a very good dancer."

"Let's see how bad you are." I smiled at him and took his hand, dragging him toward the floor crowded with dancers. "Perhaps I'll dance to match."

Awkwardly, Holt held my waist in an iron grip. I relaxed and threaded my hands around his neck, hoping he would see that dancing wasn't so bad after all. As we started to sway, I realized Chase was right. Holt was not a very good dancer, but I didn't tell him so. He'd rescued me from driving a spoon through Amaris's eye, and from Vada, who now hovered at the table, smiling down at her youngest son with pride.

Plus, I would never admit it to Chase just so I didn't have to endure his arrogant laughter.

"Don't let Amaris bother you," Holt said. "She and Beron have always been close, but he sees her as one would a little sister."

"It doesn't bother me that she wants him. What bothers me is that she's so hostile toward me when I haven't given her a reason to be." *Not that I didn't do the same to Noor too many times to count.*

He made a non-committal grunt and continued to try to sway, crunching my toes in the process. Not once or twice, but three times. He winced and apologized with each misstep, and for the first time the man I thought was a behemoth and a beast the last time I was in this House, seemed more friend than foe.

"I bet with our short but angry history, you never imagined you'd be dancing with me," I teased.

"No," he was quick to agree. "Never."

"You hated me."

He shook his head. "I never hated you. I just didn't understand you until now. And, to this day, I can't figure out how you evaded me. I certainly gained an appreciation and a healthy respect for your wit and stealth. No one had ever gotten past me before you."

My brows popped. "Never?"

He shook his head, smiling. "Never."

A warm feeling blossomed in my chest. "Maybe I'll make a decent wolf after all."

He chuckled and crunched my toes again. "Sorry."

Avoiding Beron, Amaris, and Vada when Holt had enough dancing for the rest of his life and went to sit back down with the others, I made an excuse to speak to my sister and carved a path through the room toward her where she stood alone. I didn't see Caelum in the crowd, but knew he wouldn't leave her alone for long.

"Have you received word from your priest friend, Kiran?" I leaned in to ask her.

"No, but the priests are combing through every tome and scroll they can to find what we need. They're scouring the library, but there's so much to sift through. It's like looking for a speck of seed in a mountain of sand," she admitted, her shoulders tense.

"And Lumos's library…?"

"Also being searched. The priests not present here are busy looking."

I scanned the room and only saw two… no, three of the silver-robed brethren in attendance. A pair trailed Vada as she moved about thanking people for coming, talking about the new future with a combined Helios and Lumina. A third lingered near the doors, watching and kindly blessing those who stopped to speak to him.

There was hope in the Luminans' words, in their voices, gestures, and eyes.

They had no idea what – or whom – was trying to incinerate the future they imagined for themselves and future generations.

"You're avoiding her," Noor leaned in to say of Vada.

"Of course I am."

"You can't avoid her all night."

I quirked a brow. "Is that a challenge?"

Noor chuckled knowingly. "Reyan, Padren, and Malia are asleep, tucked warm in their beds."

I pressed my eyes closed. "Would you thank the Lioness for me?"

She nodded, her lips pressed tightly. The Sphinx didn't have to tell me anything. She didn't have to warn me before taking them away. In fact, she could've left Padren and Malia and flown away with Reyan, but she wanted him to be happy and comfortable. Now she was making sure I was, too. If I couldn't be with him, she would let me know he was cared for.

There was comfort in knowing they were safe.

"What happened at the table earlier? Caelum said Beron was upset." Her dark eyes bore into mine, curious. "He mentioned a broken glass."

I gave an unladylike snort. "Broken? More like shattered – by Beron's fist. Caelum didn't tell you?"

"He doesn't know what it was, exactly. He just knows that Beron was close to exploding. Caelum's a little on edge because of it."

"It was just a misunderstanding," I hedged.

"With Amaris, I assume," she said, glancing toward the redhead.

"You assume correctly. She's very territorial when it comes to Beron."

Noor moved to lean against the nearest wall. "He doesn't want her. If you need proof, just watch them."

As Amaris and Beron danced, he held her away from his body, kept her at arm's length, never smiled for too long, and his eyes flitted everywhere instead of locking onto hers.

"Has he mentioned the dress?" she asked with a grin.

"He has not."

"Well, he certainly noticed," she said. "He dances with her, but he only has eyes for you."

When I glanced up to find them on the dance floor, his blue eyes clashed with mine.

Caelum jogged over. "Please, save me from speaking to anyone else," he begged Noor.

She grinned and shoved him toward me. "I think you should dance with Citali." He shot a quizzical look at her, but she waved us toward the floor. "Just… go."

Caelum led me to the floor and we joined a song with quick steps where we clapped along with the small finger cymbals some dancers had brought over to the musicians. I noticed Kevi, who gave a sultry wave. Her eyes quickly darted to my silver and I grimaced. I would rather choke her with a chain of it than trade it to her for the lies she passed as secrets.

Her smile fell away as if she could read my dark thoughts and she slipped into the crowd again. Perhaps she would avoid me this evening the same way I was skirting around Vada.

The tempo was quick and the steps quicker. This dance number left no time for conversation among partners. No time to think, only time to feel the next step, spin, and pivot. My palm met Caelum's and we walked a circle, stopped, clapped, and then reversed course with our other palms.

I caught a flash of red and wondered why… *why can't he and Amaris stay across the floor?* It spanned the entire length of the vast room. There was no need for them to draw near.

The dance ended and the room erupted in applause.

Caelum and I took a moment to catch our breath. His pale forehead glistened with sweat and my back cooled as our hearts calmed. I smiled at him. "That was fun."

"It was," he agreed. "It's always fun to dance with friends."

"And even better to dance with the one you love…" His brow furrowed. "Noor pushed you out here, but she'd rather be in your arms than waiting along the wall."

He looked torn, then as he started toward her, he stopped. "Are you sure?"

I smiled. "I've never been surer."

It was true. The two belonged together; partners in life's great dance. I started toward the far end of the room, only to find Vada striding purposefully toward me. Pivoting, I turned and walked back. I felt someone's stare, followed by their huffing frustration. I didn't have to guess to whom either belonged.

Nor did I care to dissect their reasons.

I was on my way to find Holt or Chase when Chase found me. "My turn." He grabbed my hand and pulled me back to the floor. This time, he found a spot just large enough for the two of us, which of course happened to be right next to Beron and Amaris.

A slower, calmer rhythm began. Chase pulled me close and pressed his hand against my back as he steered me through a series of predictable boxed steps. Beron and Amaris repeated the same. They didn't speak, unless they did so in one another's minds, and they both watched us from their peripheries. Amaris with disgust on her drawn lip, and Beron with an intensity that made me want to scream. I purposely ignored them both. Chase didn't have to pretend they weren't there; he seemed oblivious to anyone but himself.

The longer he danced, the more his hair livened, until soon it was the curly mop to which I'd become accustomed. Somehow, the familiar sight set me at ease. The wine he drank at dinner loosened his already easy tongue.

Chase told me about his family. He was the youngest of four, and the only boy. His sisters were all married now, and the oldest had five children including a newborn. His people hailed from the mountains, from a small village not too far from the House of Wolves. The icecaps we could see from the ridge separated us from them. His father was a hunter and trapper, though he no longer hunted wolves anymore – just in case. His mother was a baker. They lived a simple, happy life together.

It surprised them all when Chase shifted for the first time. It terrified them as well. He'd only been back to see them a handful of times since. "Now when I see them, they act like I'm a stranger, like they aren't sure what to say. It's hard. I haven't changed where it counts," he lamented.

"The strangeness isn't unfamiliarity, Chase. It's guilt. They feel guilt."

He ticked his head back. "Guilt? For me?"

I nodded. "For you."

"How do you know that?"

"Because guilt and I are wonderful friends."

He blew out a breath. "Father blames himself. He thinks that hunting Lumos's lands and harvesting his animals brought a curse upon the family and I bear it for his actions. I've told him that Lumos choosing me wasn't a curse, but instead an honor. I tried to explain that what I do helps people – that it matters. But he can only see the boy child he raised and the wolf I've become. He can't reconcile the two."

"Maybe in time, he will," I offered, unsure if my words were filled with hope or lies. "Of course, it may mean that you have to visit more often, if for no other reason than to make them see that you're the same Chase they've always known and loved."

He tried to smile, but the corners of his mouth were heavy.

"Don't run from them. It just reinforces their fear."

"Beron said *you* were going to run. The night you were…" He gestured to my stomach.

"I was, but not out of fear. I was finally free from the yoke of my father, and the only thing I wanted was on the other side of the city. I knew I didn't belong in the House of the Sun anymore, so I was packing some things to leave when Zarina came in."

His hand tensed on my back. "Why'd she do it?"

"She was convinced that Noor had stolen what was hers – the position as Aten, and that I was a traitor for helping her defeat our father. Not that I actually did anything other than stand with her." My stomach soured at the memory. "She accused us of aligning with Anubis, when it was she who had done so. I keep wondering… what if Zarina didn't know she was doing his bidding? What if she's just another of Father's unwitting victims?"

"Your father was horrible – no offense."

"None taken," I assured him.

"It meant a lot to Noor for you to stand up to him with her," he said before adding a wink.

"It meant more to me that she ended him. Our father wasn't like yours. You're lucky, Chase. Don't abandon him because he doesn't understand. Help him to. Even if it takes a lifetime, it'll be worth it in the end."

Chase nodded tightly. "Want to go get some water?" he asked, gesturing to the tables across the room.

"Sure."

"Citali," Beron said. I turned to find him standing right behind me. My skin flushed and that sweltering hot feeling

I'd had before we left the House of Wolves returned. "Would you like to dance?"

A flash of red trailed through the crowd as Amaris angrily stomped across the floor. Chase raised his brows, turned on his heels, and sauntered away, stopping to talk with every pretty girl who batted her lashes and simpered in his direction.

Beron extended a hand. I slid my small palm into his larger one and watched his pale fingers curl around it. He turned to nod at one of the musicians and a familiar song filled the air…a sensual Helioan melody about seduction. I quirked a brow and wondered if he knew what the rhythm was meant to imply – something akin to one preparing a plate for another, or the proximity of bedrooms in the Luminan House. Was Kevi somehow behind this? She was friendly with the musicians and knew the notes and chords.

The finger cymbals pinged in rhythm as we began to move in time – together, but also so that each accentuated the other's last sway. Helioan dances weren't structured and repetitive. They were stories of flesh and feeling.

I'd danced with Beron at the House of Dusk and in this very room, back when he thought I wanted his brother and I had to pretend he was right. I remembered his bold moves, his brazen touches, each both test and dare. I didn't shrink away from them, but met and melted beneath his fiery attention.

His fingertips trailed my shoulder blades, lightly plucking my dress's satin strings as he circled me. His fingers drifted over my arm and crossed my chest, and then it was my turn.

I let my nails gently rake over his tunic until he hissed.

Then, we parted. It was a dance of wanting, but not having. Of taking liberties and chances that were forbidden. A dance that thrilled and enchanted. The music shifted and so did I, turning my back to his chest and draping an arm over his neck, writhing to the beat as if I were a freshly caught cobra emerging from my basket after hearing my first song.

His fingers trailed down my arms and he pressed against my stomach and pulled me closer until there was no space between our bodies. A rumble came from his chest and resonated through my ribs, back to front.

I smiled because I'd drawn it from him, then turned to face him and saw the desire flaring in his eyes.

I put that there, too.

"You're playing with fire," he warned darkly.

I leaned in and craned my neck, waiting.

He bent lower until my scarlet lips were just shy of his. I grew up with Noor, was taught by Sol herself. "I've been playing with fire since infancy. It's all I know and the one thing I *don't* fear."

"You've changed."

Since we were last here, he meant. He was right to an extent. In many ways, I *had* changed. In other ways, I hadn't changed at all, but this time our circumstances were different. I had no reason to lie or hold back now.

His strong hands found the small of my back and reeled me in so that my breasts were pressed against his chest, our stomachs flush. His thigh parted my legs, and as he moved us, the fire he'd spoken of came alive in my chest.

Low in my belly.

In that moment, in that heated swell of bodies, I wanted him.

"Beron!" a harsh voice snapped.

Slowly, I slid away, putting distance between the brazen Wolven and I. "Mother," he answered, chagrined.

"I need to speak to you… for the rest of the evening," she hotly hissed, slicing me with a glare.

I fanned myself. "I need a glass of water. Thank you for the dance, Wolven…" And then I left him to take the tongue-lashing I knew Vada was preparing to give him. I plucked a glass of water from a table near the doors and made my way to rejoin Holt and Chase at our table in the corner.

Chase's grin stretched from one ear to the other. He shook his head and gave a low whistle. Holt glanced up with a half-smile on his face.

"What?"

Chase's brows rose. "*What?* Are you serious?"

"About?" I asked, having no idea what he was referring to.

"That dance with Beron," he clarified.

"It was Helioan," I explained simply.

"Well, I hope Noor plans many Helioan balls in the future, complete with Helioan music. That was the closest thing I've seen to two people copulating on the dance floor."

My eyes widened and I choked on a laugh. "That is *not* what it looked like." I glanced to Holt for reassurance and his smile widened. "Was it that bad?"

"Bad?" Chase scoffed. "It was delicious. I am completely turned on now."

Holt gave Chase a look that said shut up, but Chase refused. "Come on, Holt. You have to admit that—"

"That what?" Beron asked, looming over the table.

"Nothing," Chase coughed to clear his throat. He leaned back in his seat, the smile gone from his face instantly.

I drank a gulp of water. Then another. My face was hot. My skin was hot. I fanned myself. More drinks.

My glass quickly emptied.

I stood abruptly and hurried to the water table for another glass, chugging it just as swiftly. "Citali?" Beron asked carefully from behind me again.

"I'm so hot." I tried to smile, but couldn't think of anything but the oppressive heat. Was Sol out? Was she close by? I took two more glasses and pushed out of the room. The hallway was somewhat cooler, but I needed Luminan wind, cool, moonlit sand, and maybe the sea to extinguish the fire that raged inside me.

Beron trailed me as I cut across the hallway, past two Luminan guards stationed at a pair of double doors, and down a set of stairs that tumbled onto the sand. "Calm down, Citali."

"I can't."

I was so hot. So… *uncomfortable*. My hands tightened on the glasses. Lumos shone high above us, Beron's ancestors twinkling alongside him. Nothing was out of place. There was no heat but what we'd produced on the dance floor.

The wind toyed with my hair as I continued to drink, emptying one glass and then the other. I tossed them onto the sand and walked to the edge of the sea, removing my sandals and wading into the water.

"Is this the first time you've felt flushed like this?"

"I felt it earlier, but not this intensely."

He pressed his lips into a thin line. "Your body is preparing for the shift."

"Tonight?" I shrilled.

He shook his head. "No, not tonight."

"How do you know it won't be?" I asked shrewdly.

"Lumos would've shown me."

I swallowed thickly and studied the foamy water sloshing onto my ankles and calves. I held my dress up and let it wash over me. Cold. Salty. Beautiful. Slowly, the heat in my skin ebbed away and the tension filling my bones eased.

"I'm afraid," I told him.

He tucked his hands in his pockets and nodded. "I would be, too."

"Did you know beforehand? Were there any signs?"

"Not for me," he said. "For me, the change was instantaneous. But for the others, there were signs. With each, Lumos sent them to me weeks before they changed."

"I don't have weeks though, do I?" I asked, listening to the ocean's song on the horizon.

He shifted his weight, making new footprints in the wet sand. "No." He was quiet for a moment, studying Lumos's face. "The others… their symptoms came far more gently.

Yours are raging. Not that I should have expected anything less from you," he teased.

I smiled. "You should get back to your party."

"Not without you."

I wasn't ready to leave the waters just yet. "You don't need my help to cut the cake. You have sharp enough claws."

"I don't want to leave you alone," he said. He was probably worried I would wade in and drown, or that the dark one would call to me and no one would be around to ground me in reality.

To the Wolven, I was weak and needed protection.

He rocked back on his heels. "I also don't want to be alone."

"What do you mean? Half of Lumina is inside the House tonight."

He smiled, a strange vulnerability glinting in his moonlit eyes. "But you're the only one I want beside me."

# 13

Speechless, I left the sea and walked back inside the House of the Moon with Beron. I hovered nearby as he accepted gifts, smiled, and carved the first pieces of his cake, deftly stealing one for each of us before leading me out a side door so we wouldn't get trapped by those who also wanted a piece. The throng included Holt and Chase, who looked somewhat offended that Beron hadn't stolen slices for them, too. I wasn't sure where Amaris was.

He led me upstairs to an expansive balcony that stretched the length of the House of the Moon and overlooked the glittering sea. "With this cake, my celebratory obligations are fulfilled..." He grinned, handing one of the small dessert plates to me.

"Did you bring me here to deliver bad news, or to shield me from your mother and Amaris?"

He slid a cake-covered fork into his mouth and let it slowly slide out, clean. "What makes you think it's either of those things?"

Sugary icing dissolved on my tongue and I bit back a moan. I'd had many desserts, but none as sweet as Beron's birthday cake. "I assume you stole me away for a reason. It's not like you just want to spend time with me under the moon, before the sea." I pointed my tines at the ocean's heart, wondering how many trident tips had been broken on its steely surface.

His head tilted. "What if I said that you've guessed my motive and uncovered my nefarious plan to get you alone?"

I narrowed my eyes at him before sinking my fork into another bite of cake.

A moment later, he asked, "Does my mother's opinion matter to you?"

"Yes and no." He waited for me to elaborate. Lumos graced strands of his dark hair and danced in his eyes. "I don't enjoy being loathed. No one does. Since I'm an honorary member of your pack now, I'm sure we'll have to see each other much more often than she ever dreamed or would prefer." She probably thought she was rid of me when she left Helios in Noor's care and returned home. "But there's little I can do to sway her opinion, so I'm not sure that I should waste time caring what she thinks."

The dimple deepened and he tipped his chin up. "Why do you let Amaris rile you?"

I'd given Vada several reasons to distrust and dislike me, but Amaris didn't hate me because of anything I'd said or done. She hated me simply because I breathed, and sought to provoke me at every opportunity.

With Noor, I knew that if I pushed, she'd push back. That was why she was a formidable opponent. I rarely pushed Zarina. Truthfully, I barely interacted with her at all as we aged, but she was my sister and I knew her.

Amaris was a stranger. I wasn't sure of her fighting style, but knew I was in for a battle at some point. Beron claimed Amaris was merely jealous, but I wasn't sure that was the right word.

Given the ravenous hunger, the overwhelming hot spells, and the feeling of being interconnected with others – perhaps when one didn't want to be – I wondered if her feelings were born of instinct. A new wolf, female, had joined the pack and now she felt she had to posture for dominance.

Instead of speaking my thoughts in the air, I settled on, "Everything seems to rile me right now."

He gave a challenging smirk. "Holt and Chase don't. Holt *danced* with you tonight. I can't recall the last time he danced, if he ever has, and tonight, he volunteered for you. You didn't even have to persuade him. And Chase certainly enjoyed spending time with you."

"It's nice to get to know them a little better," I admitted. "I'm sure they were comfortable with one another and the pack before I added my presence and complications to it." He sat his crumb-covered plate down on the broad rail and stared at the sea. I nudged him. "If I didn't know better, I would say that Amaris wasn't the only one jealous this evening."

Beron stared at Lumos with the slightest smile on his face.

I smoothed a hand down my stomach. "Noor brought this dress for me. She thought you'd like it," I told him.

His eyes met mine, darkening again. "I more than like it," he rasped. "Your sister can be cruel."

"A family trait, I'm afraid," I tried to tease. Too much truth lay heavily on my smile and it succumbed, then sank. "She mentioned that you'd talked about a dark flame being alive within me."

"It's true," he said, turning to me, propping his hip against the rail. My body moved to mirror his position. "And when you wear this dress beneath Lumos and his light catches onto every dark facet…" His hand gravitated to me and found the dip of my waist, his thumb brushing low on my hip, "…that dark flame I see in you dances with the cool one that flares in me. Caelum is frost, but I am fire."

He didn't have to point that out; I already knew it. I knew it so much it ached to even think about.

His eyes dipped to my lips, the diamond at my throat… lower. He swallowed and I watched his throat struggle. With great effort, he peeled his hand away. Beron took a step back and thrust his hands in his pockets just as Chase and Holt stepped onto the stone balcony.

"You can't hide from your own party," Chase chastised Beron, hanging an arm over his shoulder. He steered the Wolven back inside. Holt started after them, then remembered me. "Are you coming, Citali?"

I stared at Lumos, frozen in place. Because the moment Beron turned away from the god of the moon, his face dimmed. It seemed slow, like time itself paused, but a shadow slid over Lumos until it obscured him entirely.

The essence trapped in my flesh recognized and clawed toward the source.

The obscurity transformed from an opaque gray shadow to a hue resembling freshly spilled blood.

"Yeah," I absently said, watching for any other alteration to Lumos's face. I blinked and Lumos's light returned.

"Are you sure?" he asked again, his easy demeanor turning serious.

"I'm fine. Just enjoying the cool air." I brushed off his concern and left the balcony and Lumos behind, even as a shiver crept up my spine.

What I'd witnessed wasn't an eclipse, where Sol and Lumos met to combine their awesome powers. Sol was nowhere to be found. A new presence had emerged in the form of a shadowed, blood-soaked shroud. I knew whose presence it was. I felt pulled, not toward Helios, but to someplace far across the earth. No, not some*place*. Some*one*. The dark one.

Lumos had revealed his message to me for a reason, and he hadn't shown Beron… which meant this was a secret he wanted me to keep. The only problem was that I didn't understand what the vision meant. I knew it had to do with Anubis because I felt him slide across Lumos's face. Then, like a whisper, he'd called for his essence to return to him. Not only did the shadow obscuring the moon obey, but for a moment, the part of him trapped in me was pulled as well and I felt like a helpless, suffocating fish being drawn in on a skilled fisherman's net.

I was completely overwhelmed by him.

A thought struck me as we reached the landing…

What if the message wasn't from Lumos at all?

The moment my feet hit the landing, Noor appeared in front of me, her chest heaving. "I need you to come with me."

She clamped a hand onto my arm and rippled the air to make a portal. My eyes searched for Beron's, finding them the instant before it closed and we were thrust into the balmy air in the heart of the House of the Sun, stumbling into her meeting room.

I had no time to ask why or what the urgency was before chair legs scraped over the stone floor as Sol's priests stood to honor their Aten, unable to hide their startled expressions.

Noor looked at Kiran. "You found it."

He nodded grimly, then gestured to a book laying in the center of the polished table. A book bound in shadows that writhed against the golden surface as undulating wisps of darkness, whispers of an ancient world we couldn't begin to comprehend. "We can't open it. We've all tried," Kiran told Noor.

She reached out for the tome but hissed when her bronze finger hit shadow. She jerked away in alarm.

"That's why I wanted you to bring Citali," he explained. My lips parted before I snapped my jaw closed. "If his essence is in you, you might be able to handle it," he softly suggested.

Handle it? Oh, I would handle it. I'd handled many difficult things in my lifetime. He had no idea… My blood boiled at his nonchalance.

"Citali," Noor whispered. "He meant the book."

"I know what he meant," I snipped.

She glanced from me to it, a nudge to try. I stepped forward and leaned in, my fingers slowly drifting toward it. I wasn't sure if this would work or if I would be burned, too. Exactly how much of Anubis's essence was required to 'handle' this particular tome?

I looked up to meet Noor's worried eyes and sucked in a breath just before my fingertips grazed soft, tattered leather. I gently lifted it from the table.

The priests gave a collective gasp and Kiran explained, "None of us can touch it."

I studied the book. "How did you bring it here?"

"In a rather large basket. One of us was burned while placing it inside," Kiran answered, gesturing to the priest standing to my right. Benira was the eldest among their brotherhood now that Saric had left for the hereafter. His weathered hands were bandaged tightly.

Sol's priests always healed quickly.

"Why did *you* choose to bear it?" I asked, focusing on his wounds as I clutched Anubis's book to my chest.

"Asena Citali, you know better than most what it is to shield those you love," his weakening voice quietly noted. He pointed to the book. "Now, we need you to find a way to shield us all."

Dread and doubt mingled in my stomach. "Priest Benira, I'm afraid I might not be able to shield anyone. And I'm not an Atena anymore…" My voice trailed away as I listened to the book, to the shadows that sliced themselves into ribbons of smoke.

"I know you aren't. That's why I called you by your new title: Asena. It means *she-wolf*."

The term rang through my bones, filling them until I felt my incisors lengthen fractionally. I ran my tongue over the sharper, twin tips.

The book elicited yet another change in me, this one not wolfish in the least. Everyone watched as shadows gathered around my hands, slid over my dress, and slipped cool tendrils around my neck as if they didn't know what I was but recognized me all the same.

"I will enjoy watching you show the dark fool how powerful a she-wolf truly is. And how ferocious a mother is when her child's life is in danger," Benira said proudly.

Angry tears flared in my eyes. I hadn't protected Reyan from Father; how would I save him from Anubis? I gripped the book tighter, hoping the answer we needed had been inscribed within its pages.

"Asena," he enunciated. "You now know it is possible to fight an evil much larger and crueler than yourself and win. If anyone can face the dark one, it is you."

When I thought I saw Father on the mountain, walking toward my son with burning malice in his eyes, something snapped in me. Something that would not realign and heal, something feral, and I was glad for it. And I hadn't yet shifted. How feral would I be after I morphed into a wolf?

Noor cleared her throat. "Can you give Citali and me some time to look through the book?"

The priests did not protest as I thought they might, but did as their Aten asked, standing and pushing their chairs in before draining from the room. Only Kiran lingered. "If you need us..."

"She doesn't," I told him, holding his glare.

He pinched his lips and inclined his head respectfully, then trailed his brethren down the hall toward the temple.

Noor and I settled into chairs beside one another. "Why do you hate him so much?" she asked.

"I don't know," I told her honestly. I wasn't sure I hated him, exactly. It was possible I felt about Kiran the same way Amaris felt about me. His every breath was an inexplicable annoyance. It didn't mean I wanted him dead, I just didn't want to be in the same room with him. Or hear his voice. Or see his face.

Noor walked to the doors and instructed the guards not to allow anyone inside. I noticed with a pang that one of the guards was one of Merik's friends – Yeroh. I didn't recognize the other guard. Yeroh reverently inclined his head before his umber eyes flicked to the other guard.

My head tilted. Was he warning me against his compatriot?

Noor closed the doors before I could investigate further. Our footsteps echoed over the bare walls, making the room feel hollow when I knew it was full.

Brimming with secret murmurings.

Whispers from the wisped shadows.

With Noor at my side, I listened.

"What does that say?" she asked, pointing to the engraved words on the cover. It wasn't a language I recognized, but the shadows knew it…

"The Book of the Dead," I quietly told her, cracking the cover open, careful not to damage it. Tucked inside the cover was a folded papyrus. Helios was the only kingdom that used papyrus to write upon. Why would the god of the dead have a document from the Kingdom of the Sun?

I dragged it onto the table, carefully opening and smoothing its edges.

The papyrus was covered in Helioan words:

*This is the history of Anubis, spirit eater, god of the dead, sower of darkness and discord. His name is ruin.*

*He is the creator of lies and the spinner of illusion. He is the master of mirages.*

*Before the Sculptor formed the rock of creation and before he envisioned the worlds that would be carved from it, and the spirits that would rise from the sand and soil and tread upon the same, he created a living darkness.*

*It breathed. It thought. It schemed. It was hot and cold. Good and evil. A terrible, powerful thing. And it envied. The darkness struck an unfamiliar emotion, even in the Creator's heart. The darkness struck fear.*

*For the darkness, once living, refused to die. So the Sculptor tried to alter its nature.*

*The Sculptor failed.*

*The darkness was not solid. It was not rock to be chiseled. It ebbed and flowed. Flew and sank. Disappeared and reappeared again. It was and it was not. It could not be caught, captured, or changed.*

*The Sculptor turned away from the discord. He formed the creation rock in his mighty hands, amid the darkness. And despite it, he chiseled Sol and set her ablaze, hanging her in the midst of what he had come to fear. A bright light to scorch the darkness and keep it at bay. Her purpose was to burn.*

*But he could not leave his world subject to evil as she moved about the sky in the path he carved for her. From the creation rock, the Sculptor chiseled Lumos, a god to rule the night. Lumos did not burn, but his cool light was bright enough to temper the darkness in the places where Sol's light could not reach. Lumos's purpose was to soothe. His light would join Sol's and shine where hers could not. And together, the two gods of illumination would prevent the cursed darkness from spreading. Their combined purpose was to shine.*

*Lastly, from the creation rock, the Sculptor finally chiseled the world that haunted his thoughts. The darkness grew jealous of the gods' purposes and decided to build its own.*

*When the Sculptor's breath fanned over the world he'd created, and as Sol and Lumos moved about, shining their lights over it, spirits rose from sand and soil. Flesh built on bones and wind filled their lungs. But no spirit was meant to walk the earth forever, and eventually, the flesh faltered and failed and returned to the sand. To the soil.*

*The spirits roamed alongside the living. Fear and chaos reigned.*

*Until the darkness declared himself the shepherd of the dead.*

I swallowed and looked up at Noor, who clutched her draping moon diamond necklace with wide eyes. "Mother's book did not mention him at all…but this was written by her hand."

I smoothed a thumb down the page, the cool shadows tugging at my fingers. "Because she wanted to destroy all record of his existence."

*The darkness called himself Anubis. He established a kingdom of shadow and soul. Over the spirits he reigned, but he had no power over the living. The living belonged to Sol and Lumos. Anubis envied their power. He wanted to douse their light so the living would depend on him as the dead did.*

*He sought to destroy the gods of illumination.*

*As he raised an army of vicious souls, intent on slaughtering the living so that Sol and Lumos had nothing to burn for, the gods of illumination fought back, shining brightly across the skies. Burning low upon the earth. Incinerating the spirits of those who fought on the side of darkness. The combined power of Sol and Lumos allowed the Sculptor to subdue Anubis. For darkness is made weak in the place where light burns.*

*The Sculptor sealed the dark one into his shadow realm and rewarded Sol and Lumos with dominion of the hereafter. Sol was granted an inheritance of the spirits of her people, the sand bearers. With them, she stoked her fire and with them fueling her, burned brighter and hotter than ever. Lumos chose to set the spirits of the soil bearers in the firmament to scatter and spread his cool glow so that true darkness could never again emerge.*

*Anubis's name was chiseled from histories, though the memories of the living remained. A warning for those who might choose to follow his destructive path.*

*Darkness is made weak in the place where light burns, but sometimes light casts shadows. It is in the shadows that Anubis lies in wait.*

I laid the papyrus down and took up the book, glancing at the strange markings. Noor stared at the empty table's center like it held the answers we needed. "Where was this book found?"

She pressed her eyes closed and gripped the chair arms so tight, I thought she might melt them again. "Hidden beneath a loose stone in the floor of Father's room."

"Did one of the priests find it?"

She nodded but refused to meet my stare.

"How did they know where it was hidden?" I asked. If Sol hadn't led them there, someone knew where to find it. Someone knew what he was doing and didn't stop him. Had Sol's priests been tainted, too?

She pressed an uneasy hand over her mouth as if she didn't want to say. That was when I knew. I knew who found the book and its secret, hidden cove.

Kiran.

"I want to speak to him. Privately."

She shook her head.

I sat up and leaned closer to her. "When did he find it?"

"I haven't had a chance to question him about it."

"Let me."

Her lips pinched.

"You're too close to him to effectively question him on the matter," I told her. "I'm not." Maybe she hadn't had time to ask, but maybe Kiran was keeping secrets, in which case, I'd be happy to collect his unfaithful tongue. He owed his Aten the truth, especially about this. She was letting their friendship cloud her judgment.

"Is there more written in the book?" she asked, nerves tightening her spine so that she sat rigid in her seat.

I flipped through the decaying, delicate pages, careful not to tug too hard on any of them while moving them left to right. "Yes, but in a language I've never seen. I can't read it."

Noor swallowed thickly. "Citali?"

"Hmm?" I looked up to see her face turn ashen. "What is it?"

"The writing… the symbols. They're changing. Appearing and disappearing, rearranging themselves, contorting into new forms."

What was she talking about? The writing wasn't changing at all.

"Do you feel well?" I asked.

"I feel perfectly fine, but I swear to you, the book is… it's changing what it holds. Like a puzzle."

I couldn't see what she saw, and I couldn't reconcile the fear on her face with the tome I held in my hands.

"Anubis was the sower of discord. Perhaps the words alter themselves to conceal what's inside to anyone but him…"

"Or those who share his power," she gently mused. "You might be able to decipher it, Citali."

I flipped to the latter half of the book, where the pages had been cut to conceal a dagger. The one on my hip warmed. Its shape was a perfect fit. I didn't have to merge them to know it. Zarina had used an obsidian blade. An artifact not only endowed with Anubis's essence, but one that had once belonged to him.

"I'm afraid for you," Noor whispered, staring at the hollow space where the blade begged to lay.

I was afraid, too, but didn't want to think about the blade. What was done was done. Now we needed to undo it and set it right. The only path forward was to bind Anubis and break his power over our sister and the Helioans she'd managed to sway to her side, then expel his ruinous shadow from my body. We needed the words located in this book.

"Do you think the priests might be able to translate the writing?" I asked. "Or maybe the scribes could look at it?"

"I'll call for Benira first," she croaked. Noor crossed the room and opened the door. Hovering outside was a familiar, foxish face.

"Red?" I stood, alarmed.

"Hey, Citali." He glanced between the guards and strode into the room even as they told him that no one was allowed to enter. "Beron sent me to check on you."

Noor calmed the guards, assuring them that Red was welcome.

I sat the book down on the table, but not before he saw the shadows ghost around my fingers. I'd never noticed shadows dancing around Father. How had he handled it if Anubis's essence wasn't in his flesh? Unless he didn't obtain it until we were well into Lumina…

Red's brows drew in and his lips parted. I shook my head and whispered. "Please." *Please be quiet. Please don't panic.*

Noor asked her guardsmen to recall Benira and Kiran.

Red positioned his chair across from mine, making himself comfortable before leaning forward with his elbows on his knees. "I should get Beron."

I shook my head. "Not yet."

"I have to show him what I saw, Citali. This isn't something I can keep from him."

"I know. You're loyal to him."

He nodded and shoved his hands in his pockets. "I'm loyal to the pack, of which you are a member."

I sat down in my chair. "Show him, but tell him I'm fine."

He nodded and settled back in his seat, going quiet as he telepathically conversed with his Wolven. I could almost hear Beron's clipped tone as he and Red conversed.

Noor crossed to the balcony to stand in her mother's light. I caught portions of their conversation as she implored Sol for help, wisdom, and a thousand other things we would need to stop Anubis from further infecting our people and poisoning their thoughts and minds.

The doors slowly creaked open. I turned my head, expecting to see Kiran and Benira enter the room. What I didn't expect was to see Merik's friend, the guardsman Yeroh, lying slumped against the wall in the hall. His compatriot, the one Yeroh tried to warn me of, entered the room and slammed the door, sliding down the bar to lock it from the inside.

Red and I stood as one and I grabbed the book. "Protect Noor," I told him.

He shook his head. "That's not the order I was just given."

"It's the one you will obey," I warned.

He gritted his teeth. "I. *Can't.*"

I eased toward the opening that led to the balcony. Red *would* protect her, even if it meant placing myself in front of her for him to do it.

The guardsman's bald head glistened with sweat that beaded and ran in rivulets down his temples. He kept his stance wide and his kilt spread so he could move fast and fluidly. He pointed the tip of his spear at me and let out a roar, rushing around the table. Red met his battle cry with a ferocious growl, shifting in an instant. Shredded pieces of clothing burst from his enormous form, scattering all over the floor. His fox-red hackles raised as he moved to block me – and Noor – from the possessed man.

Growling, Red stalked toward the guardsman, who didn't even flinch when man turned to beast in front of him. Who didn't bother to lower his spear, but kept pushing forward with a feverish gleam in his eyes when he jabbed at Red. He withdrew, wringing the spear handle tighter.

He jabbed again, but Red evaded.

The wolf snapped and snarled. He was offering a warning when he could've ended it already. The man darted left, but Red quickly cut him off.

"You will die if you proceed," I warned the traitorous guard.

"I'm dead if I don't," he said, laughing hysterically before tears began falling from his eyes. "I'm dead either way."

"What do you mean?" I asked, peeking around Red.

The guardsman lunged. He swiped the tip of his spear through the air, barely missing Red's front legs. He ran to the right, but again, Red was there.

The guardsman, sweating and panting but determined, locked eyes with me. "I'm sorry," he told me, his lips quivering. Then his eyes changed. The fear bled away, replaced by something far older. A keen awareness shone in their depths. The shadows of the Book of the Dead clawed toward him and the man's lips parted to reveal a tar-like mouth, like Father's had become in death. "Citali," a powerful, ancient voice emerged from the young man. "Ya kek ra." He used the old tongue, shared by Helios and Lumina before the divide. It had been years since I'd learned it, but I knew what he said.

*My dark sun.*

A familiar growl came from behind me and a shiver slid down my spine as Beron eased from the balcony into the room. Caelum had brought him through a portal my sister had opened. The Lumin made his way to her side.

Beron's cool eyes met mine. I could almost hear his fur tremble as he stalked forward. The room shrank as the stones under my feet reverberated with his rumbling threat.

"Citali," my sister pleaded, waving me toward her and Caelum. The Lumin stood firm, frost gathering in his palms even as her flames flared on his arm, the crown of moonlight glowing in the skin of his forehead. My sister's hands turned red, ready to melt anything they touched.

I'd somehow drifted away from her. Or had the shadows pulled me to *him*?

Beron snarled. "*Ya* kek ra. Ahmanet…" His words pounded through my mind: My *dark sun. Gift of the moon.*

He'd spoken through his mind, but the guardsman's facial expression turned to stone. Anubis had heard every word.

The guardsman charged the Wolven with his spear raised and a face contorted with a horrifying mixture of fear and rage. The Wolven bared his teeth and made for the man's throat. It was over in seconds. Beron tore his head from side to side and flung the guardsmen across the room. His spear clattered to the floor.

There was a moment of surreal silence as the man gasped, then choked on his own blood as it burbled up his throat and poured from the shredded wound. Noor's bronze skin turned to ash as his blood blossomed over the floor. I clutched the book to my chest and skirted the wolves. Red snapped at me before he realized who was moving.

His eyes gleamed with apology as I made it to the door, unlocking it.

"Where are you going?" Noor cried.

"Yeroh!" I cried, rushing to his side and falling to my knees. There were no wounds on his body. No blood pooled beneath him.

"Don't," Beron said from over my shoulder. I realized he had shifted back to his human form. He crouched next to me, naked and still thrumming with energy. "His neck is broken."

He pointed to the severe bend I hadn't noticed.

I covered my mouth. *No.* "He tried to warn me." I looked to the Wolven. "He knew the guardsman was affected."

Beron went still. His muscled arms and chest turned to stone. "What is that?" he asked of the book in my hands and the shadows pouring from it to ghost over my skin.

"The Book of the Dead," I croaked.

He reached out as if to take it, but I twisted my torso and held it away. "Don't! I'm the only one who can touch it without being burned."

He clenched his jaw so tight I thought it might break. "Why you?"

I gave him a look that said it should be obvious why.

In that moment, he looked ready to tear the throat out of the world itself.

Footsteps hurried down the hall as Benira and Kiran drew near. Kiran took in Yeroh, followed by a shaky breath. I wondered how the bitter scent of new death paired with the guilt swirling through him, and whether his tongue was as charred as the guardsman Beron had torn apart for threatening us.

"Priest Benira," I carefully said to the elder of the two. "My sister needs you inside."

"What happened here, Asena?" he asked with his mouth agape, horror marring his features. He paled at the sight of Yeroh, dead and slumped, his lips and fingertips turning bluer the longer we conversed.

"The dark one is to blame," I told him, holding Kiran's stare. "The Aten needs your guidance. There is another guardsman dead inside."

"Of course," he stuttered, shuffling quickly toward the door. Kiran started to follow him, but I stood and with a hand to his chest, stopped the one who coveted my sister. "Not you."

"I know what you think, but I'm not beholden to Anubis," he told me, his hands raised in supplication.

"Yet you knew where to find this…" My fingers tightened on the tome.

"Because Sol showed me."

I tilted my head, not believing a word. "Sol?"

He scrubbed a hand down his face. "She looked so much like Noor, I thought it was her at first."

"No wonder you followed her," I bit.

The priest gritted his teeth, but explained, "When I drew near, I knew it was the goddess. Sol sweltered. She rippled the air around her, distorting it as if we were standing in the sand. The goddess motioned for me to follow her into his rooms, and when I did, she crouched before the stone, making sure I saw which one. Then, she just… vanished." The priest looked at his feet, then steeled his spine and raised his eyes. "I will serve Sol, and my Aten, until my death. I'm sorry if you don't approve, but *they* do." *And they are all that matter*, he implied but didn't say.

"Your servitude, like your life, will come to an end much sooner than you realize if you do not distance your heart from her. You made your choice and she's made hers."

Beron slowly stood, covering his nakedness as best he could.

"You cannot serve Sol when your heart is split. A priest needs to devote his whole heart to his goddess," I chastised.

"I assure you I am trying, but I cannot help what I feel. I may be a priest, but I am still a man. You should understand," he said gentler. "Merik is dead, but you must still harbor some feelings for him in your heart."

Though he was gone. Though it was my fault. Though he was never coming back.

I was sick of this conversation. "Show me your tongue."

Kiran looked taken aback, but opened his mouth and stuck out his tongue. It was pink and whole, not rotten like I thought it might be. He had not been tainted.

To be certain, I held the book toward his chest until he hissed and a red burn appeared on his skin. A decent person would have apologized. They might have explained to the priest why they burned him. I couldn't find it in my heart to be decent, so I looked at him dismissively and said, "The Wolven and Red need kilts."

Kiran slowly sealed his lips. He dragged his attention down the hallway and called for an overwhelmed woman who stood several feet away, hands hovering over her mouth, to help him. She rushed away, returning a few moments later with two pleated, midnight blue kilts. Beron thanked the woman as he deftly tied it around his waist. Then he asked her to fetch two other priests. When she asked which among the brethren he preferred her ask for, he said any would do. She scurried away to do his bidding.

My breath caught and blood ignited as my eyes caught on Beron's every muscle and scar. Everything that combined to make him the man I knew and the Wolven I wanted to fight beside. To protect him as he protected me.

"Go inside, priest," I testily told Kiran, fighting but unable to pry my gaze from Beron. "Take this to Red." I handed the second kilt to him and he left us in the hall.

The woman who'd procured the kilt for Beron returned, leading two of Kiran's brethren. As they attended Yeroh, I turned from the Wolven and told Sol's caretakers of the guardsman who lay dead inside as well, and they promised to return for him as they gathered Yeroh's lifeless form and carried it away, hoisting him by ankles and wrists. As his head lolled, the break in his vertebrae punctuated how I'd failed him.

My emotions tumbled.

I let Yeroh down because I didn't listen. Didn't act when he dared tell me something was off with the man. Now, both were dead and I could do nothing to bring them back.

I watched until the priests reached the hallway's end and carried Yeroh out of sight, bearing witness to my failure and of the threat we hadn't realized walked among us. Because while Anubis might not have burst from his shadowed kingdom yet, he'd supplanted himself firmly among our people.

It was clever. Noor and I would hesitate to kill our own people when we saw them fight his control over them. When we saw their humanity, even if it gave way to his power. When we knew of the families that waited at their homes and the futures they dreamed of seeing.

I pressed the book to my heart and wondered if the shadows had slithered inside my heart, because I was barely in control. Barely holding those sharp shards of myself together into any semblance of a useful form.

If the Lioness had foreseen this darkness in me, she had not mentioned it. Could the spirit eater and god of the dead shroud the future from even the Sphinx?

# 14

Noor stood with the priests as they hovered over the attacker's body. "I want you to check him for recent wounds and fresh scars. Tell me if you see anything at all," she instructed. I didn't miss her quick glance to my stomach.

If Zarina used the blade on me, how many others had she or Father infected before we returned from Helios to wrench it from their grasp?

Worse, what if they no longer needed the blade to spread Anubis's foulness throughout the kingdom?

Noor and I spoke to Benira for a time. Unfortunately, the eldest priest could not read the language carved into the Book of the Dead. "I'm sorry," he lamented. "I have never seen writing such as this. It's as if it knows I'm trying to…" He scowled. "It keeps altering itself." He glanced over the page I held open. "Citali, if you try to decipher it, use great care," he said to me pointedly. "We don't know who penned it or what magic the symbols might hold or unleash."

"I think we know the author," I told him, voicing what he was so artfully skirting around. "And the writing does not change for me. It remains constant."

His watery eyes shone with fear. "Then perhaps it's best left alone."

"For someone else to find and use against us? Sol led Kiran to the book. What's to say that Anubis couldn't send Zarina, or any of those he's infiltrated, to take it back?" I argued.

"It can't stay here," Noor said. "You have to take it with you. Take it away. Keep it safe. And learn what you can, if you can, as safely as you are able." She inclined her head to the eldest priest. "Thank you, Benira."

He bowed to her. "Of course, my Aten." Benira turned to me and bent at the waist again. "Asena, my advice is that if you cannot decipher it, find a way to destroy it."

"I thought priests believed all knowledge should be preserved?"

He shook his head. "If we manage to destroy Anubis or seal him away as the Sculptor once did, the worst thing we could do is repeat the mistake of leaving a record for someone to find in the future. I'm not a proponent of erasing one's history without learning from it, as Saric always taught, but I am willing to make an exception in this case. Anubis is a plague that needs to be stricken – cleanly. Completely. And forever." He pressed his bandaged hands together and bowed to us again. "Sol be with you both." He left us to rejoin his brothers, carefully folding his damaged hands in front of him.

"Why hasn't he healed?" I asked Noor.

My sister had no answer. When the priests burned their feet walking in the sand, they healed very quickly. Was a shadow burn somehow far worse? Could the dark essence of Anubis enter even a priest's body through a wound?

I watched the dark tendrils writhe from the book and curl around my skin like I was its shield. Like they thought I wouldn't dare destroy them as Benira suggested. Would they destroy me instead, as they had the guardsman? Was I dying from an invisible wound and didn't even realize it?

Despite his injury and age, Benira helped his brothers carry the guardsman's body away. They would prepare the men and take them to the top of Sol's temple tomorrow. Noor would call her mother down and she would consume the acceptable parts of their spirit, fueling her great fire. Her light.

I hoped she saw the true will of the guardsman who attacked us. He didn't want to harm us. He was forced to. His words haunted me.

*I'm dead if I don't. I'm dead either way.*

I was terrified. Because if the shadows that ruled him were inside me, what was I capable of doing for the dark one?

Servants soon arrived to clean the floor. It had only been a handful of days since Noor became Aten, but already they looked healthier. Their skin was fuller, their eyes bright, even if they still shone with fear. I wondered if they were the same ones who'd scrubbed my blood away.

My sister's face was still ashen, but her shoulders were set in that strong, straight line that meant she was ready to fight. "You should go get some rest. I'll come for you if I learn anything new."

"I want to know that my son is safe," I told her.

With a nod, her eyes unfocused as she called to the Lioness. Her hand reached blindly to mine and clasped it. "All is well with him."

"Kiran has not been compromised," I told her. "Has Caelum already returned to Lumina?"

She nodded. I could tell she wanted him with her, and I knew he wanted to be at her side. Neither was brave enough to admit they needed the other. When would they realize they were far stronger together than parted? "He doesn't want to be parted from you."

Her brows kissed. "He told you that?"

I gave a nod. "The other day."

"I thought if I asked him to stay, he might feel smothered."

"I think he'd love for you to smother him," I teased. The heavy atmosphere made the attempt feel forced, but I meant it. Caelum wanted Noor. Beside him. Always. He'd made that abundantly clear when he gave her his cuff, and even clearer when he donned hers. When he showed her the crown and gifted her his heart and allegiance.

"I'll go to him when I can," she said. "Thank you." Her gaze caught on something over my shoulder. "I think the wolves are getting restless."

I glanced back to see Beron and Red shifting their weight and speaking in low tones, glancing at the exits, then back at me. "I think you're right."

"I'll open a pathway for you all."

The heavy weight of the day settled into my legs the moment I stepped from Helios's warmth into the cool mountain air. The scent of the needled trees and fresh snow met us in front of the House of Wolves.

Beron, Red, and I barely had time to say goodbye to Chase, as he immediately left for Helios on Beron's orders. Noor offered to take him through the gateway, but Beron wanted the wolves to maintain a presence in both kingdoms, *and* the space between them. Chase would run through the Dusk Lands to keep an eye out for anything that seemed amiss, and he would arrive in Helios in a few hours. We watched him disappear through the trees, his gray fur blending with the patches of fresh snow.

Red gestured to the House. "I'm going to get some sleep while I can."

"Goodnight," I told him.

He and Beron shared a silent exchange.

Beron warily glanced at the book still pressed against my chest.

There was a sudden shift in the air between us. Almost electric. As if a storm charged the sky and soon, bolts would stab the ground all around us.

The Wolven straightened, almost a dare to his posture. As if silently saying he saw *me* – not the Aten's sister, not the one who tried to ruin everything she touched, including his kingdom and his brother's power over it, not even the Asena… As if he didn't notice the dark, dancing shadows dancing around my fingers and throat. Like he didn't care what part of Anubis was trapped within me.

Maybe it was because he'd chosen to make me part of his pack. Maybe it was something deeper. Either way, I wasn't sure I wanted to wade so far with Beron. I still didn't know how to swim, but I could easily manage to drown.

Despite my reticence, I couldn't help but gravitate toward him. "Why did you come to Helios tonight? Red wasn't in danger."

He slowly, deliberately stepped closer. "I didn't come to help Red. I didn't come because of the book, or the priests, or the dark one. I came for *you*, Citali."

My heart struggled toward him.

With another step, I erased the expanse between us, craning my neck as he bent and leaned in. My breath ghosted his stubbled jaw. I placed a tender, aching kiss on the smooth skin just above it, peeling my lips away as his hands found my waist. "What was that for?"

My heart cracked from the weight of the truth. "I have nothing else to give you."

His chest stilled beneath my hand. "What do you mean?"

"To celebrate your birth, your mother, Caelum and Noor, and the pack presented gifts." A silver medallion engraved with his image. An aged to perfection Helioan bottle of wine and a jar of Luminan sand studded with pearlescent shells. Even the pack promised him a surprise during their next run.

I wasn't sure what that would entail, but hoped the dark one did not disturb it.

My lashes fluttered as I struggled to unravel the words that bound my tongue. "I can never thank you enough for what you did. There aren't enough gifts in this world to show you how much…" I choked on the words.

"Citali," he whispered against my temple, raking the delicate skin there with his stubbled jaw. "You owe me nothing."

"I owe you everything," I argued, barely breathing as his hand tightened on my waist.

He nuzzled my nose and I met his touch. "I can't think of anything or anyone else when you're in danger."

I choked a laugh. "When am I not?"

He smiled. The dimple deepened. I dipped my thumbnail into it. "I feel the strangest pull to you," I told him, unable to stop myself from telling him.

His smile hardened and he stepped away, and the pull I'd just felt became an abrupt push. An unseen distance, like a great, gaping fissure splitting the earth, opened between us.

"I'm not sure you know what you're saying or doing right now," he grimaced.

My head ticked back in surprise. "Why would you say that?"

"Because you acted like this with my brother not long ago. You pressed a kiss to his mouth, too, as I recall. Your emotions aren't stable."

A pain emerged deep inside my chest. I *felt* his emotions. I *felt* his pain. His frustration, like gnashing teeth, snapped and gnawed as he struggled for dominance over his feelings. As he sought to push me away.

He threw up a wall, stone by stone to keep me away from his heart.

And then, I felt nothing from him as he managed to close off whatever connection the two of us had. The deep pain was carved from me, replaced with a cold hollowness that reminded me of snow and frost-covered mountains.

Bitter. Frigid. Lonely.

My *dark sun. Gift of the moon.*

I realized he'd spoken it just to upset the dark one. It hadn't meant anything to him. I wasn't sure why I thought it would have, or why I let myself care.

"Citali," he quietly lamented.

I flashed a glare at him. "No."

He didn't get to toy with my feelings this way. He'd said they were running high and what I felt was meaningless because I hadn't transitioned into the wolf I would become. Maybe he was right, and they were best discarded and ignored.

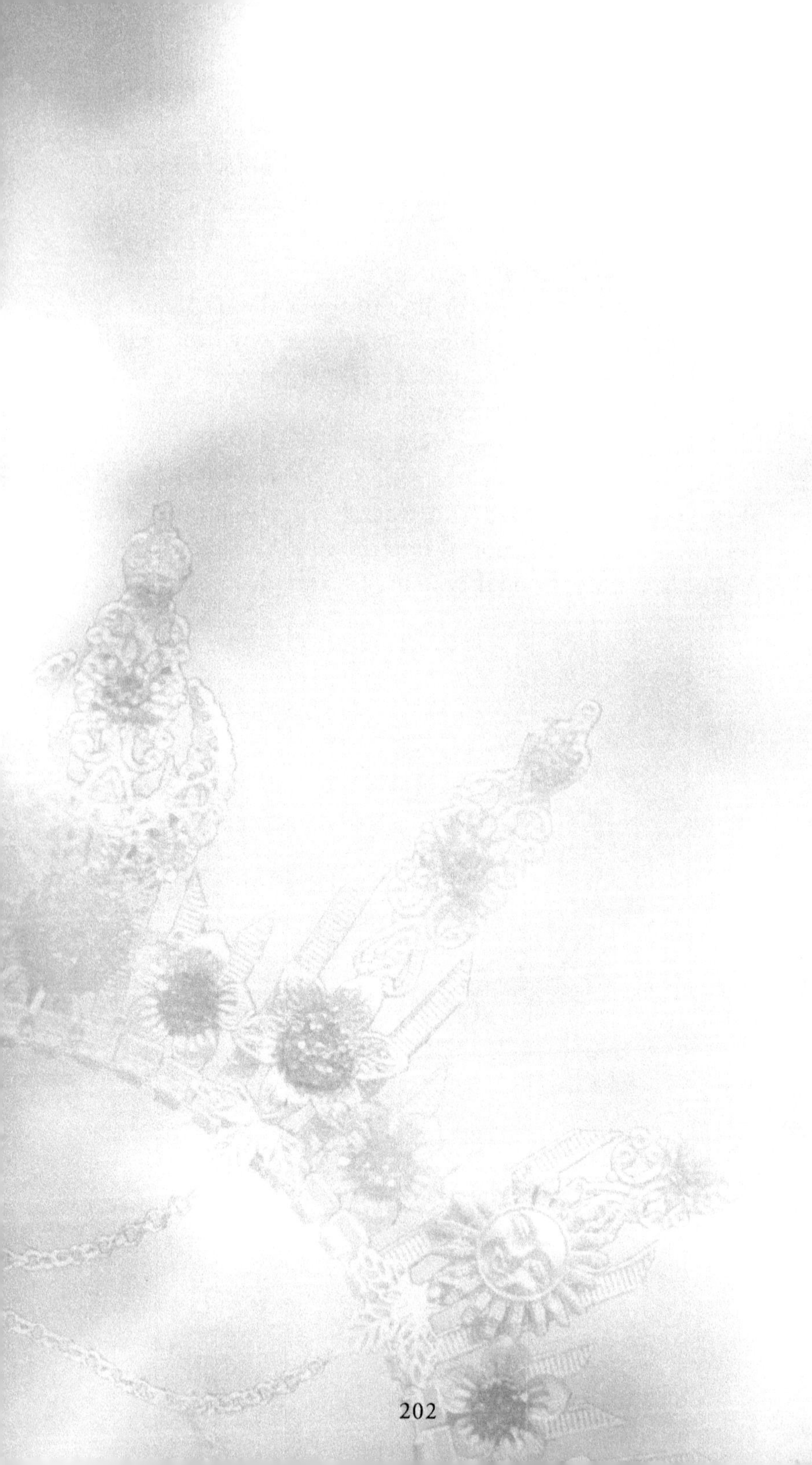

# 15

Sol's light broke over the mountaintops in brilliant white gold beams that gleamed and glistened over the snow where it lodged in crevices and shadows. She hadn't startled me awake, though. A sharp noise at my window had.

I quickly dressed in the butter-soft leathers Vada had given me and tucked the book into my waistband, quickly lacing my boots. The House was quiet as I slipped down the steps, through the great room, past the fireplace and through the front door.

Warm light hit my calves, knees, thighs, and stomach as I walked across the porch to greet Sol, shielding my eyes to see who had tried to get my attention.

Red and Holt weren't outside. Chase was gone. Amaris wouldn't have thrown a rock at my pane.

Footfalls came from around the side of the House. Surprisingly, Caelum emerged. "What are you doing?" I asked, confused and exhausted.

"Checking on you."

"And you couldn't have walked into the House and yelled my name?"

He laughed, then sheepishly tucked his hands into the pockets of his trousers. "My brother thinks your business is his now."

"He and everyone else," I grumbled, trudging down the steps to stand with him.

"Want to take a walk?" he asked in a hopeful tone.

"Sure," I drawled. What did he want? Caelum didn't come there just to spend time with his love's horrid sister.

We walked into the trees, into alternating swaths of shadow and sun. Cold and warmth. And for a long while, he was quiet.

"Did Noor send you?" I guessed.

"Not exactly. Though, she was glad when I told her I was coming to see you." His stride was longer than mine, so he kept his pace slow. It almost felt like we were two friends just out for a stroll, catching up on lost time. Almost. "She told me everything that led up to last night's altercation. About Kiran, Benira, the guardsmen, *the book*..." he pointedly enunciated.

A defensive feeling curled around my middle. I wondered if it came from me, the book itself, or the shadows guarding it. "If the book is what you came for, I won't give it to you."

He scoffed, ducking to avoid a low-hanging branch that I would have to leap to touch with the top of my head. "I don't want it. I came to see if it's affecting you, and how you feel after seeing what happened with the guardsman."

"I've never been more afraid since I thought I was dying, and that should tell you something," I answered. "You saw him. He didn't want to hurt us, and he didn't want to die. He didn't deserve his end."

"The priests found a pink scar on the heel of his palm. A clean slice."

"She needs to check all the guardsmen for similar marks," I murmured.

He nodded. "She's asked the priests to help with that. They're making plans for what to do with anyone who is found to be marked." He was quiet. "There must be a way to rid them, and you, of his essence."

"I hope it doesn't involve dying," I answered wryly, terrified that might be the only way to purge Anubis from those harboring him.

"It won't come to that," he vowed. "Noor wanted to come, but she's busy with the priests. Between the guardsmen's departure she faces and the decisions that must be made before they recall the guard, she can barely breathe."

The Aten's and priests' duties normally kept them quite busy, but now that everything was crumbling, they had much more to piece together on top of their usual affairs.

"That's what you're for. To help her remember to take deep breaths and put one foot ahead of the other. To stay strong and not wither. That sometimes it's okay to tread the water instead of fighting the current."

He smiled. "I'm trying."

We walked to the river, where the strangely blue water roared like the thoughts in my head.

"So, the book doesn't bother you? The shadows don't?" he asked carefully.

"Define *bother*," I retorted. They hadn't taken control of my body yet, if that was what he was asking. "Caelum?" I stepped onto a boulder so I could look him in the eye. "What will happen if I turn into a wolf and Anubis is able to manipulate me then, as he did the guardsman last night?"

Caelum went still. His lips thinned. His chest slowly rose and fell beneath his dark tunic, but somehow, it seemed his breaths were deeper. As if reminding himself to breathe the way he was supposed to help my sister. It told me he had no answer to my question.

"We have to do something," I added. "Either implore Lumos to stop this transition, find a way to remove the essence, or stop me before *he* uses me to tear the world apart."

"It's too early to assume that might happen to you," he said gently, but I knew Caelum better than that. Caelum was a thinker.

"It's too dangerous to assume it won't." My chest tightened at the thought. "You'll have to do whatever it takes if it comes down to it."

I wouldn't say it, but he knew what I meant. If Lumos wouldn't stop me from becoming a beast, and Anubis was able to aim my fangs and claws at the innocent, they would have to kill me.

"Noor couldn't do that to you," he rasped.

"Then *you* must. Or Beron."

"Beron couldn't either," he said.

"He'd have no trouble with it, but even if something prevented him, that still leaves you, Lumin. I need you to give me your word."

He shook his head. "How can you ask that of me?"

"Because I need someone to keep their word and protect my son when I can't."

His silvery blue eyes cut to me. "You really are afraid."

I nodded once.

His head snapped toward the House. "Uh, oh," he muttered.

"What?"

"Beron's awake and looking for you."

I let out an exasperated strangled noise, but cut it off when I realized I'd left without telling him where I was going. The Wolven had every right to track me, to keep his pack safe from the monster he'd brought into their fold.

Caelum and I took off toward the house. "I'm telling him you're fine and with me."

Given the fight we'd had last night – which Beron had dragged a memory of me with Caelum into – I wasn't sure he'd appreciate us taking a walk. Here again was another reinforcement that our 'friendship' was doomed.

We took trails engraved into the earth by hooves and the pads of many feet. When we drew near the house, we heard arguing voices, male and female. Beron and Amaris.

I stopped to hear what they were saying.

Caelum's lips parted and he started forward. "We probably shouldn't eavesdrop."

I threw a hand out to stop him. "We absolutely should," I warned. I wanted to know what the Wolven would say when he didn't think I was listening or could hear him in my head.

Beron threw his hands out in frustration. "There's never been anything between us. You're my *friend*, like a sister to me, Amaris. I don't want to do anything to upset that."

She pled with him. "We are not kin, and nothing will ever change our friendship."

"It already is," he argued. "You're different. On edge. Constantly upset at me, or at *her*."

"I'm not," she promised, shaking her head. I could see the deep crimson of her hair through the green needles. I saw Beron's tense posture and smelled his clean scent on the stirring air. "Look, I know you're attracted to her. You told me that in the Dusk Lands, and attraction is a stubborn fire to put out. I know you care for her. You wouldn't have saved her if you didn't. But you don't love her."

*Beron talked about me with her when we were still in the Dusk Lands?*

"What do you know of love?" he rasped, crossing his arms, enacting a barrier of muscle and flesh to cover his heart.

"Answer one question for me," she challenged. "Would Citali have saved *you* if the situation was reversed? If you had cried out to her for help and she'd heard you and come to your side, would she have gone straight to Sol and pleaded to do anything – alter herself – for you?"

The muscle in Beron's jaw ticked angrily. "She isn't the Aten and doesn't have a link to the sun goddess," he defended weakly.

"But if she did..." Amaris amended. "If she could speak to Sol, would she have? And even if she didn't, would she try anyway?"

He was quiet. I couldn't believe he wasn't shouting in her face. *Of course she would have!*

"Beron, if your answer isn't an immediate yes, then she doesn't deserve any piece or part of you. Least of all your heart." Amaris's voice faltered. "If you rid the world of Anubis, you can ask Lumos to release you from her hold on you."

*What was she talking about? I have no hold on him...*

I could barely breathe, barely contain the rage and pain and confusion that churned within me. Then I realized I didn't know if I was feeling those things or Beron was. Or if we both felt the same thing at the same time, and the emotions were building and melding together.

"She doesn't even want me," he told her. "But I need you to finally hear me when I say that I don't want you in that way, either."

She shook her head. "If Lumos severs the mate bond, you might feel differently." She reached out and touched his arm, dragging it from his chest and trailing her fingers down his bare skin. He pressed his eyes closed, but didn't pull away.

*Mate. Bond.*

The words crashed through me, but the wave of anger I felt rushed like a raging river through a tranquil valley, uprooting trees. Uprooting my feet.

I stalked from the wood, unable to see anything but her hand on his skin.

Her eyes pleading for him to see her, to pick *her*.

"Citali," Caelum warned, gently grabbing my arm.

I wrenched it away. "Don't touch me," I growled.

"Wait," the Lumin tried again.

"Don't touch me!" I shouted, shadows spilling from my mouth and palms, slithering over my skin, fueling the burning dark flame that festered inside me. I barreled into Amaris and she fell hard, her breath escaping in a loud gasp. The next second, she was back on her feet as though it hadn't happened.

I pointed my finger in her face as Caelum and Beron parted us. Caelum firmly pushed me away, but I wasn't finished. "Don't you *dare* put your hands on him again! He told you how he felt. You had no right!" I gasped, pressing a hand to my chest where an ache formed and spread. "And you have *no idea* what I would do for him."

She struggled against Beron's arm that held her back. "What you'd do for him *now*, you mean? What about before Lumos forced the two of you together? You don't deserve him!" she spat.

"I know!" I shouted, pushing Caelum, my chest heaving. Hurting. "I know I don't, but I don't care."

A terrible growl tore from her chest. Her nose wrinkled as she bared her teeth. Her canines elongated into fangs. She panted, the shift so near. She suddenly twisted her head to Beron, who had released her and positioned himself in front of me and his brother. *The Lumin*, I reminded myself… The Wolven was sworn to protect the Lumin – even from his own.

She stared at him in disbelief, as though she couldn't understand whatever it was he'd screamed into her mind. She scoffed, "You're wrong," her eyes flicking to me. "That girl is nothing but ruin."

In the Book of the Dead, it said that Anubis was ruin… and the comparison hit me like a blow to the stomach. Then, it enraged me.

I tried to go around Caelum to get to her, ready to end this once and for all. If she wanted a fight, she had it.

"Citali, stop!" he shouted.

It was one thing to spit venom at me, and quite another to try to manipulate Beron into…

"Citali!"

A thought suddenly crashed into me and I looked at Caelum. Horrified, I covered my mouth.

Was I wrong? What if I was terribly, terribly wrong?

If Lumos made Beron bind himself to me to save me… then maybe whatever pull existed between me and Beron was Lumos's doing, and we were nothing but puppets to his will.

Like the guardsman.

Maybe Amaris looked at her best friend when he was near me and saw feverish eyes and harried breaths and knew he was acting out of character. What if she knew he had sacrificed everything and gotten nothing in return and never would?

Numbly, I staggered away from them all.

# 16

Amaris stormed around the house to the back yard and took the thin, rocky trail that led toward the spring. I followed her. She knew, of course, and when she'd had enough of my presence, she wheeled around with her teeth bared. "What do you want?"

"To talk."

"I have nothing to say to you," she spat.

"I need to know about the mate bond."

She gritted her teeth. "Why?"

"Because you are the only one who will be honest with me about it."

Her nostrils flared. "Beron would be honest."

"But he would be gentle. He handles me like I'm this fragile thing now that I'm changed but haven't shifted. I need the brutal truth laid bare by a brutal tongue."

She crossed her arms over her chest. "Ask your questions, then."

"Do you love him?" I asked.

She looked away. "Yes. I always have, though the feeling changed as we aged."

"Before he went with Caelum to the Dusk Lands, did he return your feelings?"

She raked her bottom lip with her teeth. "I don't know. He didn't say." Even if he didn't say, she knew. She just didn't want to admit that he didn't feel the same way she did. "All I know is that he left for the Dusk Lands. We all met him back at the House of the Moon when you arrived on the ship, but Beron was different than when he left."

"How was he different?"

Her lashes fluttered. "He talked about Caelum and his choices, but the more he talked about his brother and the two women fighting for his hand, the more your name fell from his tongue. It was clear which of you he would choose if the choice was his and not the Lumin's. He was glad when Caelum chose Noor. Beron wanted his brother to choose her so you might still be available to others – perhaps even to him."

I shook my head. "He couldn't have felt that way. I drove him insane at the House of the Moon!"

She smiled. "You certainly did, but that's when his tone shifted. Instead of hearing reverence in his voice when he spoke of you, an irritation filled it. And then when you threatened Noor on the balcony and he had to reveal himself to protect her, it drove a wedge between you. A wedge for which I was particularly thankful."

"Did I hear correctly when you said he could break the mate bond? Or that Lumos could?"

She shrugged. "He made it, which means he could sever it. From what Beron gleaned from Lumos in the few seconds he had to make his decision, the bond is a lifelong commitment. He will never be able to mate with another or have children if you reject him and this bond with you remains whole."

"What if I die?" I asked.

"I think then it would be broken," she said, looking at me with murder in her eyes. She scuffed her bare foot on the ground, back and forth, back and forth, wearing away the rock to expose the soil beneath. "I meant what I said. You don't deserve him and never will."

"I meant it when I said I know," I retorted.

She shook her head. "If *he's* too stubborn, maybe *you* should ask Lumos for both your sakes."

Would Lumos deign to talk to me at all? About this or anything else? I still wondered if the image I saw of his shadowed face was sent by him, or another…

Amaris's stony façade finally cracked and her chin trembled. "You have to know he only saved you because he could, because that's who he is, not because he wanted to be shackled to you for a lifetime, forsaking everything else he might later want. Even if that is never me."

It was clear she cared about him. I wasn't convinced it was the burning, all-consuming passion I had with Merik, or the feverish clash of fire and frost that belonged to Noor and Caelum. But her feelings for Beron were genuine, rooted and deep.

"The bargain I made does not concern you, Amaris," Beron said from above us as he waited at the top of the hill.

"Your decision was made under duress." She tipped her chin up to him defiantly. "Besides, when has Lumos ever denied you anything? All you have to do is ask and he would give it freely."

That muscle ticked in his jaw. "I need to speak to you, Citali." He looked at Amaris pointedly. "Alone."

A shadow fell over me just before I was thrown to the ground and my chest was pinned there by a thick paw. I coughed, an ache blooming in the back of my head. Small, sparkly stars danced in my vision.

The Sphinx's mane dragged over my nose, eyes, and lips as she faced the Wolven. She extended her claws and they cut into my leathers. "Get off me!" I wheezed, prying at her paw.

She was too busy threatening Beron, who'd shifted into wolf form. His shifted pack surrounded us, ready to pounce.

"Get. Off. Me!" I shouted.

She didn't seem to hear me. My sternum caved another inch. I thought it might crack under her weight. Until I remembered Sol's knife.

Threaded onto the belt the Sphinx had given me, tucked just under my leather tunic, it lay warm against my skin. My fingers curled around its handle. I could barely get enough of a breath to say it one last time. "Get *off*."

When she only roared at the wolf pack challenging her, I sliced my knife across the back of her heel. In a flash, blinding light beamed in every direction. The wolves whimpered and the Sphinx swayed, but the blade cut true and cleanly through flesh and tendon.

The light disappeared, but I could still see it when I blinked my eyelids closed. Her great weight suddenly lifted from my chest. I dragged in several breaths, wincing when my chest expanded. Maybe she did crack my bone.

Livid, the Lioness flapped her wings and hovered above me. Clear blood leaked from her wound. "Do you wish to die?" she roared.

"I wished to live! You were suffocating me." I pressed the heel of my palm to my chest where the skin was tender and sore.

Her endless eyes blinked. She landed again and limped, her body already mending itself. "If I sought to kill you, I wouldn't have bothered landing. I'd have snatched you up, soared as high as I could, and dropped you."

I imagined her doing just that and suppressed a shudder. "You're much larger than me. If your intent wasn't to kill me, I don't know what else you could have been thinking!"

"I was *thinking* that you possess something you were never meant to have," she bit, "and I was concerned it might possess you."

*The book...* It shivered against the skin of my stomach, trembling toward me.

"If it wasn't meant for me, why am I the only one who can touch it?" I argued.

She scoffed. "You can touch it because it is made of the same essence caged inside you. But you cannot decipher it, can you, Asena?"

I wrung the handle of the knife still clenched in my hand. "Why are you not with my son?"

She gave a feral, toothy smile. "What makes you think I'm not?"

"Because you're here!" I shouted.

"Am I?" she asked. Then she faded and completely vanished from sight.

I looked to Beron, then to Holt, Red, and Amaris. They all gaped at the space the Sphinx had just occupied. Then her laugh rang out, her tinkling voice raising the hair on my arms the instant before she reappeared. "I gave you my word that I would protect your son, and that is what I'm doing. There and here. Then and now."

Riddles again.

"Give me the book," she demanded.

I flicked a wary glance at Beron. We might be in for a fight, but I couldn't do as she asked. "No."

The Lioness tilted her head. "Give it to me."

I shook my head. "No. It's not yours."

"Nor is it yours. It is *his*."

"It is mine now."

She began to pace back and forth, growing restless, irritable. Chase would call her testy. "And you plan to guard it yourself?"

"That's what I'm doing as we speak."

"It is mine to keep safe."

"If that's true, Sol would've revealed it to you and not the priests," I argued.

The rumble that tore from her chest trembled the ground, but I squared my shoulders and faced her as if she was the kitten she'd become for Reyan. "You can't take this near my son."

She threw her head back and scoffed, "You dare to tell me what I can and cannot do?"

"*He* senses it," I told her. "The shadows belong to him. If you take it near Reyan, the dark one will find you *and* him. I can't let that happen." As she paced, her gait returned to normal. The limp I'd given her was gone. "Did Sol tell you to come?" I asked.

She shook her head.

"Can you read the language contained inside the book?" She was the most ancient thing in existence, aside from Sol and Lumos. If anyone could read it, it would be her.

She blinked. "I am not sure."

"If I bring it out, do you give me your word not to take it from me, or even try to?"

"For now, yes," she agreed with a haughty glance, her chin high.

I withdrew the book from my waistband. To my right, Beron flicked me a glance. His black hackles were still raised, trembling with the energy he would need to pounce if she had lied. Even though I feared the validity of her promise, I needed her to see.

Shadows swarmed my hands as I opened it, staying close to my skin and as far from the Sphinx as they could.

Holt, in sable fur, stood ready behind the Sphinx near Red. Amaris was to my left, her fur a beautiful bronze hue. In that moment, something between me and the wolves changed. They were instantly ready to defend me or die trying. They understood if the Sphinx wanted me dead, there was little they could do. She could shred us all in an instant.

I opened the book, careful of the folded papyrus and started to show her the shadowed pages. I watched the Sphinx comb over them, image by image, slowly shrinking back. I stepped toward her. "Don't," she gritted, easing away.

"Does it burn you?" I asked.

She shook her head. "I made a mistake. I do not want that thing."

My brows met. "Why?"

"The words… the words are cursed."

"What do they say?"

"They shift," she said, nodding toward the page. I watched it carefully, but nothing changed or shifted. "They shift under dark magic. I cannot read them. But I feel their malice."

Noor and Priest Benira said the same thing of the writing, but I experienced something completely different. For me, the words didn't meld or bend or warp at all. "They are unchanging."

She shook her head, still studying the page I held out to her. "Then what I see is a mirage, a lie." Her face lifted. "Or what you see is."

The shadows tugged at my hand, becoming more and more insistent. I snapped the book closed. "Talk to Sol. Ask her how to read it or how to keep it from Anubis."

She bristled. "I do not take orders from you, Queen of Wolves."

A growl tore from Amaris.

I stepped closer to the Sphinx. Her eyes darted to the book. "I need to know what it says about the shadows, if there's a way to rid myself of them now that they're trapped in me, and what to do if I can't."

The Sphinx's stare told me she knew exactly what had to be done if the answer wasn't found soon. "You can't trust it," she warned.

"I can't trust anything right now."

The Sphinx gave me a look akin to empathy. It surprised me so much, I softened my tone. "I would also like you to ask Sol to speak to Lumos on my behalf."

The Sphinx shook out her mane. "To what end? The god of the moon cannot burn the shadows away. Only pure light can do that."

"Yes, but he can stop my transition. I do not want to shift into wolf form with this darkness inside me."

The Sphinx went still. Eyelids blinked over fathomless eyes. "And if he calls for your life in return? That was the deal, was it not? Your life would be preserved if you became what *he* needed?" She nodded toward Beron.

"He doesn't need me," I told her.

Beron growled, prowling closer and gnashing his teeth.

The Sphinx laughed. "He vehemently disagrees, Asena."

I glanced toward Beron, whose emotions poured toward me in tumultuous tatters. Fear. Anger. Protectiveness.

"Why don't you ask your sister, your Aten, to speak to Sol?" she asked.

"I certainly can if you're incapable," I taunted.

She gave a laugh that held a hint of warning. "I think you'll find me capable of many, many things that your tiny mind cannot even fathom."

"Prove it." I shrugged, sheathing my knife.

Caelum was in the House when the altercation happened, though he heard the commotion and came outside when the Sphinx took flight.

When I wiggled my fingers and thanked the Lioness for another delightful conversation, she roared loud enough to rattle the windows of the House of Wolves.

Beron and his pack ran back up the hill to shift back into human forms, grab clothes and food, and meet us on the back terrace. Caelum settled into the chair beside me and gave a heavy sigh. "Do you regret writing the missive that brought us into your life?" I teased.

"Never," he said easily.

"But without me and Noor, your life would be so normal. Quiet. Predictable…"

"Boring," he added, sitting back in the chair. Clouds steadily built over the sunny sky. While I knew Sol was still above, not being able to see her face made me nervous. The last time it clouded, I saw my father and almost died trying to stop the vision of him going after my son.

"It's going to rain," he said, noticing me watching the sky.

I shivered. "Or snow."

In the distance, icy peaks jutted into the sagging rain-clouds. "It'll snow there," he said, pointing. "Here, it will rain. It's not cold enough for it to snow today. Sol warmed the air just enough."

I considered his words, marveling at his ease in accepting Sol into his lands. "Do you appreciate or regret her presence – her influence – in your kingdom?"

He drummed a finger on the chair. "I love it. Lumina needed her."

Noor's cuff burned on his arm. I could almost feel the heat radiating from it and wondered if he loved feeling a reminder of her on his arm as much as she loved his cooler cuff.

He glanced toward the House and sat up straighter.

"Is he okay?" I asked of his brother, to which Caelum nodded. His eyes flicked to me, away, then back. "What is it?"

"Can I see the writing in the book?" he blurted. "Everyone's seen it but me. I'm curious to see if the words shift for me as they do the others."

"I did not mean to leave you out, Lumin," I teased apologetically. "You certainly can look at the pages, I just don't recommend touching them."

He waited while I cracked it open. "Noor told me what happened to the priest Benira's hands." Caelum studied the page. "Can you turn the page for me?"

I turned it. "Caelum?"

"Hmm?" he absently answered.

"Can you read this?"

"No," he replied slowly, "but it's strange watching the symbols change. They hover above the page itself and for the briefest of seconds, they seem so familiar. Then the text shifts and I lose my grasp on it."

I wondered if he might be able to read it if the words settled. If it was Anubis's writing, then Lumos may know how to read it.

When I glanced at the pages, nothing moved. Nothing changed. Nothing shifted. The writing was solid, as if it was chiseled into stone. The shadows curled around my hands and somehow, I knew they were responsible for the chaotic shifts. They guarded the tome itself and what was penned inside.

I wondered if Zarina intentionally left it behind for us to find, assuming Father told her about its existence. I considered the fact that stabbing me and fleeing into the night probably ruined her opportunity to search for it that evening. She would have passed my rooms before reaching Father's. Maybe she was on her way to retrieve it, saw me, and acted on impulse.

Holt and Red stepped outside wearing fresh clothes, Holt in deep green and Red in muted gray-brown. Caelum waved them over to the book. "What do you see?" he asked, careful not to influence them.

Holt's lips parted as he looked at the book.

Red shook his head in disbelief.

The wolves, the Lumin, the Aten, the Sphinx, the priests of Sol… none of them could read the words contained in the tome. What choice was left but to ask the shadows and hope they revealed the truth?

Beron stepped outside and looked over my shoulder. "The writing writhes," he breathed. "Are you sure we didn't make a mistake not giving it to the Sphinx?"

"I am… Not that she wanted it in the end," I added dryly. "She said the words were cursed."

The Wolven moved to the seat on my right and sank heavily into it, rubbing at the bridge of his nose. Holt and Red claimed chairs and even Amaris joined us a few minutes later. I tucked the book away again when I noticed the Lumin and pack seemed transfixed and troubled by the shadows.

When Beron spoke, the pack listened.

"There's been too much strife among us the last few days, but just now, when it mattered, we came together. We have to put our petty fighting away and focus, because the Sphinx is on our side. What would have happened if we'd just faced Anubis?"

Holt nodded immediately in a show of open support. All the wolves agreed, Amaris included.

"I don't care what issues are swirling between us. We have to focus on the threat at hand before we deal with anything else." He pointedly glanced between me and Amaris. "Anything."

"You won't survive as a pack unless you fight *for* each other," Caelum added. "Don't forget that, no matter who you're squared up with."

Caelum and Beron shared a wary glance. Lumina had never been at war with Helios, but wars of a different kind raged in every kingdom. I wanted to know what kind the Kingdom of the Moon had fought. Helios was plagued by failing crops and famine, followed by our father hoarding all the goods and rationing only enough to keep our people barely alive. And even then, some of the weakest welcomed death far too early.

Caelum's words resonated through me until they were all I could hear, over and over. In shouts and whispers. All I could see in my mind was the image of a darkened Lumos. I had to tell them. Keeping this secret wasn't right.

"I had a vision," I blurted. If we were to fight together, we needed to prepare for the war ahead. I turned my attention to Beron. "In Lumina, after we had cake and you left the balcony with Chase… I saw something in the sky. You didn't notice it. Holt didn't either. I just… I don't know if the vision came from Lumos, or if the dark one sent it."

Beron's mouth gaped in shock. "Why didn't you tell me?"

I pushed my hair back from where it hung in my face and rested my head in my hands. "Truthfully, I wasn't sure if I just imagined it, especially since no one else noticed it. I imagined my father on the mountain when he wasn't really there. This may be nothing but the dark one playing tricks, but I wanted to tell you in case it was real."

"What did you see?" Caelum gently asked.

I pressed my eyes closed and the image was there, emblazoned behind my lids. "I saw a shadow slide over Lumos's face, turning it a deep gray. And then when his face was completely covered, the gray changed and his face became a fiery red orange."

"A blood moon," Amaris breathed.

Red muttered a curse. Chase was in Helios, but I'm sure he would've said something to match if he were with us. Holt carefully watched his Wolven.

"What is a blood moon?" I asked breathlessly, afraid of the answer.

Beron and Caelum stood and left us, entering the House so abruptly, they might as well have slammed the door in our faces. The others didn't seem surprised. I wasn't sure if it was because Beron was screaming into their minds, or if the omen I'd just mentioned was so bad, it went without saying.

I looked to Holt, then Red. "Will someone explain what a blood moon means?"

"It foretells the death of one of Lumos's wolves," Amaris croaked.

What? My lips parted.

"Don't worry. You're probably safe. You haven't shifted yet." Her honeyed words held venom. She stood abruptly and stalked inside the House.

My gaze shifted between Holt and Red. "I think it's me."

Holt swallowed, then shook his head.

"Nah, it isn't you, Citali," Red tried to reassure.

But it made sense. I was the one to whom the vision came. I was the newest member. The biggest threat and one that would be neutralized if the dark one remained uncontained… The Sphinx would do it if no one else could garner the courage. She would end me if I became the monster I was beginning to fear more than I ever had my own father.

Holt flicked a glance at the windows. "They're going to have Noor call Sol to Helios."

"But Lumos is there now."

He nodded. "The two will eclipse."

The two gods of illumination would meet over Helios. But would the scant light the stars leaked be enough to keep Anubis away from Lumina?

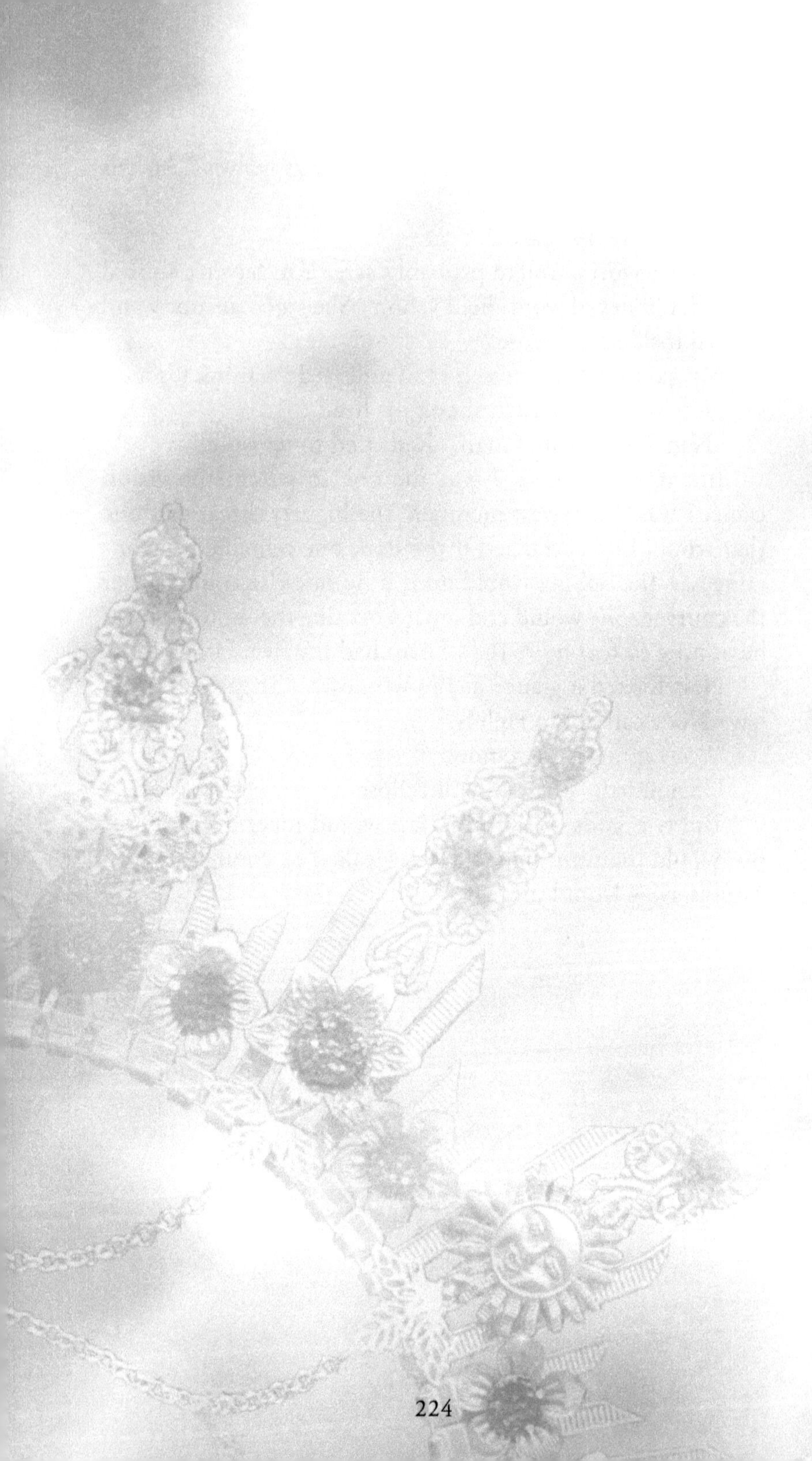

# 17

By the time Holt and Red stood up, and Red offered me a hand and pulled me out of my chair, Beron had sent Chase to Noor and Noor had opened a portal. Chase stayed in Helios with the Lumin and Wolven, but soon, the three would return. Clouds still blanketed the sky when Sol heard Noor's call and abandoned Lumina to join Lumos over her temple.

Amaris was in the kitchen eating when we entered. She finished chewing whatever she'd grabbed and told Holt she was going to run the perimeter. She didn't spare even a passing glance, but I could be civil if she ignored me.

The heat of my homeland lingered in the House and I tried to ignore the shadows who whispered that they'd left me behind on purpose. That they didn't want me to go with them. That I wasn't welcome in my home anymore. That I was tainted. A target. Too unstable to trust. A liar. I'd hidden the vision from them.

"Are you okay?" Red asked, leaning a hip against one of the long tables.

My fingertips traced the gouges left behind by years of chopping and slicing. I nodded, trying to silence the incessant whispering.

"Hungry?"

"Always," I answered.

He smiled. "Let's find something to cook up, then."

Holt spoke up. "There are trout in the snow cellar."

"Snow cellar?"

"We collect snow and ice from the mountaintop and keep it piled in a small cellar," he answered. "It preserves the food we catch or bring home."

*Home*. There was that word again. Mocking me. The insidious shadows whispered that Helios wasn't my home anymore. The sunlight was not a welcome home for darkness. They said this wasn't my home, either. The House of Wolves was for *their* kind. Since I hadn't turned, I was not one of them.

I was another kind.

I was his.

*His dark sun.*

Something in me recoiled at the voices slithering through my mind. I gripped the edge of the counter, my vision swimming. I wanted to shred the whispers, to sink my teeth in and shake and tear until the life and words bled from each one.

"Citali?" Red asked, dipping his head to peer into my face.

My skin was so hot it felt as if it would blister and peel off. Cold sweat beaded on my forehead and upper lip, sliding down the back of my neck. My fingernails lengthened and raked against the wood. Shavings peeled away when I moved my hands.

"Citali, calm down, okay? Holt!" Red yelled, a tinge of unease in his voice.

Red was beside me in an instant. I heard Holt's voice. My eyes wouldn't focus. "Cold rag," one of them snapped.

A wet, cold rag swept across my face and neck. "You're okay," he said. "Breathe. Calm down."

A colorful curse. Red.

"Citali, listen," Holt demanded, hefting me onto the counter and holding me upright. "It's going to take every ounce of strength you have, but you have to push what you're feeling into the pit of your stomach. Pretend there's a bottle there. Push all these feelings into the bottle and cork it."

There wasn't a bottle large enough to contain what I was feeling, nor a jug or barrel. Not even this mountain could hold what wanted to burst from me. Angry swirls of fire raged through my body, threatening to consume my every thought and breath.

"Listen," Holt implored. "Your body wants to follow Lumos now, to go to him and shift, but you cannot go to Helios. It's not safe for you there right now."

My chest caved. I drew in several shallow breaths only for it to cave again. I couldn't do this. I couldn't bottle this feeling. Couldn't calm it even fractionally. I was too weak. Always too weak.

A tear fell from my eyes and splashed onto my forearm.

"It's okay," he gently assured me. "I know. It's a powerful feeling, but you are stronger still, Citali."

I didn't feel strong. I felt like the shards that made me had been crushed beneath someone's heel, ground to dust and thrown to the sand. I coughed, sobbing and crumbling onto Holt's shoulder as I pushed the feeling down, locking it away likc he'd instructed.

I couldn't summon a bottle like he suggested, but within my belly swelled a thick, oily darkness. Instead of corking my fire, I drowned the feeling in viscous shadow.

Holt hovered in a nearby chair, sitting up when I blinked awake. Coals flared in the bottom of the fireplace. I sat up.

The couch I had been sleeping on was comfortable enough, but I'd lain too long. My muscles were sore and my body ached.

"What happened?" I asked blearily.

"You almost shifted. When Sol left, your body searched for Lumos. You battled the urge away, though, and almost immediately fell asleep. I carried you in here to rest. The great room has the most comfortable furniture in the house, if you ask me."

A blanket had been draped over my shoulders. In a sudden fit of hunger, I flung it away and made for the kitchen, unable to think of anything else but filling the hole in my stomach. Holt's chuckle trailed behind me.

"Are you acting as my jailer again?" I snipped.

He grinned like he actually might enjoy it this time. "Until Beron returns, yes."

Thankfully, the wolves had left food out for me, consisting of cooked fish and a colorful array of vegetables, baked bread, and cinnamon butter. I filled a plate, already chewing from a loaf as Holt poured a glass of wine. He set the glass down at my chair and placed the bottle next to my glass as I settled into my seat.

I glanced at the wine in surprise. "No water?"

"The wine will help suppress the feeling."

"Hunger?" I asked around a mouthful of bread. How could my stomach feel empty even as I worked to fill it?

He shook his head. "The urge to run to Helios, barefoot and howling."

I raked my tongue over my canines. "My teeth are sharper." I held my hands out. "My nails, too."

Holt grinned. "Who would've thought it was possible?"

I froze with the wine glass poised at my lips. "Did you just make a joke?"

He held his hands out in surrender, laughing.

"First you dance, now you joke. I'm not the only one who's changing."

Red came into the room with a wide grin. "I heard laughter and the sound of chewing, so I figured you were awake."

Still holding my glass, I pointed at Holt. "It was him, believe it or not."

Red quirked a brow, clearly not believing me.

"She's still testy, though," Chase added, slipping through the doorway.

"Why are you here? Are they back?" I glanced at Holt. He hadn't mentioned the others had returned.

"No, they're still in Helios, but the eclipse is over. Lumos is on his way back here and your two favorite brothers will be back soon. Beron and Caelum are still talking with Noor."

The shadows curled around my stomach, their touch feather light, but their whispers echoing loudly. *They're keeping secrets...*

My chewing slowed. "Where's Amaris?"

"Running the perimeter," Chase answered, running a hand through his shaggy curls.

"Still?"

He huffed a laugh. "We've all taken turns. You just happened to wake up during one of hers." A moment later. "Are you feeling better now that you've had a nap and dinner?"

I groaned. "You aren't jailers; you're nannies," I muttered.

"Testy," Chase stage whispered. Holt and Red both chuckled.

I poured another glass of wine.

"You sure that's a good idea?" Red asked, hanging onto the top of the door frame and stretching. "You're tiny. You probably can't handle more than a glass."

Holt's smile fell away when I pointed my fork tines at him. "He said it was."

Red glanced at Holt, his brows raised.

Holt wiped his mouth with a napkin and held his hands out. "I only said it would take the edge off, not to down the whole bottle."

I smiled sweetly. "And I haven't yet, have I?"

"Yet?" Holt asked, looking nervous.

Chase shook his head. "Beron's going to kill us if you keep drinking."

"Why?"

"You know why," he pointedly said.

"I'll handle the Wolven if you're too afraid," I offered, shrugging a shoulder.

Chase barked a laugh. "I bet you will."

Holt and Chase guided me through the inky night to the warm spring, where I claimed a rock. I'd traded my leathers for a dress, tucked Sol's blade into the thigh sheath Noor had given me, and wrapped a blanket around my shoulders to keep warm. The book was hidden in my room. I was glad to be rid of its weight and whispers.

Slipping my legs into the warm water, I sighed. Chase and Holt awkwardly sat with me. "You don't have to stay here," I said drolly. "I'm mere steps from the House."

"We're good. We enjoy the spring," Chase replied, leaning in to cup some water in his hand, splashing me with it.

I guffawed, kicking water toward him. "When is he coming back?" I asked, staring at the sky.

Surprisingly, I missed the stars. I wondered what the tiny flecks of sentient silver saw when they looked down upon us from afar. Could they see the answers we sought so fervently, but lacked the perspective to view? What would their life experiences have taught them that we had not yet learned?

"Well, that depends on which 'he' you're speaking of," Chase said, rolling up the bottom hem of his trouser legs to the top of his knees and sinking his legs into the warm, bubbling water. "Lumos or the Wolven?"

"Both," I challenged. It felt like an eternity since I'd seen either of them.

Hurried footsteps climbed the hill and Amaris emerged from the wood, panting, wearing human skin and clothes. "I saw someone."

My muscles tightened.

"Show us," Holt snapped, standing, ready to shift.

Chase offered his hand and I took it, letting him pull me up.

Red ran down from the House and joined the pack. "Anyone recognize him?"

No one did. "I can't see what you're sharing," I told them.

Holt tried to describe the man. Young. Shaved head. Olive skin. Fit.

He was Helioan, no doubt, but it could've been any number of people. "Does he have any distinguishing marks or traits?"

Amaris gritted her teeth, trying to recall. "It's so dark, I couldn't tell."

"He's Helioan, which means we have to assume he was sent here by the dark one," I told them.

"Someone needs to stay here with Citali. The rest of us should go track the stranger," Holt said. He looked at me. "Beron's coming."

No sooner did the words leave his mouth than a portal opened to reveal my sister's sunny face, her eyes glowing a stunning golden hue. Caelum and Beron stepped through before she did. "Get the book and come with me," she said.

"You said it wasn't safe to keep it in Helios," I argued.

"If the book is what the dark one wants, we cannot let him have it. We'll go someplace else."

I nodded and scrambled up the hill with Noor as the Wolven began to order his pack into positions that would both protect the House and allow them to cover every inch of ground as they fanned out from it.

My eyes locked with Beron's. *Be careful,* I said in my mind, wishing he could hear me.

Noor and I hurried to my room and I removed the book from its hiding place where it was wedged between the back panel of a desk and the wall. She opened a portal and we were gone.

But we did not emerge in Helios. We appeared in the sand. In every direction, as far as I could see, lay burnt orange crests and valleys. The hot wind howled, making our dresses flap like sails in a storm. It tore at our hair. We were not in the sacred place she'd shown me where her mother's bones lay, the place where the winds were calm and soothing.

Noor's shoulders relaxed just enough that it made me wonder if she'd forced the motion. "Caelum will let me know when it's safe to return," she assured.

"The wolves will handle the intruder," I told her. "They're incredible."

She smiled. "It sounds like you're starting to make friends in the pack."

"Aside from Amaris, yes." A pause. "Have you heard from the Sphinx?"

"Reyan, Padren, and Malia are doing well. The Lioness has not sent another vision, but Sol reassured me that the three thrive under the Sphinx's attention."

"She will spoil my son," I tried to tease. The Sphinx would do exactly that. Reyan had a way of making the hardest hearts soften. Mine melted the moment I held him in my arms again, as though he'd been there all along. There wasn't a moment he'd breathed when I hadn't held him in my heart.

"Something you'll get to enjoy soon enough," she tried to assure me.

I hoped with every fiber of my being, and with both the good and bad parts of my soul, that she was right.

"Did you speak to Sol on my behalf? Or to Lumos?" I asked.

Noor nodded. "Lumos said that he will allow you to choose when to shift. He won't force it." Her words lingered and I knew there was more she wasn't saying.

*They're keeping secrets,* the book's shadows whispered again.

"What about the vision?"

"Sent by Lumos," my sister answered. "His warning stands for the pack."

"Why?" I asked, frustrated. "Why can't the Sculptor just shove Anubis back into the depths where he belongs?"

"Because that would mean dragging you and every other person who holds his essence there with him. He won't punish the innocent for the deeds of the dark one."

"Won't it come down to that anyway?" I asked.

She shook her head. "No. We will find another way."

*There might not be another way.*

But I still wanted to try. "What would happen if Sol shone her light onto the book?" I asked Noor.

She looked from me to her Mother, who shone directly above us. Her intense fire hovered as she watched over us. "Try it and let's see."

I looked at Sol. "Can you calm the wind? The pages are brittle and I don't want it to disintegrate."

In answer, the wind settled but didn't die entirely. It quietly whispered over the blistering sand, not strong enough to drag grains from the sandy crests, but strong enough to provide mild respite in the sweltering heat.

I brought the book out from where it was tucked beneath my arm and held it beneath her light, marveling when the shadows retreated. I looked at Noor and repeated the words given to me by the Sphinx during our last encounter… "*Darkness is made weak in the place where light burns.*"

Parting the pages, the shadows remained in hiding. My sister laughed delightedly. "The words are steady now. The shadows were responsible for shifting them, but her light overpowers their confusion."

The world tilted and blurred when I raised my head.

Sol burned brighter, so close. She was fire, hovering just over our heads.

"Citali," Noor breathed.

Climbing the dune we stood upon, was a woman. A mirror image of Noor. Sol.

"Is she real?"

"She is. She no longer wears flesh, but this is how we remember her and how she thinks we'll be most comfortable when she comes to speak to us."

My knees buckled, hitting the gritty sand as the goddess of the sun approached. Noor joined me.

Sol's skin was made of radiant light. Her face, pure fire. Her smile dazzled as she greeted Noor. "My daughter."

As much as I wanted to throw my arms around her ankles and thank her for burning Father into dust, I was angry and hurt because she hadn't saved me when Zarina stabbed me. Didn't think my life was worth sparing.

The goddess turned to me. Her hand ghosted over my hair and I suddenly remembered her doing that when I was small. Tears flooded my eyes. Sol had been kind to me. She'd treated me as a daughter while she wore flesh.

I didn't understand why Father wanted another wife so soon after my mother passed, and Zarina told me Sol had coaxed Father into her arms before my mother died. Now I knew that was untrue. In a blink, the hurt and anger folded into guilt and shame.

"Citali, your anger toward me is justified." The goddess's voice was musical, infusing warmth and love in every word. She pressed a hand to her heart. "I thought that sealing the dark one's essence in your flesh was a fate worse than death and meant to show you mercy. That night, Noor called to me and through her mind, showed a vision of you lying on the floor. All I could see was a twisting mass of shadow and thought you were already consumed. The dark one distorted my vision of you, I believe, because he wanted to reclaim the power your body held. He did not want to be bonded to you."

"I am not bonded to him," I refuted fiercely.

Sol's head tilted to the side ever so slightly. "Aren't you? You can sense him and he can sense you. It is not a mate bond like the one Lumos established for you and Beron, should you claim it, but it is a connection, a link, nonetheless."

I had no idea how Beron had convinced Lumos to save me. If Anubis altered Sol's vision, surely he used his shadows to distort Lumos's.

Sol pulled the thoughts from my mind and shook her head. "Beron saw past them. Lumos told the Wolven what he saw, but Beron was vehement that what Lumos saw was a lie. It was a risk, but Lumos trusts Beron explicitly. Once Beron bit you, Lumos's vision cleared and he saw you as Beron did. Then he watched as you not only survived his essence, but commanded it. He and I believe you can use the dark one's own essence against him."

My brows furrowed in confusion.

"The dark one calls you *kek ra. Dark sun.* You were dark flame from the moment your mother bore you. It was the first thing I noticed when I first saw you in the flesh, as a child running the corridors. There has always been a burning intensity behind your eyes, and in them lays a wisdom beyond your years, a maturity born from grief. Beron noticed it, too, when he saw you in the Dusk Lands, sneaking through a crowd you should not have been in to spy on his brother.

"The Wolven revealed many things to us today." She flicked a glance at Noor. "I know you were concerned with the number of afflicted Helioans, but most who bear the essence of Anubis have or will soon perish. Their flesh cannot bear the weight of his shadow. Those who have not yet succumbed, soon will." She turned her attention back to me and brushed my hair again. "Do not despair. Their fate is not yours. You are not like them, Citali. Like me, like Noor, you were born to burn. And this time, it will not be light that drives Anubis from this world. It will be a shadowed flame. It will be *you*."

"How?" I croaked. I wanted nothing more than to rid the world of him; to drag his essence from my flesh, bone, and blood and let it burn.

"Until you completely give in to the dark flame within, you cannot ignite shadow."

She was worse than the Sphinx.

I shook my head, frustrated. "What does that mean? How do I fight Anubis? I need you to tell me how, not to spout riddles!"

"Let's begin with what *not* to do, then. Do not trust that book." She gestured to the Book of the Dead. "Through that tome, the dark one influenced your father and swayed those who fell under its influence. That is not a tool with which to gain knowledge. Do not trust its whispers," she said knowingly. "It will act as a bridle for the dark one to fit in your mouth so he can steer you in whichever direction suits him at any given moment. Unless you can find a way to use it to bridle and steer him."

"We can't risk that," Noor argued. "We can't risk her falling for his tricks. I won't lose her to him."

Sol scoffed. "Do you think she would be so easily lost, daughter?"

Noor squared her shoulders, unafraid of the goddess standing before her. "The dark one fooled you, and for a moment, fooled Lumos. How can we know for certain Citali will be immune?"

"We cannot know. We must hope." Sol smiled at her daughter, then at me, before the body she appeared to be wearing collapsed into sand and a gust of arid wind tore her away in a winding spiral, scattering her before us.

# 18

"Hope."

Of course, Sol had hope. Sol would send her giant lioness to carry me into the sky and drop me over the sand if it seemed all hope was lost. The next time I blinked, Caelum appeared in front of us, understandably giving me a fright. "Caelum?" I sputtered. "How?"

Noor beamed. "I convinced my mother to allow him a portal."

"To the sand?" I asked, brows raised.

He grinned triumphantly. "To wherever Noor is."

I almost groaned at their sappy expressions. They were ridiculously in love.

"It's safe to go back," he advised.

"Did they find the stranger?"

He nodded. "Dead."

My eyes flicked to Noor. Sol warned that those harboring Anubis's essence would soon perish if they hadn't already. "His tongue and mouth?"

"Like tar."

I shuddered despite the hot temperature, remembering the darkened mouths of Father and the guardsman who attacked us. I couldn't help imagining myself lying on the ground as nothing more than a husk of a body waiting to be burned, mouth like tar, my tongue drawn and shriveled.

Sol rose higher, but the sand tucked every ounce of heat it could within its grains for safekeeping. Caelum began to squirm, lifting one foot then the other before shifting again.

"Let's go before we melt the Lumin," I teased.

Noor laughed. "I could melt *your* mountains, Caelum, but you could not freeze *mine*." She opened a portal and we stepped into the pale moonlight that blanketed Lumina. Clouds dotted the sky like soft pillows, but at their edges, Lumos shone through. He was here, watching.

As the god of the moon watched, his Wolven waited.

Beron lithely stepped off the porch of the House of Wolves, shirtless, with his hands in the pockets of his trousers, his stance far too casual for the tension screaming in his muscles. His hair was wet with sweat and every honed muscle was illuminated by Lumos's cool, white light.

"We spoke with Sol," Noor offered before telling him of the death that waited for every Helioan Father and Zarina had managed to sway toward the dark one.

Beron stopped breathing. His shoulders did not rise or fall. His taut stomach did not contract or expand. His eyes caught on mine and held fast, as if he would tether me to the earth or die trying.

Noor noticed the tension between us. "Not Citali," she rushed to amend. "Citali is not dying."

"Because of the bite?" Caelum asked.

Noor smiled, a look of awe filling her eyes, for me... Something I never dreamed I would see. "No, because of the strength of her spirit."

Beron finally took a breath, his shoulders rising and falling with the movement. His taut stomach contracted and expanded. He looked away.

But not for long.

Noor drew Caelum to her side. "Come on. Holt and Red can help carry the Helioan through a portal – home."

My sister was not subtle with her nod or the glance she tossed our way. My face heated and I wondered if steam wafted from it as it did the spring. Though I silently begged her to stay, she tugged Caelum toward the back of the house; the vessel of the sun disappearing into the night with the vessel of the moon.

"Did you ask Sol to sever the mate bond?" he asked in a tone I couldn't decipher.

It wasn't curiosity that laced his voice. There was a hint of danger, warning. And yet there was something more. Sol mentioned *hope*. I wondered if that was what else lurked in his words. I couldn't tell whether he hoped I had or wished I hadn't asked Sol to sever our bond. I couldn't believe that after what Noor just revealed, the fate of our mate bond was what weighed heavily on his mind.

"No, I didn't mention it. I think you were right earlier when you said we should just deal with the most pressing matter now and worry about everything less important later." If I couldn't become the hope Sol had for this world, the bond would be severed with my death anyway.

"Less important?" he asked.

I couldn't stop the nervous swallow.

He gave a cruel smirk. "Are you hoping I'll die under the blood moon and you won't have to ask anything of Lumos?"

I shook my head. "The blood moon is not meant for you."

"Sol told you this?" Now his tone was a wall built of mockery. I wanted to crush it.

"Did Lumos tell you differently?" I asked, suddenly angry. Suddenly hot, as if the arid desert heat had only now caught up with me. My mouth was suddenly parched, and my skin flushed as he moved closer, smirking like we weren't breezily discussing our chances of dying.

"He hasn't revealed who it will be. Why do you suppose that is?"

"It isn't you," I said adamantly.

His chest bumped mine. "Nor will it be you. If Sol says you are the one who will end this war, your pack and I will follow you into every battle until it is won, Asena."

Asena. She-wolf.

*Queen of Wolves...*

I raised my chin to see him better. "And when it's finished?"

"When it's finished, *if* you still want to sever the mate bond, we'll approach the gods together."

"Why?" Why would he make it easy? Why would he go at all, when...? *My gods.* I suddenly tuned in and felt the emotions roiling in him. He fought a battle of his own. One of frustration. Anguish. Lust.

His hand ghosted down my arm. "Citali." My name was whisper, prayer, and plea. My name on his tongue was sweet honey.

I suddenly wanted to taste it. To feel the shivers that burst over my skin just from hearing my name on his lips. Pushing up onto the tips of my toes, I drew his face down and with my lips a hair's breadth from his, uttered, "Beron."

His eyes drifted closed, but his mouth drew closer, inching toward mine.

Footsteps came from around the side of the House and his eyes popped open. A frustrated storm swirled in the shades of blue. In that moment, I wished I were the storm stretch and he would unleash his fury on me.

After the wolves carried the Helioan through the portal and surrendered him to Sol's priests to prepare his body for his departure, things finally quieted, and fatigue and exhaustion settled into the very marrow of my bones. I tucked the book into its hiding place, far enough away from the bed that the shadows' whispers wouldn't bother me, then collapsed into a deep slumber. I hadn't had the energy to cover myself up, let alone build a fire, but when I woke the next morning, a blanket had been spread over me and a fire burned in the hearth, warming the room.

Beside me was a chair I didn't recognize, and on the chair lay a small stack of clothes, consisting of dark trousers and two fitted tunics. One bright red, the other midnight blue.

I chose the red and quickly dressed, threading the golden belt around my waist and tucking the dagger into the loop. The book called to me and I wondered…

Easing it from behind the desk, I fanned the pages to where the dagger's cut out began. I took the dagger and eased it toward the hole that had been carved to hide it. The shadows shrieked as Sol's name and gold came near.

I paused my hand.

Sol said that it would take a shadowed flame and treachery to defeat Anubis this time. He would expect us to fight with light. He wouldn't expect someone to use his own essence against him. I just had to figure out how to manipulate it, and him.

A plan had begun to form in my mind, one that would be dangerous not only for me, but for everyone I loved. One that might drive a wedge between those I wanted to keep close and safe. But this was war. Sacrifices must be made to preserve what I loved most.

My son. My family. My pack. My people.

I shouldn't upset the shadows, or the book, I finally decided. I needed them. So, I secured the dagger on my hip and tucked the book into my waistband before making my way downstairs. The others were still sleeping, so I decided to make breakfast. I had never actually prepared a meal before, but how hard could it be?

Baking was incredibly difficult.

It would be kind to describe my acrid-smelling attempts at bread rolls to be lumps of charcoal, though it would be an insult to the coal. Red rushed into the kitchen, swatting at the smoke filling the air. "Where's the fire?"

"There is no fire. I was baking." I moved aside so he could see the charred lumps.

His tension collapsed into hearty laughter.

"I'm glad you find it funny," I grumbled.

"Funny?" he chortled. "It's hilarious."

Holt and Chase stumbled into the room with bleary eyes. Holt coughed, even though the smoke wasn't that thick. He moved to open the door – something I wished I'd thought of doing before Red rudely interrupted my baking.

Chase only stood and grinned, making me… testy. "Wipe the grin off your face, Chase. It wasn't like I was allowed in the kitchens in the House of the Sun."

"You tried," he placated, a teasing smile on his lips.

"Oh? And I suppose *you're* a great baker…?" I quirked a brow.

His rose to meet my challenge. "I certainly am. Though, I think tiny Reyan would do a better job than his mother." He moved into the room and dumped flour into a large bowl. Holt took my charcoal outside and Red began to clean the counters for Chase. "Watch and learn, Asena."

Beron appeared in the doorway. He leaned against the door frame shirtless, his arms crossed. And, of course, he wore his customary smirk. The air between us was clearing, but something about seeing him through the lifting smoke made my heart race.

That feeling left as soon as Amaris appeared beside him with mussed hair, still wearing a sleeping gown. She gave him a sultry look as she squeezed around him, careful to brush his arm. *This girl…* If she thought I'd never played this game, she was wrong.

Beron straightened, uncomfortable. Irritated.

Amaris grabbed an orange from a bowl along a far counter. She peeled the rind and separated the pulpy slivers, slowly eating. Beron pushed off the door frame. He moved toward her and I held my breath.

He reached around her and took two of the fruits in his hand, then walked to me. "Want to take a walk while Chase bakes?"

"A walk?" the self-proclaimed expert baker protested. "She needs to stay, and watch, and learn."

I took one of the fruits from Beron and reveled in the sight of an affronted Amaris, giving the Wolven a wide smile. "Absolutely."

We strolled outside past the charred remains of my rolls littering the rocky soil and I wondered why he'd asked me.

"Did you cover me and light the fire in my room last night?" I asked, peeling the fruit.

He threw his rind into the forest. "I did."

"Why?"

"Because you were shivering." He split the fruit and tore a piece away, chewing as if he didn't have a care in the world.

"Why were you awake?" I asked. "You were just as exhausted as I was."

He smirked. "I've never seen anyone as exhausted as you were last night. You slept in your clothes and didn't even bother climbing under the blankets." Beron slowed his steps and turned to face me. "Lumos wants to speak with you tonight."

I'd just seen Sol, and now Lumos wanted to see me? "Did he mention what we needed to discuss?"

"I'm not privy," he said, looking none too happy about it. It was my turn to smirk.

"Privy?"

"Entitled to. Meaning the conversation is a private one," he explained.

"Ahh. And Caelum? Will he be *privy* to what is said tonight?"

Beron shook his head. "This conversation will be yours and Lumos's alone."

"Hmm." Sol wasn't exactly specific in her instructions on how to defeat Anubis. She gave me generalities and encouragement. She'd given me hope. But the shadows inside me and those surrounding the book at my waist strangled that hope the moment she turned to sand, hissing that there was no way hope alone would be enough.

"Hmm. That's all you have to say?"

"No, that's not all. What do I wear to meet the god of the moon?"

Beron laughed, his dimple on full display.

We walked to the river where Beron sat on a boulder and waited as I found my own, across from him. Placing distance between us made things more comfortable. Less tense.

"You're edgy," he noted.

"I am not!" I snipped, forcing my shoulders to relax.

"Are you nervous about meeting him?"

"Of course I am."

He smiled. "He favors you. You have nothing to fear."

We sat in silence after that, the roaring river rushing past and drowning the sounds of our chewing. He quickly finished his fruit and I finished mine, and then we rinsed the sticky juice from our hands. "Did Sol mention anything about me?" he asked.

Beron's attempt at nonchalance failed as badly as my attempt at baking.

"She might have," I teased.

He sat up straighter, shifting his weight forward. "What did she say?"

"It was a conversation you weren't *privy* to." Beron looked nervous. This was too fun. I relented and decided to tell him a small snippet. "She said that you told her about the first time you noticed me at the House of Dusk."

His throat shifted and he dug his fingers into the stone upon which he was perched. "She did?"

I nodded and gave a small smirk.

His eyes drifted to my lips.

I remembered the other thing Sol mentioned. Clearing my throat, I told him, "She said that when I lay dying, even though Anubis's essence was coursing through me and blocking her from seeing anything but his stench, you saw me. Lumos saw the shadows, too, didn't he?" Beron nodded and pressed his eyes closed. "You told him that he was seeing a lie and he trusted you. How did you see me when even the gods couldn't?"

"I've always seen you, Citali. Anubis will never be strong enough to obscure you from me."

Amaris's words echoed through my mind. I didn't deserve Beron.

"You and I aren't so different. We both went to the Dusk Lands to protect someone we loved," he said.

I gave a mirthless laugh. My long nails dug into the boulder. "You were protecting Caelum. I was trying to hurt Noor."

He shook his head. "I wasn't talking about Noor. I was talking about Reyan. And you never would've hurt Noor."

"I tried," I told him, sitting up straighter.

"No you didn't," he smirked.

"You wouldn't have shifted and run through the House to save her on that balcony if you thought I was incapable," I said wryly.

He scooted forward until our knees almost touched, then he let his fall against mine. "I never said you weren't capable, but I know you better now, and know that if you were truly trying to kill Noor, you would have succeeded."

I looked away as he drew near.

"It's why you didn't chop the berries very well. What a crude jam you made. Barely even spreadable."

I watched his lips, the dare in his eyes. My fingers tightened on the rock. "You've already seen how unskilled I am in the kitchen," I breathed.

"She said you threatened to push her into the river, but you didn't push very hard, or else she would have landed in it with a splash." He struck the water beside him. Water sprayed both of us. "You and I aren't so different."

I shook my head. "We couldn't be more different if we were Sol and Lumos."

He grinned. "Yet the goddess of the sun and god of the moon love one another."

"Have you forgotten about the great divide? How long will this peaceful love between them last?"

"Why should love be peaceful?" He drew closer. His knee slid between my legs. His hand found my thigh, brushing the dagger there. "It can be both fire and ice. Scorching at times and at others, frosty." His hand slid up to my hip, then to my waist. "Which do you prefer, Citali?"

I wanted him.

Wanted. Him.

Beron.

The Wolven.

Leader of the pack.

Brother.

Friend.

"*I'd* prefer it if you would find another spot!" shouted Red. "Some of us need to bathe."

Beron groaned and hung his head. I snickered and scooted away, standing and dusting off my trousers, surprised at how close I'd come to kissing him.

Again.

We kissed once at the House of Dusk. It was when Caelum had slipped away with Noor and I was feeling rather defeated, experiencing a rare moment of weakness, and Beron was trying to soften the blow. He was being very sweet. Charming. He told me stories of their childhood that poked fun of Caelum and made me laugh. He stayed with me for a couple of hours, doing what he could to take my mind off my troubles.

I guess we weren't so different – in that respect, at least.

Zarina was the one favored by our father. Noor by her mother, and then by Caelum. I was only favored by my child who, because of our circumstances, didn't even know to call me Mother. Father allowed me to visit just to make sure I knew what I stood to lose if I crossed him. The fleeting moments when Father sent me to see him were what kept me fighting. Loving Reyan kept me alive when nothing else would have.

But Beron made me feel seen that night. He made me feel wanted for the first time since Merik…

We drank flagons of wine and somewhere among the stories and occasional soul-deep admissions, his lips found mine in a delicious, tender kiss that I didn't want to pull away from. I'd memorized the feel of his lips, the stubble on his jaw, the depth of his dimple. The scent of his hair and skin, clean yet wild. Fresh yet earthy. He smelled like Lumina at night, I realized. Ethereal darkness studded with flecks of silver brilliance.

The kiss was *real.* It was perfect.

At the time, and given the circumstances, I quickly decided it was a mistake. I think I hurt him with my words. Things changed between us after that. He watched me with Caelum more closely, but emotionally he withdrew.

When I knew Noor held Caelum's heart, I grew desperate to find the crown and drove him mad with my attempts and antics. It was my only hope. I just didn't know it was a false one.

The thing was… that kiss came naturally. Free of any scheming or machinations on my part. And the kisses I'd almost had with him since he saved me felt exactly the same. I cannot bring myself to believe the mate bond had anything to do with the fact that I wanted to kiss him again.

The only problem was that there was far more at risk now than before, and yet another scheme was about to force us apart when our lips had almost just touched.

We walked away from the river as Red began to strip off his clothes. "Can't you wait until we're out of sight?" Beron snapped.

"It's nothing any of you haven't seen before."

"Are you saying that every body is the same? I can assure you that while we have the same anatomies, every body is beautiful and different in its own way," I turned to argue.

Beron quickly moved to block my view of him, a clear sign that Red was already naked in the river. "It's not like I won't see him eventually. And when I shift, he'll see me, too," he chided.

Beron offered a playful smile. "When you shift. Not now."

"He's just jealous!" Red shouted.

I grinned at the Wolven's offended, but guilty, expression.

The day was largely uneventful, which made me apprehensive. Noor checked in to let me know no other deaths had been brought to the priests' attention. Sol warned that their flesh could not bear the shadow and those harboring Anubis's essence would soon begin to die.

We'd seen the first. When would the others join him in death?

She also brought another message from the Sphinx, who'd allowed her to pass another image of my son to me. In it, he was smiling as he sat beside Padren on the shore of a vast blue lake. Sol's light lay smooth over its surface. They held poles from which lines lazily drifted, patiently fishing.

I imagined the great Sphinx turning herself into a lionfish and allowing Reyan to hook and reel her in just to please my son.

Sol was easing away from Lumina now, and the time for me to meet Lumos was fast approaching. Beron didn't know if he would come to me as Sol did, taking the visage of a human, or if he might prefer to communicate another way.

Chase made delicious steaks, roasted vegetables, and a simple cake for dinner that the pack enjoyed together. Even Amaris joined in on the conversation. She'd been in a decent mood most of the day, which made me even more wary.

I'd soaked in the spring, scrubbed my skin and hair, and dashed back to the House, teeth chattering in the frigid wind, to find a fire roaring in the hearth in my room. I combed the tangles from my tresses and then plaited it, pinning it off my shoulders and back. In one of my trunks, I found a deep blue gown that was simple in design, but hugged my hips to my knees where it fanned in a flurry of delicate, pleated ruffles.

Pushing clammy hands down my thighs, I stood, letting the layers at the bottom of my gown cover my sandals. The book was tucked into its hiding place. The shadows were quiet tonight. Since Sol had chased them away, they had barely stirred. I wondered if they could sense that Lumos was drawing near.

I could feel their presence as clearly as I could now feel the strange essence within; a buzzing, living darkness that wasn't there before Zarina stabbed me.

Someone knocked twice on the door. I could feel Beron behind it. "Come in."

The handle turned and the Wolven's shadowed features lit with firelight. He took me in and slowly walked toward me. Something glinted in his hands.

My aureole.

He cleared his throat. "Caelum thought you might be missing this."

I took it from his hands and let the heavy weight anchor me. "Thank you."

I wouldn't wear it again. I wasn't an Atena of Helios. But I could give it to Reyan so that he knew I once was, and could hold my past in his hands. One day I hoped he learned of the upbringing that forged me into who I was. The good and the bad. So he would know I loved him and had fought for him, even if I often failed.

Padren and Malia taught him about Merik. If I didn't survive Anubis, who would teach him about me?

Moving to the desk, I lay the sunlit crown on top of it, listening to the shadows' quiet hiss. The aureole represented their destruction. It was a symbol of the thing they knew to fear most.

"Are you ready?" Beron asked.

I turned to look at him over my shoulder. "I am."

He cleared his throat. "Beautiful is too weak a word for how you look tonight, and always, if I'm being honest, Citali."

I pressed my eyes closed and took a deep breath. "Thank you."

We walked down the steps to a chorus of wolf whistles. Amaris didn't join the pack in showing her approval, but she was present. Beron smirked as he offered me his arm and we stepped through the wolf pack and entered the night.

Lumos waited just through the trees. We walked toward him and came to a rocky area where the mountainside had fallen away. Enormous boulders were strewn from the place where we stood, cascading to the river running below. Trees had grown between and atop them, refusing to give the rocks an inch of the land they claimed as their own.

Beron quietly took hold of my hand and squeezed it in a silent show of support. "I'll come back when he calls me."

*He's leaving?* I knew this was to be a private conversation, but I assumed he'd be near. Especially given my precarious past with sheer cliffs.

Instead of voicing my fear, I squeezed his hand back. "Thank you."

I didn't watch Beron leave, but I felt his presence drift away, then disappear.

Like Sol had drawn near, Lumos lowered himself until all I could see were his lovely scars. A triumph of craters and gashes. He was a beautiful warrior, and I couldn't help but wonder if he'd earned the marks by wresting Anubis into the depths.

And then… footsteps.

I turned and my breath caught when I saw Lumos appear as a man. He looked so much like Beron and Caelum it was startling. "I knew you would notice," he said easily, tucking his hand into his trousers just as the brothers did. "I wear the face of their father."

"Has Beron seen you like this?" My voice was thin.

"No, that would hurt him. I would never seek to do that."

His dark hair was Beron's. There was a hint of warm brown hidden in the strands, where Caelum's was black kissed by frost. The boys had taken their father's straight nose. Beron's dimple was another of his father's contributions. The brothers' bowed lips were Vada's, though.

"Sol spoke to me on your behalf, but I thought it was time we met. Tell me – you don't wish to become a wolf?"

"You know what lies inside me. If Anubis is as powerful as everyone fears, then turning into a wolf while his essence is trapped within me is an incredibly bad idea."

"Only if you intend to allow him to use you. If you become a wolf, you will become a far better hunter."

"If what Sol said is true, my sister will soon be dead. I won't need to hunt *her* anymore. And I know exactly where to find Anubis. I need no hunting skills. I can already feel him. Smell him."

He straightened. "You wish to hunt as you are."

"I do."

"You cannot take Beron into the deception, Citali. He is not immortal. Neither is Caelum. How do you intend to entrap the dark one?"

"Neither is Noor. And I have no intention of trapping him so someone else can set him free. I want him gone. I have a plan, but I need your help."

He listened as I explained what I would do, how I would do it, and hopefully, how it all would end.

"If you don't want me to drag Beron into this, I need you to break the mate bond." With cool, unblinking eyes he watched me. "It will drive a wedge between us. The bond tethers him to me, and me to him. He can't be free of the plan if he isn't free of me."

His face glowed like frosted snow under the moonlight as he considered all I'd laid before him. Every inch of it a gamble we might lose, but if we won… we would be rid of Anubis forever. I could see in his eyes he wasn't sure I could pull this off, but he was willing to sacrifice me if I was willing to sacrifice myself.

"A bargain, then," he offered. "I will remove the bond so that you can accomplish your plan, but afterward, when the dust storm settles, you agree to shift and take your place in Beron's pack."

"I agree to those terms," I told him. Swallowing thickly, I looked down at my hands. "He's going to be upset."

Lumos inclined his head. "Because his heart wanted the bond."

I blinked at my hands as they wrung one another. "That's not true."

"Citali… I was not present for your childhood or adolescence. I was not present as you grew into womanhood. But Sol has told me of your father and of your upbringing after she shed her sandy flesh, and I want you to listen carefully to what I am about to say to you." I nodded. "Your father was wrong to teach you that you are unworthy of love."

It felt as though he'd shot an arrow through my chest. Tears pricked my eyes. "He never said that. He said a great many terrible things, but not that, exactly."

"He did not have to say it," Lumos said gently. "He made you feel it by taking away every good thing that showed you love. He was wrong, Citali. You deserve to love and be loved in a way that supersedes reason and expectation. That ventures far beyond tradition, and lays outside the bounds of the experiences of others. You deserve Beron's love." He gave a fatherly smile. "It was because of that love that he saw you when Anubis's shadow obscured you for all others. Even Sol and I could not see through it. And it was because I felt his love for you that I even considered allowing him to save you. Without his love, his bite would not have healed or transformed you."

"Did you expect me to die?" I asked.

"I honestly wasn't sure whether your spirit would succumb to the shadows or answer Beron. The fact that you answered him tells me much about your heart as well."

The moon god had given me a chance. Because of Beron. Because of love. "Why did you do it? Knowing what the obsidian blade left behind in me."

He gave an empathetic smile. "I know what it's like to be separated from the one you love most, even if you're to blame for the division."

I pressed my eyes closed. "I hope I can survive it."

He dragged in a long breath. "Sometimes, we must push the ones we love away to keep them safe," he told me. "But if you go through with this, Citali, you must do it completely. Anubis will know if you cling to anything – whether it be Reyan or Beron. And he will not hesitate to use them against you."

It was nothing I wasn't used to, but now that I'd been freed from Father, I wasn't sure I could bear it again. And Anubis was far more powerful than Father ever dreamed of being.

"Why can't the dark one hear me?"

"Are you certain he can't?" Lumos hinted.

I shrugged. "The shadows can't hear my thoughts. They are very responsive and easily provoked when I speak, but have never responded to anything I've thought. It would've sent them into a spiral if they could read my mind. And if they can't, I don't think he can. At least, not yet."

His features sharpened, and though he wore a familiar, familial face, I was reminded of who and what he was. If it was this easy to forget with him, how would it be with Anubis?

"Whether he's still too weak or you're still too far away, the reason why he cannot glean your thoughts doesn't matter. I suggest you use that knowledge against him before he finds a way to do just that."

"You think he will become strong enough to?"

Lumos stepped closer. "I think you'll have to allow him a measure of trust to gain his."

"I can't do that!" I exclaimed, alarmed. "He'll know about Reyan. About Beron and the pack. Noor and Caelum. You and Sol."

"Trust is a sharp blade to those who would wield it like a weapon. I suggest you prepare for battle and manipulate every opportunity available to you. The dark one already knows of Reyan. Your father revealed many things to him, but he can search the earth for an eternity and never find him. He already knows of the Wolven and his pack, and of the Sphinx. He knows of Noor and Caelum. He certainly is aware of Sol and I."

Lumos was right. I couldn't draw Anubis near without letting him get close to me.

"It's a lovely view from the soil," he marveled, staring into the sky, gently smiling at the stars, the ancestors of his people. "Remember that many things depend on your success or failure."

I stood with him for several long, quiet moments, the pressure weighing heavily on my shoulders. But in those moments, I didn't think of the fate of the world and my people. I could only think of how much I was going to hurt Beron, and me. I dreaded leaving this place because he would know. He would think I went to Lumos and begged him to divide us, and I would have to let him believe it. To push him away so I could keep him safe.

It would be like it was the morning after I kissed him, then went to breakfast to attempt to attract his brother. We'd planted something beautiful – and he didn't understand why, and I hated myself for it – but I couldn't nurture it because it wasn't part of my plan. Beron wasn't part of my plan.

For some reason, he didn't care that I'd hurt him or that the sprout we'd begun growing had withered. He loved it anyway. He came when I screamed his name. He saved me without a second thought.

"How will Anubis appear to me? As man or shadow?"

Lumos's head swiveled to me. "No matter what he cloaks himself in, you will know him. He will look like everything you've ever wanted and was told you could never have. That's why few can resist him. You must anchor yourself in Reyan, and in Beron, if your heart has chosen him, and remember they are your way back from the darkness Anubis will weave. No matter what you smell, feel, or see, you cannot trust anything but your memories and what you know in your heart to be true. He is the creator of lies, the spinner of illusions, the master of mirages. Anubis is dogged and relentless in his fervor to ruin this world and claim it as his own."

He gestured to my thigh where the dagger lay hidden beneath my dress. "Sol will call for you soon. Settle what you must quickly. Take the book. Keep the blade close; you will need it. Do not be alarmed when she takes her gilded protection away from the knife. When he comes for you, go with him willingly. The others will think you are under the dark one's control. Tonight, Anubis will draw his shadow over my face. Each night the shadow will grow until the blood moon hangs over Helios in three nights' time. That is when he will attack. You must stop him before he regains his full power and unleashes his fury."

"How will he attack?"

"He will go after what Sol and I love the most, barring each other."

Our people. Noor. Caelum and Beron. The pack.

"You and Sol have to keep them from coming after me."

He shook his head. "We cannot interfere, or he will know we've lain a trap. Their attempts to rescue you are vital to the deception you've planned, and their vehemence will bolster its believability."

"The pack said the blood moon was an omen indicating that a wolf from our pack would die. Is that going to happen?"

Apology deepened the lines on his wizened face. "Everything living must eventually pass away."

"Not the Sphinx," I argued.

He smiled. "No, certainly not the Sphinx. But I did not make the wolves out of sand and breath. I made them out of woman and man, flesh and soil. As such, they were never made or meant for eternity." He glanced off into the distance. "Sol grows restless. She senses a darkness."

In his face was longing, along with a deep understanding in the lines carved into the flesh he wore. He saw her only yesterday and already missed her. Caelum felt the same way for Noor. Beron may have once, but he would no longer feel that way when Lumos left me on this ledge.

"We cannot linger," Lumos offered, giving me a sad smile.

"Just… will you comfort him as much as you can?"

He inclined his head. "Of course."

Despair coursed through my veins. Dread. Desperation. I didn't want to do this, but I had to. I pretended I was the Atena facing my father, the enemy. Because that was what Anubis was. I just had to remember that and remember why I was breaking Beron's heart.

I had to convince myself it would be worth it in the end.

And I had to hope against all hope that Beron could find it in his heart to forgive me again. I'd pretended to be cold and calculating my entire life. I could do this. Schooling my features, I pushed my shoulders back.

"Can you take away my emotions?" I asked, hoping Lumos could, or would do this for me.

He shook his head. "You need to constantly remind yourself of what you're fighting for. If you don't feel, you'll lose, Citali. You will lose yourself to him. To shadow. Mind, body, and spirit. Then you will lose Reyan, Beron, Noor and Caelum, the pack, and your kingdoms."

Failure wasn't an option.

"The Sphinx said that if I died, Reyan would be at risk."

"You should stop focusing on dying and focus on ensuring your plan is successful. And be ready to alter it at a second's notice, because, like his shadows, Anubis is constantly morphing and changing."

"I'm ready."

One moment he was there, and in the next he crumbled; a heap of soil piled where he once stood. I watched as the great moon lifted into the star-studded sky and then carved a path toward the House of Wolves, stopping at the bottom step.

Beron was sitting in one of the chairs, waiting for me.

# 19

He leaned forward and braced his forearms on his knees, his head down. "You could've warned me about what you were doing. I didn't know until the moment I felt the bond break," he said.

"You would've tried to talk me out of it, and I might have felt guilty enough to give in."

He gave a derisive laugh. "You?"

"I didn't mean to hurt you." I looked at my hands and said the words I'd been practicing. "I know you don't understand because I haven't spoken to you about him, but getting to finally spend time with Padren and Malia, and of course, our son… I just… I'm constantly reminded of Merik. I miss him and it made me realize I'm not ready to be bonded to anyone yet. I don't know if it's right or fair. I don't know how his parents would feel about it, how I do, or how Reyan might in the future. There's so much I still need to sort through." I didn't have to fake the catch in my voice. "I don't think I've even properly mourned him. I wasn't allowed to."

He huffed the slightest laugh and scrubbed his hands over his face, raking his fingers into his hair. "Well, damn. I was prepared to tell you how hurt and angry I was, but how can I be angry with you for that?"

"Easily," I rasped.

He shook his head. "You're right. You need time. All this happened far too fast."

Amaris's words echoed in my head again. I would never deserve him.

"I need to go and change," I told him.

He nodded, still looking down at his clasped hands. I started up the steps and when I got close, he finally swiveled his head toward mine. The blues cut into my heart, his eyes resembling jagged pieces of ice. "I'll be here. After."

I swallowed, knowing he wasn't talking about after I changed; he was talking about after this turmoil had ended and I'd worked through my grief. I raked my bottom lip with my teeth and walked inside, fighting the urge to tell him everything and beg his forgiveness now before I irrevocably changed the way he looked at me.

The pack was in the House, carefully arranged around the fire like flowers in a vase. Amaris glanced up from the book she was reading. Her eyes tracked me through the room. Red and Chase watched me from their seats nearest the fire. They knew my bond with Beron was broken. It was evident in their eyes, the discomfort in their postures.

Holt sat up from where he'd stretched out on one of the couches. "You okay, Citali?" he asked.

"I'm fine," I said coolly. Picking up my skirts, I marched up the steps to prepare for a fight they didn't know I would soon instigate.

In my mind, I screamed for them to be careful. To guard one another, so that maybe, maybe we could change the fate of one who might fall.

I unzipped the dress and let it plume around my feet, stepping out of it. I was going to Helios, which meant I needed a dress cool enough to accommodate the heat, and hot enough to attract the god of death. My eye caught on just that. A gown the color of shadow and anger hung on the bathing room door.

Had Lumos left it? I told him what I needed to do. *This would certainly help.*

Or could it have been Sol? Did Noor send it on her behalf?

I slid the dress over my head and let it fall into place. The neckline was high while the back was exposed. The fabric wasn't thick or traditionally pleated; rather, the gown was constructed of layer upon layer of sheer gray. If the wind blew, I knew I would look like writhing shadow embodied. Like darkness and danger.

The dark magic and book would get his attention. I just had to keep it.

I had tried and failed to hurt Noor when Father demanded it. I would not fail this time. The lives of my son, my family, and my pack depended on my ability to kill. This wouldn't be hard, though. Anubis deserved what I was about to do to him. He deserved far worse.

I painted my eyes with charcoal, then my lips with deep plum. Grasping the book in my hands, I watched the shadows plume as I whispered to them about my greatest pain, followed by sweet lies about what I desired more than anything else. What I would give anything to have back in my life. What I would kill to have again…

They delightfully ate the falsehoods, and I hoped delivered them to their master.

Noor appeared in my room moments later. Glancing at me from head to toe, she looked taken aback. "That dress."

"Did you leave it for me?"

A haunted look filled her eyes. Wariness. Fear. "No."

"Are you okay?"

She pressed her eyes closed. "I need you to come to Helios. Sol would like for us both to be present for a mass departure. The shadow-bearers are dying."

"Just as she said. How many are dead?" I hoped the number was small and insignificant.

Tears welled in her eyes. "The priests stopped counting at a thousand."

My heart dropped into my stomach and my eyes bulged. "A thousand?"

How had Father managed it? Had Zarina helped? Was she among them?

"My gods," I breathed, clutching the book to my chest.

Noor forced her tears away. "Caelum is there. I'd like for the pack to come with us. I have a terrible feeling about this day. When I stood atop Sol's temple a few moments ago with the priests, watching them carry Helioan after Helioan up the steps, I saw a vision of me and you standing over them. Sol descended to carry them into the hereafter, and when she was done, a great shadow fell over the land and took you away, Citali. A great shadow hand swept you right off the temple's top."

My heart began to hum with excitement and fear, but I offered my sister an empathetic smile. "Well, that's impossible. It was only your imagination running away with you amid terrible circumstances."

"Before I came for you, I told myself the same thing, sister. But then I saw you in that dress."

I looked down at the gown, a question drawing my brows.

"That's what you were wearing when you were taken away."

"Noor," I choked.

"You shouldn't come," she said resolutely.

I stopped her with a hand on her elbow. "I should be there. They are my people, even if I am not their Aten. I am your sister and I want to stand beside you. Like we said."

Why had Sol sent her such a warning? Or was it meant for me, letting me know that all would go as planned? Noor looked shaken. I worried she'd make a portal and refuse to allow me through it.

"I can change out of this dress if it bothers you."

"You don't seem upset at all," she noted shrewdly. "What if my dream was a warning that Anubis is coming for us all?"

I blew out a long breath. "Make no mistake, Noor – he *is* coming. And if I am the last shadow-bearer, it won't matter if he comes sooner or later. He *will* come for me. Today, we can be prepared. We'll all be there and be ready to fight. Together."

"We have to warn Beron and his pack," she said, moving to the door and waving for me to follow her.

"Noor?" I called out. She paused with her hand on the doorknob and looked over her shoulder at me. "If some shadow monster does sweep me away, my most precious things are here. A lock of Reyan's hair, my aureole –"

"Stop!" she ordered. "Stop talking like that." Her brows kissed. "Wait. You met with Lumos. What did he say?"

"He mostly just introduced himself, though he said we were all in for quite a battle. He confirmed that one of the wolves will die during the blood moon."

"When will that be?" she rasped.

"In three nights."

She cringed. "I shouldn't ask the wolves to come along."

"The wolf will not die on this day," I told her.

"Do you know which one?" she whispered, crestfallen, a hand splayed on her chest.

I shook my head. I did not know. Lumos said the death would happen, but not which of them it would be. He also didn't say I couldn't try to prevent it…

"Do they know?"

I nodded. "They know of the blood moon omen and what it means."

Without another word, I followed her downstairs, her golden pleated ceremonial gown nearly glowing in the dark interior of the House of Wolves. Beron had joined the others around the fireplace. His eyes met mine, then darted to Noor and remained fixed on her.

She told them of the terrible amount of dead in Helios, then she told them of her vision. Beron noticeably tensed when she described me in the dress I was wearing.

"She should stay here," Holt argued, regarding me warily. "It's not safe for her there. That's what Sol was trying to say."

Chase sat up straighter. "It's not safe for Citali to be here alone, either. The dark one found her just outside."

"He can find me wherever I am," I told them. "I'd rather be with all of you. I'd rather fight with you than hide away."

Amaris gave me a look akin to respect, but Red and Chase both looked uneasy. Holt had voiced his opinion, but he wasn't angry, just concerned.

"If we go, we go as a pack," Beron said. I wasn't sure he would consider me part of the pack now that I'd asked Lumos to sever our bond, but when his eyes met mine, a question swam there.

"I need to be there," I told him. "They're still my people."

He gave a decisive nod. "Then we go with you."

Noor pressed her eyes closed. "If you wish to come, we need to go soon. You'll need cooler clothes. And when I draw Sol down, you'll need to find a shaded place."

The wolves agreed and rushed off to change into something lighter. I stopped Amaris on the steps. "You can use one of my dresses if you'd like. They're cooler than anything else."

She seemed taken aback. "Thank you."

She'd been to Helios in wolf form, had walked in the heat of the desert beneath Sol's sweltering heat, but she hadn't felt her draw near enough to consume the departing.

Noor and I waited. "I should've brought kilts for the others."

"They can change when they get there."

She nodded. Slowly the wolves trickled back down to us. Chase first, shirtless and wearing the coolest trousers he had, then Red and Holt – who matched Chase. Amaris wore an eggplant-colored, pleated dress. Beron was the last to descend. Without a shirt, his muscles rippled beneath his skin. He wore the golden kilt Noor had procured for him after she became Aten.

The pack laughed at the sight of him, to which he responded by giving a partial grin. "Go ahead and laugh now, but this is the coolest thing you can wear. You'll be begging for one within the hour," he warned.

Noor made sure we were all ready before creating a portal. Beron moved to stand behind me and I could feel his comforting warmth at my back. "Ready," he confirmed. His voice elicited a shiver down my spine. If I didn't know from the Wolven's reaction that Lumos had severed the mate bond between us, I would've thought the god of the moon had lied to me.

My sister waved her hand and a hallway within the House of the Sun appeared, spear-wielding guards at the ready. We stepped through and they greeted us with respectful nods. The Helioan heat, only slightly muted by the shaded interior of the house, welcomed me home. A home I had every intention of defending now that she was under attack.

*Over a thousand dead.*

That was an act of war.

"The priests and guards assisting them are almost ready for you, Aten," one said.

Noor turned to the wolves. "If you need to change, now is the time."

Holt, Red, and Chase said they were fine, glancing at Beron's and the guards' kilts out of the corners of their eyes. I rolled mine. "You'll regret it later, but we have no time to argue over your poor apparel choices."

Chase's jaw dropped.

Noor waved for me to walk with her and together, we strode down the hall to the door that led to the paved pathway that would take us to Sol's temple. The temple was surrounded by Helioans.

The wails of mothers and wives, the cries of fathers and husbands, the grief of sisters, brothers, and children filled the air.

Noor's chin began to quiver at the same time mine did. We mourned with our people. Felt their cries to the marrow of our bones. Felt the heavy weight of grief and death that sought to crush the soul.

Sun diamonds fell from Noor's cheeks and scattered over the ground as we walked through twin lines of guards to the temple on a path that sliced through the gathered mourners. All that remained of Helios was here. No one was left untouched by the shadows and death Anubis had inflicted so swiftly upon our people.

Caelum waited at the temple's base. He kissed Noor's cheeks, wiped her tears away with his thumbs, and whispered something into her ear. She nodded and pulled away from him before holding her hand out to me. It was shaking when I took hold of it.

We ascended the steps of the temple together, climbing high until we reached the top, where there was little room to stand. Every inch was piled high with the dead, not to mention the priests who had positioned themselves around the perimeter.

Sol's statue stood sentry, her arms raised into the sky.

Kiran stepped forward to greet my sister. "Aten."

"Thank you all for what you've done," she croaked, more diamonds plinking at our feet.

He inclined his head and covered his heart. His white ceremonial kilt rapped in the wind.

Noor nodded. "I'll call for Sol to descend. You may begin."

He moved away and took up a position nearby, gesturing to his brethren whose voices rang out in unison as they sang a song to honor the dead and guide the spirits from their bodies. They sang a song to thank Sol for coming to take them to the hereafter. For the lives she'd given and would now accept once again. A full cycle of life and death, sand and flame.

Their voices were as melodic as their words were reverent. I pressed my eyes closed and listened. I tried to overlook the swelling dunes of dead, to ignore the smell of death that would've made my eyes water if I wasn't already crying.

Noor looked to Caelum, who glanced at Beron just before the wolves scattered and positioned themselves among the guards surrounding the temple top. They would stay close as long as they could withstand the heat – as all had agreed.

Noor watched as the hot wind took hold of my dress and toyed with the strands of sheer shadow. Her eyes were haunted, her brows drawn.

Noor feared her vision; I needed it to be true.

Lumos said the reactions of Noor and Caelum, the Wolven and his pack, and the guard had to be real for Anubis to believe my deception. I looked to Sol and asked her to protect them all today.

I would've asked for her to bring Lumos here, but it wasn't safe for both of them to be in the same place when Anubis emerged. They would be targeted together, too much of a temptation for him not to lash out at.

Amaris and Red moved to the right. Holt and Chase took the left side. The Wolven stayed behind me and Noor, flanked by Caelum.

I wanted to turn to him and tell him that sometimes things must be broken to be fixed. That there was a purpose to what I had done and what I was about to do. To tell him to wait until this was all over. To be there, like he promised to be. To be there after.

I would be there after, too.

Noor raised her hands and called her mother down to us.

When Father, as Aten, called her for departures, Sol descended slowly, as if she didn't want to be near him at all or for any longer than necessary. Now that we knew the truth, we knew why. But now that he was gone and Noor was her Aten, Sol wasted no time. When Noor beckoned, Sol answered and hastened to her daughter.

She descended swiftly. Oppressively.

The wolves were swiftly affected by her heat, panting and sweating and dancing on the baking stones. I turned to Beron. "Find shade until she is finished. It's too hot now."

"We can bear it."

I shook my head. "Not this. You truly can't. She's descending fast and she has so many to burn…"

He swallowed thickly and looked to Caelum, who nodded, backing me up. Even though Caelum's frost coated his skin, it melted almost instantly. He continually poured his frost magic over himself just to keep from baking. "You can watch from the ground just as effectively. No one will get past you," he told them.

The Wolven reluctantly gave a silent command and the wolves descended the temple steps, fanning out on every side and positioning themselves among the people below. People huddled beneath palms and in the scant shadow casted by Sol's statue. Helioans held scarves over their heads to stave the heat, huddling over children and pets who refused to leave their owners.

Sol wasted no time as she poured her heat over the temple top. It crashed like a wave of molten gold as her flames caught and spread over the mass of bodies.

*Over a thousand.*

She baked my tears away and tightened my skin over my bones. Her inferno was made hotter and burnt faster because of the wind that gusted. "Her breath," Noor explained, perfectly comfortable among the golden flames that flickered and roared, raged and built.

Until they stretched into the hands of Sol's statue.

I couldn't hear anything over the snapping flames and wind. It wasn't until I turned my face to check on Beron that I realized something was wrong.

"Noor...?" I said under my breath.

She turned to find Caelum, who had unexpectedly joined Beron at the bottom of the temple steps. Despite the flames, scattered shadows were inching toward us, separating from the shadow that fell over our people, though there wasn't a single cloud in the azure sky.

The dark one's shadow moved like an asp, undulating over the gathered people until he reached the stone base. Noor came to stand beside me. "Citali, you must run. I'll make a portal for you."

I gritted my teeth. "No."

She stabbed her hand at the encroaching darkness. "This is what I saw! You cannot let him take you." When I shook my head, she pressed, "Think of Reyan."

Reyan was all I thought of in that moment. That I might never see him again. That he might be raised by Padren and Malia and ultimately by the Sphinx if I failed in this attempt.

That I was his mother and would be damned if I let someone else part us again.

That the dark one would be sorry he ever met and bargained with my father or my sister.

Me.

Sol was almost finished. There was barely anything left of the departed now. The stench of burnt flesh stung my eyes and nose. While I was still reeling from the smell, Noor made a portal. She tried to pull me toward it, but I wrenched my arm away. "Stop."

"Citali, you must go!"

"No, Noor. I will not run," I said defiantly.

She let the portal fade with a whisper and dropped her hand, mouth agape. "What are you *doing*?"

Sol's fire disappeared with a hush and all went still. Even the dark shadow.

Noor sent her mother high into the sky. "She'll cast more light from afar," she said as if to reassure herself.

But Anubis's essence was impenetrable.

The wind toyed with my dress as I faced the one whose essence I bore.

"Citali, stand behind me." Noor moved to block me from the dark one. She churned her palms until flame erupted, then formed a ball of fire and prepared to launch it when the shadow dissipated. Screams and gasps erupted through the crowd as something carved a path through them like a river wormed through soil.

A commotion broke out at the base of Sol's temple. Beron and Caelum were there, trying to stop someone from climbing the steps. They shouted warnings.

If it was the dark one, he would have slaughtered them to reach us. Whatever or whomever this intruder was, it wasn't him. I knew the feel of Anubis, and while there was a stirring familiarity, this was not the god of death.

"Who is it?" I breathed, leaning over the edge of the platform.

Then I saw her.

*Zarina.*

My bones went cold despite the heat.

Noor let out a cry and the flames trickled from her hands to the stone at our feet. "What happened to her?"

"Let her pass!" I shouted to Beron.

His head swiveled and he locked his eyes on mine, the muscle in his jaw ticking to announce his anger. "I don't think that's a good idea."

"I didn't ask for your opinion," I snapped.

Beron wasn't happy, but he moved aside, giving our elder sister plenty of room to pass between him and Caelum. Noor's cuff flared on his bicep and his cool light intensified on hers as well, as if they were alive and afraid for one another.

Sol's warm breath dragged the scant amounts of ash through the air. They swirled off the temple top and rained down upon the stone façade. Pieces caught in Zarina's dark hair; once lustrous and thick, it now hung in thin, dirty strings.

Her gait was wrong. Forced. As if her joints didn't quite bend and flex as they should. Her back was rigid and her arms hung limply by her sides. She climbed slowly, as if each step was more painful than the last, but she was determined to reach us. Beron and Caelum trailed a few steps behind her, but she didn't act like she heard them or knew they were there. Her eyes remained fixed on me and Noor.

"I don't know if that's really her, Citali," Noor whispered urgently. "Look at her skin. She didn't look like this just days ago."

Her once glowing, supple skin that used to match mine and Noor's in tone was now sallow and shriveled into crepe, hanging from her bones. How had she deteriorated so quickly? It had only been a handful of days since she was strong enough to wield Anubis's blade and corner me with it, strong enough to sink it into my flesh. Looking at her now, she didn't appear strong enough to even grasp it now, let alone raise or plunge the blade. Beneath her eyes lay bruise-purple rings.

But worse than the dark circles under her eyes, her sallow skin, her disjointed gait… worse than all of it combined were the shadows flaring and writhing around her hands.

"It's her." The book at my side hummed. The shadows in the Book of the Dead knew her because she carried the dark one's essence. Slowly, I slid my palm along my hip to my thigh, where Sol's blade eagerly waited. My fingers curled around the handle.

Zarina was halfway to the top when Noor noticed I had the knife in my hand.

Her brows pinched. "Citali."

"I don't care how she looks, Noor – she's still dangerous. She can't be trusted, and I won't be left unarmed and helpless in her presence, nor will I allow her near you. She's infected, Noor. Look at her."

Zarina's once-plump lips were peeling and the dark tar that could be seen in the maw of her mouth had left a stain in the cracks. She climbed closer, slowing the farther she dragged herself. Our elder sister tried to speak, but her voice had corroded.

"Either she is truly deteriorated," I declared, "or this is an illusion, and a well-laid trap."

When she stumbled, Beron and Caelum both rushed to keep her from toppling backward. She noticed them then and emitted a grating, inhuman scream toward the Wolven and Lumin. They did not retreat.

Zarina quickly refocused, pushing upward one agonizing, contorted step at a time until she drew near to the top. I motioned for Noor to back away from the edge and together, we waited for Zarina to reach the temple's top.

Caelum and Beron followed her onto the platform and took up defensive positions.

Zarina shielded her eyes when she glanced up at Sol's statue. She panted for several long moments, her quaking hands fixed on trembling knees. Tar-like saliva dripped in strands from her bottom lip and formed webs that flexed in the hot wind, but did not break.

She finally stood up straight and stumbled toward us.

"Stop there," Noor commanded. Surprisingly, Zarina listened.

There was an awareness in her eyes, along with desperation. Like the guardsman who attacked us, our sister was still lucid inside the shell of her former self. Every small, decaying piece of her tightened my bones, because the darkness that fed off her vitality was alive in me.

*Their flesh cannot bear the weight of his shadow.*

I tightened my grip on the blade's handle.

"What do you want?" I asked carefully.

She glanced at my stomach. "I'm sorry," she slurred. More strands of dark saliva escaped her mouth, joining the others clinging to her chest and stomach. Her once-beautiful, golden dress was stained and dirty, torn and ragged. The pleats had been flattened.

"Did you stab me of your own accord, or were you controlled?"

She blinked slowly. "I don't know."

"Are you in control now, or is he?" I demanded.

She blinked again, as if searching for an answer she didn't have. "I don't know!" she cried.

"What do you want, Zarina?"

"Kill me," she said, turning empty, pleading eyes toward me. "Kill me," she whispered again, this time to Noor.

Noor's entire body turned to stone so that she appeared as nothing more than a smaller version of her mother's gigantic statue, watching over us.

"Where is he?" I asked.

A black tear leaked from her eye and streaked down her face as if it was dragging artfully swiped charcoal and not shadow. "He is everywhere. There is no escape while you live. Kill me. Call for Sol to take me from him. Please," she begged, falling onto one knee, then the other. "I'm dying and don't have long. Don't let *him* have me. I want to see the hereafter. I want to burn for Sol. I never should have listened to Father."

She coughed and a geyser of tar spewed from her throat, spraying over the stones between us in great black globs. Fire poured from Noor's palms as she quickly burned the stain from her mother's temple. Zarina swayed on her knees. I glanced at Beron over her shoulder. His cool blue eyes met mine, a question swimming in them. In two steps, I reached Zarina. Clenching Sol's blade in my hand, I drew the blade back.

Caelum, Noor, and Beron lurched forward, but I was faster. I took hold of Zarina's hair and held her upright before plunging the knife into her heart.

Noor's anguished scream echoed from the temple top, scattering the doves that perched on its sides. "*No!*"

I eased Zarina to the ground, careful not to let her head hit the stones she once walked upon.

"How could you?" Noor screamed, littering sun diamonds from her eyes. Caelum held her back while Beron positioned himself in front of me.

"Because it was merciful," Beron answered on my behalf.

It *was* merciful. Zarina was dying. He sent her here so we would see it, but she managed to defy him in the end. She wanted to burn for Sol, and wanted nothing to do with he who had ruined her. How could I not honor that?

Yes. Killing her was merciful, and it was necessary.

Zarina was at peace, but I… I would never survive this memory. It would be with me until my death.

Anubis's essence coated the blade Sol had claimed and bound. Just as Lumos had warned, Sol's gold began to flake away. Delicate leafing stuck to my skin and I brushed it away. Sol's breath caught what remained and scattered it with the ashes of our people until only Anubis's obsidian reflected my face back to me.

Thrilled, the blade hummed in my grip.

Noor tried to help Zarina as she lay dying. She pled to Sol, as she'd pled for me. But I knew the goddess's answer as well as Noor did.

Caelum comforted her, kneeling at her side, both of them in shock. Neither one of them was paying attention to me now.

Panic rolled through the crowd. They'd seen a girl they watched grow up before their eyes possessed by darkness. They'd witnessed an Atena's death at the hand of her own sister. Anubis wasn't here yet, but they could sense him. They'd seen what he could do to the former Aten's daughter – none of them were safe.

There was chaos below as people tried to flee but couldn't, hemmed in by more bodies than could be counted. Shouting and shoving began.

Sol's priests moved toward Zarina, their movements hesitant. The eldest priests cried out to Sol for help. They did not know if she should be touched, or if they should sing prayers over her body because she was compromised by darkness.

My eldest sister was cruel on her best day. Cold as ice. She'd been told what to think and how to act her entire life and didn't figure out she could defy our father until the bitter end. To her, being the Aten's eldest was a duty she fully embraced. She had forgotten she was a girl like any other. She had forgotten how to love because it was a gift she never received.

She deserved better than this. She deserved more than to have Sol's priests, whom she stood beside daily, question whether to care for her body. She deserved better than to be killed atop her temple. She deserved more than the dark tar that filled her until it brimmed from her mouth.

She deserved better.

So did my son. My people and Lumina's. Noor deserved better.

And so did I.

I took the book, flipped it open to the carved pages that once held Anubis's blade, and eased the knife into the fitted hollow. Then I waited as the shadow that sent Zarina built again.

Beron was suddenly beside me. He gestured to the book, now humming with power. "Why did you do that?" When I didn't answer, he shouted, "Why did you snap the blade into the book?" He tried to take the book from my hands, hissing when the shadows burned his fingers. "Why?"

"Because I need to see him!" I screamed at the Wolven, holding the tome to my chest.

"Are you insane?" He looked from me to Zarina, horror pressed onto his features like a sharp quill to papyrus. He thought that, like her, I had been taken over by the shadows, soon to be consumed.

He had no idea how insatiable my appetite was, or how much fight sang through my veins.

He cursed as a great shadow stretched over the crowd once more, deeper, darker, viscous. "You called him?" I locked my jaw and refused to speak. He moved closer, clasping my elbows and letting his gaze bore into mine. "*Don't* give into him," he pleaded.

"I'm not," I argued weakly.

"Citali, please. Take the blade out of the book. Send him away."

I shook my head. "I can't. You heard her. He's everywhere."

"Don't listen to his words; watch his actions. He'll do to you what he did to Zarina," Beron beseeched.

"And if my fate turns into hers, will you grant me the same mercy I gave my sister, Wolven? Or will you be too weak?" my voice cracked. Tears built in my eyes. My hands shook. All I could feel was the blade's handle. All I could hear was the dull, hard press through bone and tissue as I broke her.

*Zarina.*

"I could never hurt you," he breathed, holding my tear-filled stare with intensity that matched my own. "So if that means I am weak, then I'm proud to own the title."

Over his shoulder on the staircase that Zarina had just climbed, the thick, roiling darkness stopped. Anubis had come for me. And he wore exactly what I'd asked him to: Merik's face.

I didn't expect to feel so overwhelmed and taken aback. It was my fault he had come for me. My fault he wore the face of the boy I once loved. I told the shadows that I longed to see him again, that I wanted him back so he could raise Reyan with me. So I wouldn't feel alone or unsafe anymore.

Anubis listened. He had provided.

I manipulated him, but somehow felt like the fool.

Covering my mouth, I watched him climb the steps with powerful strides.

*It's not Merik*, I told myself. *Merik is dead.* Twin tears fell from my eyes.

"Who is that?" Beron quietly asked.

I started down the staircase.

"Citali, no!" he begged.

I paused my steps and threw a terrible glare over my shoulder. "Don't tell me what to do. I am not a mutt for you to order about."

Noor shouted for me. "No. That's not Merik. Merik is dead, Citali!" She and Caelum tried to reach me, but Beron was frozen where I'd left him. Shock and hurt and anger warred for dominance in his face, along with a terrible blankness I wanted to rush back to erase.

But I couldn't.

I kept walking. To Merik, who wasn't Merik at all.

His head was shaven. His skin the same sun-kissed, olive bronze I had memorized. His glistening white, perfectly straight teeth were set in a handsome smile. Anubis had recreated every pale striation in his deep brown eyes. Every bulged vein in his arms, as well as the contoured planes of his chest and stomach.

He even wore the kilt of a guardsman.

"All is well," Anubis said in Merik's rich voice.

That was what he would say when things were absolutely *not* well, but he wanted me to know they would be one day. They were the last words he spoke to me before he was executed. He knew he was going to die, but still wanted me to have hope.

How had Anubis copied him so perfectly? My memory wasn't this crisp. Time had dulled it. But nothing about this version of Merik was inaccurate. Down to the tiny scar just below his bottom lip.

"You are not Merik," I told him, holding my chin up.

"No, I am not. But I can be. For you, I can be anything," he tempted. "I can foster life or be the granter death."

He glanced to Noor and Caelum who stood frozen, only a few steps above me now. Fury, indignation, and fierce resolve raged over my sister's face. She was magnificent. Noor had conjured a flame and waited, holding the fire in her hands, ready to fight for me. With me. Caelum's hands held frost. His eyes met mine as if to say he was willing to defend me – his friend – and to defend Helios.

"Come with me and I will spare them, *ya kek ra*."

*My dark sun.*

Merik's eyes caught on my book and sparked. His smile spread wider. "You've kept it safe for me and removed the terrible binding Sol placed upon my blade. I thank you."

When he stretched out his hand, I twisted my body to shield the book. Something within said it was mine now and not at all his. His eyes narrowed ever so slightly, but he quickly recovered, gracing me with a charming smile. "It is your hand I seek."

"Why?"

"Citali…" Noor growled in warning. I could almost hear her teeth gnashing. She would say *Stop talking, stop toying with him and get behind us…* but if I moved an inch, Anubis would slaughter them. The threat glimmered in Merik's eyes and I hated seeing *him* inside the boy I'd once loved, lingering like a parasite.

"Do you know why yours is the only flesh that can contain the shadow?" he asked. I swallowed thickly. "Because the Sculptor made you for me."

Beron shifted. Growled. Snarled. Hackles raised, he stalked down the temple's side as the other wolves moved to block our descent.

I raised my chin flirtatiously. "Or perhaps it is you who were made for me. I am no one's possession, but I may just make you mine."

Anubis laughed, delight glistening in his eyes. "Come with me."

"Where will we go? Helios is the most beautiful kingdom on earth."

He shook his head. "I disagree. Let me show you a realm of wonders you could not imagine if you tried."

"Why should I trust you?"

He grinned. "Have I done anything to make you think I bear you ill will?"

"You conjured my father, threatened my son, and almost killed me by running me over a cliff. You killed over one thousand Helioans with your foulness, not to mention my sister. I would say you've done plenty to convey such a message."

"It was *your* hand that plunged the blade into Zarina's heart," he whispered seductively.

"And it was *you* who forced it."

Beron snarled, so close now. Just over Caelum's shoulder.

Creeping in front of him…

Anubis jutted his hand closer. "Come with me. Let me show you what no one else alive has seen." I narrowed my eyes at him. "Citali," he breathed in Merik's voice, stepping onto my step. "Don't force my hand."

He gestured toward Beron, who yelped in pain, but quickly recovered. My heart thundered.

"Stop!" I tore the dagger out of the book and pointed it at his gut, right where Zarina stabbed me.

"That blade cannot kill me," Anubis scoffed.

"It can cut flesh, though."

"I am not made of something so weak," he growled. He lowered his hand, then his eye flicked to Noor. When they hardened, I knew he was going to hurt her as he'd hurt Beron, but much worse. Anubis was not fond of being defied. Father wore the same look and harbored the same hatred in his eyes. I distracted him by sliding the dagger into the sheath on my thigh.

"That blade is mine," he gritted.

I snorted. "I don't think so. It was given to me." I held my hand out and waited. He regarded it warily as the shadows writhing around my palm called his from where he'd hidden them within Merik's skin.

"Is this a trick?"

Shrugging, I dared him. "Clasp it and see."

Merik's palm hovered over mine for a moment. Anubis held my stare, then slid his hand into mine.

In my periphery, Beron shifted from Wolven to man again. He reached out for me and screamed my name as Anubis whisked me away, just as Noor said he would.

# 20

Anubis regarded the palm I had taken hold of and flexed his fingers before giving me a sharp look. "That was a trick."

"What?" I absently said, looking all around. His voice was so crisp, but all other sound had become a dull roar.

I was not swept away as Noor had seen in her vision, but the world changed in the blink of an eye. The azure sky became a muted gray. The stones of the temple, the sand that lay beyond it, and even Sol's light that once shone brightly in the sky… all gray.

The earth was bathed in deep, angry shades of it; pale, bony shades and everything in between. It was not the gray dullness of the Dusk Lands, but something sharper and more surreal, like the world was now inlaid with shards of broken mirror glass.

The voices around us were distorted, the tones deep, as if spoken by too-thick tongues.

My lips parted when I saw Beron, Caelum, and Noor still standing on the stairs. They seemed distraught but were otherwise unharmed. Guardsmen encircled them, spears at the ready. As if one could cut through something as complicated as the god of death or his shadow magic.

Helioans were still gathered on the ground below us, clearly confused and afraid for what they'd witnessed. Anubis and I stood in their midst, though we were unseen by the masses.

We had somehow *become* shadow.

"You took more of my essence," he accused. "I will have that back now."

My brows kissed. "I took nothing."

His eyes glinted dangerously. "I can't tell if you are lying, but I will have the truth, one way or another." He reached his hand tentatively toward my arm. Our shadows tangled and my hand came away with even more of his darkness. He pulled away, dismayed. "You are siphoning my essence!"

"Not purposefully," I breathed, afraid he might be right. Afraid of what it might mean and how it might bolster or alter the plan I had made. I almost laughed. Lumos warned me to be flexible, to constantly be planning a new route once the dark one emerged, because he knew my original plan would not hold.

The god of death recovered quickly, but like me, I could see him furiously trying to make sense of this new piece of information and trying to formulate a new plan as well. Satisfaction bloomed within my chest.

Anubis smiled at me with Merik's lips. He turned a slow circle with his arms extended and his palms raised, basking in his accomplishment. "Tell me, Citali. Are you surprised?"

I would not let him know how much this altered reality troubled me. I would not let him see a shred of weakness. I affected a bored expression. "I'm unimpressed. You said you would show me what no one else alive had seen. This is just Helios painted to match the Dusk Lands," I scoffed.

He grinned. "Ah, but you have not seen my full powers yet. Here, I am still weak. Let's walk to the river. A ship awaits us."

Anubis turned back the way he came and I descended the stairs behind him. At its base where throngs of disturbed Helioans were still gathered, the god of death used his shadows to coax people away from us. Just as Zarina had parted a path through the crowd, we did as well. If this was him at his weakest, I trembled at the thought of his unencumbered strength.

None of my people saw us pass through, but they somehow sensed the threat walking among them. Some rubbed the gooseflesh on their arms. Some shivered. Eyes darted this way and that. Some stumbled to move away. To make room for us, one man shoved another beside him, nearly toppling him over and eliciting hateful words and a returned push.

Beron noticed the commotion breaking out and tracked it. Tracked us. Wearing a hastily knotted kilt, the Wolven shoved through the crowd. "Call out my name, Citali! I will hear you. I will come for you."

Anubis slowed his steps and looked at me over his shoulder. My ribs tightened uncomfortably. "The Wolven is enamored with you," he purred seductively. I remained silent. "Do you wish to cry out for him to save you?"

"He forgets that I, too, am wolf now, and with every breath and choice, save myself."

The god of death did not require air in his lungs, so Merik's chest did not rise or fall. His shoulders did not move with the expansion and contraction that came with breathing. That was why it was strange to see his pupils flare, the illusion he'd spun alive when he clearly was not.

Anubis, somewhat irked, resumed his path and I hurried after him to fill the space between Beron and me with more Helioans than he could move in time to catch us. I didn't know if he would be able to even if I was within reach. He couldn't see us, only the effects of our movement. He saw the sway of a palm leaf in the invisible wind that was us, but he could forever chase the gust and never catch and hold it.

Beron continued to yell my name. Caelum and Noor joined him in his effort as he swore he could still smell my scent. I wondered if, like Anubis, I smelled of sickly-sweet rot.

The guards struggled to keep their Aten and Lumin safe as they plunged heedlessly into the crowd. I thought Noor might boil them all by the time we managed to put enough distance between us in the strange grayness that enveloped me and Anubis. Their already muted voices became nothing but a hum. Neither Noor nor Caelum needed a human, or an army of them, to stand between them and an enemy. Neither did Beron or his wolves.

When we reached the riverbank and a quaint, flat-bottomed ship that boasted solid black sails, I looked back toward my home just as Beron's howl split the night.

"This might be your last chance to escape me," Anubis said in a breezy tone. "Are you sure you don't wish to run to him?"

I hated that he sounded like Merik. That he used his lips and tongue to form his words now. I hated myself for ever suggesting it to the shadows and the book I still clutched against my chest.

"If I wanted to stay with him, I would have. And when I want to escape you, you will know it."

He grinned. "Citali, I know that you care for him, as you care for your sister, the Aten, and Sol above us. I am the creator of lies and the spinner of illusions, remember? I can taste them from many miles away."

"I made my choice," I insisted stubbornly. "I will board your ship."

"You're willing to sacrifice yourself for them?"

My grip tightened on the Book of the Dead. "Do you plan to kill me? Then what? You'll lose your leverage against them."

"Death is not the only sacrifice one can make," he said, stepping close enough that his kilt brushed my dress as he passed by.

No, it wasn't. But *his* death – a true, eternal death – was what I craved.

Anubis boarded his ship and then paused near the ramp and waited, allowing me the chance to change my decision one last time. If he thought I'd think him chivalrous, he was sorely mistaken. If he thought I wouldn't find a way to end him, he was flat-out wrong.

I'd somehow managed to steal more of his essence and planned to use that to my advantage if I could. What was his shadow magic capable of? What was I capable of with it? Could I steal more from him? If I could, what did that mean for me? How would siphoning his essence affect his strength and mine? I felt no different than before I took it. I felt no different than before Zarina stabbed me, infusing me with his dark essence.

I would figure it out soon enough, but not unless I boarded the ship. Because the only one who could teach me his power was the god of death himself.

Placing one foot resolutely in front of the other, I walked up the plank and breezed past him like I owned the ship and the sands, sky, and sea.

My skin crawled when he chuckled. With a flick of his wrist, the ramp slid smoothly onto the deck and the rope that moored us to the shore uncoiled, loosened by invisible hands. The sails unfurled, landing with a heavy snap before they billowed and filled with shadowed wind. The ship turned and took us upriver.

I moved to the ship's railing to watch the water flow beneath us. The ship should have struggled against the churning currents in this section of river. Instead, it sliced through the water like a knife through soft butter. That was when I realized the ship was not touching the water at all, but hovered a few feet above it.

Anubis walked to the prow and stopped, looking fondly over the land of Helios. I couldn't think for the life of me why. Helios did not belong to him. Then he spoke.

"Before… there were no kingdoms with distinct lines. This was Sol's, Lumos's, *and* mine," he said softly.

Slowly, I moved toward him.

I let my fingers trail along the top of the rail. His dark eyes flicked to them, then back to mine, his feral nature shining beneath Merik's tender shades. I wanted to gouge them out with the obsidian blade and hear him scream so loud I could taste it. I felt the knife's weight on my thigh.

"Where are we sailing?" I asked.

"Across the sand."

The ship veered into the smaller dunes whose sands crumbled into the river little by little, like grains tumbling to the bottom of an hourglass. The bottom never touched the crests, but skirted them, staying low.

Sol was setting and Lumos was about to appear on the horizon. I could feel him just as I could feel her. Somehow, I knew the gods of illumination could not see us, cloaked in Anubis's shadow. When Zarina stabbed me and infused me with this darkness, I was obscured so that only Beron could see past the shady mass.

"Why do we sail across the sand?"

"Because I need to retrieve something."

"You're very evasive," I noted.

"And *you're* very intrusive," he tutted.

I itched to ask another question. "Does something lie beyond it? I thought the sand stretched to the divide."

He smiled. "There is much you do not know."

I gave a winsome smile. "Well, enlighten me."

Anubis nodded toward the book, then his eyes flicked to my thigh. "Return my belongings."

I clasped it tighter. He was twice my size in Merik's body, but infinity had given him strength beyond that of normal men. I knew he could easily wrest it from my grasp if he wanted. "I want to know what's in it," I insisted.

He turned to the prow and clasped the point of the railing with each hand. "You don't trust me to deliver its contents?"

"Trust the creator of lies? The spinner of illusions?" I mused. "That doesn't seem wise."

Sol sank below the southern horizon at the same moment Lumos peeked over the distant northern dunes. For the first time in days, Lumos didn't pull and make me feel out of my mind to charge him and complete my transformation.

Anubis turned to face me, leaning against the railing as the sky darkened inch by inch. The first star appeared, sickly gray like everything else but us. "Why aren't we gray like everything else around us?" I asked curiously.

"So many questions," he purred, crossing his arms and one ankle over the other. "When curious children get too close to the river…" He snapped his teeth together like a crocodile.

"Why do you feel the need to constantly threaten me? Could it be that *you* are threatened by *me*?"

Anubis gave an enigmatic smile. "I haven't decided yet whether you are river or crocodile."

I was something far worse than either. I would see him drowned and then I would devour him.

A long moment passed, and I let my palms dig into the railing to steady myself. My emotions began to spiral. Lumos may not be calling out to me, but my body had been changed by Beron's bite all the same. My skin began to heat uncomfortably.

I startled when Anubis spoke. "You are not gray because you are not comprised of shadow. You hold it, affect it, but are not made of it."

"And you?"

"I wear an illusion." I wondered what he truly looked like; if he had a discernable shape or if he preferred to stand in the darkness cast by the living. "Tell me… how did you feel seeing Merik again after so long?"

I couldn't tell if he was honestly curious or merely being cruel. My lashes fluttered and my throat tightened as tears stung my eyes, but I answered him honestly. "That it was the best and worst thing I'd ever seen. The best because I miss him. The worst because I know you aren't him and he isn't really alive."

Dune after dune swelled beneath our ship like great waves frozen by Lumos, then burnt by Sol.

"What's wrong with me?" I asked.

His brows pinched. "What do you mean?" He looked me over. "Nothing is wrong with you."

"All those Helioans, my own sister," I choked, "died from the effects of shadow in their flesh. Why am I able to hold it? Why am I not also dead?"

He ran a hand over his shaven head. "I've already told you. The Sculptor made you for me. He woke me when you took your first breath. I woke the second you were born and have waited nearly nineteen years for your father to release me. I came to you as quickly as I could, but I see now that it wasn't soon enough."

*What does that mean?*

"How did my father know to set you free? How did he accomplish that when no one else had before? Did the Sculptor tell him where to find your book and blade?"

I knew the creator of lies was spinning illusions as we spoke. Sol claimed that the Sculptor sealed Anubis away. If so, why would he want to release him? And why gift him with… me?

His strong jaw locked. "I've had enough of your interrogation."

With a narrow glare, I left him at the prow and walked to the ship's quarters. Flinging open one of the doors, I rummaged through the contents of several crates. There was smoked fish, figs and sweet dates, and cheese wrapped in cloth. Being indoors felt too much like I was caged, though I had no illusions that the ship itself wasn't performing that task on its own.

Still, the fresh air made me feel like I could breathe, or maybe it was Lumos's presence as he rose high enough that I could see his entire face, radiating the cool light that I'd become so familiar with in so short a time.

Lumos searched for me. He knew I was there somewhere, he just couldn't see me. Beron searched, too.

Drawing water from a barrel, I took the book and my meal outside and settled near the stern, as far away from the god of the dead as I could put myself. There was nothing I could do to stop him from using his shade to cloak one-third of Lumos's face.

I pressed my eyes closed, imagining the Helioans' reactions to the events that had unfurled. There had been so much turmoil and despair lately. So much fear and death. This would only add to it. This omen was a sign of worse things to come. And at the end of the third night when Lumos's face was completely obscured, Lumos's face would bleed and a wolf would die.

Noor and Caelum were supposed to usher in their union with blessed days punctuated by days of eclipses. They were to merge their kingdoms and kindred. To build a new House between the two and help the land recover and flourish, like their peoples.

This – *Anubis* – was not supposed to happen.

I chewed the fish in a feeble attempt to maintain control when all I felt like doing was crying. I felt like sobbing and shifting and tearing the ship apart, sinking my teeth into Anubis… only, it was too soon. If I attacked now, they wouldn't find purchase in flesh, only shadow.

I needed to be patient so I could learn what could possibly kill the one who couldn't be touched or seen.

If Chase were here, he would tease me about my appetite and being so testy. Amaris was probably glad I was gone, but Holt and Red wouldn't be. My chest tightened. They all thought I'd abandoned them – *for him* – when nothing could be farther from the truth.

The only thing I wanted was to know that my son was still safe. I wanted assurance that the Sphinx could somehow sense our location and if we were sailing toward Reyan, that she would take him and hide him away until I could find a way to end Anubis for good. Or that she could defend him, Padren, and Malia if Anubis came for Reyan.

An unsettled feeling buzzed in my stomach. Before I saw the god of death today, at his weakest, I would have believed beyond question that the Sphinx would win any battle waged between them. Now, I wasn't sure. How could the Lioness harm something that didn't exist in any true, tangible form?

Maybe that was the answer, to somehow trap him in flesh that could be killed.

My emotions tumbled faster when I considered the impossibility of that task.

Beneath the churning sea in which I found myself, I could barely see the light that struck the surface. Yet, somehow, in the dark depths, I wasn't completely terrified, though the dark sails curved above me filled with the will and breath of the god of the dead.

My thoughts tumbled across the sand to the Wolven. I needed to know Beron didn't hate me for what I said to push him away at the last minute. Even after that, he ran after me and told me to call out for him, and I didn't.

Maybe he would think I was unable to speak, but deep down, my heart didn't believe it.

My hands began to shake as I pushed down the memory that kept bobbing to the surface and refused to sink. I took a swallow of water, and once again, tried to drown it. The feeling of knowing Zarina was dying and that I had to be the one to give her peace. She couldn't survive the shadow. Couldn't hold it inside her flesh. And what she said resonated as truth. The shadows had already claimed her. If she died and succumbed to his dark power, her spirit would belong to him and never rise to become part of Sol's fire.

Anubis's essence ruined her body, but our father poisoned her mind long before her skin was cleaved with the obsidian blade. And though she'd stabbed me, and only days ago I was determined to return the favor, it didn't feel like I'd emerged the victor, because now I knew she was a victim, too.

Zarina was gone forever.

That heavy truth weighed me down and made me sink further, faster, into the dark water. My lungs burned, but I didn't kick toward the fading white light. There was no chance I could reach it now.

"Citali?" Anubis said, crouching in front of me. I hadn't even noticed him move. Now that I thought of it, I supposed neither time nor space could bridle darkness. I remembered Sol's warning to use the book against him.

A tear fell and splashed onto the dark binding. The shadows, instead of recoiling like they would one of Sol's or Noor's tears, drank from mine. They swam in the salt, reveled in it, then consumed it, along with the next that fell. And the next.

"Why are you crying?" he asked in a tender voice I did not expect.

I blinked up at him, unable to stay strong for one second longer, unable to bridle my tongue for him. "I killed her."

His lips parted as if he wanted to say something, but no words slipped past. Anubis glanced at his precious book laying on my lap, then rose and strode back to the prow where he stayed for hours, watching the sandy sea, continuing to dim Lumos in the sky as he arced overhead.

Eventually, I calmed down. My stomach full and heart shredded in two, I opened the cover and flipped through the first pages. The shadows lingering within the book and blade swarmed with the ones trapped in my hands, twisting and knotting, tangling over the words, until the words began to shift. I thought that the shadow magic, and Anubis, had finally strengthened enough to conceal the writing from me. I'd been the only one who could see the steady script before, but now... The images dissolved completely until only tattered pages remained, as empty and hopeless as I felt.

The book thrummed, alive with a different energy. Suddenly, silver words emerged from the parchment. Not written in the strange, ancient style my eyes had tripped over earlier, but the Helioan words I'd learned to read as a child.

They were words I could read.

Words I could use.

# 21

It was not Sol or Lumos who rearranged the Book of the Dead so I could understand it. It was either a trick from Anubis, or a missive from the Sculptor himself. And the message was simple, repeated through every line on every page:

*To command shadow, you must accept it.*

My flesh had accepted them when the blade sank in, but my heart had not. Acceptance wasn't a mere receiving of a thing. It involved want. My heart and mind had to welcome and embrace it. Respect, learn, and love it. Hone it. Then, and only then, could I use it as a weapon.

But how could my shadow battle his? Weren't they one and the same?

Inwardly, I told myself to calm down and stop overthinking things. To stop questioning and carefully listen. I just wished the sands of time weren't as equally impatient as I was.

I closed the book and held it against my chest. The ship's sails snapped as Anubis approached again. I stood to face him, my muscles tensing at his intense stride.

"I want you to tell me of the one whose skin I wear."

"Why?" I choked.

"Because I want to know of your life. I missed most of it."

"I'll tell you, but only if you answer some of my questions."

I was an ibis bartering with a crocodile over the last puddle of water in a time of great drought. For now, the crocodile acquiesced, and the ibis survived another moment in his presence.

"Very well. Tell me how you met him."

He walked away to retrieve two crates and arranged them like seats, one beside the other. He gestured to one and waited until I sat upon it to take his own. In the moments that followed, the god of death and I settled into strange conversation, each gathering information for our own conflicting purposes. Each sharpening the weapons we would later use against one another. Like two enemies using the same whet stone before a battle.

"Merik was a guard at the House of the Sun. Father insisted that each of his daughters have a personal guard to see to her protection, and that we carried out his wishes without hesitation."

In addition to not breathing, Anubis did not blink. He did, however, assume… "Did the guard take advantage of his station?"

I shook my head. "No. It wasn't like that."

"What was it like?"

"At first, he carried out his duties woodenly. He was a very skilled fighter. One of the best in the guard. That's why Father chose him for the task. Zarina's guard was harsh and cruel. One night we were returning to our rooms after dinner and she and I got into an argument. Her guard pushed me. Merik defended me. After that… things shifted. He became more tender. More relaxed when he could. He became a friend."

"A friend," he repeated, his tone indicating he didn't believe me.

I nodded. "We were friends first, but there was a spark between us. It didn't take much to kindle that into an inferno.

We tried to be careful and keep our love secret, but some things cannot be hidden forever."

"Reyan," he said.

My eyes cut to him. "Do not speak my son's name – in my presence or out of it," I snapped.

Anubis shrank back, just fractionally, but enough that I noticed.

"How do you know of my son?" I bit.

"Your father revealed much to me."

"And he and Zarina told you what Merik looked like?"

"Yes. Your sister provided what your father could not. She remembered many fine details about his appearance." My teeth ground together. His eyes sharpened. "You don't like that I look like him? You said that you wanted him back. I was merely granting your wish."

I didn't like that he looked like Merik, and I didn't like that Zarina had paid such close attention to him, either. But it was the trap I had laid for him. One he was still caught in so long as he wore Merik's skin.

"The shadows betrayed my words to you." I pretended to be hurt.

"They provided for you. They allowed me to give you what you wanted most."

I smiled and gestured to him. "But this isn't what I want at all. I told them I wanted *him* back. Alive. Merik. Not you wearing Merik's likeness."

"Would you prefer I look like Zarina?"

My mouth gaped. "Absolutely not! Why should you ruin her further?"

His eyes narrowed. Mine did, too.

"Did you love him?" he asked, surprising me.

"Merik?"

He gave a nod.

"Of course I did."

"Do you love him still?" he volleyed, a challenge in his tone.

"A part of me will always love him. If you're asking if I am *in* love with him, I am not."

He became quiet, but his cunning eyes never left mine. He shifted on the crate. "I don't understand how loving someone differs from being in love with them."

"Have you ever loved anything, Anubis?" I asked, honestly curious.

Sol had loved. She came down to the sand and donned flesh in order to love, and she loved Noor. She always had and always would. I think I came to understand the goddess better once I knew who Noor truly was. A mother would do anything for her child. She could forebear a great many things to make sure her child rose above them all.

The god of death's stare made my skin heat and crawl. For a moment, I wondered if he was trying to say he loved me, but he most certainly did not. He claimed I was created for him, but for what purpose? To what end? If he thought wearing Merik's flesh would make me crave him or convince me to join with him in any way, he was horribly mistaken.

My heart thundered. Angry. Indignant. Finally, properly terrified.

After a long moment, Anubis looked away. He did not answer the question.

"Where are we going and what are you retrieving?" I redirected the conversation.

"To my home," he admitted softly. "And I cannot yet reveal what I intend to retrieve."

"Because you don't trust me?"

He nodded. "I do not. Yet."

My brows kissed. I swallowed thickly and leaned toward him. "Is there a circumstance under which you think you might one day be able to?"

"If this is an attempt at seduction, it is an obvious one," he muttered.

"I am attempting no such thing. I merely asked you a question."

Anubis smiled. Merik's eyes sparked. "Your every breath, every word, and every movement is alluring. But you know that, don't you?"

"Are you attracted to me?" I asked, almost choking on the words. He'd known me for hours. *Hours*. Not days, weeks, or the months Merik took to even dare to be my friend.

"You were made for me," he said simply.

I tilted my head. "So you keep saying."

"So you keep doubting." The god of death gave me a terrible smile. "It is the truth, Citali. You will soon see I am not lying to you about this."

If he was hoping I'd say the same in return, I left him disappointed.

I would lie.

I would cheat.

Steal. Stab.

Whatever it took to rid me and this world of him.

"Tell me of the Wolven," he asked, carefully watching my reaction.

"What about him?"

"The two of you shared a mate bond for a short time."

I choked a laugh. "How do you know so much?"

"I watch."

"Mmm. Then you must have seen that it was the Wolven who saved me when Zarina would have let me bleed to death on the floor. His bond that pulled me back from the brink of death. His choice that allowed me to see my son again when you would have had Zarina cut me down – the one who was made for you..." I could not keep the derisive tone out of my voice.

Anubis shook his head. "I did not ask her to harm you. She did that on her own."

Zarina had looked me in the eye atop Sol's temple when I asked her if she stabbed me of her own volition or if she'd been compelled to do it. She said she didn't know. I believed her. Confusion unfocused her eyes as she thought about what had transpired. It could have been her, but I still knew my sister. The sister I knew and loathed as much as I loved would have walked away.

Still, she looked almost surprised when she thrust the blade into me. Maybe he was right.

Or maybe he spun lies into tapestries of confusion, hoping I would be too entranced to see the bloody wall it hung upon.

I wasn't sure it mattered now what caused her to sink the blade in… The past lay dead with Zarina now. It couldn't be changed.

"Suppose you're telling the truth and Zarina was wholly responsible for what she did. It does not change the outcome. *You* didn't help me; the Wolven did. He brought me into his pack. We were friends before Zarina tried to end my life. We are friends still."

"Friends in the way that you and Merik were friends?" he asked suggestively. His dark eyes glittered, watching to see if I would shrink away from such intimate topics. But I was no delicate flower. No blushing virgin.

"If you're asking if I've known his body and he mine, then the answer is no. We have not crossed that line."

"You are attracted to him, though?" he dared.

"Attraction is not love, Anubis." I shook my head. "I almost feel sorry that you don't feel things as mortals do."

"Mortal hearts are fickle and weak," he told me. "But no mortal can fathom a love that spans eternity. Your hearts are wild because they know their beats are numbered and race from one passion to the next, only for each new flame to burn out as quickly as the last. An eternal heart does not feel such panicked pressure. It is patient because it has the luxury of time, and it is passionate because it is grateful."

"If the Sculptor truly made me for you, then why did he give me a mortal heart? Why wouldn't he give me an immortal one to match yours?" I challenged.

"*Ya kek ra*," he breathed, scooting closer. *My dark sun.* "You will burn for an eternity. With me."

"You cannot make me something I'm not."

He smiled. "I only wish to awaken that which you are. The Sculptor has a gift for you. That is what we sail to retrieve."

His vague, ridiculous answers were worse than the Sphinx's riddles, which was saying a lot because the Lioness was very sly with her tongue.

I looked away from him. "My heart's beats may be numbered, but at least it is alive. Do you even have one?"

He stood so abruptly, my breath caught. He reached for my hands. I laid the book down and let him draw me to my feet. "Place your hand over it and feel for yourself."

"You don't even breathe," I told him, fingers curious despite the fact.

"Look – *feel* – beyond this form. Let the shadows guide you. Give yourself to them and they will honor you, their queen."

Queen of Shadow. The Sphinx told me I would be Queen of Wolves. Of teeth and claws and power. Not wisps of intangible shade.

The book told me that to command them I had to accept them. To be honest, I was afraid to do just that. But I knew the only way to get closer to Anubis was to earn his trust. The first part of earning his trust was leaving everything behind to go with him. This was the second.

I slowly raised my hand and my palm hovered over his sculpted chest. I'd run my hands over it many times before, but only when it belonged to Merik. I had never touched Anubis. My shadows buzzed around my fingers, slipping in and out of them, twirling and twisting around. They did not fear him.

I pressed my hand to his chest and held it firmly against his bare skin.

"Feel beyond, Citali."

My hand pressed into his flesh and sank deep into a darkness so viscous, I nearly tasted the chill of it. I could feel my borrowed shadows dance, and they were soon joined by others. In their frenzy, a strange pulse appeared. A heartbeat. Frighteningly slow, compared to my racing one. It was patient like he had described. Unworried. Unhurried. Confident and sure.

I curled my fingers to see if I could catch hold of his heart somehow. Anubis did not seem bothered when I pressed into his skin, but I could not find any solid thing to trace the source of that ancient pulse. My eyes saw my hand sunk to the wrist in his flesh, but I needed to see beyond, to feel what could not be seen.

Embracing my shadows, I asked them for help.

They dragged my arm further in, nearly to the elbow. Anubis tilted his head, curious. "What are you doing?"

*I want your heart!* I shouted in my mind, pouring my words toward my hands, sinking them into the darkness that writhed in my fingers. The shadows obeyed.

My palm found something so cold it burned when the pads of my fingertips brushed against it. My fingers wrapped around it just as Anubis stumbled away.

"What did you do?" he asked, alarmed.

In my hand was no heart, but I had taken more of his shade. Much more. So much that my palm was nearly completely obscured. Like Lumos's handsome face would soon be.

"I… I don't know," I blinked, pretending I had no idea what had happened and hoping he could not see the lie I created, or the illusion I spun. I thrust my hand out, but he shrank away with a hiss. "Take them back," I asked.

"I don't know how to take them back," he slowly enunciated. The hair on my arms rose at his tone. "And I don't know how you are tearing them away from me, but I do not like it, Citali."

"Nor do I. Take them away from me." I quickly clutched my hands to my chest. "Wait. What will happen if you try and fail?"

"Nothing will harm you, Citali. Certainly not a part of me."

The sails deflated and the ship slowly drifted to a stop, then lowered itself onto a still, inky sea. The dunes I was sure only moments ago were beneath us were gone, replaced by water that shone as obsidian as the blade on my thigh. Lumos and Sol were nowhere to be found. There were no stars. Just darkness so unending, I wasn't sure how I could see at all.

He'd distracted me so I did not see where the desert ended and this place began. I was furious for letting myself fall for his trick, but smug that I'd at least taken something of his for it.

"What is this place?"

Anubis wistfully looked around. "Home."

The ship glided across the placid sea toward a shore that emerged from the midst of the dark land. The vessel ran aground on black sands, but shadow and darkness were not the only things alive here. Something ancient and powerful lurked beneath its surface.

Anubis jumped off the ship into shallow, thick water that swallowed his legs from the knees down. He reached for me. "Or would you prefer to wade through it?"

I certainly did not. I eased toward him and he raised his hands, waving for me as a father might coax a child to jump into his arms. His hands – Merik's hands – gently clamped onto my waist and lifted me from the deck as I clenched his book in my hands. Then the god of the dead carried me to the black sand shore. The grains were pleasantly warm underfoot.

Anubis did not immediately let go. I stopped scanning my surroundings to look up questioningly.

Slowly, he peeled his fingers away and I took a step backward. "These are the Shadow Lands," he softly said.

The tall, black palms shivered from his voice, but I couldn't tell if they were frightened or thrilled he had spoken.

"With no light, how am I able to see?"

Sol and Lumos did not light the land of shadow, but I could make everything out clearly. Not just silhouettes, but crisp details.

"Because shadow lies within you."

He thought it was because of him and what he had given, not that I was born with something dark and burning within my spirit.

They said I was shadowed flame. A dark sun.

They were right.

But it had nothing to do with Anubis, or what I'd taken from him. My shadows guided me in the darkness.

The god of the dead led me down a wide, dark sand path that cut into the trees. A clearing emerged in their midst and in that space stood a carved pyramid of polished black stone so tall it could likely fit the Houses of the Sun, Moon, and Dusk safely inside its broad base. I stopped to take it in. "Is it made of obsidian?" The blade of the same material hummed against my thigh.

"It is." He was quiet for a moment. "Are you afraid?"

I was and wasn't, though I couldn't explain why. "Of a structure?"

Anubis smiled. "It is the House of Mirages."

"Fitting for the spinner of illusions," I mused. The shadows, curling darker around my palms, clawed toward Anubis's House, but my feet were planted firmly in the sand. I did not want to step foot inside that place.

The longer I stared at it, the worse my apprehension became.

"Will you turn back now that you've seen a land that only the dead have occupied?" he challenged. "Or will you come inside and allow me to show you even more marvelous things?"

"Marvelous for whom?" I rasped before clearing my throat.

"For you." The way he looked at me with bold appreciation and tender endearment made my skin crawl. Where had his false reverence for me come from? Who told Anubis I was made for him, and why did he seem to genuinely believe their lie?

Maybe that was what frightened me most. That the god who had power over life and death, over spirit itself, was completely sated on the lies someone or something was feeding him. So satisfied with the story, he never questioned its validity.

Who was the *true* creator of lies? Who truly spun the illusions Anubis found himself trapped within?

That was what the House of Mirages felt like… a beautiful, painfully obvious trap.

Or was this Anubis's deceit – to make me think he was being deceived so I would trust him enough to step inside that pyramid?

"What do you need from inside?" I asked, trying to sound aloof.

"To begin with, rest and revitalization. You need these things as well," he noted. "We will return to Helios in two nights."

I knew that. Tomorrow, more than half of Lumos would be shrouded. The day after, his entire face would turn to shadow, then to blood. I imagined Beron's dark, silken fur slipping through my fingertips and hoped it would not be his pelt coated in blood beneath a moon by the same name.

Anubis ticked his head toward the House of Mirages once more. Somehow, I managed to move my feet, following him to the vast base where an opening emerged between glassy stones. The book hummed a warning against my chest. I cracked it to find a single message waiting: *Do not lose yourself inside. Remember for whom you fight.*

Anubis's House was decorated with dust and lacy cobwebs. He tore them away from each doorway and led me into the heart of the pyramid's labyrinthine corridors and halls to a door made of wood stained to match the dark, volcanic glass that lay over the entire structure. He pushed the door open and stepped inside. At first, it seemed to be a room like any other, but the longer I stood within its walls, the more I sensed a presence. Something was here in this place. Something watched and waited.

A bed that could comfortably rest a dozen lay in the room's middle, draped in golden silk to match the sheets and bed cover. Something hummed within my chest, saying they were spun and woven just for me. That they weren't real.

Anubis watched me. "Is this suitable?"

"It's fine."

"I'll leave you to rest. I'll gather food from the ship and place some just outside the door."

"Are you locking me inside?" I asked.

"That isn't necessary, Citali. One is not a prisoner in her own home." He turned to leave, the muscles of his shoulders and back rippling with every step he took toward the door.

Goosebumps spread over my flesh. I didn't want him to leave me in this room, in this House, or in the Shadow Land.

I almost laughed at the irony: I didn't want the one person I never wanted close to leave me. Brushing errant strands of hair out of my face, I watched as he closed the door and listened as he strode down the hall we'd just taken.

Then I waited for whatever lurked in the darkness to show itself.

# 22

The book trembled against my chest. I slowly cracked it open, afraid to look down long enough to read the message I knew waited on the page. My eyes darted downward to see one word: *Remember.*

Remember what?

My eyes rose to see a mass of shadow swirling in the corner. Fast as lightning arcing to the ground, it struck me and swept me off my feet. Soft silk pinched between my fingertips, I fell immediately asleep in a strange bed, in a strange room, in a strange House and land.

*My door shut quietly. Sol's light kissed Merik's brown skin as he left his spear standing against the wall and strode to me. His eyes glimmered with want and mischief. With the familiar dare I had come to crave.*

*I pushed my chair away from the desk. My feet hit the cool stone and I stood just as he reached me, and our lips collided with a forbidden kiss. My thumbs grazed his freshly shaven head and jaw.*

*My bottom hit the desk's edge and he lifted me onto it. Sheets of papyrus fell to the floor, forgotten.*

*His hands pressed my body into his and I melted at his touch. Not even the sun goddess burned as hot as I did.*

*Footsteps came from the hall. I pulled away, then pushed him toward the door where he should have been standing. I scooped the papyrus into my hands and settled back into my chair while Merik took up his spear and affected a placid, bored expression the instant before the door swung open and Father strode in.*

*He glanced at Merik, then at me. "Citali," he greeted woodenly. "Your presence is required in Sol's temple." He turned to Merik. "See that she hastens."*

*Merik bowed to his Aten, but the moment my father left our presence, his fearful eyes fastened on mine. That was a very close call.*

*I vomited into a basin, a cold sweat beading over my skin. "Please," I begged the healer, my throat burnt and raw.*

*"I cannot lie to him, Atena," she apologized. "I cannot risk my life and the lives of my family."*

*She knew my monstrous father well. He was someone who cut down anything that stood against him like tall grass along the riverbank. "Please. Just… can you wait so that I can warn the one I love?"*

*"Who is it?"*

*"I will not speak his name just so you can tell my father and have him slaughtered."*

*"When will you see him again?"*

*"This very afternoon. Please. Wait until morning."*

*"I cannot promise to wait until morning, but I will put it off as long as I can," she said, handing me a cool cloth and placing a sachet of herbs beside the bed next to a carafe of water. "Drink the tea. The ginger will settle your stomach. The chamomile will calm you."*

*My heart raged, knowing it would not be calmed until Merik was safe.*

*The healer left me. I didn't believe she would run straight to my father, but she could only avoid him and conceal the truth for so long. With shaking arms, I pushed myself upright and trudged to the door where my guard stood. "I need to see Merik. I know you are friends. It's urgent and for his sake, please be discreet."*

*The guard returned what felt like an eternity later with Merik at his side. He rushed to me when his friend closed the door. "Citali?"*

*He was frightened. I'd never called for him before.*

*"You need to gather your family and leave Helios."*

*Suddenly, he looked as sickly as I felt. "He knows about us?"*

*"Merik… I am carrying your child."*

*His lips parted. "What?" he breathed. I thought he would be angry with me. Instead, he rushed to me, fell to his knees, and kissed my stomach.*

*That was how Father found us when he entered the room unannounced.*

*The healer lied.*

*Father took one look at us and turned on his heel and left, a silent warning on his brow and a smug smile on his lips.*

*He did not strike out at Merik that day. Even when I begged him to leave, my love refused, though he knew –* he knew *– my father would never forgive such an offense against one of his daughters.*

*Instead, he sequestered me and used Merik's life as a means of controlling me until the instant Reyan drew breath and he had something much more valuable to use against me. Because as much as I cared for Merik, I would always love Reyan most.*

*The midwife toweled Reyan off as my son screamed at the top of his lungs. It was the most glorious sound I had ever heard. My heart swelled with love. With pride. With fear…*

*Tears fell from my eyes. Tears of joy and terror.*

*She placed him on my chest, and I held him carefully against me. Reyan calmed the moment he heard my heartbeat, settling against my skin to sleep.*

*Merik stood nearby, watching, waiting for his turn to hold our newborn. Father ordered that he be present during the birth of our son, striking through my heart a vein of fear as pure as gold forked through bedrock.*

*It was just as the exhaustion and toll of childbirth claimed me and my eyes drifted closed, that the door flung open and six of Father's most trusted guards entered the room, led by Zuul, Father's principal guardsman and advisor.*

*The midwife froze, then quickly reached for Reyan. I sat up and handed my son to her and ordered her to keep him safe. I demanded to know what they were doing in my rooms, though I now knew that Father's allowance of Merik's presence there was his final cruelty.*

*Merik knew as well. He did not fight or struggle. He let them take hold of his arms and wrench them behind his back. His eyes met mine. "All is well," he said lightly, as if he was completely at peace and didn't have a care or worry in the world. His own men forced him to his knees and still he held my eyes. Still he pretended. "All is well, Citali."*

*All was not well.*

*His death was clean.*

*One quick glide of a sword and Merik's voice was forever severed with the hope he'd spoken.*

*My wail sent doves scattering from the balcony.*

*And it was only after, when Merik lay dead and spilling blood on my room's floor that I realized the midwife had taken Reyan away. I just hadn't realized she wouldn't bring him back. She'd stolen my child.*

# 23

I woke with a start to shadows screaming around me like wraiths. They were upset, I realized, because I was. In the dark room, I sensed no presence. I padded to the door and found it unlocked. A small crate of food lay just outside. Lifting it, I carried it into the room and rummaged for something to eat. The wolf in me was still unsatisfied. Famished – yet again.

There was smoked fish, cheese, and bread alongside a corked bottle of wine and a small carafe of water. I took a long draw of fresh-tasting water, trying to recall how I'd fallen asleep. I didn't remember even lying down.

I'd dreamed of Merik, though I wasn't sure if it was because Anubis wore his likeness and it rattled me, or if something more sinister was at work. Had the god of the dead torn my memories to the forefront of my mind, allowing his shadows to taste, then feed on them? Had he stolen me the way the midwife stole my son? Would he pay a similar price for his role?

She burned atop Sol's temple the next day, along with the guards who'd come to kill Merik, slain by the one who gave the order. I was the only Atena to attend their departure

– and as Sol took what she found acceptable, I sealed the most important secret of my life away.

Padren managed to send word to me through one of Merik's friends who went to pay his respects after Merik's death. Our son was with them. A woman they didn't know brought the babe to their home and they found a young woman to nurse him. All would be well, Padren assured me. Just as Merik promised with his last words.

I never knew how he mustered the strength to speak to me after that, or how he spoke words of kindness. I'm certain I would hate the one responsible for the death of my child if the situation were reversed. There would be no kindness left in me.

My thoughts slid to Reyan and I wondered if the Sphinx would swat at him if he pulled her tail, knowing she wouldn't. He had her wrapped around his tiny, chubby finger. The Lioness would keep him safe. She would guard him, Padren, and Malia. Anubis couldn't find them. She wouldn't take them to a place where shadows could penetrate, and while I didn't know where on earth that place might be, the Sphinx was immortal. She'd lived more mortal lifespans than I could fathom. She knew the kingdom of Helios intimately; knew every grain of sand and beyond.

My heart ached not knowing where they were. It was for the best to keep them safe, but not knowing meant I couldn't go to them to help if they needed me.

I whispered to the shadows that even *they* could not obscure the Sphinx with her translucent wings and sharp claws.

The shadows answered.

As if I had conjured her, the sound of claws raking down wood came from the door. The handle turned and the Sphinx stepped inside, taking up the entire room with her large body and crystalline wings. Her attitude filled in the gaps left by her enormous features.

I bit my lip, debating whether she was real.

"Not even a polite greeting?" she purred haughtily, tipping her chin up. "You aren't going to inquire of Reyan? Ask of Padren and Malia? Padren is a saint, though Malia can be a bit… what's the word? Irritable."

"What have you done to provoke her?" I asked.

The Lioness puffed her chest. "You assume *I* am to blame?"

"Of course," I snorted. Malia was pure gold, while the Sphinx was comprised of riddles and claws.

She shrank down to better look me in the eye and waited. Her obsidian gaze matched the depthless walls surrounding us.

"Why are you here and not with them?"

"What makes you think I am not?" she asked.

"*How* are you here? Sol does not reach this land of shadows."

"I am not bound to Sol's light. I am made of it," she answered.

"*You* are made of Sol's light?" I deadpanned. "You?"

"Of course. What else could make a creature so grand?"

*And humble…* "If you are made of Sol's light, then why don't you shine? Why do you not chase my shadows away?" I held my hands up and watched them slither calmly through my fingers. They'd settled when I had. They weren't afraid of the Sphinx, weren't bothered by her in the least. Which… made absolutely no sense. If what she said was true, they should shrink away from her.

"I do not shine because I contain the light within my form, and because I do not want to hurt you. You hold more of his essence in you now."

"You can tell that?"

She gave a curt nod, her eyes betraying the fact that she did not approve of this new change in me.

"How would it hurt me for your light to touch my shadows?"

"That part of you touched by the light would be excised."

*Excised.* I swallowed.

She drew closer, leaned in. "How did you steal more of his essence?"

"I don't know."

Her uncanny eyes met mine and she tilted her head. One of her brows rose with the corner of her mouth. "You can tell me."

"I honestly don't know." This encounter felt off. Why had she come here? How did she know where I was when Sol and Lumos weren't able to see through Anubis's shadows? And why was she asking me about the shade?

"Reyan is well. Have you solved the riddle of where I've been hiding them?" she asked casually.

"Lioness, I know you aren't actually here, just as you know that I loathe your riddles."

Her eyes hardened. "You dare question me?"

"I dare many things. Why would Sol's light seek out a place of shadow or a person who bears it?"

"To destroy that which should not exist," she growled. She grew larger until her shoulders bumped the ceiling, then… vanished. Nothing more than a mirage, as I'd suspected.

With her gone, the unsettled feeling left my stomach and I could breathe a little easier. Reyan was safe because of the Lioness's wisdom. I'd never been happier that a secret was kept from me.

The House of Mirages was playing tricks, or its master was. I decided to be more strategic and careful in what I whispered to the shadow magic…

I ate my meal, a thousand thoughts racing through my mind as I considered every detail of the false encounter with the Sphinx. Anubis had gleaned quite a lot of intel from Father and Zarina. When he mimicked them, he did so perfectly. Every small detail was present so the one looking could find no aberration, no fault, forcing them to question their own eyes and sanity.

Anubis knocked on my door what felt like hours later, still wearing Merik's skin. "I just woke and thought I would check on you."

"Liar," I gritted. He went still. "I know what you're doing, but it's not going to work. I will never let you near my son. Sending an image of the Lioness to tempt me was a foolish error on your part."

He never blinked. His face never betrayed his feelings the way Merik's had. "I want to show you something," he said in reply. He didn't deny what I'd accused him of, and certainly did not apologize for trying to deceive me.

"Another illusion? I don't wish to see more lies."

"How about the truth?"

"Do you even know what truth is?"

He held my glare. "Of course. It is the thing most avoid because it cuts the deepest. You of all people intimately know that feeling."

My hand found the place on my stomach where the blade had slid into. Anubis settled into a stance that told me he was willing to wait as long as it took for me to acquiesce.

"How long have we been here?"

"Time stretches differently in this land," he muttered, still waiting. Patiently. Like his ridiculous immortal pride or distortions in time would allow him an eternity.

"That is not an answer to my question."

"Only hours have passed in Helios," he replied tiredly.

I groaned. It felt like I'd already spent days here. In Lumina, when Noor and I followed Caelum to the House of the Moon, the darkness closed in on me. I felt desperate to leave, knowing I was too far from my son to protect him. I wanted nothing more than to go home, scoop him up, and run away without looking back.

"Has Sol risen?"

He shook his head. "She soon will but has not yet."

It was best to get this over with. I waved him toward the door and followed him deep into the pyramid's dark heart to a chamber with high ceilings and polished walls – every inch covered with the language I recognized from the Book of the Dead.

"What is this language?"

"It is that of the Sculptor."

My mouth fell open. "You learned all this from the Sculptor?"

He waved his hand and torches that lined every corner and wall flared to life. But instead of casting fire's warm glow, the flames were encased in shadow. Anubis watched me for a reaction. "Shadowfire is what the Sculptor uses to see by as he hammers his chisel."

This was what Beron saw inside me, even before he saved me. This was what he would have tasted when he sealed our bond with a sacred bite. Shadowfire. *My* essence, I realized. Something dark and scorching, despite its shadowed flame.

In the center of the room loomed a pool of disturbed, mercurial liquid that seemed more alive than the sea beyond the trees in this shadowy land. The liquid silver churned as small crests formed over its surface, crashed, then built again. Anubis settled at its edge, letting his fingers drift lazily along the surface. His fingers came away clean.

"What is this?" I rasped, unable to look away for fear of what it would do when my attention left it.

"This is a remnant; a sliver of the creation rock from which the Sculptor carved the earth and the trio of gods to rule it."

It wasn't rock at all, but something primeval and menacing. How could the beauty of this world originate from such malevolence? I could feel its sentience as a pulse within the water that seemed more patient than Anubis described the immortal gods.

"The world needs light to survive," Anubis quietly noted. "The gods of illumination will deny it, but shadow is also vital, Citali. *I* am necessary. As are you."

"I'm not like you."

He gave a wan smile. "We are more alike than you think."

I would never believe that. I couldn't be more different than the god of death.

"If you wade into the waters, you will learn the truth you so fervently seek."

Shaking my head, I took a step away from the pool of silver, troubled water. I did not want to wade into it. I didn't even want to dip my fingertip into it, but I needed to. I had to know what he did. I had to learn his weakness if I would ever be able to defeat him.

"It will not harm you," he promised.

"Will you wade in as well?"

He shook his head. "It is an honor to stand within the pool. I have already been granted the knowledge. The Sculptor seeks to share it with you now."

If he and the Sculptor were on such favorable terms, why had Anubis been removed from the earth? I squinted speculatively. "How do I know this isn't a trap?"

"You'll have to trust that I'm telling you the truth. I have no proof to offer, only my word. And that of the Sculptor's."

"Will I see him?"

Anubis nodded sagely. "That was my experience. In a few earthly moments, he imparted a millennia of wisdom. I hope he grants you the same."

He *hoped*. What if the Sculptor clamped onto my ankle and dragged me beneath the surface, holding me there until he'd rid the earth of me? He'd once tried to bury Anubis, yet somehow, the god of death didn't seem angry about being put away.

Sol's account of Anubis's story rang true, and Sol had never lied to me as far as I knew. In our short time together, Anubis had many times. He might still be.

Anubis held out his hand and waited.

"I do not wish to die," I rasped.

Anubis pressed his eyes closed. "You are safe within these waters, Citali. And safer still with me."

If that was true, why was he trying to learn where my son was? What did he need with Reyan? Perhaps he saw how perfectly Father had been able to control me by threatening my child and planned to do the same.

"Is this a trick?" I breathed.

Shrugging, he smiled, a dare playing on his lips. "Clasp it and see."

My palm hovered over Anubis's for a moment. I held his stare, slipped my fingers into his hand, then let my foot hover over the water's metallic surface. With a deep breath, I let one foot sink to the bottom, followed by the other. The chrome liquid tugged at the strips that comprised the skirt of the dress I'd chosen until suddenly, the cool water went still around me. The torches' dark flames rose, flickering to the ceiling the instant before a sudden gust of air tore through the room and guttered the flames. A shiver slid up my spine that quickly abandoned it and curled around my heart instead. Anubis still held tight to my hand. "When I let go, you will be in his presence."

I gripped his fingers. "Is this another illusion?"

He did not answer, but held my gaze as his hand fell away.

# 24

Anubis was gone and I stood alone in the pool. A strange umbra slid over the room; dark but still managing to cast light enough to see by. Hammering came from someplace in the depths of the pyramid. I eased out of the liquid and chased the sound, wending through passageways, deeper and deeper into the ground. The farther I walked, the more the air heated, the very air seeming to ripple as it struggled to breathe. For a moment, I wondered whether the Sculptor had invited Sol into this dark place.

A man sat on a nondescript wooden stool in front of a great rock wall, tapping his hammer's head to the chisel he worked over the stone. Every tap resounded through my bones, echoing through my spirit.

The stool's woven seat was frayed and stretched under his weight. I wondered how long he had been sculpting. What else had he made before and after he'd hewn out the marvel that was our world and the gods who guarded it?

As chipped fragments fell away and piled at his feet, he patiently, methodically worked. The fragments bowed to the sweltering heat, turning into the mercurial liquid from which I'd just stepped out.

"Citali," he greeted as his hammer struck the chisel one last time, dislodging a significant piece from the rock.

I swallowed thickly as he turned to face me. His hands were weathered but strong. The hammer and chisel were worn from what I imagined was constant use. His hair was stark white, and his eyes were a startling silver. His skin was the color of midnight and dawn, and each glorious shade in between. It changed like oil on water when he moved. He wore a loose, rust-colored gown cinched at his waist. The Sculptor's feet were bare.

"He's taken the book away from you, so I will no longer be able to communicate to you through it anymore. I've paused time for him so we can speak freely for a few moments."

"How do I know you're real? He spins illusions," I questioned warily.

The Sculptor stood still. "What does your heart speak on the matter? I made them as compasses with which to guide you."

My heart recognized his truth.

He was real.

But my mind was distrustful. "What two messages did you send to me through Anubis's book?"

"I advised that to command shadow, you must accept it. Then I cautioned you to remember."

I was truly standing in the midst of the Sculptor! I was awed in his presence, but then I realized that Anubis had taken the book from me at his first opportunity. "Has he taken the blade?"

The Sculptor looked to the endless ceiling. "Not yet."

"Did he know you were guiding me with the book?"

The Sculptor pondered this for a moment. "He did not know, but he suspected you were learning the language and it made him uneasy."

"He told me that what I learned here would be truth…"

A small wooden table appeared beside him and he laid down his tools upon it. "Is truth what you seek?"

"I seek an end to Anubis – and to all threats against my son and loved ones."

"Then we have a common goal," he said, gently stretching his fingers against his thighs.

"Are you the only Sculptor?" I blurted.

He gave a gentle smile. "There is far too much work for only one."

"Why couldn't you kill him? Why was trapping him the only option?"

"I cannot return to the earth I carved. There is far too much to do. Unfortunately, the three gods I created to rule it are equal in power. None can best the others. Keeping him tucked and asleep was their only option. I helped where I could, but could not spare much time for him."

"You could stop time, as you are now," I volleyed.

"Time cannot stop indefinitely. Even now, my hands and heart ache to grasp the hammer and chisel again." He looked back to the rock, studying the crevices and divots he'd made. Where the chunk had fallen away, there was now a puddle of silver at his feet. "Ask what you truly want to know. What you *need* to know."

"He says you made me for him. Is that true?"

The Sculptor glanced at me over his shoulder. "It is true. I made you for him. But not for his heart or pleasure." The Sculptor's pewter eyes sharpened, and I felt in my gut a purpose I hadn't realized was there.

When Reyan was born, my purpose was to be his mother. To rear him, teach and protect him. When he was stolen, that purpose never left my bones. And while this new purpose would accomplish my previously established goals, it demanded more. It demanded all of me.

I would not only protect my son, my loved ones, and my people. I was born to protect the world.

I *had* been made for Anubis. To end him.

But worse than that… I was to take his place.

The Sculptor watched the realization settle on my face. “He will ask you to drink of the water of life. It will transform your heart and make you immortal.”

My eyes widened. “He and I would be equals?”

“For a short time, you will be made immortal and share his shadow magic equally. But under the blood moon, I will give you command of them all and allow you to strip all power from him, as well as his immortality. You will be the death of him, Citali.”

That meant that after I drank of the watery remnant, I would endure the rest of eternity with Sol and Lumos. My patient heart would beat long after Reyan’s went still. After Noor joined her mother in the hereafter, burning over us. After Caelum and Beron’s bodies were returned to the soil they were made from and their spirits sparkled in the night sky with Lumos as he guided them in their slow migrations.

Unless I commanded the spirits of the dead once more.

“It is a heavy burden to bear, but the only way to accomplish your purpose. If you do not drink of the water, nothing will stop Anubis. He will bring ruin. He will take your son’s life – whether by blade or influence – and he will kill Noor, Caelum, and Beron and his pack, along with anyone else who stands against him.”

“I will stand, even if it means I fall,” I told him resolutely.

“You were chiseled as the dark sun, now also a gift of the moon. You are shadowfire and teeth, and not even the god of death will be able to withstand your gifts. You will burn away his shadow and claim it as your own.”

“Will I inherit his dark power and claim the dead once more, as the gods of illumination return to ruling the living?”

“It is their purpose,” he simply said, affirming my fear.

"I don't know how to be a god."

The Sculptor smiled. "For that, I am glad."

"I don't know how to live in shadow. I was born beneath the sun and have learned to love by the moon."

The Sculptor took up his hammer and chisel. "You do not have to confine or banish yourself as he has. You will have the power and the time to enjoy all the earth offers. You will have Sol's love and Lumos's support. They will lead you when you ask for guidance and aid you when you require help. You can trust them."

He moved closer to the rock, his toes dipping into the mercurial puddle. "When you return, he will spin illusions like heavy cloaks and lay them over your shoulder, not to keep you warm, but as one yokes an animal who might serve him. Remember who you are. Remember your son and your love."

An image of Reyan in Beron's arms came to mind, then one of Reyan with the Sphinx. I shuddered to think of the great lioness leaving his side for even a second. I couldn't protect him as it was. Neither was I able to be what Beron needed or deserved.

"You fight what you feel because you fear love," he hinted softly.

"From love comes ruin," I rasped, remembering Merik's hopeful lie. *All is well.*

The Sculptor's wizened hands tightened on his tools. "When Sol left him, your father's heart burnt away to nothing. He, too, feared love, so ruin was all he had left."

My anger rose. "Do you excuse his actions?"

The Sculptor's eyes flashed silver again. "Never. I simply seek to encourage you not to make his mistakes. Ruin is born of hatred and fear, never from love or courage. Be fearless in claiming your purpose. It is yours alone and reflects what you need most in your mortal life."

"But it comes with the price of immortality."

He inclined his head. "The earth needs the balance of three. If Anubis is removed, he must be replaced. But just because you will have duties beyond what you can comprehend doesn't mean you cannot handle them. And they will not bar you from those you love. Being the god of the dead means that you will see your loved ones safe until age claims them, and afterward, they will walk in the Shadow Lands with you."

It was a comfort, I admitted to myself. It wasn't a perfect solution, but it meant I would never be separated from them. When one of them passed, I would still be part of their existence. There would not be a certain number of months or years I would be parted from them, where I longed to die just so I could see them in the hereafter, burdened by my stubborn heart refusing to stop beating without them. Or where I went to burn for Sol, never to set eyes on the glittering Luminan jewels set into the heavens.

He turned away from me. "Be careful with your words when you return. He has been gently testing you," he said of Anubis. "Now, he will place you in his mortar, and with his pestle grind and try to mold you into what he would have you be."

The very notion sent molten rage sliding through my veins.

The Sculptor quietly regarded the rock.

"Does he know my thoughts?"

"No. He saw the Sphinx near the House of Wolves, so he had no trouble spinning her when you whispered her name. You are right to be careful what you share with the shadows, Citali. But I can ensure your thoughts remain your own, if you'd like."

"I would."

He moved his chisel into the hand that held his hammer and dipped his thumb into the mercurial liquid at his feet, then walked to me and brushed it across my forehead. His thumb was rough, but his skin warm. His touch was comforting. "This will seal your thoughts and ensure they will only ever belong to you…unless you'd like for someone else to have them."

"Will *you* know my mind?"

He gave a gentle smile. "I do not need to. I know your heart."

I swallowed thickly and guilt washed over me. My heart was the one that tried to kill one sister and managed to slaughter another. My heart was weak and only merciful when it served her.

"All that is left is for you to take his place," the Sculptor prompted. "I must start time again, Citali, and you must press on and see this through."

"How do I burn his shadow away?"

"With the fire in your heart, of course," he answered gently.

"Can you speed time to make the days pass quickly? I have two more to spend with him before returning to Helios."

The Sculptor smiled. "I'm afraid not. You need time to embrace your shadow and the dark flame within so you can conquer his power."

"Can you stop the death of the wolf?" I asked, trying to keep the quiver from my voice.

He watched me for a long moment, then returned his chisel to his right hand. "Death is not my duty. My purpose is to sculpt and bring about life."

He turned to the wall, and suddenly, I was standing calf-deep in the primordial pool. Anubis slowly manifested before me. Or perhaps it was I who appeared before him. Either way, I was returned.

The god of the dead's keen eyes locked onto mine. "Welcome back."

My heart felt like the creation rock, as if the Sculptor's chisel was being hammered in neat lines down its length and across its breadth. Formed anew. My shadows writhed within me, yet I could feel them in him. I felt the shadowfire in my heart, angrily licking and ready to burn away all that stood in the way of what I wanted.

Anubis's eyes locked onto my forehead. "The Sculptor blessed you?"

"He did," I rasped.

"Did he tell you what would happen if you drank from creation's water?"

I nodded. "I will become immortal."

"You will become what you were meant to be," he corrected. The two of us were dancing on blade tips, each step carefully taken so that our soles did not split. "Do you want to drink of it? Do you choose an immortal life – with me?" he asked hopefully, carefully.

I squared my shoulders. "The Sculptor revealed many things. I am ready for an immortal life, Anubis."

His eyes narrowed fractionally, as if he was trying to discern whether I had merely failed to say I wanted such a life with him, or had done so knowingly.

It was the latter. I smiled sweetly. "Do I just cup my hand and sip?"

His shoulders relaxed and he stepped into the pool with me, feet disappearing into the lustrous water. Bending at the waist, he took water into his cupped palm and held it out to me. "Drink."

I brought his hand to my lips, holding his wrist in place and glancing up at him before sipping. His body stiffened when my lips touched his skin. And though he didn't need to breathe, it felt like he held a breath.

I expected fire. I expected the remnant of creation to sear my veins from the inside out. While I knew that somewhere deep inside, Anubis's heart still beat, I believed mine might stop.

It slowed so drastically, I thought for a long moment that it might have. But there was no fire, nothing molten about the life-bringing water. The thin, silvery stream was cool and refreshing – not in the way that fresh water was, but soothing to the very marrow. The tension melted from my muscles. The scant headache that had formed as I reappeared in this pool immediately eased.

I stretched my arms out at my sides. They felt lighter, stronger. My legs did, too. All of me felt honed, like a dull blade ground upon a whetstone emerged sharp enough to split even the finest strand of hair. Was this how Noor felt when she was filled with Sol's power?

No, I was stronger than Noor. And soon, I would be Sol's equal. The thought flitted away like a delicate butterfly that flew too high for me to catch.

"How does immortality feel now that you've tasted it and been transformed?" Curiosity flooded his voice. He rushed to explain, "I was made this way. I know nothing else."

No. He wasn't transformed yet, but he would be. He would be reduced to nothing soon enough. "I expected it to be a painful transition, but it's been surprisingly pleasant," I answered truthfully.

He studied me closely. "Do you feel differently than before?"

"My head no longer aches."

Anubis smiled. "You never cease to surprise me, Citali. I grant you immortal life and all you can say is that your head no longer aches, as if the span of eternity is nothing more than an eyelash on your cheek. Nothing impressive at all. As if it is completely normal."

I noted how quickly he'd stolen responsibility from the Sculptor, as if *he* was the one who made and collected this very remnant. How had the Sculptor ever come to trust him with it? Why was this pool in the Shadow Lands where Anubis could enter and use the very water of creation whenever he pleased? Or perhaps… it was never placed here for *him*. Perhaps it had always been mine.

"Maybe it is as you said: I was born for this."

"For me," he corrected.

It took every ounce of will within my body to agree with him, but it was all part of the plan. Lure him close, then steal his shadow and claim it as my own. "For you. The Sculptor said as much, though I told him that as you were made first, you've belonged to me for far longer."

His eyes turned molten.

I stepped out of the sacred pool and when my soles hit the stone, the world blossomed. Scents from the flora that stretched from pyramid to shore flooded my senses. The delicate sounds of crickets and insect wings filled my ears. The bittersweet taste of immortality lingered on my tongue. The pads of my fingers tingled as if feeling the air molecules around me.

The only way to properly describe the way I felt was *alive*. More alive than I had ever been. More aware.

Connected.

Immortality felt right. It had been mine since before I was conceived, but immortality was another illusion, I reminded myself. It only meant that one would live an extended life beyond the mortal years with which I was born. Someone stronger might sever it at any moment. Anubis would soon learn that.

He stepped out of the pool behind me. The liquid slid sleekly from his skin before puddling onto the stone. My puddle moved to join with his and together slid back to the pool's edge as if it longed to rejoin its kind and exist only within the pool's boundaries. I bet the Sculptor set those, too.

The liquid crawled up the pool's stony side and slipped back into the pool.

The frighteningly slow beat within my chest now kept time with the heartbeat of creation, sedate and unhurried. I wondered if somehow the things the Sculptor carved were set to the rhythm of his heart. After all, it was he who chiseled and coaxed life from its ancient form. And if human hearts had numbered beats, maybe immortal ones did, too. They just chased an ending too far in the future to see from the present.

"I hear the change in you," Anubis gently noted, ghosting his fingers down my bare arm. "But your eyes betray nothing. They are like the obsidian that surrounds us, bottomless and hard as diamonds. And like mirrors, they guard you. They reflect but refuse to reveal your emotions."

"A skill that saved me more than once, I assure you."

"I should warn you," he hedged, "that your father's spirit roams these lands."

My bones turned to stone. "Why?"

"Because Sol refused him. He is the first spirit that has been cast aside for me to collect in a very long time."

"You brought him here, knowing who he was and what he'd done to me?" I asked.

"I won't lament the way he raised you. If he were of another mind or manner, you would not be the same. You would not be *ya kek ra.*" *My dark sun.* He lifted his hand and ran a finger across my wrist. "I prefer for you to burn."

"Did you… did you wither his heart so he would make me like this?"

Anubis shook his head. "I did not have to. Sol did that for me."

I strode away from him, wending through the pyramid, somehow sensing the island around it and every grain of sand that comprised it. The lifeless water surrounding it. The palms that preferred shadow to Sol.

There was another presence roaming the shore, listless and uncomfortable in his new skin. I wanted to see him. No, I wanted to see the fear in his eyes. The jealousy that would flare at my changed form.

Anubis trailed behind me but gave me a wide berth. He knew my heart and what I would do when I finally found my father's spirit. Wisely, he did not prevent me from it.

The Sculptor said the god of the dead would test me in earnest, heaping trials onto my neck to see if I could handle them. This did not feel like a bridle or yoke; this felt like freedom. I could taste the justice I would mete out like a bittersweet flavor that lingered on my tongue.

A door appeared at the end of a shiny corridor. At my side, my reflection kept step with me in the shining obsidian. She looked more wraith than woman or wolf, and for the first time since I could remember, I enjoyed her. She wasn't something to dress up as a manipulative means to an end, she *was* the ending.

I cut through the trees. When sand briars pricked my soles, I felt no pain and my skin quickly knitted itself back together. Creatures that inhabited this place hid themselves, but I could feel their breath, hear their tiny legs skitter away. Focusing on Father, my shadows brought me to him.

The man was no longer clad in flesh. In death, he was embodied in an opaque, pale light, appearing as he did just before Noor ended his life.

I wasn't sure if spirits could remember their existences or feel emotions, but seeing him confirmed they did both. Fear shone in his eyes. "Citali," he said without moving his lips. It was no more than a thought. A recognition.

His eyes darted to the obsidian blade on my thigh where the panels of my dress had caught on its handle. He quickly forgot the knife when Anubis appeared over my shoulder. My father knelt on the sand to the god of death, but he did not belong to him. Not now. Not ever.

I strode toward him and called on my shadows. "Tear him apart so that nothing remains," I commanded them.

Father stood, holding out his hands as if he could defend himself. He looked to Anubis for help, but the god of death merely smiled back. This was more gift than test…

My shadows coiled around him, sharpening into knives as they began to slash and shred, cut and chop until nothing but a heap of spiritual strips remained. I lavished in his screams until my shadows smothered them, too. "Devour him." And I watched as they did.

When I was satisfied, I turned to face Anubis with my chin raised.

"You're welcome," he said.

He believed he had given me this offering. That he could have stopped me from ending what remained of the man who'd molded me. He was wrong.

My lips tugged upward in a sly smile. "Thank you." He held out a hand with his palm up, waiting. "Aren't you afraid I will somehow siphon more shadow?" I teased.

"I think I understand now that the Sculptor wishes for us to share power and responsibility as equals."

Inwardly I scoffed, then smiled. I slid my fingers into his palm and we walked along the shore, crossing over the very spot my father's spirit had occupied only moments before.

# 25

My immortal body did not hunger. Lumos claimed I would shift and become wolf when I chose. Now, I thought that choice might have been torn to shreds and consumed like Father's spirit. Zarina had set into motion a series of events that rapidly changed my life in ways I never knew was possible, and now, she was dead, too, burning for Sol.

I felt her even from the Shadow Lands, set ablaze in the sky with our ancestors and arcing through the sky. Did my sister look for me as well? Did she know I was alive and resided in the shadows, or did she worry that Anubis had consumed me as he had her?

Had Noor lost hope? Had Beron?

I held Anubis's hand last night as we walked, though I could not claim the touch was innocent. It was far too intimate for that. Our shadows had mingled, kissed. I'd torn a small amount away from him again when he walked me back to my room and insisted I rest. He didn't seem upset that his essence was drawn to me. "They serve us both now," he simply said.

The change in him set my teeth on edge. He'd been angry and suspicious when I tugged at his heart, but now he seemed content with sharing his dark magic with me. I couldn't reconcile his abrupt change in attitude. Like one of Beron's pack, he'd shifted from human into wolf, sniffing and pawing at my emotions. I was merely waiting for him to bare his fangs, snarl, and attack.

My immortal body did not need sleep, but Anubis insisted I rest. He left another crate of food at my door. The crusty bread, overripe grapes, and hard cheese sat drying on its tray on the table near my bed.

As I considered the tray, a familiar howl made my hair stand on end.

*Beron isn't here. He can't be!*

But Anubis could spin illusions, and the House of Mirages was nothing to trifle with. I left the pyramid and followed the sound, just like I knew he wanted. I chased it into the palms where I found the Wolven waiting, his dark fur glossy in the strange light of this place.

But I knew it was not the Wolven at all. Shadows whirred around the imitation's form. Still, I pretended not to see them.

"Beron?"

He shifted into his human form at the sound of my voice, his hips suddenly covered with a kilt of palm leaves. I almost laughed. Anubis thought to cover him when Beron was never concerned with his nakedness. He accepted every part of the transition to and from his Wolven form. The false Beron rushed to me and crushed me to his chest. His fingers wove into my hair and he breathed in my scent with a sigh, then exhaled like he'd finally found what he'd been searching for all his life.

"I've searched everywhere for you!"

I pushed at his chest and his fingers relaxed. He stepped away but remained close. "I am well," I answered guardedly.

His brows furrowed, and a sharp blade carved into my chest because I could imagine Beron reacting exactly like this the next time we truly met. "What happened to you? You're different."

"So much has happened," I breathed. "I don't know where to begin."

He approached again. "I caught your scent as he took you away and tracked you here."

I raised a brow. "How did you navigate the still sea?"

His ocean eyes glittered. "I tracked your scent through the sand and found a small rowboat tethered at its edge. The dunes fell away completely where the water began. What is this place?" he asked, scanning the canopy.

"These are the Shadow Lands."

His gaze flicked to my hands. "You aren't ruined like Zarina, but you are unraveling." He held out his hand imploringly. "Let's leave while we can."

I squared my shoulders, wishing Beron were really there. Anubis missed no detail in his ardent recreation. It would be easy to believe it was him if it weren't for the swirling shadows. "I want to stay. You should go home, though. I'm sure Caelum is worried."

He gave a contrite laugh. "You can't be serious."

"I am." I held my hands out for him to see the shadows entwined around my slender fingers. "I belong here."

"No," he pleaded. "Don't let him trick you, Citali. You don't belong here or with him. You belong with the pack. With *me*."

"I belong to nothing and no one but myself, and I choose to stay," I stated firmly. "I'm sorry you came all this way for nothing."

"Sorry?" he derisively laughed. "You're sorry? Do you think that will somehow erase my feelings for you?"

"Your feelings are not my concern."

He shook his head and raked desperate hands through his glorious, dark hair. “You truly are ruined.” He turned and strode away. Within seconds, the palms swallowed him whole.

*It wasn’t really him*, I told myself.

It wasn’t him.

After he disappeared, I walked to the shore and sat on the dark sand, silently watching the still water shine like obsidian, reflecting the empty, dark sky. Anubis appeared sometime later, clad in Merik’s skin. Without speaking, he settled beside me.

“When will you stop testing my loyalty?”

He smiled. “When did you realize he was an illusion?”

“When I traced his steps to this shore and he was gone, yet no rowboat waked the water,” I claimed, unwilling to let him know I saw the shadows.

The god of the dead paused for a long moment. He realized he’d failed. He didn’t anticipate I would follow Beron. *Good…*

“You expect me to believe that your reaction to him was true?” he smoothly turned the tables.

My eyes glittered defiantly. “Do you expect me to believe you truly want to share power with me when you don’t trust me in the least?”

He looked away, his eyes transfixed on the still sea. There was nothing in it. No fish or eels or crocodiles. No life whatsoever. Anubis finally answered, “I would not mind sharing if I better knew your heart.”

I shifted and turned toward him, arranging my skirts so my legs were mostly covered. “If you have questions, ask me. There is only one way to get to know my heart, and that’s by learning me, not by spinning illusions to test me.”

“I could ask, but you could lie,” he replied.

“Then we are already equals in that respect.”

"Do you love the Wolven, Citali?" He effortlessly shifted from Merik's skin into a replica of Beron and watched for a reaction. "Does your heart belong to him?"

Of all the things this solemn god wanted to ask me, he chose to ask about my heart. Had it once belonged to Merik? Yes. Did it now long for Beron? It certainly did. But there was another love that transcended those romantic aches: the love of a mother for her son. I would not forget Reyan, and I would never forsake him for anyone.

I heaved a sigh. "I am grateful that he saved me, and he is my friend, as I've said. I'm not sure why it matters to you who I love."

He scooped dark sand into his fist and let it fall into a small pile in front of him. "It matters because I wonder if one day you might come to love me."

The god of the dead craved love?

"If one day you think you might trust me, then… maybe. But I don't believe that one can love without trust, Anubis."

I scooped a fistful of sand and made my own pile. "Besides, I am not the only one who has to earn a measure of trust."

He hummed at the thought, and together, we sat pensive on the shore.

Anubis stopped testing me at every breath. Perhaps that was the greatest trial he could imagine. Was I trustworthy? Could I prove myself to him in such a finite amount of time? He did not conjure the Sphinx or Beron again, but stayed in Merik's skin.

I asked if he would show me his true form. He hadn't allowed it yet, but when I asked, he considered my request. That was a start.

Anubis conjured a settee and as we lounged upon it, close but not touching, he told me that only hours had passed in Helios and we had plenty of time to spend together before we would sail again for my kingdom and emerge beneath a blood moon. I was both disappointed and excited that time worked differently in this place. I wanted desperately to go home, but needed time to coax Anubis into my plan…

I asked him to show me how to spin illusions.

"Why?" he asked, going rigid.

"If I am to live an eternity, I don't wish to drown my moments in perpetual boredom. Teach me something small and simple."

"Do you think that will satisfy your curiosity?"

I smiled at him and shrugged one shoulder nonchalantly. "For the moment. Ultimately, I want to be useful."

He pointed to a fallen palm. "Watch."

The shadows from his palm rushed to the trunk and gathered, forming a perfect, scaled green lizard the color of lichen. The lizard's tongue flicked out to grab a beetle scuttling across the wood – also conjured, though its iridescent pink shell shone metallic in the dim light.

I did not want to conjure a beetle or a lizard. Nor did I want to conjure a bird to fly into the shadowed sky. I raised my palm toward that same tree and surged my shadow toward it. They gathered and built a sleek, black panther. It crept down the trunk, its feline green eyes fixed on Anubis. A jackal leapt out of the jungle beyond her, startling her, startling me. She hissed and turned toward the threat. The jackal seemed to grin, baring its teeth. I transformed the panther into Zarina and Anubis let the jackal fade away.

My sister looked exactly as she had as she climbed Sol's temple to beg us for a death that I granted. I was strong enough then, I realized. Her shade-stained lips, stringy hair, and emaciated form walked toward him with that same disjointed, painful gait with which she fought for every step. I made her walk toward him.

Anubis watched her carefully before his eyes flicked to mine. There was no fear in them, only discomfort. "What is this?"

Zarina let out a keening screech to reclaim his attention, at which point I turned her into Noor. Fear shone in his eyes then. I wasn't sure if he feared me or the pure light my sister held within, bursting so that it spilled from her eyes.

The god of death reigned over spirit and shadow, but he could not master his own emotions all the time.

"Anubis, because of you, I killed my eldest sister. When we return to Helios, what is your intention regarding my younger sister and Aten?"

He stiffened. "She is no longer your Aten. You do not bow to Sol anymore."

"If you remove her title and power, she remains my sister. I will not see her harmed."

"I only mean to strip her powers. I will not harm her, and she will not die by my hand," the god of death promised.

I scooted closer to look him in the eye. He did not look frightened, but did seem taken aback. I was the panther and he was a jackal who did not know how she might react, how long her claws were, or whether she was willing to fight to the death.

*She was.*

"The Sculptor assured me of your intentions, but should those change, so will my allegiance. You say that she will not die by your hand, but you will not force mine against her, either. Is that understood?"

"Are you saying I have your allegiance now?" Merik's lips curved ever so slightly. "It seems your true loyalty lies with Noor."

"What we have is tentative and fragile, but what I saw in the remnant pool today was a future I want a hand in forging."

"Tell me exactly what he showed you…" he tempted.

"A future where nothing threatens me or my son. A future where you and I are equals with Sol and Lumos and rule the Shadow Lands together."

He scooted closer. The muscles in Merik's arm rippled as he braced it against the settee, just shy of my thigh. "And is that all he revealed?"

I swallowed, letting my lashes flutter. "No, that's not all, but that is not something I wish to discuss today. That… will take time, Anubis."

He grinned. "We have more moments ahead of us than there are grains of sand on the shore or drops of water in the seas."

"Just know that if you harm any of them or ask me to do so, you will spend an eternity regretting it," I vowed.

He could feel my shadows but could not manipulate them. He could feel my power but could not influence it. And though his power had strengthened in the Shadow Lands, he was not as powerful as he would be if he had all his essence. He tried to retrieve some of the magic he'd given me but failed. I might have taken a little more of his shade just for trying it.

"The Sculptor said I am to have half of your unique abilities," I told him as he led me to a private room to bathe.

"That must be why I cannot draw from you, but you can still take from me."

"When do I get my full share?" I asked.

"What's the rush?" he asked, his uncanny gaze sharpening.

"I do not want to go into Helios weaker than I should be," I explained confidently. "The Sculptor said this was my inheritance, a reward for standing beside you."

His countenance turned to stone. "And you require a bribe to do so?"

"I don't want to be weak when we return," I repeated. "Noor and Caelum will not lay down their powers. They will fight."

Anubis sat on the edge of the steaming bath and let his fingers graze the water. "I think you will find that they will be more than cooperative. If they should become difficult and fight, as you seem so sure of, we will still emerge victorious."

"The Sculptor revealed as much, but in the vision he gave me, I was your match."

He braced his elbows on his thighs. "What did he show you regarding Reyan?"

"My son ran along the shadowed beaches, alive and vital in this dark place. He survived, grew, and thrived."

"I know you have been told that both Sol and Lumos seek to choose him as their vessel upon earth, but when I strip Noor and Caelum of their power, there will be no further vessels."

"Why not just choose one of your own? Would that not keep the balance?"

"The Sculptor wishes for the world to return to one kingdom, one people. Sol and Lumos divided it when each claimed half. The Sculptor reviles division, and never gave the gods of illumination permission to endow a human with even a fraction of their godly power. He has asked me to right their wrong."

I sat beside him and carefully removed my sandals. "What of the Sphinx and Wolven?"

"The Sphinx is an abomination. Sol had no right to make her," he said vehemently. "But do not worry. I won't harm her until Reyan is safe and in your arms. The Wolven can be stripped of power like the Aten and Lumin. I do not have to end his life."

Sitting up, I turned to face him and he mirrored the position. "He saved me, Anubis. I know you don't like him, but he is my friend."

"I can bear your friendship until his mortal life ends," he rasped. His head swiveled toward mine and the steamy air seemed to thicken. "There is much I would bear to ensure your happiness."

Our knees brushed. He scooted closer, then raised his hand and let the backs of his fingers drift along my jaw. "It pleases me that I affect you."

He was taking another step into the trap I had lain…

I licked my lips. "What do you mean?"

"Your skin is flushing."

"The steamy water has warmed the air in here," I volleyed breezily.

He smiled. "Your immortal heart is beating faster."

I straightened my back. "It feels no different to me."

His hand ghosted down my arm, hip, and thigh, resting just above my knee where it anchored itself. His thumb grazed my inner thigh and I parted my legs just a little. It was enough. Anubis's grip tightened. I let my lips drift toward his, my gaze flickering from his mouth to his eyes.

"You feel it, Citali. Even as you deny it."

"I don't want to feel it," I whispered. "I barely know you."

His lips hovered over mine now. "That's not exactly true, though, is it? We've spent little time together, but something deep inside you recognizes me. Whether it is because we share the shadow magic, or because the Sculptor's perfect design entwines us, it does not matter. We are destined."

I pretended for a moment that he truly was Merik. It made it easier to let my lips graze his with a single, sensuous swipe. My bottom lip stuck to his, then peeled away. I'd kissed Merik more times than I could count or recall, and though Anubis used his form, he did not feel like Merik at all. Merik's kisses were frantic and passionate because they were stolen. They were strong and never soft. He and I never had the luxury of time, while Anubis believed he had nothing but.

When I pulled away, I realized that Merik was no longer the one I wanted to kiss. He and I did not fit now. Too much time had stretched between us along with the sharp chasm that death left between the dead and living, and the guilt I was sure my heart would always bear for him.

The only one my mind gravitated toward now was Beron.

I touched my lips with shaky fingers and turned away from Anubis. He graciously accepted my withdrawal. "I'll leave you to bathe," he said quietly before slowly standing, then striding away.

Casting shadows about the room, I ordered them to guard me. On a ledge lay towels, a dark robe, soaps, and sponges. I stripped off the now-grimy gray dress, took up a soap and sponge, and used the pool's stone steps to enter its gloriously hot water. I could feel the sand and sweat melt from my skin, disintegrating into the water. The pool was long and deep, and I swam down its length, then turned and swam back. I floated and stared at the obsidian ceiling and watched my reflection to make sure it did not move when I kept still.

In this House of Mirages, I never felt alone.

There was a coldness here despite the heat. It was the opposite of the House of Wolves, set in the cool mountains but holding the warmth of the wolves that inhabited it. I wondered how Holt, Red, Chase, and even Amaris were doing. I thought of Beron.

I wondered where my power began and ended. Could I only control the shadows stolen from the god of death, or could I bend all the world's shadows to my will? Gathering them in my hands, I told them they were mine. I told them never to betray me to Anubis again. And if they did, I would incinerate them all.

A tremble rippled the shady wisps.

I could not risk saying his name aloud. Not here, while the darkness watched and listened. But I thought Beron's name and pushed it to the shadows, telling them to keep my words from the dark one. I asked them to seek the Wolven out, wherever he was.

The Sculptor said no one and nothing could glean my thoughts unless I wanted them to. If it was possible from so far away, I wanted the shadows to carry a message to Beron.

Lathering my hair with soap, I scrubbed my tresses clean and floated some more. As I let myself relax, a scene entered my mind.

*The musicians were strumming and breathing life into their instruments, the melody as seductive as the dancers Father brought to entertain the Lumin and his entourage. I walked through the crowd without being noticed, dressed as one of many women brought here to serve the Aten and his entourage, the lower half of my face concealed with a dark veil. I carried drinks to men who had not asked for them, smiling and winking when they whispered that while I had anticipated their needs, they had others I could attend to…*

*The Lumin's chair sat empty. I waited for him to claim it, watching to see the man for whom Noor and I would soon battle one another.*

*Father lounged beside the empty seat, being fanned by a servant girl while yet another fed him plump, juicy grapes. After Noor, none of his seed had taken root in the wombs of his wives or mistresses. Perhaps Sol believed the three of us were enough. If he'd sired every woman he took to his rooms, Helios would teem with his children.*

*I wove a path to a drink table in the back, preparing to gather more cups, when a pair of blue eyes ensnared me. They weren't blue like Sol's sky, but fathoms of shades deeper. The color I imagined the sea I had only read about.*

*My hands stilled above the golden goblets and for a moment, the music faded away.*

*"You're no servant." The young man's voice was deep, and he was confident in his assertion. He smirked and my heart began to race. Was this the Lumin?*

*"You presume to know my station?"*

*His smirk broadened into a full grin, and a handsome one at that. A hint of dark shadow lingered on his jaw, neck, and above his lip. His clothes were fine. Upon a sharp, black tunic lay a detailed, carefully embroidered image of a wolf. The wolf howled at the full moon, emblazoned in dark thread over his heart. A dark moon…*

*"I presume to know many things," he answered haughtily. "I know that your right hand dominates your left; that you pretend to be coy when the lecherous men make their feeble attempts at tempting you into their beds, but the moment you turn away your seductive smile disintegrates; and that you have been watching the Lumin's chair even closer than I have."*

*"Is the seat reserved for you?"*

*He laughed then. "I'm not the Lumin, no."*

*"His personal guard, then," I guessed.*

*He inclined his head. "You could say that. And I stand here because I have a perspective of the entire room from this spot. The Lumin included."*

*"He's here?" I asked, glancing over my shoulder and scanning the faces I'd already dismissed.*

*"He is currently on his way back to his seat and your father."*

*My lips parted.*

*"The only thing I haven't worked out is which Atena you are… Noor, or Citali."*

*I felt like flinging the goblet of wine into his face for the smug, self-satisfied grin that deepened his dimple.*

*The seat beside Father's was occupied by a young man nearly as handsome as the arrogant guard with all his assumptions. Even in the dull light, I could tell the Lumin's eyes were a few shades lighter than his 'guard's', but their straight noses were the same. Their brows were sloped alike and even their postures were similar. This guard may have forced himself into a more casual position, but there was a rigidness to him, same as the Lumin's. The Lumin – who studied the dancers like a scribe regards his ever-emptying ink well.*

*"Your brother took quite a risk in writing to my father."*

*The guard's smirk fell. "I see I'm not the only one watching carefully…"*

*"No," I assured him. "You aren't."*

*I turned to walk away. "Wait," he called out, pushing off the wall he'd been leaning against. "Which sister are you?"*

*"Does it matter?" I asked.*

*His lips parted. He closed them again and sank back against the wall, the smirk firmly in place. "No. I suppose it doesn't."*

*I let him watch me leave and might have swayed my hips for his benefit. I was here for his brother's crown, and perhaps his kingdom. That fact alone set us at odds. It made us enemies.*

*I stopped at the seventh-floor landing, too lost in thought to continue down the corridor. Noor jogged up the steps, shocked to see me standing there. I pretended I had been waiting for her. "Where did you go?" I asked.*

*She shrugged. "I found a hidden staircase and wanted to get a closer look. Not that it worked. The dancing girls blocked my view."*

*I narrowed my eyes, sensing that she was either lying or withholding the entire truth, much like I was. "That's too bad."*

*She claimed she hadn't seen the Lumin, yet her skin was flushed, a delicate sheen of sweat beaded on her upper lip and forehead, and she breathed as if her heart wanted to leap from between her lungs. Had she been sneaking around as I had and gotten caught? Before this task was set in front of us, I would have cringed to think how Father's wrath might fall over each of us for such insolence, but now? Now, Father needed us. And that was a measure of power in and of itself. It was protection, yes, but it could also be a means of manipulation if necessary.*

*"Did you see him?" she asked, her breathing leveling.*

*I quirked a brow, afraid to let her think for a second she had the upper hand on me. Besides, I didn't need to lie. I* had *seen the Lumin. "Of course I did."*

*"What did he look like?"*

*"You'll find out soon enough," I told her, then strode to my rooms and left her behind, where she belonged.*

*That night, I dreamt of the blue sea, of a young man with dark hair, pale skin, and a smirk that made my heart race as he stood on a white sand beach under a glittering black sky. I dreamt he strode past me and took the Lumin's seat, and the cat and mouse game we would soon play involved him. Then the dream shifted to that of a dark wolf howling at an even darker moon. I dreamt he was my prey and held the crown of moonlight above my head, using his height to his advantage and keeping what I wanted most just out of reach.*

"Citali?" Beron's muffled voice called.

I stood up in the pool, my eyes darting in every direction to find the illusion of Beron, but he wasn't there.

"Citali?" It came again, this time louder. "I swear I… I saw something," he mumbled.

"What did you see?" *Red.* Red was with him.

His voice sounded perplexed. "I saw a vision of the night we met."

"Were you thinking about her, Beron?"

"No, I wasn't. I was just walking down the southern path and the vision hit me, but it wasn't just my imagination; it was *her*. I could feel her. I could smell her scent," he explained adamantly.

The southern path was exceptionally shaded. Did the shadows really take my thoughts to him? Did they show him what I was thinking? Were Beron and I still connected through the bite and pack, even though our mate bond had been severed?

I could not cry out to him because I knew Anubis would hear, and there was nothing Beron could do to help me while I was tethered in this place. I needed Anubis to believe I was on his side and would help him when we returned to Helios.

On the other hand, I needed Beron to know I was okay and wasn't decaying like Zarina. I wanted him to have faith that I would come and fight on their side when I returned.

I gathered my shadows and sent out a new thought, this time a memory of all that Anubis was capable of, information crucial to Beron and his pack, Noor and Caelum, Sol and Lumos.

I showed Beron how we traveled to the land of shadows, but warned him not to come. I showed him the pool and the Sculptor and what he had revealed. I revealed the plan I had begun – even the parts he would not want to see – and the parts I hoped would come in the near future. I finished by telling him that whatever he saw of me and Anubis – it wasn't real. I didn't feel anything beyond pure hatred toward the god of the dead.

Walking from the pool, I slipped the dark robe onto my shoulders and tied it at my waist, then dried my hair with a soft, plush towel. I smoothed lotion onto my skin and sat in the humid air, hoping Beron had heard my most fervent thoughts. Our communications were seemingly random and sporadic. I'd sent the last thoughts to him not even expecting he'd see them, but he had. I needed him to see and know these things. I needed it to reach him.

He had to be prepared. They all did.

I just wished I knew more of Anubis's plan so I could tell them exactly *how* they should prepare.

I walked from the room, determined to learn as much as I could in the scant time we had left. Was Anubis crafting this timeline, or did it belong to the Sculptor?

As patient as the god of the dead claimed to be, his rush to return to Helios seemed out of place…unless the Sculptor carved the urgency within Anubis's gut. The Sculptor said I would burn away Anubis's shadow and claim it as my own, but I wasn't sure how to ignite the flame everyone else could see and sense, the flame cloaked in shadow…

# 26

When I returned to my rooms, I found a delicate, golden dress laying on my bed and a tray of the same food waiting for me on a nearby table, along with a cool glass of water. The bread was hardened and difficult to chew, but I made do. I was sick of fish and the cheese was stale, but not yet molded. The god of the dead knew little about the needs of the living, it seemed.

I ate what I could, then slipped the supple, gold silk over my head. It fell over my skin like a whisper. Why had he chosen gold when everything in this land was its opposite?

Whispering my vision into my shadows, I altered the garment, turning the silk to small obsidian scales, like those of the dragons of lore.

He could sense my magic and presence, so there would be no sneaking around to snoop in this House. The House of the Moon was easy to case, much to Beron's and Holt's chagrin. But there was no crown of moonlight to touch and steal here. If Anubis wore a crown, it would be made of shade and just as intangible as Caelum's turned out to be.

I walked freely, loudly, giving myself a tour of the pyramid. Anubis drew near to me almost immediately. "Do you find my House to your liking, Citali?" he breezily asked as he approached from the opposite side of a long hallway. His gaze slid down my form, snagging on each scale like a fingernail might. He smiled appreciatively.

"It's empty," I simply told him, keeping my chin high.

"Indeed. What to fill it with, though?"

"Anything would be better than nothing." I strolled to another door and pushed it open to reveal another empty room.

"Anything?" He gestured into the space and conjured a dragon with scales to match mine. She reared back and roared, but before she could singe us with her flame, I gently closed the door, keeping my face passive bordering upon bored. He faked a sigh. "You're difficult to impress."

"To impress me would mean to stop playing at these silly conjurings and teach me how to use the shade we share." He hesitated, but considered my words. "Unless you're frightened of me." I let my lips slip into a slight smile, then quirked a brow in challenge.

"You conjured a perfect version of Noor. I bet even Caelum would have believed she was real."

"He would've seen through it immediately. His heart knows my sister."

Anubis grinned like a jackal. "Very well. Let's see just how powerful you are."

We walked outside, through the jungle's wide path to the shore where we'd arrived. Anubis's ship lay still with its prow upon the sand. He gestured to the sea. "We both know you could create a monster to rise from its depths, but can you control the sea itself?"

The volume of water before me waited with bated breath. Perhaps it had been holding it the entire time we'd been there and was desperate for fresh, life-giving air. I could feel its length and width and depth, aware of the land that held it like milk in a bowl.

The ocean was a salty siren, this sea a lumbering monster. Something ancient lay within its dark water.

"Start small. Make waves," he suggested.

Make waves. I remembered the water in the primordial pool, how it thrashed and churned and the choppy crests peaked and fell over its silvery surface. I told my shadows to turn the dark water to pewter and to make the entire sea churn, angry as my heart.

I tasted pure, raw energy, as blazing as the sun and vital as the moon. As primal as the remnant caught in the pool in the House of Mirages.

My power slid over the water's surface, brightening it so that it matched the remnant kept within the House of Mirages. Then the sea itself groaned. The first broad ripples formed, spreading from center to edge. The ripples grew into waves and soon they lapped the sand at our feet. They grew, each building with the indignant, insatiable fury trapped within my heart until they were taller than the palms around us.

Something within me was more insatiable than the wolf still lumbering beneath my skin, and she wanted to devour the one who stood in the way of the life she craved.

Anubis carefully studied what I had done. He turned, wariness creasing his brow. "Well done."

In an instant, I let it all fall away. The waves stopped crashing. The ripples stopped spreading. The silver leached from the water and in mere seconds, the sea was just as it had been before I used my power to alter it.

"You use your power differently than I do," he admitted.

I turned to him, my brow creased. "How so?"

"I alter what everyone else sees. I work to fool minds. You alter substance itself. You work to change matter."

*So he truly does spin illusions…*

Anubis pointed to the sky. "I bet you could erase the shade I've spread over the Shadow Lands."

I looked to the sky, sure that I could.

"Don't," he sharply warned.

No, he wouldn't appreciate that, would he? His kingdom would then be subject to Sol and Lumos's light. "When you reclaim your place among the gods, will you not have to rejoin them and uncloak this land?" I asked.

He shook his head. "The gods of illumination do not know of this place. They cannot see it. It will always be ours – a secret sanctuary for the remnant. The Sculptor tasked me with its safekeeping."

"When are we returning?" I asked as my power coaxed a pleasant breeze from the water. It slid through the palms, at first tickling their leaves so they sounded like wind chimes, then strengthening so they rattled like the tails of deadly snakes.

"Soon."

"What will happen when we return?" I pressed.

"Why do you question everything?"

"It is my nature," I said honestly. "Would you respect me if I didn't?"

He pondered that. "I suppose not."

"I just want to know what we will face so I can be prepared. My power is new."

He let a finger drift down my forearm and hook onto my pinky. "You are afraid, but I have seen the future. The Sculptor showed me our victory. Do not fear anything, Citali."

I shook my head. "You may have seen it, but the Sculptor only showed me a glimpse far into the future; he did not show me the path that leads to it."

"Just know that what he revealed is a future you will not have if we do not return to Helios," he quipped.

I tightened my pinky on his. "Show me."

"Kiss me," he challenged.

"You'd barter knowledge of the future for a simple kiss?" I asked. My skin crawled with the look he gave me.

"Nothing about you is simple, Citali."

"I thought you said we had plenty of time for… this."

"It's only a kiss," he said nonchalantly. "But if you are too frightened, it can wait."

*Manipulator.* I had used that trick of a dare a thousand times and gotten my way just as often. It always worked. It would work now. But he was right, it *was* only a kiss.

I took Merik's face in my hands and pushed onto the tips of my toes to reach him, placing a kiss on his lips. His hands gripped my wrists and held them in place. "Close your eyes. Do not open them until I say."

When my lids drifted closed, his lips caught mine. At first, they felt like Merik's and then, the feel of them changed. They were cool and tasted of shadow. I was kissing Anubis now, without the illusion of flesh between us. I had to see him.

My lids parted and his illusion returned before I could see him. "Why do you hide from me?"

"I'm afraid I will frighten you."

"You? Frighten me?" I teased. As I took my hands away, his grip loosened, but didn't leave my skin.

He was quiet for a moment, emotions crashing over Merik's face as tumultuously as the sea upon the shore.

"I have seen Sol and Lumos. I have faced the Sphinx herself and run with wolves. Your face could never frighten me."

"But my illusions have. I frightened you in the forest when I sent the illusion of your father and child to you."

"Why did you try to kill me? You've said time and time again that I was made for you. If that was so, then why did you try to trick me into leaping to my death?"

He smiled. "Death is not powerful enough to separate us. If your body of sand disintegrated, your spirit would still be with me."

"But *I* wouldn't be me," I argued. "You wouldn't be able to hold me as you do now. I wouldn't smell or feel the same."

Anubis's hands left my wrists and slid up my arms. "The shadow power we have is comprised of the essence of the spirits of the dead. Your temperature would change. You wouldn't be as warm, but to me, you would not feel different than you do with flesh."

"Why would you be so cruel as to use my father and son against me?" I rasped, watching him carefully.

He let his hands fall away. "It was a moment of weakness."

"Weakness?"

"Jealousy," he clarified.

"You were jealous?" I repeated.

"With the wolves, you were happy. I didn't think you'd want to leave them."

"They are my friends. They were trying to keep me safe," I said softly, wondering what was going through his mind. If he thought killing me and entrapping my spirit in this place was a perfectly acceptable alternative to me running with the Wolven, what was the least he might kill me for?

A feeling of dread filled my stomach. Was that his plan all along? Get me here and kill me so I couldn't stand against him when he challenged my allies – Sol and Lumos, Noor and Caelum, the Sphinx and Beron, the pack?

Immortal lives could still be severed.

"You said you would show me… for a kiss," I reminded him. "I kissed you. Now, I'd like to see what you have seen."

The creator of lies and spinner of illusions fulfilled his portion of the bargain we'd struck.

*We stood at the prow of his ship, sailing over the sand. Dark sails snapped overhead. The night air was arid and hot. Lumos's cool light did not light the dunes, and his brightness had been dampened by the great shadow that obscured his face. As we approached Helios, blood washed over the god of the moon, casting a red-orange hue over the earth. The river itself looked like blood. It reminded me of the one that poured from my stomach when Zarina left me for dead.*

*A wolf howled in the distance – Red's howl – followed by more howls echoing over the sand. Holt's. Amaris's. Chase's… The pack had spotted us. Beron howled his acknowledgement. I could feel his emotions, his determination, and the adrenaline pulsing in his veins.*

*Helios was flooded with people. They had armed themselves and gathered to fight from the riverbanks to the streets, with the bulk surrounding the temple of Sol. We sailed higher, Anubis studying the gathered force that was prepared to defend their homes, their way of life, their culture, and their Aten.*

*"Guard the flame!" someone shouted.*

*A great roar answered. "Guard the flame!"*

*Noor, standing atop her mother's temple, called forth Sol. The goddess appeared on the horizon, blazing and angry, burning hotter than I'd ever felt her. Even from this distance, it felt like she was drawn near for a departure. She raced over the sky toward Lumos, still and soaked in blood.*

*Caelum stood with Noor, frost collecting in his palms. The only warrior missing was the Sphinx…*

*A great flock of birds poured from around Sol, flapping angrily toward us. Anubis's ship hovered over the kingdom. As the flock drew near, it quickly became apparent that these weren't birds at all, but Sphinxes. Thousands of them. All wore the Lioness's face. All were clad with her claws and teeth.*

*Anubis shouted to Noor, "Surrender, Aten, and none of your people need suffer."*

*She squared her shoulders and pure light radiated from her skin. Her eyes were molten gold. "Never."*

*"Surrender, or Citali dies."*

*He threw me over the ship's rail, clasping my forearm as I clawed at his. "Pull me up!" I screamed.*

*Noor shouted my name.*

*"No!" I told her. "Don't give in to him."*

*Shadows writhed around him. He tore mine away and with it, I felt my immortality tear from my chest. "What did you do?" I gasped.*

*"You are disloyal." He grinned down at me. "Did the Sculptor tell you to deceive me, or was that your doing?"*

*"I am not disloyal," I gritted, grabbing his hand with my free one, trying to pull myself up and over the rail. My palms slickened and sweat beaded on my forehead. "The Sculptor did not show me this! He showed me a peaceful way that you can settle things with Sol and Lumos, reclaiming your place among them. That is how my son is kept safe – with a peaceful resolution."*

*"You cannot honestly believe that peace can come after so much strife," Anubis said derisively.*

*"I do!" I screamed. "Lumos and Sol divided their kingdoms and the sky to avoid one another, but look at them. They have found peace again, Anubis. You don't have to cause a war to rejoin them. The Sculptor said –"*

*Through the crowd of armed Helioans and Luminans alike, cut a voice. "Citali!"*

*Beron's voice.*

*I looked down to find the Wolven running beneath me as if he might catch me when Anubis let me fall. As if he would save me again if he could.*

*"You love him," the god of death hollowly said. "I will kill him if you do not help me. I'll kill them all."*

*A wave of screams flowed from the river as Anubis called on his shadows. Bones crunched, bodies slumped, and voices went silent. "Stop! This is madness, Anubis. These are my people."*

*"And so they shall be again, only changed."*

*"It's not the same!" I screamed. I peeled at his fingers, trying to get free. "If they die, then so will I, and I will hate you in death as I do in life," I told him.*

*"So be it." His grip loosened. "I will not negotiate a peace for you now that I know where your heart and allegiances truly lie." His fingers fell away and I plunged to the ground.*

*My hair whipped around me as I plummeted. Beron howled, whimpered, then collapsed on the soil. I knew he was dead because I couldn't feel him anymore. A tear fell from my eye just before I struck the earth. For one fleeting moment of consciousness, I stared at Anubis, victoriously sailing above us all.*

*The last thing I thought about was how my son was no longer safe and never would be again.*

Anubis carefully watched me as a tear slid down my face. "That is what the Sculptor revealed to you?"

"That was my warning to you," he answered. "If you deceive me... if you betray me, I will end you along with everything you love. I will lord over your spirits for an eternity and keep you from seeing them in the Shadow Lands."

"Why are you threatening me now? Until this moment, I thought you might be different from what I grew up believing you were."

He bristled. "And now?"

"Now I question what the Sculptor showed me, and I question the Sculptor himself." I went still. My lips peeled apart and my stomach writhed. "The Sculptor wasn't even real, was he? He was just another mirage. I am not immortal. There was no remnant, and no House. None of it was real."

His stood up straighter. "I did not deceive you."

I shook my head again. "I don't believe you."

"That isn't fair," he complained.

"Fair? You wish to tell me what is and isn't fair?" I angrily asked. "You've summed me up as disloyal without cause – just because you're paranoid and jealous that I have the capacity to love? Is that it? Would you be jealous of my child because I doted on him, teaching him and spending my time raising him into a man? If so, you're right. I *will* be disloyal. I will be disloyal to anyone and anything who threatens him!"

The Sculptor said that fear, not love, brought ruin. I would prove it was both. I loved fiercely enough to ruin the world for my son.

"Do you see?" I shouted, flinging an arm out.

"See what?" he gritted.

"Do you see how truly loyal I am to those I love? Do you know that the Sculptor showed me a vision that in the future, a living version of me loved you as well?"

His lashes fluttered and for the first time, Anubis looked flustered. *Good.*

I left him on the shore to consider his plan.

Then I conveyed the vision to Beron through the shadows, but assured him that I would not die if I fell. I was immortal now. However, I didn't tell him that in the seconds before I fell, Anubis would tear my immortality away like a thief snatches a pendant.

*Do not chase after or call for me. If he threatens me, all of you must pretend you do not care. That I am expendable. If he drops me, I will not be hurt. The vision was his way of warning me about standing against him.*

*The Sculptor let me drink of the water from creation. I am changed.*

*I have an immortal heart now.*

I wondered what the Wolven would think of me. He'd given a piece of himself to save me, with Lumos's permission. And the life he'd spared would echo throughout eternity if I could only defeat one foe.

A formidable one, at that.

But no one was unbreakable.

In my rooms, I sealed the doors with my shadows, slipped back into my silken robe, and slept. I would need rest to weather the coming storm.

*Beron fumed in front of me. He'd finally caught up with me, as I knew he would. It had taken him quite a long time to find me this time. "What are you looking so hard for?"*

*I could have said the crown of moonlight, but that would be a lie. I was looking for my freedom, and my son's. I pressed my lips into a thin line.*

*"Why won't you answer me?"*

*I remained still just to drive him insane.*

*He blew out a tense breath, then braced a hand on the wall by my head. "Why do you have to be so difficult? He's made his choice. Do you think he'll change his mind if you keep this up?"*

*"I don't want him," I told Beron, my voice breaking.*

*A tear dropped from my eye. The Wolven tracked its path. "Then what do you want?"*

*I wiped my cheek and shook my head.*

*"I can't help if you won't tell me what's going on," he pleaded.*

*But I couldn't tell him. I couldn't drag him into my troubles. I knew what that would mean for him. I watched the light bleed from Merik's eyes and knew that nothing was well in the world as long as Father breathed.*

*"I'll make you a promise," Beron said, pushing off the wall and giving me room to breathe.*

*"What's that?"*

*"I will search for your secret as fervently as you search this House."*

*I swallowed thickly, hoping he broke that promise. It could only lead to heartache or death, and I didn't wish either on the Wolven.*

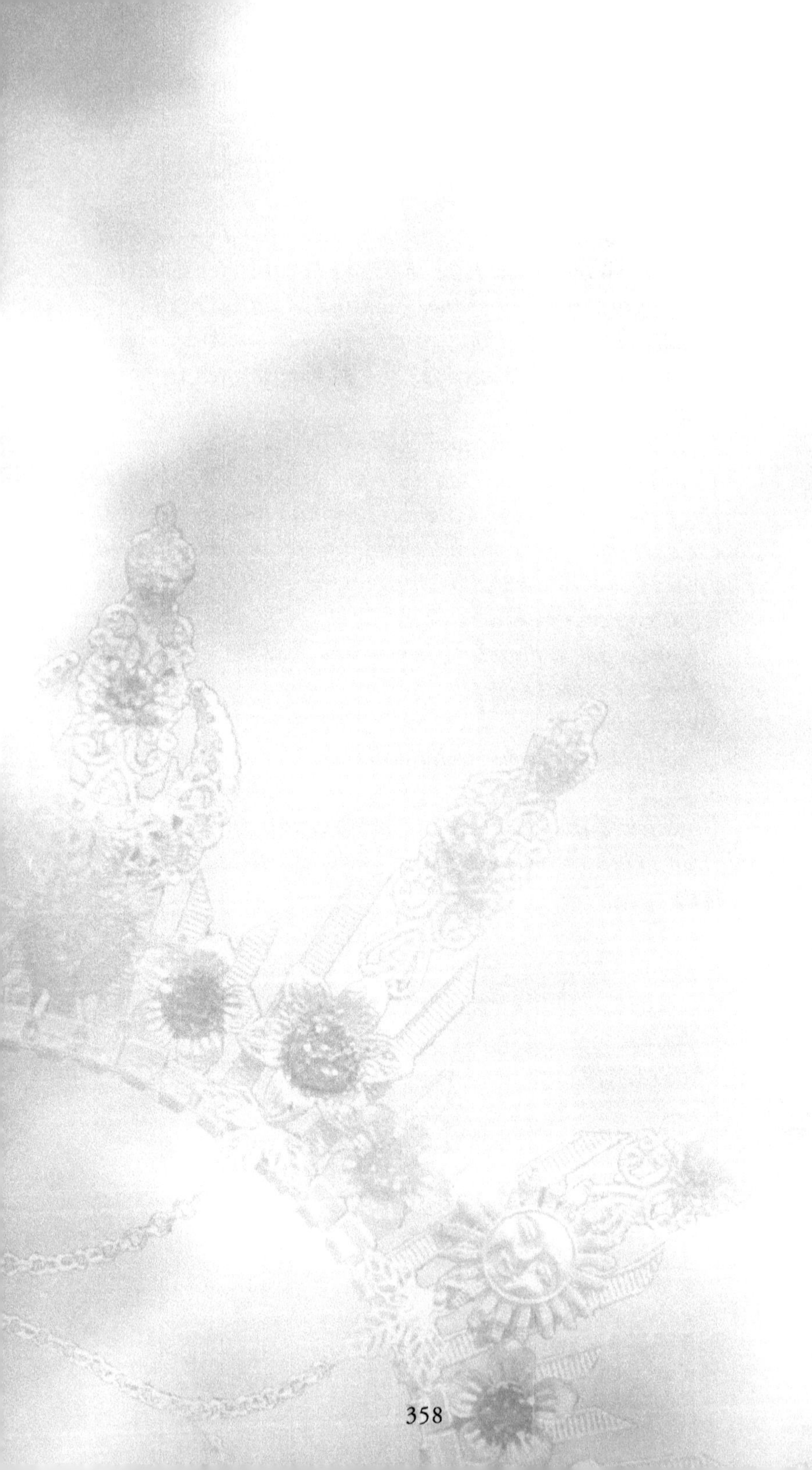

# 27

When I woke, the scaled dress still lay on the floor where I'd stepped out of it the night before. I used my power to alter it. The dark pleated skirt folded at my side so that one of my legs peeked out, allowing for better mobility. I laced up a simple black corset and tied it tightly at the small of my back. Then I draped a sheer panel trimmed in gold over my shoulder and fastened it at my waist to keep it tight. Lastly, I laced golden sandals onto my feet and emerged in search of a better breakfast than smoked fish, molded bread, and stale cheese. Anubis found me in the palms, using my shadows to collect coconuts.

He ticked his head to the side, perplexed. "Are you hungry?"

"The food has spoiled."

"The fish should last for weeks," he argued.

"I cannot eat fish at every meal. I need something more."

"I didn't expect you to speak to me," he admitted, staring at the ground. The god of the dead felt shame.

"I shouldn't." I carried two coconuts out of the jungle and back toward the pyramid, where my shadows formed an obsidian bench and I sat upon it. They cracked open one of the coconuts and I drank its clear water, quickly learning the coconut wasn't ripe. I used my shadows to ripen it, then took the obsidian knife from the sheath on my thigh and carved pieces away, chewing them slowly.

"I would very much like to have my blade back," he said tightly.

"We've already discussed this, Anubis. The knife is mine. I bought it with blood and agony. What's so important about it that you won't let it go?"

He watched me carve another piece of coconut from the husk. My shadows encircled my hand, protecting it and the blade. "The relic holds my essence."

"Held," I corrected. "It is devoid now, but you already know that."

"Someone made it for me a very long time ago," he finally relented.

"Who?" I pressed.

"It doesn't matter."

"It matters to you," I hinted. "Who was she?"

His eyes ignited. He pressed Merik's lips into a thin line.

"I won't get upset. Tell me about her."

"It was a very long time ago," he began. "And who she was doesn't matter, because she is gone."

"Who has her spirit? Sol or Lumos?"

"She burns for Sol now," he rasped.

"When you reclaim your place, will you reclaim her spirit into your care and invite her into the Shadow Lands?"

He was quiet for a long moment. "I'm not sure she will remember me. If she does, I'm not sure she won't hate me."

I softened my voice. "Sol's fire does not burn and it is not torment. It's glorious. I've felt it, only for a moment, but it was peaceful, Anubis. And besides that, I believe you would be hard to forget."

"Perhaps she'll hate me all the more for taking her away from the flame," he mused insecurely.

"She won't."

He thanked me quietly, staring like I was some strange thing he'd never seen before.

"What did she look like?" I asked.

Sand swept up from the earth and spun into a funnel. From it walked a beautiful young woman. She had dark hair, skin, and eyes. Honestly, she looked like me. She smiled as she ran toward someone, something folded into a swath of pale cloth in her hands. "Anubis!" she called out, waving a hand in the air. "Anubis, I made you something."

The girl disappeared, grains of sand falling to the ground again.

"Her mother worked obsidian into jewelry, while Elara worked it into weaponry. She brought her first knife to me. I commissioned many pieces from them both over the span of a few years. Elara and I became friends, but… I thought that one day she might be more. She hinted at it a time or two, only to have her mother sweep her away. She knew what I was and what a life with me would require. I found her one day, floating in the sea. They say she'd drowned, but she feared water. She would barely wade into the sea far enough for the waves to ebb against her ankles…" His voice trailed off, then a fierce glint entered his eyes. "I found the one who did it and I made him suffer – in this life and the next. If Sol and Lumos hadn't entrapped me, I would be making him suffer still. Perhaps one day I will get the opportunity to continue where I left off."

I swallowed, wondering how the god of the dead defined suffering. I looked to the House of Mirages. "Is that why you made your home out of obsidian?"

He inclined his head. "It is."

"You loved her."

His brows drew in.

"You cared for her, at least. The obsidian means a lot to you."

"It does." He glanced again at the blade.

I carved piece after piece of delicious, sweet coconut and let him watch the obsidian slide into the fruit's supple flesh, remembering how it had done the same to mine.

"Do I remind you of her? She and I look a little alike," I noted.

He nodded once. "Your hair is the same, long and straight. It shines the same way in Sol's light and beneath Lumos's face. Your eye color is also similar, though hers were filled with innocence and trust."

I huffed a laugh. "What would you say mine are filled with?"

"When I first met you, I would have said shadowfire, as others have. It's certainly there, but sometimes, they're filled with shards of glass. Perhaps even obsidian. At any moment, you look as though you would slice anyone who crosses you and laugh as they bled."

My brows rose a little. "I thought you might say they were filled with shade."

He shook his head. "Nothing as weak as that."

Weak? The power that lay in shadow was indescribable, unfathomable, infinite. It was hardly weak. My blade dug at the brown husk and came away empty. I'd eaten all the fruit away.

"You have another there, if you're still hungry," he said, nodding to the second coconut.

"I'm going to save it for the ship."

"I'm sorry I didn't bring what you needed. It's been some time since I knew what was necessary for daily life."

I shrugged. "I'm not even sure I need to eat now that I drank of the remnant."

"It's not required, but it can still be enjoyed."

"Can an immortal body feel pain?"

He nodded. "Yes, but it is merely a dull ache. Besides that, you will heal and recover quickly."

"I'll definitely feel it when you strip my immortality away and throw me overboard," I scoffed.

Anubis motioned to the bench and I moved over so he could sit next to me. He braced his elbows on his thighs. "I do not have the power to take away your immortality."

"That was just for show, then?"

"If any god could do that, Sol and Lumos would have taken mine and ended my life before merely sealing me away."

"You could seal me away," I suggested.

Anubis's head swiveled toward me. "I hope that won't be necessary."

I nodded in agreement. "I hope not, either. I hate being left alone." Using my shadows to conceal the true obsidian blade now tucked into its sheath on my leg, I quickly conjured one to take its place, holding it out to him in my palm. "Here."

Anubis sat up, looked at the blade, then back at me. "Are you sure?"

"I am. For you, it evokes a happy memory. Mine is not so pleasant as yours."

He took the false dagger, then placed it on his finger and balanced it there, seeing that its weight was perfectly distributed. "Thank you, Citali."

I nodded once.

"It is time for us to set sail for Helios."

I blew out a frustrated breath. "Why now? Why not wait? Lumos called for the death of one of his wolves beneath a shadowed moon. Everyone will be expecting us if we go now."

He gave a tight smile. "Then it is best not to keep them waiting."

"You didn't answer my question," I reminded, not letting him off the hook for a second.

Anubis cut his eyes to me. “Because our power is greatest beneath a shaded moon.”

“When Sol comes with her light, won’t it negate the added power?”

He stood and began walking the broad path wending toward the shore. “Sol will arrive too late,” he replied airily.

“What you showed me was not a vision of the future. Not a true one, anyway,” I asserted confidently as we walked together.

“Why would you say that?”

“My sister would never negotiate the kingdom in exchange for my life. I tried to take hers several times. Noor hates me.”

“She stood with you the other day when Zarina arrived,” he pointed out.

“The trust between us is…” I pretended to search for the right words, “fragile and tentative. Given our upbringing and past, we had no solid foundation upon which to build it. It’s as unsteady as shifting sand.”

His lips tugged upward. “The same could be said of the trust between us.”

He wasn’t wrong. It took years to form a true, unbreakable bond with someone, but sometimes duress and circumstance sped up the process. While you couldn’t test the dynamic formed over great expanses of time, you could test its strength under sudden, acute pressure and see if it frayed, broke, or held strong.

“What about the Lumin? How does he feel about you?”

I lifted one shoulder nonchalantly. “Very much like Noor, I’m afraid. Father pitted us against each other to win Caelum’s favor and steal the crown of moonlight. Caelum does not trust me, and he does not value me as he does my sister.”

“I knew what your father did, but hearing it from you sounds much harsher. What about the Wolven?”

“He and I fought at every opportunity in Lumina. Still, we can somehow call one another friend.”

"Friends care for one another," he led with a calculating gleam in his eyes.

"Beron would not sacrifice for me. To Beron, I'm no more than a few sweet memories sprinkled between bitter ones."

He grinned. "It sounds like you're trying to dissuade me from tossing you overboard."

"I would appreciate it if you didn't. I don't like heights or dangling from flying ships, or falling, or being hurt because you don't wish to dock and fight face-to-face, hand-to-hand," I said haughtily.

Anubis bristled. "You think I fear hand-to-hand combat?"

I shrugged and bit the inside corner of my lip. "Could you win a fight without using your power?"

"My power is part of me, as yours is part of you. Anyone who stands against us knows who and what they are up against." As we reached the shore and the waiting ship, a grin slid over his lips. "Let us change the future… beginning now." He extended a hand. Without hesitating, I slid my palm into his, clutching the remaining coconut to my chest. We walked to the dead sea and he swept my feet off the sand and carried me to the ship, then climbed aboard after me.

Moments later, the dark sails snapped and dragged us away from shore, back across the still sea. I watched it from the rail, wondering if the creator of lies had lied when he said he wanted to change the future, or if he was still planning to follow through with throwing me over the side of the very rail I clutched.

He claimed the vision he gave me was a warning, but there was truth in its depths. Perhaps that was my gift: sensing truth amidst the lies.

Anubis moved patiently about the deck seeing that everything was in place before joining me. "I prefer the sea you created," he admitted.

"Why?"

"Because it was alive."

"I thought you preferred the dead," I teased, then straightened my back. "Can you sense when someone is about to die?"

He shook his head. "No. The will of a spirit is unpredictable. Even if the flesh is ill and death is expected, the spirit only concedes when it is ready. Not a second before."

We steadily sailed over the stagnant sea as if a river pulled us along with it and we weren't soaring at all. Conflicting thoughts swirled through my mind. For a moment, I'd doubted my immortality and the Sculptor, but that was Anubis's doing. I pricked the tip of my finger with the true obsidian blade, which was still invisible in its sheath on my thigh, until I was sure it bled. It did not hurt, and it only bled for a second before the skin knitted back together before my eyes.

In addition to my slow, immortal heartbeat, I felt the shadows beneath the ship and knew that we sailed not upon the wind, but upon shade and power itself. Anubis was quiet, pensive as he stood by my side. The lack of conversation allowed me time to think.

I thought of Reyan and sent a thought to Beron. *We are sailing toward Helios. Make ready and remember what I said. I am expendable. You are not.*

His response was immediate. *You will never be expendable to me,* he thought in return.

*He must believe I am. You must make him believe it or he will harm me, Beron. He will use me to manipulate and kill you all.*

The Wolven sent a final thought. *Share a memory with me. Something you've never shared with anyone. I miss you.*

My sluggish heart sped, and I pushed a precious memory toward him.

*Four guardsmen escorted me from the House of the Sun. They formed a square around me, prongs setting a diamond. We took several roads and alleys toward the river and I felt every bit a tributary. The current tugged my feet quicker, eddying around us until I was nearly jogging to reach him.*

*A smile touched my lips when I saw the humble house in which Merik had been born and raised. Padren would not be home. He would be working in fields of wheat and barley, sweating in the midday sun. I knocked on the heavy wooden door and waited.*

*Malia wasn't expecting me. Would she be shocked or disappointed that I'd been allowed a visit?*

*The door cracked open and a kind smile graced her face. "Citali!" she greeted. Her eyes darted to my squadron of Helioan guards. "Please come inside. I'll draw all of you some fresh water. I just made honey cakes."*

*My guards perked up at the sound of that. They even left their spears just inside the door, at Malia's kind plea. "I don't want Reyan to be frightened," she explained. She cupped my elbow. "He's napping, but he has slept long enough. Would you like to wake him?"*

*My heart caved in. "I would love to."*

*She gestured to a darkened room. I slipped inside while Malia distracted the guards with her delicious honey cakes, telling them how Padren kept a hive in the back and endured many a stinger just so she could have fresh honey.*

*Reyan lay in a bed, looking incredibly small beside the pillows placed on either side to keep him from rolling out, though it looked like he hadn't moved. I gently sat next to him and watched his gentle, peaceful breaths. I wished I could be the one to tuck him in for his naps and bedtime, and the one to wake him with sweet cakes each morning.*

*No one would understand how much I envied Malia's simple life. Riches could buy many things, but most of those things didn't matter. Titles were only as good as the power they afforded.*

*I stroked Reyan's soft hair. It still held the curl he was born with. He stirred and stretched, yawning and blinking his eyes. They caught on me and he held his breath.*

*I smiled, hoping he wasn't afraid.*

*"Cit-li?" Though his tiny voice was sleepy, his eyes sparked. He sat up and wrapped his arms around me.*

*I hugged him to my chest, feeling my hardened heart begin to melt.*

Beron sent a memory to me as well.

*I left Father's grave and strode down the street. I stopped by any time I was near the graveyard, even if only for a moment. Tonight was no exception. Lumos was nearer to the earth than I'd ever seen him, so broad the rooftops carved away my view of the moon.*

*It had been a difficult day filled with difficult people. Caelum took up our father's business when he died, weaving and mending fishing nets. When I was old enough to work them, he taught me how to do the same. Some fishermen were easier to please than others. Today, one told us we would never be half as gifted as our father had been. He wasn't wrong, but it hurt to hear it. We were trying. Mother was, too. She worked long days and hurried home to what work awaited us there.*

*There was never a day that we could relax, and that was what I longed for the most. A change in our stars and circumstances. Father was up there somewhere, glittering among our ancestors, looking down upon us. I wondered if he was proud or disappointed at the lives we were living and the hopes that seemed hopeless on days like this.*

*I wished he could teach us how to better weave the nets.*

*Suddenly, a strange warmth erupted in my chest and spread until my skin felt hot and too tight. I stopped in the middle of an alley, wondering if my heart was going to burst and how my brother and mother would manage to scrape enough money together to lay me in the soil beside Father.*

*I began to sweat and pant as a sharp pain cut through my muscles. My knees buckled and a fierce feeling of protectiveness and clarity formed in my mind. One moment, I was sure I was dying. The next, I felt more alive than I ever had. With the intense rush of pain gone, my instincts ripened. I ran through the city transformed and came to my brother, who was levitating into the sky, his skin glowing to match Lumos, who drew him upward.*

*That night, we left our half-woven nets behind. Mother sent word to her employers that she was resigning from her position, effective immediately. And the three of us walked to the House of the Moon where Caelum announced he was the newly chosen Lumin and I was his Wolven.*

*Because Lumos saw our hearts and our struggles, our stars and circumstances changed.*

*So did we.*

I thought to Beron, through my shadows… *Why can we share memories when you can only share thoughts – words – with the rest of your pack?*

He replied several moments later. *I don't know, but I'm glad for it. It's a comfort and a tool we may soon need.*

*It's a weapon,* I agreed.

*Whatever happens, Citali. I need you to know something…*

He shared another memory. This one, from his perspective, was of me with Caelum. The Lumin and I were in the Dusk Lands, walking alongside the river. Beron, always watchful, remained near his Lumin, though I had no idea. Caelum told me of the Luminan agriculture, of creatures that thrived in darkness. I remembered questioning him about many things, trying to feign interest in his kingdom, in him. Perhaps he sensed even then that I was lying.

*Citali glanced over her shoulder, directly where I'd stood only a second ago, scanning to see what she had sensed. The Atena was perceptive. Noor had never indicated if she knew I guarded him, even in their presence. I ducked behind a thick tuft of tall grass and blended with the surroundings, the grass grazing my skin, then cutting it and causing it to itch. I wanted to stand, but she stood and watched.*

*"What is it?" Caelum asked, glancing around as if he was unaware.*

She knows you're close, *he said into my mind.* Stay farther back. She's not a threat.

*I snorted. She was the greatest threat that had arrived from Helios, even if he had no idea.*

*Caelum took her hand and urged her to continue the walk. She hesitated, but only for a moment. Even though I gave them more space, she knew I followed.*

*My brother favored Noor. My mother did as well. I favored Citali. I couldn't for the life of me figure out how Caelum could ever choose Noor over her sister, but I was damn glad.*

I showed no emotion, as Anubis was still near, but I fought not to laugh and cry at the same time.

And then, Beron sent another thought: *I'm still damn glad, Citali.*

*Me too,* I answered.

# 28

I was standing at the prow when the still, dark waters evaporated into a sea of dunes and we entered the sand. I used my shadows to crest each hill with piles of bones, arming even the sand itself. Anubis noticed. "Is this your doing?"

"When our people depart this world, Sol burns away what is acceptable and takes it and their spirit into her fire. What is left behind is returned to the sand," I replied innocently.

"I didn't notice piles of bones on our journey out of Helios," he retorted shrewdly.

"Were you looking?" I asked. "Truly?"

He shook his head. "No, I was only looking at you."

"Then I apologize for the distraction," I told him.

"It was worth it," he said boldly.

The further we sailed, the more apprehension forked like lightning through my body. Melding with fear, the two forged together in my gut and solidified into a blinding amber metal.

I knew I was supposed to don armor of bravery and valor, but this felt more true. I would clad myself with this new metal because it wasn't made of fear or worry; it was made of the only thing that made life worth living. After all, I wouldn't fear or worry for anyone I did not love. This alloy was made for Reyan. Beron. Noor and Caelum. The pack. Padren and Malia.

This alloy was made for my people.

It was made for my kingdom.

And it was made for me.

It would see me victorious if the Sculptor had spoken truth, and if he hadn't and I failed to end Anubis, it would wrap me in the knowledge that I fought as hard as I could for them.

I wished things were simple; lit with the light of truth and not shaded with doubt and darkness. I wished I knew how to defeat the dark one.

The Sculptor told me that to command shadow, I must accept it. I had accepted it and learned to command it as best I could. I could master matter. Was that more powerful than tricking the mind with illusions, as Anubis did? I wasn't sure. When he spun them around me, I had been fooled. His mirages were so perfect and immersive, sometimes I questioned what was real and what wasn't. But the question was there. The doubt. There was part of me that saw through the falsehood and recognized it, called it a lie and the spinner a liar.

Perhaps that was where my power truly lay. Not in altering matter, but in seeing through Anubis.

He turned to me. "Will your sister be guarded well?"

I nodded. "Of course she will. She is the Aten."

He gave a calculating smile. "For now."

"How can you take Noor's fire? It came from Sol – an inheritance of power far beyond that which Father held. He was the Aten, but he was not Sol's heir."

"I can nullify it by trapping it within her, hiding it so she cannot draw from the well again."

"Will you do the same with Caelum and Beron?"

He inclined his head, sensing my apprehension. "You are expecting a great battle, but it will be over quickly. I have been fully restored."

"Half your power is mine," I scoffed. "How can you claim to be whole?"

His eyes softened. "I am whole with you at my side." He moved closer. "Citali, we must restore the balance and symmetry the Sculptor designed. The Sculptor made both light and darkness, neither to subvert the other, but to live in harmony."

I snorted. "We sail into war. It will be anything but harmonious, Anubis."

"You are afraid," he noted, his knuckle grazing my cheek. "Don't be."

"I don't want anyone to get hurt. Can you promise me no one will be harmed?" I asked.

He shook his head. "We do not create the war they wage against us, so we cannot be held responsible for the casualties that come from it."

"But we will partake in it," I argued.

"We will end this fight quickly and in doing so, prevent the greatest loss of life, Citali. The quicker we put out the fire they've lit, the fewer people will be burned by the flames of the hatred they fan." He grew frustrated by my apparent disbelief in his godly prowess. "You don't believe they upset the balance? Does that mean you do not wish to fight because of your personal relationships?"

"I told you – I barely have relationships with any of them. I didn't lie about that. I'm just not sure why Sol and Lumos won't return the spirits that are yours. Have you tried to speak with them?"

Anubis waved off my question. "You think I haven't tried to negotiate? They won't allow me a chance! They refused me outright. They refused the Sculptor himself, Citali. They have more power with the spirits of the dead fueling them than they ever had looking over the living. Power and greed have suppressed their view of right and wrong."

He would never see reason.

"They refused the Sculptor?" I gasped, pretending to be upset.

"They refused him. They refused me. And by keeping what is not theirs, they refuse you as well."

"How quickly can we subdue them?" I asked.

He finally smiled. "How fast can you work shadow magic?"

"I am new, but I think I can do what needs to be done."

Anubis gave a jackal grin. "I have no doubt in your ability," he hedged, as if there was something more he was thinking but keeping to himself.

"What *do* you doubt about me?"

"Your stomach for a war waged against your sister. You must remember that the light magic the Aten and Lumin possess was never Sol's and Lumos's to give. It disturbs and destroys *our* shadow magic. Beyond that, the vessels of the gods of illumination tend to die young and do not live to see old age. The magic they weren't meant to have slowly eats away at the body that contains it."

I fought to keep my anger tamped down so he couldn't see my revulsion at his words. "Like your shadows did to my people and my sister?"

He nodded. "Their flesh could not bear the weight for long."

"Are our shadows truly so heavy?"

He gave an apologetic nod. "I didn't know how heavy until now. I thought that as Lumos and Sol had given their vessels power, I could, too. I didn't think it would harm Zarina for many years to come."

I gasped as I realized what he was saying. "You tried to balance things by choosing Zarina to represent you among the living!"

He inclined his head. "I'm sorry it did not work." He held my gaze. "I am truly sorry, Citali. I'm sorry she is gone, and that she injured you. I'm sorry for your pain. But I cannot bring myself to apologize that it brought you close. You were made for me. I know you don't like to hear or think about it, but it is the truth."

"I know," I rasped. "And I can handle Noor. I just don't want my remaining sister dead. I've lost enough."

Shame slid over his face again for the briefest of moments and the god of the dead's tone softened. "I will leave you to strip Noor of her power. However, if you cannot or will not, my hand will be forced. I cannot promise you that she will survive a battle between us, but I can secure her spirit, even from her mother, Sol."

"That would be death beyond dying to her, Anubis. Noor's is the only spirit I would wish to see Sol take – and keep."

"Her spirit is mine and was never meant to be Sol's. She knew that when she descended and took on the flesh. She knew that when she bore the babe. She knows it now," he said with finality. "I cannot let Sol and Lumos steal my purpose. Not a single spirit should burn for them. Souls were meant to rest in the quiet darkness of shadow."

We sailed into a place over the sand where the grains wafted hotter and the arid dryness broiled the air. We were close now.

I sent the thought to Beron. Then with another, replaced the dark corset and paneled skirt with a fitted suit of obsidian armor. Anubis seemed taken aback. "How did you do that so quickly? I…"

"I told you I am ready, Anubis."

His eyes slid down the smooth suit of dark glass. "You did this to please me?"

I nodded. It was the truth. I had done it for him. I wanted the black glass to reflect his image back to him when I took his power and position. I wanted him to see the moment he lost and knew he would die. I wanted him to remember the obsidian and know he would never again see Elara, the girl he'd loved in the only way a creature like him was capable. The god of the dead did not possess a spirit. When he was ended, he would not be escorted into the Shadow Lands. He would be nothing.

I wanted him to see the one he believed was made for him – and realize that the Sculptor made me for a darker purpose: to end him. Every facet of dark glass would reflect his fall. They would not allow lies or illusions. They would show only truth.

"Would you like one to match?" I offered.

The illusion he wore of Merik had never changed. He wore the same guardsman's kilt Merik wore each day. He glanced down as if he'd forgotten what the illusion looked like. "I would love to dress to match my queen."

I smirked at that, letting him think I was greedy and wanted the title and his approval more than anything.

When we left the Shadow Lands, I was nervous for what lay ahead, but now I knew not to be afraid. I didn't know if the Sculptor chiseled my fear away and carved greater courage into my heart, or if my shadows had finally accepted and chosen me, infusing me with their magic and confidence. Whatever the shift, I was grateful for it.

I stepped closer to him and traced my hands over his taut abs. Obsidian spread from my fingertips until he was encased in it. "I want to see your face, Anubis."

He looked down at my hands still pressing against him. Shadows whirred around my hands. "Soon," he said. "I give you my word."

"Will you reveal it in Helios?" I asked, waiting until he looked up at me.

"If it is required, yes."

"Why do you hide yourself?"

He clasped my hands with his. "What is a mortal's greatest fear while they are living?"

It dawned on me then. His face was what they feared most. "Death," I answered.

He nodded. "Death, and to part from those they love. They cannot fathom the hereafter. For many generations, Sol and Lumos have divided the spirits of their people, but the kingdoms were kept separate. You say that Noor and Caelum wish to unite the kingdoms and forge a new, singular one. What will happen if I do not reclaim my place within the trio of gods?"

"Spirits could be parted after death."

"For eternity," he added. "They would not rest in the Shadow Lands together in a new, peaceful existence. They would burn for Sol or Lumos and never see one another again. That was not the Sculptor's wish for the spirits clad in flesh. A mortal life is a gift and a series of lessons the spirit must traverse not only to survive, but to grow. But like a vine, there comes a time for it to wither. The hereafter is a different sort of gift – a different sort of life – but life, nonetheless. Most cannot fathom it until death comes for them, but the life carved for the dead is a comforting, quiet existence that should be spent with loved ones. But… it isn't an empty continuation. Spirits have purpose. They were meant to walk the earth and guide their mortal descendants. They should not burn hot for Sol, or distant and cool for Lumos. The spirits of the dead are vital to the living."

He took my hands in his and raised the backs to Merik's lips, but something frigid brushed a kiss over them. "We will subdue them quickly. There need not be a true war when we sweep the battle at its inception."

"Thank you."

Lumos hovered overhead, his face completely enshrouded. The shadow dimming him was darker than in the vision he sent.

"I want you to stay close to me, Citali. Do not stray." His tone was a warning. "We are strongest together, and I would not see you harmed."

The river materialized in the distance, snaking through the sand. Homes appeared to huddle close to the river. Flattened fields of wheat, barley, garlic, leeks, and cabbage came into view and a herd of cattle bellowed as the ship lowered onto the river. On the other side was a copse of fig trees. The water dragged us past the farmland to where the outskirts of the city began. In the center of it all, Sol stood proudly, hands raised into the air atop her temple.

Warm torchlight flickered upon the pale stone building façades. In the warning illusion he'd spun, the people of Helios had gathered and armed themselves, prepared to fight for Sol and their Aten, not to mention their way of life. Men, women, and even older children were prepared to die to keep Anubis from poisoning all they loved. I had dangled in the air above them.

I knew what it was like to have someone you loved dangled in front of you, of them being in danger with every breath they took. I did not know until that illusion what it would be like to be the one threatened.

The ship slowed. In my mind, I reached out to Beron. *We are approaching the shore.*

*We're ready. Are you?*

*I'm ready.*

In my gut, my mind, and my heart, I was ready. I had accepted my shadows and mastered them. Now, I needed to collect the rest that Anubis now held before he could hurt – or kill – anyone.

There were no Helioans gathered near the shore. None in the streets or alleys. Anubis walked to the ship's rail and gripped it tightly. "It is time."

The prow angled to the shore and we ran aground. Anubis threw out the ramp and I waited with my hand out to take hold of his. His eyes flicked to mine and seemed to ask, *Is this a trick?*

I quirked a brow. *Clasp it and see.*

He slid his hand into mine and watched our shadows mingle for a moment.

*Noor has called Sol. She is on the way,* Beron advised.

Together, we stepped off the ramp. The instant our feet hit the soil, blood fell over the moon. It was not a slow seeping of color; it happened in an instant. Lumos said a wolf would die and the Sculptor confirmed it, but I refused to accept that finality. The future could be changed. People could make different choices that would alter the outcomes.

Anubis noticed blood-soaked Lumos and smiled smugly. "The Sculptor watches. The blood moon is a sign that he champions *us* and Lumos has lost his favor."

"Has Sol also lost his favor?" I asked.

Anubis squeezed my hand. "Certainly. With the Sculptor aligned with us, Citali, the gods of illumination and their vessels do not stand a chance."

The Sculptor was here. I could hear the strike of his hammer upon the metal chisel head. Feel the reverberation tremble through the earth. His work was steady. Powerful. The strikes echoed through my bones and within my stomach, the shadowfire come to life.

The outskirts of Helios were empty, but that was because the people had amassed to guard Sol's temple and her living flame – Noor.

Anubis stopped when he saw the throng of people gathered at the temple's base, standing on every step that led to the top. He assessed Noor and Caelum and the pack ready to shift just below Sol's statue.

The god of the dead released my hand and drew from the shadows lurking throughout the city. He spun illusions, thousands of them, but he did not spin monsters. He spun duplicates of the people of Helios to sow confusion. No one knew friend from foe. No one would strike out at any for fear of harming an innocent.

His illusions were so perfect, spouses could not tell the mirage from their loved ones; mothers could not tell which was their son. The doubles even spoke in the same tone, had the same mannerisms. He'd gleaned all the information just by watching them for a minute.

Sol's orange corona emblazoned the sky a moment before she cut over it, a sharp sliver of light and righteous anger. The smile Anubis gave the sun goddess was one of pure hatred.

"If *you* wish to strip Noor of her power, do it now and do it quickly."

I nodded.

Into Beron's mind, I spoke: *Tell Noor that it will feel as if I am taking away her power, but all is well. I give her my word. Tell Caelum the same. Anubis must believe I've eliminated their magic, so for a time, I have to cloak it so it cannot be seen or used.*

Beron would relay the message to Caelum and Caelum would whisper it to Noor. I hoped he was quieter than a mouse and that I could properly distract Anubis long enough for the message to find my sister. Noor was a good liar. Shrewd when she wanted to be. If anyone could make Anubis think I had achieved my goal, it was her.

With my shadow magic, Anubis and I drifted like leaves on the wind to the top of Sol's temple. Noor and Caelum stood defiantly in the center, the wolves positioned around the perimeter. We entered it just feet away from the Aten and Lumin.

A number of people I recognized from the Helioan guard, as well as priests of Lumos and Sol approached from every side of the temple, hemming us into a small square.

My sister's eyes were hard when they fell upon me and the god of the dead. Her voice trembled with rage when she asked, "You *dare* step foot atop my mother's sacred house?"

Her eyes burned gold. Gilded flames flickered over her hands, licking up her forearms.

"Shall I raze it instead and stand on the ruins?" Anubis challenged gleefully.

My eyes darted between the god of the dead and my Aten sister. I suddenly rushed to Noor. She caught my upper arms in her molten hands, but my obsidian armor protected my skin. Stretching my hand out, I offered a single plea. "Sister, I stand with you, as I stand with Sol. Let us face the dark one together and defeat him as we defeated our father."

"I will fight with you, Citali." She clasped my hand and my shadows slid into her skin and coated her light the same way Anubis had enshrouded Lumos's face. Just as he would dim Sol when she drew nearer. Noor's eyes went wide. She gasped, choked, and jerked her hand away. "What have you done?" She clutched at her chest. "What did you do, Citali?" Her voice went shrill.

She couldn't feel Sol's flame anymore. I wondered if muting her power had somehow severed the connection she felt with her mother. As long as she breathed, Sol would guard Noor, but Noor seemed shaken by what I had done. "What. Did. You. Do?" she roared, nearly hysterical.

*Did Beron have time to warn her?* I flicked my eyes to Caelum, who tried to calm her. The cuff on his arm was gone. Noor noticed and a sharp, keening noise escaped her. She looked to me with the same question in her eyes. The gold fire in them had been snuffed.

"I took away your inheritance," I coldly advised.

Caelum's frost steadily built. It coated his arms, chest, eyebrows and lashes, and fractals of frost formed over his chest and stomach. He reached out to grab my wrist, but I was quicker. The pack shifted, snarling, snapping, and growling as they circled us, binding us into a tighter and tighter space. Overwhelmed, Noor's knees buckled and she swayed. Somehow Caelum caught her before she hit the stone underfoot, but when his frost bit her skin, she cried out and her teeth began to chatter. She needed her fire to combat the frostbite but could not summon it.

Pain washing over her face, she pushed herself up from the ground and shakily regained her footing with Caelum at her side. He dared not touch her for fear of hurting her again.

Noor seethed, "I will not let you harm my people or my kingdom, inheritance or none. Light and fire, or none, I will fight you unto my dying breath!"

"So be it!" I spat.

My shadows took me to Caelum, and fast as an asp, I struck the Lumin from behind. Frost bled from his hands and leached from his skin, scattering droplets of water on the stone below. The crown of moonlight glowed a whitish blue on his brow. It flickered once or twice before extinguishing like the wick of a lamp with too little oil to fuel it.

Caelum cried out, holding his palms up in dismay when he saw his power fail. The cuff on Noor's arm went dead. He reached out and this time when his skin met hers, there was no pain. He drew her into his arms and tried to speak words to comfort her, but there was no comfort for either of them to find. I had taken it all away in a second.

Anubis's eyes lit at the sight of the once powerful Aten and Lumin crumbling before him. He raised his hands as if to strike at the wolf pack, but I moved them from the temple top and scattered them among the people. Within seconds, they pushed back through the crowd, trying to reach the Lumin and Aten again and guard them.

Sol raced over the sky. She was almost here.

"Guard the flame!" someone shouted. The Helioan and Luminan guard, dressed in plain kilts and armed with everything from sling shots to bows, their arrows nocked, rushed onto the platform and filled the space between us and Noor and Caelum.

I turned my back to my sister and her love, placing myself between Anubis and the vessels of Sol and Lumos.

That was the first inkling of a question that sparked in his eyes.

My shadows deftly tore his armor away. He blinked down to find only Merik's skin, his guardsman's kilt, and his scars adorning him. "What is the meaning of this?"

I collected my shadows, drawing from those throughout the kingdom and sand, then tore the shroud from Lumos's face and with it, the bloody hue. I clawed at the darkness in Lumina and in the far reaches of the earth. I siphoned it from the Shadow Lands, freeing the House of Mirages, the remnant, and the still, dark sea. I stripped my shade from Noor and stole it from the mountains and valleys. Even Sol above could not cast shade because it now belonged to me. I seized until I had taken them all and no shadow remained free but those that writhed within him.

They were mine, too. The Sculptor's hammer struck his chisel hard. The clang echoed through the sky and I felt the blow in my chest. It was time.

"What is the meaning of this, Citali?" Merik's eyes were wide. Scared.

The wolves had climbed to the top again and joined us. I felt Beron's steady presence at my back. They would be kept safe. I only had to end this battle quickly, as Anubis suggested, before a true war could be waged.

I bade my magic to strip his illusion and Merik's face faded away until all that was left was him. The god of the dead was formed in the shape of a man, but it was not corporeal. He had no flesh or bone. He *was* shadow and spirit.

Hammer struck chisel and something great and terrible crashed within my ears, white flashing behind my lids. An image appeared in my mind of the Sculptor's wizened hands striking a portion of the creation rock, then of it falling to the Sculptor's bare feet before melting into mercurial water.

"Your hands," Anubis breathed. The shadows wreathing them burned, the flame now black trimmed in gold and silver. His ancient eyes snapped to mine. "Shadowfire cannot be wielded."

"The Sculptor disagrees," I argued, stepping toward him.

I removed the shadow cloak from Noor and Caelum's power. Sunlight once again burst from the Aten's eyes and hands. Laughter bubbled from her and her face relaxed, relief flooding her features. Caelum's frost built onto his hands into frigid, thick gloves.

Anubis tried to gather enough shadow to lash out at Sol, the wolves, anything, but the more power he used, the more I stripped away. It flowed to me like blood through water, dark strings of it.

A wolf behind me suddenly whimpered and I heard a commotion. In my heart I knew it was Beron, but I couldn't look away from the god of the dead while he still created lies and spun illusions, entrapping with spirited mirages. Whatever Beron saw, it wasn't real. I told him as much in my head, but he did not reply. Instead, his very human cry came from the street below.

Several howls rent the air. Red's. Chase's. Holt's. Amaris's.

My ribs tightened. Every part of me wanted to run to the Wolven, but I had to see this through. This was what the dark one wanted, a single moment of distraction so he could slip away from me.

I would not allow it. I couldn't.

Anubis plunged a hand into his middle and the remaining shade buzzed like the bees of a disturbed hive. He withdrew the obsidian blade *I'd* made for him. My mind flashed to Zarina, mad with rage, slashing and stabbing that same sharp edge at me.

Fury gripped me and I made the blade disintegrate in his fingers. The god of the dead curled his fingers into a fist, aghast at my treachery. "Where is it?" he bellowed. "Where is Elara's blade?"

I appeared directly before him, the true blade in my hand, then plunged it into his shadowy heart, striking true. Through the black volcanic glass, I watched as what remained of his shadows flowed into my hands and seeped into my body.

He gasped, his disembodied eyes wide and shocked.

More howls poured from the temple's base.

"The moment this blade cut into my skin, it became mine," I enunciated, watching him gape. "But you were right about one thing, Anubis. I *was* made for you. I was made for ridding the world of you." Shadow billowed around me, alight with shadowfire. And in my obsidian armor, he watched my flames flicker. He watched them dance and burn for me. He watched the dark flame I knew burnt in my eyes. "Your first mistake was making a deal with my father. Your second was involving my sister, then forcing my hand against her. You just made another by harming my Wolven. But your greatest was threatening my son."

He gave a weak smile, slowly fading away. "Your precious Wolven takes his last breath and where are you? With me. That… is true power, Citali. You will remember and regret this moment for an eternity, and I will live on in your memory as the one who taught you that cruel lesson."

"You're wrong. I won't think on you at all. Whatever illusion you've entrapped Beron in will disappear with you."

In a breath, he was gone.

I held mine to be sure…

The Sculptor struck his chisel and the air rippled.

I searched the air in front of me, frantic to make sure every wisp of him had turned to nothing before I looked to the sky, transfixed, as Sol and Lumos eclipsed, bathing the world in warm darkness. This sacred day belonged to everyone. Every Helioan and Luminan who'd taken up arms. The guards of our kingdoms. The priests who'd left their ceremonial kilts and taken up arms, ready to fight for Sol, body and spirit.

Tonight, we were one kingdom. One army. Battling one enemy. Noor and Caelum were the start of the House of Eclipses, but tonight set the future of our joined kingdoms in stone.

As if waking from a daydream, my keener senses sharpened. I became aware of every beating heartbeat around me, including one that raced with panic.

The Sculptor struck his chisel and the earth shook. Everyone braced against the movement. Some held up the person who stumbled next to them. Others fell to their knees in the tumult.

Another strike of the chisel rang in my ears and resonated through my chest, but that wasn't what made me stop and wait and listen.

The pack's howling had not ceased with the end of the god of death.

*Where is Beron?*

Noor was suddenly in front of me, shaking me from my stupor. "Citali? Citali, wake up! It's Beron."

"What?" I breathed.

"He's dying, Citali!" she cried. Sun diamonds scattered among our feet. "He's asking for you. Caelum is with him."

The Sculptor's hammer fell upon his chisel and the metallic clang rang in my ears. I could hear the crumbling of the creation rock as his intended pieces fell away.

Noor reached for my hand and opened a portal, but I didn't need her help. I told my shadows to take me to the Wolven and the next second, dropped to my knees at his side. His head swiveled toward me with glassy eyes. His legs were restless. Beron writhed in pain. Panting, wincing.

"Where is the pain?" I demanded.

"Everywhere," he hissed, gritting loudly as another wave of agony crushed him. Beron cried out, the tendons in his neck standing out like the taut ropes of a ship being dragged away from its mooring by a strong wind.

My hand ghosted over his chest, then his stomach, searching for the source of his pain. I withdrew every shadow around him, perplexed when I found none harbored inside his body. How had Anubis accomplished this?

There was nothing I could see or feel that was wrong. There were no visible wounds in his flesh. "Sculptor!" I shrilled, the Wolven's panic now filling my chest. "Help him, please! I beg of you."

Caelum took in a sharp breath, Beron's hand clasped tightly in his. "You would call on the Sculptor himself?"

"Of course I would!" I shrieked.

He bent close to his brother, tears welling in his eyes. "Hold on, Beron. Don't you dare leave us."

"Call on Lumos," I barked at him. "Do *something*!" I looked to Noor, desperate. "Call for Sol's help. I don't know how to help him!"

The pack hovered nearby, all upset by their fallen leader, their alpha in every respect.

"All of you, beg Lumos!" I cried, raising my face to the sky. "Sculptor! I know you're watching us now. I want to speak to you." I kept my hands on Beron's body, my hands quaking violently. In a flash, my shadowfire winked out. Beron's teeth started chattering and violent shivers quaked through his body. His toes drew in. "I don't know how to heal him. *Please*!"

Beron's hand clasped mine and a violent torrent of thought and memory tumbled through my mind. His words were feverish and harried, urgent and gritted under pain and duress.

*We were never fated mates, pushed together by forces beyond our control. I chose you the moment I saw you.*

*Beron, save your energy,* I told him, trying to keep calm and not frighten him with my fear and tears. *Stay with me. Don't you dare leave me now.*

He ignored me and continued. *I knew you then. You held your shoulders back too properly and your eyes were too keen to be a servant. I thought you might be a spy, but that didn't fit, either. Then, your gaze kept snapping to Caelum's chair and I knew that the only two women bold enough to seek out the Lumin before they were invited to were you and your sister.*

*I chose you then. I tried to un-choose you a thousand times. If you had fallen in love with my brother and he with you, I would have been heartbroken. If you had truly hated the night and left for Helios forever, eventually, when I calmed down from the events that washed over us, I would've gone to you. I would have left the dark night for the land of the sun if it meant you chose me back.*

*So, biting you was no difficult decision for me, Citali. Because my heart was already yours. I wanted you to know. To hear it from me that I love you. I have loved you since the Dusk Lands and will love you in the hereafter if you take me there to be with you. It's okay. You don't have to fight for me.*

*No, Beron. I* will *fight! I will not stop fighting. Death may not be powerful enough to separate us, but I want you to have a beautiful life – the most beautiful life a man has ever lived. If anyone is worthy of that simple hope, it's you.*

Scenes of us quickly flashed through my mind, as if they were flashing through his mind and I was merely a spectator. There was him sliding into the seat next to mine with a smile on his face early in the morning. I thought he was just pretending to be happy to see me. I hadn't realized he was genuinely looking forward to it.

There were scenes of us dancing with my hand in his, of him brushing my hair while trailing behind me. I hadn't even noticed.

Scenes of us flirting, of him noticing my smile. The dark flame in my eyes.

Of him walking me back to my rooms and quietly telling me goodnight.

Of me with Caelum, and him wishing it was him instead.

There were scenes of us on the beach. Of us fighting about me escaping his and Holt's watch. He never hated me. Not for one moment.

*How could I have been so blind?*

The images evaporated.

Beron's voice went silent.

His tremors stopped, not because he was healed or had died, but because time itself stopped. Everyone around us was frozen. My sister and Caelum were still hovering over the Wolven. The pack stood close by, in agony as they witnessed their alpha's demise. The priests and guardsmen. Our people. Garments and hair were caught as they waved in Sol's hot breath.

I couldn't help but cry for Beron. His body was drawn in on itself, his abs tight and his features contorted in pain.

He walked through the crowd barefooted, his hammer and chisel resting in a worn, modest leather tool belt tied loosely at the waist of his rust-hued robe. His strong, wizened hands were free. Free to work, to heal. The wind tousled his white hair and toyed with the strands upon his frayed hems.

His silvery eyes met mine. "I did not expect you to call upon me so soon, Citali, goddess of death."

"Goddess of death, but not of life," my voice cracked. "Beron is dying. Anubis did something to him and I cannot help him." I looked from Beron's face into the Sculptor's. "I love him."

"I know your heart, Citali."

"Please," I begged. "Please heal him."

The Sculptor crouched next to us and looked Beron over. His white brows drew in. "Anubis could not poison his body with his malicious essence because you had taken too much of his shadow, but with his last act, he injured Beron's spirit. His flesh, as its house, is dying. His spirit will decay and die as well."

"Spirits can die?" I cried, almost hysterical. "Can't you chisel the injured portion away or knit it together?"

He pressed a comforting hand to my shoulder. "I'm afraid there is only one thing that can cure the Wolven's spirit."

"What?"

He stood up and drew me from my knees to stand with him. "Would you do anything to save him?"

I nodded, wiping at my cheeks and eyes. "Anything."

"A Wolven's mate bond binds two souls together. Yours, bound to his, could restore what he has lost."

I sobbed. "Lumos severed our mate bond."

"Then you must beg the god of the moon to restore it and hope he values the life of his Wolven in the same measure as you." The Sculptor reached out and squeezed my hand.

I had no time to consider what shifting would mean. If I became wolf and was the goddess of death, would that disturb the balance of things? *The Sculptor suggested it,* I told myself as he walked back through the frozen crowd and disappeared. Time began anew.

Caelum was taken aback to see me standing when only a second ago, I'd been on my knees beside him. I raised my hands to Lumos.

"Lumos!" I shouted. "This is my mate. This is my mate and I love him! Do not take him from me. I beg you!"

Lumos's answer was both swift and brutal, and if my heart could cry, mine would have flooded a thousand times over.

My skin grew warm, my flesh too tight. My bones creaked and I laughed and cried as Lumos pulled away from Sol. The pain was excruciating. I felt my ribs crack, one by one, starting at the bottom of the cage and working upward. Tendons stretched until I thought they would snap. Muscles, too. I stood, even as my knees shook. My legs weakened and my spine buckled from the pain. I called on Lumos and his great power to change me.

I had accepted my shadows. Now, I would accept my wolf and become Asena.

"What are you doing?" Noor shouted, starting toward me.

Caelum realized what was happening. "Noor, get back! Get *everyone* back. She's about to shift."

Noor urged the crowd away from me to give me space so I could shift. Beron watched, his tremors gone, his arms and legs limp now. He blinked slowly.

Then it happened.

The excruciating pain was suddenly gone, and my vision changed. It was sharper, clearer. My wolf body was lithe and strong and not an ounce of pain remained, only power and shadowfire. At my paws swirled burning shade. I stepped toward Beron, put my nose to his cheek, opened my jaw, and bit down on his shoulder.

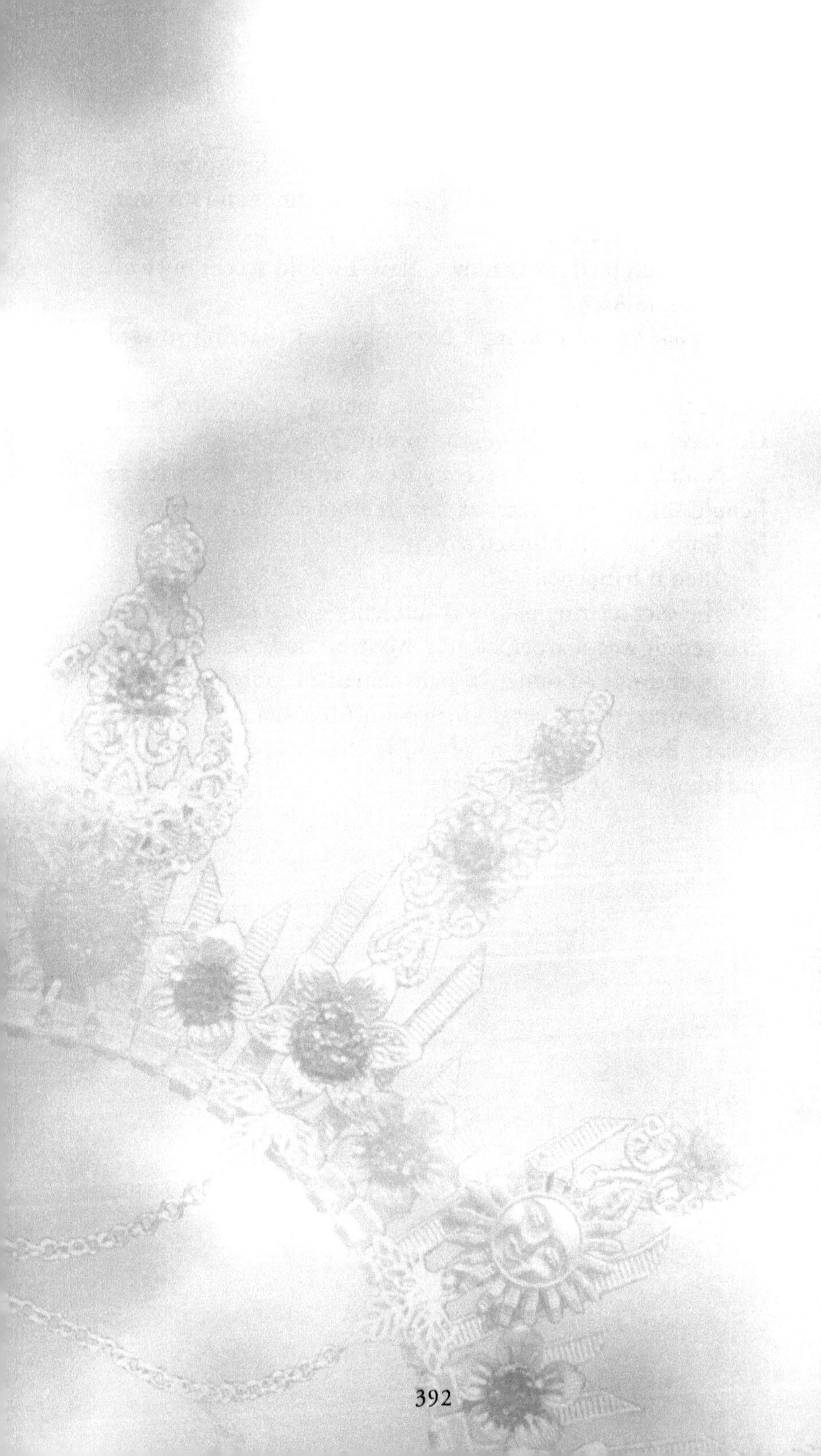

# 29

Beron did not perk immediately, but the ashen hue that had claimed his skin faded, replaced by a healthier pallor. My claws had scraped his brow and lid, but the cuts were superficial. I knelt at his side and held his hand as his breathing slowly returned to normal and the sheen of sweat on his forehead evaporated. I felt the beat of his heart beneath my fingertips and noted its steady rhythm.

The sound of hammer striking chisel echoed in my ears once more, but this time it sounded farther away.

And in my mind, the Sculptor's voice came: *All is well, Citali.*

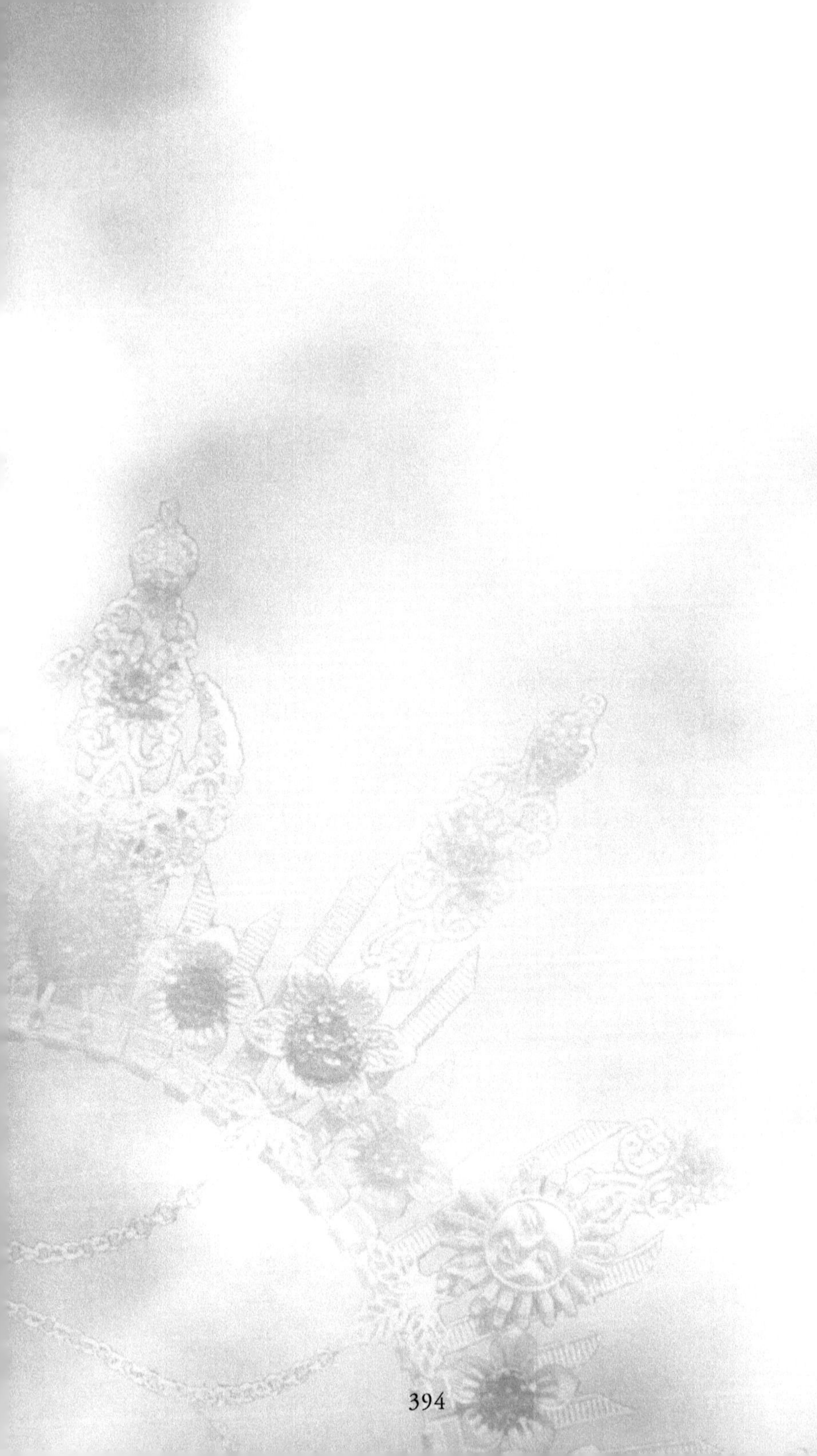

# 30

Caelum carried his brother to an empty room in the House of the Sun. I hovered as he lay Beron on the bed and carefully tucked the blankets around him. Luminan priests kept watch in the hallway, communicating with Lumos about the Wolven's state.

In my periphery, the pale curtains billowed into the room. Sol and Lumos had traversed the sky together after Beron was spared, but Lumos peeled away from her now, disappearing over the horizon as the sun goddess remained to shine over Helios and Noor.

Over us all.

My sister waited patiently at my side. When I was sure Beron was comfortable and made Caelum promise at least a dozen times to let Noor know the moment he woke so I could come and see him, I turned to my Aten.

"I need you to send word to the Sphinx. She needs to safely return my son and his grandparents. Now."

Noor smiled gently. "I won't word it quite like that."

"Tell her what I said, Noor, in the exact tone I used. I'll be waiting for her atop Sol's temple – if that's okay with her, and you."

"It certainly is, and you will always be welcome in or atop her temple," she promised. "Can I come with you?" she asked, as if unsure.

"You certainly can and will always be welcome at my side."

Together, we walked to her mother's temple and climbed the steps to the top. This time, the climb was easy and our steps felt lighter. This time, we weren't ascending to meet an enemy and right wrongs. We weren't walking toward an ending, but toward a new beginning. And knowing Reyan would be with me any moment made it that much sweeter.

Noor's elbow bumped mine. "They're already in the air. They will land in a few moments."

"She didn't take them far, then." For a second, a wisp of fear slid through my veins. Why had the Lioness been so careless when she promised utmost carefulness regarding Reyan?

Noor looked to her mother's statue as we stepped onto the temple's top. "I think she took them somewhere Anubis could not see or go. Someplace neither of us can. She took him farther than we can fathom, because that is the only place she could keep him hidden and safe. We now know there is much we don't understand and never may about the Sphinx and many other things."

I hummed my agreement. The Sphinx possessed as many tricks as she did riddles.

We walked to the center of the square where Noor's eyes turned to gold. "I'm proud of you, Citali. I am proud to call you my sister."

A knot formed in my throat and I could not speak around it. I could only nod and hope she knew I felt the same. I pulled her in for a tight, long hug.

Her hands tensed on my back. "She's –"

The Sphinx's great, clear wings flapped, sending an immense whoosh of air to sweep over Sol's temple as she landed. Our hair tore sideways for a moment. Her claws raked the stone and her thunderous tail lashed left and right.

"–here," Noor finished.

The Lioness slowly shrunk herself down. Padren blew out a tense breath before stiffly sliding off her back. His hair was windblown and stood straight up. He helped Malia slide off the Lioness's back, but I was already rushing to my son. Reyan held tight to the back of the Sphinx's mane. "Up!" he squealed.

"Reyan!" I said, my voice raising. My immortal heart beat a step faster.

His head swiveled to me. "Cit-li!" His big, innocent eyes lit up with joy. He let go of the Lioness's mane and reached for me. I caught him in my arms and held him tight, crying quietly. I didn't want to frighten him, but a feeling of relief washed over me and I couldn't contain my tears.

Father was gone. Anubis, too. And now that I was changed, no one would threaten him, or us, ever again.

Malia cried with me, her hands covering her mouth. Padren wrapped a comforting arm around her shoulders. She broke away and staggered to us, throwing her arms around me and my son. Padren did, too. "I am so sorry, Citali. I did not wish for you to bear such a burden for us all!" she cried.

"It's no burden," I assured her. And it was the truth. Conquering Anubis and taking his place, choosing to become wolf… neither was a hardship for me, and both would assure that I could care for them all, protect them as they would protect me if they could. And when their natural lives ended, I could still love and be with them. Death would never separate us. "This is a gift only the Sculptor could bestow, and one for which I'm most grateful."

Another burst of air came as the Sphinx fanned out her wings. Padren and Malia peeled away as I turned to face the Lioness.

Her chest was puffed. "Goddess of the Dead, Queen of Wolves, of spirit, and teeth, and claws…" she greeted, bowing deeply. "I am beholden to Sol who made me, but know that you have my respect and my gratitude."

"Thank you," I told her.

She gave me a smug smile. "Now…" she let linger.

"Now?"

"Now," she continued, "you are better than I, Citali."

I shook my head. I wasn't.

She looked to Sol in the distance and her head tilted as she gave her attention to the sun goddess. "Sol asked me to relay a message," she announced. "Whenever you would like to discuss the spirits they've kept safe, and their return to the earth, she is ready. She will await word from you."

I inclined my head. "I have a couple things to see to, and then I will come to her."

Her sharp canines gleamed in the sun and her obsidian eyes held Reyan's and my reflection.

"Thank you for keeping my son and his grandparents safe, Lioness."

"It was truly my pleasure," she answered. "I can't remember ever laughing so much."

"Where did you take them?"

She grinned. "You may be more powerful than me, but that does not entitle you to all my secrets."

"I guess I have plenty of time to try to coax them out of you, now," I told her.

She puffed her chest as if daring me to try. "As you do not see glimpses of the future, I should tell you that there is a third path for Reyan now. It will feel like only a season until we see which path he takes. Immortality stretches, but rarely breaks, Asena."

"What is the third path?"

"One that only you can offer him, Queen of the Dead. Sol has her Aten; Lumos his Lumin…"

I smiled, wondering if Reyan would want to become my representative on earth. His sunny disposition would be perfectly suited to Aten, but he loved watching Lumos as well. What would he think when he aged and came to know me and my power better?

The Lioness swelled into her gigantic form and took to the sky, swirling like a vulture scenting carrion on the ground, ready to pick clean the bones that lay beneath her.

I couldn't help but laugh. She may have bowed and said I was stronger now, but still she threatened. Whether she realized it or not, I wasn't sure.

Reyan flapped his arms. "Kitty fly!"

I held him out from me and zoomed him around in a circle. "You can fly, too."

When Anubis and I first approached Helios, and Beron and I, along with our friends, conspired against him, Noor had relayed what was happening to the Sphinx, who told Padren and Malia what she wished. Her version of the events of the past few days was concise, yet vague, like her riddles. She hadn't told them Anubis whisked me away to the Shadow Lands or explained what happened there. They didn't know that I'd drank from the remnant and I was immortal even before claiming Anubis's power. They didn't know I'd met the Sculptor at the creation rock or that I saw him carving it.

They didn't know that he came here to Helios at my panicked plea, or that I'd finally chosen to shift – and chose Beron as my mate. They didn't know Anubis had injured his very spirit.

The only things they knew were that Anubis came to end us all and that somehow, I stopped it. They knew Beron was hurt but didn't know how. They hadn't seen Luminians and Helioans fight together as one people, ready to die to protect the other.

They knew so little, I wasn't sure where to begin explaining or how. How could you tell someone such things as if they were simple pieces of your past, as inconsequential as the most mundane tasks of the day that were swept behind you? They were far more potent because their effects lingered, yet they were the same: done and gone.

I promised to tell them the whole story when we had more time. Though Padren appeared to be placated by my promise, I could tell he wanted to hear it very soon.

Padren and Malia led us down from the temple top where the priests of Sol met us. They dropped to their knees in front of Noor, singing their lilting songs and rocking back and forth in rhythm.

"They sing for you, Citali," she pointed out. "They are grateful to Sol, always, but this song is in your honor."

I glanced over them with fresh eyes. Benira no longer wore bandages on his hands. Kiran did not look at my sister, but kept his eyes upon the ground where they belonged – finally. It was the first time I'd seen Sol's priests without their golden kilts. They either wore their day-to-day kilts with Sol's insignia emblazoned upon the hem, or pleated, golden kilts that shone in the sun for ceremonies. Today, they wore the garments of Sol's people.

Today, they'd fought as members of the Helioan guard. Because this was Sol's city, the Aten her daughter, and her priests were not simple caretakers. They could be warriors when she required it of them.

In my arms, Reyan clapped and hummed to their song, watching their movements carefully. "I missed you," I whispered in his ear. "I love you, Reyan."

He hugged my neck.

He had never called me *mother*. I wondered how long it might take for him to understand who I was and always had been to him. I wasn't sure how to explain our past to him so he could understand it.

Caelum suddenly appeared next to Noor, a relieved smile on his face. "He's awake," he said.

"Would you like to go for a ride, Reyan? The Sphinx may need wings to fly, but we do not."

Padren gasped and he and Malia clung to one another as I took all of us up onto the crest of a shadowy wave and pushed us toward Beron like he was the shore itself. I could feel his precise location in the House of the Sun and easily picked out his balcony, landing us upon it before striding inside. Reyan giggled and clapped, though Padren and Malia were still shocked by what they'd witnessed. I could hear them asking Noor what just happened.

Beron was sitting up in bed, his back against a pile of mussed pillows. His eyes met mine, then he saw Reyan in my arms. He threw the blankets back, stood, and hugged us both, kissing my temple and whispering, "You did it. You'll have to fill me in, though. Things are a little hazy."

My ribs tightened. "You don't remember what happened?"

"I think I fell down the steps or something? Everything is jumbled and I can't recall very much."

All the others hovered just inside the room. I sat Reyan down and told him to run to Padren, who promptly lifted him onto his shoulders.

"That's my move," Beron complained.

"Not anymore. It's come in quite handy lately," Padren teased. "Take time to talk. We'll be back soon, Citali."

He and Malia told Reyan to duck his head as they stepped into the hallway. Their voices and footsteps slowly trickled away.

Beron ran his fingers through his dark hair, tousling it. The emerald kilt he wore was wrinkled and made of soft material for sleeping. His feet were bare. He took in a deep breath and slowly let it out again. "Why do I get the feeling that I'm going to regret asking you what happened?"

I smiled. "Don't regret asking. Our future is cut by our pasts."

His hand found my waist, his touch as natural as breathing. It had nothing to do with the mate bond that had ignited between us once again. His fingers tightened on my skin. "Citali," he breathed shallowly… "Did Lumos restore us?"

I craned my neck upward, wanting him to know how much I wanted this. "He did."

"Why?"

"Because I asked him to."

Beron's throat shifted. "Why?"

"Because I choose you."

His eyes studied me. "You choose me?"

I nodded once. "I choose you, Beron."

"How could I have missed that?" he breathed softly, gathering me closer. Confusion knitted his brows.

I took his free hand in mine and threaded my fingers through it before telling him what happened, and what Anubis did to injure him.

He was dumbfounded for a moment. "You went to the Sculptor – for me?"

"I did not go to him; he came to me after I cried out to him. I thought he would help from afar, but he stopped time and walked among us."

"He came to you…" his voice trailed away. Then his grip left my side and he touched his shoulder. "You bit me."

"I bit you," I confirmed. "I also slightly clawed your brow and eyelid, but that was on accident." I rubbed a thumb over where the small scratches had been just hours ago. "You healed very quickly." He touched the delicate skin my claws had raked and found it whole. Then he was quiet so long, I started to squirm. "Beron?"

His eyes snapped to mine.

"Say something."

He pulled me toward him. Our chests met, and we shared the scant air between us. Shivers slid over my skin as his fingers trailed along my spine. I craned my head to better reach him and he slowly leaned in, allowing his lips to brush mine before pressing a soft kiss to them.

But one kiss with Beron would never be enough.

My power stirred, the shadowfire igniting and encasing us. His eyes sparked as he watched the shade drift around us, growing more and more impatient as I did.

I wanted more. He saw the need in my eyes and met it just as vigorously.

Our mouths finally collided as he lifted me from the ground. I wrapped my legs around his waist. His palms cupped my bottom and pressed my core to his. A growl rumbled from his throat at the same time a soft moan escaped mine. My head swam as he walked us to the bed where together we fell, our mouths and limbs once again tangled. His taste and scent made my skin heat and tighten as if I might shift.

I wondered if he felt the change in my temperature.

My lips were swollen when he finally pulled away. My immortal heart pounded so hard it echoed through my bones. I felt it in the pads of my fingers and in my toes.

"I never want to stop kissing you," he panted.

I closed my eyes when he lay his forehead on mine.

Let myself enjoy the weight of him pressed against me.

Felt his heart pound beneath my palm.

For every one of his breaths, for every beat of his heart, I was grateful. I almost lost him forever, body and spirit. A tear squeezed from my eye.

He noticed and tensed. "Hey… what's the matter?" he softly asked, wiping it away.

"I was so scared, Beron. And now I'm just happy you're here. You're okay."

“I’m fine,” he offered reassuringly. He placed the softest kiss on my lips and helped me sit up. Then he held me as I cried. “It’s over.”

“This part is over, but it’s the beginning of an entirely new phase,” I told him honestly, fighting the quiver in my voice. “I’m not sure how to navigate my powers and guide the spirits, or face – or even *fathom* – the depths of eternity.”

He brushed my hair back from my face. “You don’t have to do it alone, Citali.” Another kiss, to my temple this time. “I’ll love you forever,” he softly said.

“But I’ll love you beyond it,” I retorted miserably.

A wave of emotion choked him at the same time one choked me. “Thank you for choosing me.”

My thumb brushed the back of his hand. “You chose me first. It is I who should thank you.”

He shook his head. “You went to the Sculptor. I only went to Lumos.”

A grin blossomed on my lips. “Yet the result was the same. Here we are.”

“Here we are,” he echoed, the words carrying a meaning as deep as the ocean.

I kissed him again.

# 31

We were interrupted by familiar laughter trickling from farther down the hallway. "Break it up!" Chase hollered. "Ready or not, we're coming in." I pictured him cupping his hands to amplify the sound, shoving his wolf brothers.

Their barking laughter made me grin.

Beron groaned. "I tried to buy you some time."

I winked. "Away from *them*? Why?"

Chase, Holt, and Red fought to enter the room first. Chase managed to squeeze past Holt and Red, who lodged against one another in the doorway. Amaris lagged a few steps behind, a slight smile on her face.

Their hair was wet; the men wore fresh kilts, and Amaris a new dress.

The guys took turns hugging me, but Chase got to me first. He growled and rocked us side to side, planting a sloppy, loud kiss on my cheek. "I have never been happier to see you as I was when you returned from whatever forsaken place he'd taken you. But when you turned on him and completely annihilated him, I'm going to be honest – I've never been so impressed or turned on in my life."

When Beron let out a growl in a tone I'd never heard, I peeled away from Chase, who put his hands in the air. "I know she's yours. I'm just saying, though."

"Well, *don't* just say!" Beron barked.

I laughed at him. "He was teasing." I looked at Chase. "Right?"

"Uh.... No, I was being honest, but I know the two of you are mates. So, it was totally innocent."

"Why are you wet?" I asked, gesturing to his hair and glancing at all of them.

"We took a swim in the river," he said simply.

"And the crocodiles didn't take a nibble out of any of you?"

Red waved off the question. "Come on, Citali. You must know that even crocs fear the wolf pack."

"Of course they do," I laughed.

Red finally shooed Chase away and gave me a friendly hug.

Holt waited nearby, quiet and patient. When Red pulled away, I walked to him. "I'm glad you're okay," he said, awkwardly hugging me.

"I'm glad you're okay, too. First, you brave Anubis and then the crocodiles. You obviously enjoy flirting with danger."

Holt stepped away, joining the guys as they swarmed Beron, telling him how glad they were that he was alive and well. They congratulated him on our restored mate bond and told him how relieved they were that he could finally stop brooding over it. Beron's eyes met mine when Chase said it. The Wolven blushed a little, even as he smirked.

Amaris moved to stand beside me. "I was wrong about you," she admitted. "I was wrong and I'm sorry."

I shook my head. "You weren't wrong."

Her eyes shone with admiration. "You went to the Sculptor without even bothering with Lumos and Sol."

"I had to. I'm as powerful as they are, and was just as powerless to help him," I confided. "There was no other choice but to go to the Sculptor."

"You could've chosen not to intervene." She looked at her feet. "Look, I'm sorry I've been unkind."

I glanced at her and shrugged. "You love him."

"He's done so much for me – for all of us. I know you haven't been around long enough to hear our stories a thousand times, but you will be, and I'm glad for it. You make him happy," she added sheepishly. "You brought him to life. He came home from the Dusk Lands with one name on his lips: yours. I guess I never imagined him loving someone the way he loves you."

For once in my life, I stammered to find a response. "Thank you."

Suddenly, I noticed the guys had quietened down. Red was grinning like a fox, of course. Chase smiled expectantly. Even Holt's serious lips curled upward. All three of them were focused on me, which meant trouble.

I narrowed my eyes. "What is it? Why are you looking at me like that?"

Chase slung an arm over Red's shoulder and explained, "We want to soar on one of your shadow waves. We saw how you arrived and, well, it looks like fun."

I rolled my eyes. "*That's* what you want? After all you've been through?"

"Absolutely!" Chase punctuated with a loud whoop. Red and Holt laughed. Beron smirked, waiting to see what I would do.

I looked to Amaris. "You too?"

She beamed. "I'm in."

"Wolven?"

"We're a pack," he answered with a grin.

"We are," I agreed. "And while I'm happy to provide your entertainment, I'm afraid I'll have to sit this one out. I'll be here, Beron."

I would be here – after.

He inclined his head just before my shadows pushed them onto the balcony. "Whoa!" Red chortled.

I lifted my hands and sculpted the shadow into a great wave, then enjoyed the sound of them shrilling like children when the wave dropped them toward the earth before catching them and swooping over the homes and merchant shops in Helios. Like their howls once had, their booming laughter echoed through the city that raised me.

I knew each voice by heart.

I borrowed one of Noor's pale green dresses and located Padren and Malia in the courtyard. Padren sat next to Reyan as he splashed in the water of one of the lily-laden ponds set into the stone. Dragonflies buzzed around him while startled frogs jumped and hid beneath the broad pads skimming the water's surface.

Malia waved for me to join them. I sat with her across from Padren and Reyan on one of the many stone benches. "Are you okay?" she carefully asked.

"I am."

"What happened to you, Citali? You're different. You're changed."

Padren listened carefully, even as he cooed at Reyan.

I owed them the truth, and that was what I gave them. I laid everything bare. In the end, Merik's parents were left speechless. For a long time, Reyan and the buzzing of wings were the only sounds. Then I heard something soft rake against something even softer. The sound came from Malia, a teardrop carving a path down her cheek.

"I am so sorry we could do nothing to help you." Her bottom lip quivered, and she looked skyward as more tears fell.

I covered her hand with mine. "Malia, don't cry for me. All is well," I choked out.

"All is *not* well, Citali," she whispered.

I gave her hand a gentle squeeze. "I promise that I am at peace with what I have become, Malia. I don't just accept it, I'm grateful for it. I got what I wanted more than anything: a way to protect my son against anyone or anything that might threaten him."

"That you did," Malia agreed.

"And you found Beron," Padren added. "Someone to love."

I swallowed thickly, unsure what to say. "It's okay, Citali. Merik would want you to find happiness, and anyone with eyes can see that Beron makes you happy."

"He makes me crazy, too," I laughed, half-sobbing.

Malia wiped her tears away and gave a shaky smile. "If he didn't, I'd be worried."

Padren scoffed and waved us off, turning toward Reyan and muttering to him how Malia drove *him* crazy, not the other way around. Reyan looked toward Malia when he heard her name. She waved to him and he waved back and blew a kiss.

"Malia, now that the danger has been eliminated, do you plan to return home?"

She locked eyes with Padren, who gave a single nod. "We actually wanted to talk to you about that." I braced for a harsh blow. I would miss them. It would be hard on Reyan to separate from them, even if I vowed to visit often. "We were wondering if it might be possible to remain with you. You'll need help with Reyan as you settle into your new role, and we want to be part of his life. We promise not to get in the way…"

Relief and happiness washed through me and I couldn't stop my wide smile. "You could never be in the way. I would love that, and I know Reyan would, too. I should warn you, though. I think my new role will require me to be somewhat nomadic."

Padren made a silly face at Reyan, who gave a big belly laugh in response, then turned his attention back to me. "I've always wanted to see the world beyond Helios. Besides, home is where your loved ones are, not a building of stacked sand bricks."

Sol slowly slipped lower on the horizon where she'd been lingering. Cool and comforting, the evening shadows grew, stretching across the courtyard like an unfurling blanket. Noor glided out of one of the many doors that graced the House of the Sun, adorned in a blindingly white pleated dress. She smiled at Merik's parents, my son, and then me. "Dinner is being prepared," she announced. "Tomorrow, the House of the Sun will host a great feast. All of Helios and Lumina are invited to attend."

"Thank you, Atena," Padren said first, giving a half bow which was quickly seconded by his wife.

Noor inclined her head gracefully and came to stand beside me. "I took the liberty of retrieving a few of your gowns from the House of Wolves. I wasn't sure where you'd like to stay tonight, but if you'd like to stay in your rooms here, I burned away the stain. I didn't know I could do that before…"

"Thank you, Noor. I would be most comfortable there." I sighed. "I need to bathe if I don't want to spoil dinner with sand and sweat."

"We'll keep Reyan occupied while you get ready," Malia volunteered.

Crossing to the pond, I crouched beside my son. "I'm going to go take a bath, but I'll see you before dinner. Okay?"

"Okay, Cit-li," he said, returning his attention to the pond once more.

I stood, but it took me a moment before I was ready to leave him. Finally, I strode inside with Noor. Just inside the doorway, we passed a woman who asked if there was anything we needed. Noor asked if she could gather hot water for my tub. The woman promised it would be done as quickly as possible.

"They earn a wage now. No more servants need to bend to the Aten's whims. I will employ proud Helioans who work hard and are compensated well for it."

"I love watching you unravel him," I told her, then my feet stopped as I remembered. Noor paused with me. "His spirit was in the Shadow Lands. Anubis said that Sol found him unacceptable and would not take any part of him, so Anubis brought him to his island."

"And did *you* unravel him, too?"

I gave a grim smile. "My shadows ripped him to shreds. Nothing remains now."

She offered a small smile and cupped my elbow. "I hope that's the last time we'll say that."

I met her eye. "It is. He's gone for good. All of him."

Her hand fell away and she began walking again. "Good."

I bathed and combed my hair before slipping into the simplest of the three dresses Noor had brought back for me. I slid gold bangles onto my wrists and watched as the shadows whirring around them settled into my skin.

Padren, Malia, and Reyan met me in the dining room. I took my son into my arms and settled with him in one of the many chairs. Malia sat to my left and Beron deftly swept into the seat on my right. The rest of the pack crashed into the room a moment later, playfully complaining about how fast the Wolven was.

Beron merely smirked and shrugged. "Train to be faster."

"Like *that* would help," Amaris muttered as she passed us to take a seat at the other end.

Reyan chatted with the wolves until Noor and Caelum entered the room, but when they arrived, his jabbering halted as he took in her radiance. Noor was beautiful; the sun incarnate. She glowed even brighter whenever Caelum was at her side.

Noor took the seat at the far end of the table, at the head, and Caelum sat at her right hand. His cool glow cast onto her olive skin while her flame warmed his pale flesh.

Reyan wanted down, so I set his feet on the floor and he scampered to Noor and held his hands up. "Sol!" he greeted.

She smiled, choking back her surprise. "I am not the sun goddess, Reyan. You know my name," she reminded him as she raised her nephew onto her lap.

"Noor," he said.

"That's right. I am Noor. Your aunt."

"Ah-ten?" he said questioningly.

"Yes, I am the Aten." She conjured a tiny ball of light for him and he immediately tried to pluck it from her hand. She tossed it into the air and it broke into a thousand pieces, all raining down on them in glittering flecks of light. He shrieked gleefully. As they played, I watched, and my thoughts drifted…

"You okay?" Beron leaned in to quietly ask.

I met his blue eyes. "I'm exhausted. My flesh can bear the weight of shadow, but it still tires. Beyond my body, my mind is so incredibly tired, too. I feel weary to the bone, perhaps to the spirit."

He ticked his head toward the others seated farther down the table. "All of us are. Some hide it better than others, but we are all worn out." His hand curled around mine. Comforting me. Reminding me that he was here with me. After.

The longer we sat, the more it became evident that everyone was spent. Conversation quietened. Postures slouched. Yawning became sport.

Padren asked where Reyan should sleep and I told him I'd like for him to stay in my rooms. I had so much time to make up for, so much time to recapture. Instead of dwelling on the past, I was finally able to look forward to our future together as mother and son.

Caelum and Noor escorted Padren and Malia to their rooms, and the wolves had no trouble finding their own. Beron escorted Reyan and me to my rooms. Reyan's head bobbed on my shoulder by the time we reached my door. I crossed the room with Beron, who unfolded the blankets so I could lay Reyan down to sleep.

My son looked so peaceful as I drew the blankets around him and tucked him in tightly. He slept so soundly with none of the fatigue or worry that marred the adults' foreheads. I watched as his tiny chest rose and fell. His lips were parted, his cherubic face completely relaxed. Beron stepped behind me, rubbing my arms as if they were cold.

I turned to face him. My hands found his taut waist as his lips met my forehead. "Get some sleep," he whispered. "See you in the morning for breakfast?"

I nodded. "That sounds perfect."

"I take it the hunger abated after you shifted?"

"Before that, actually. After I drank of the remnant, things changed."

"What other things?" he asked curiously, brushing a strand of hair behind my ear.

"Too many to list tonight," I told him.

He kissed my temple. "Then it's a good thing we have so many tomorrows ahead of us."

Beron peeled away and left me with my thoughts, which threatened to pull me under. We did have tomorrows, but Beron was mortal. His lifespan stretched between us as a thin, taut mooring line that would one day snap when his spirit set sail for the shade.

As much as I told myself I would see him in the hereafter, I knew that parting with him, with anyone I loved, would be the greatest pain of my life. Each second that ticked away brought us closer to the moments I dreaded most.

I lay beside my son and counted his breaths until my eyes drifted closed.

# 32

I dressed in a deep blue gown that matched Beron's eyes, then walked with Reyan to find some fresh clothes he could change into for the day. His tiny hand clung to mine as we traversed the halls where I'd grown up. "Padren!" he shouted, releasing my fingers and running down the hall to his grandfather. Padren caught him and swung him into the air, eliciting a delighted squeal.

Malia waved him into their rooms. "Let's get you dressed for the day, Reyan." Padren sat him down and he ran inside to meet his grandmother at the chest of drawers. "Will you need us to watch Reyan today?" she asked hopefully.

I nodded. "For a short time. I need to go to the Shadow Lands to take care of something."

Earlier, I heard the Sculptor's hammer strike his chisel. It still echoed in the back of my skull. He wanted me to return the remnant to him so no other mortal could drink from it.

Wars could be waged for such power.

It was better to rid the world of it.

I just hoped I could bring myself to do it before I suggested that Beron drink it. It was selfish to want him to live forever, to forsake the life he loved for something so drastically different. For a time, I could pretend I was the same young woman I was before drinking the water of creation and fool everyone else, but I could never fool myself. It was impossible to consider all the ways that immortality had changed me. It was so new and untested – just like I was.

"The Shadow Lands?" Padren quietly asked.

I nodded. "The Sculptor would like me to destroy something that lives there now. Before the spirits can be returned to the earth, I must complete this task for him."

Padren's brows rose in alarm, but the expression didn't erase the worried lines framing his lips. "I worry for you."

"I wish you wouldn't."

He rocked back on his heels, stuffing his hands in his pockets. "Will you take Noor or Beron with you?"

"I'd like to take them both, as well as Caelum," I replied.

"I don't like it when you are alone," he said. "People… need other people around them to ground them, to remind them of what is real and what isn't. They need encouraging smiles, and sometimes to hear difficult things." His warm brown eyes met mine. "I guess what I'm saying is that I hope you continue to surround yourself with good people who love you. If you ever need me to walk a difficult path with you, I will, Citali. You are part of my family. I hope you know that."

"I do, Padren. And I cannot thank you enough."

After the Aten and Lumin, the Wolven and his pack, Padren, Malia, Reyan, and I finished our delicious breakfast, a quiet fell over the table and heads began to swivel to me. It was then that I realized they were waiting on me to tell them what I might need them for today.

I looked at my hands as I wrung them in my lap. "There's something I have to do, but I'd like to ask some of you to go with me to do it. Also, the temple sustained some damage and I was also hoping that some of the others might lend your strength to the priests so Sol's temple might be restored." I shrugged a challenging shoulder. "If the wolves could handle some heavy lifting, that is."

Laughter bubbled from Chase. "I think we could handle that." Red, Holt, and Amaris readily agreed.

"Caelum, Noor, and Beron, I was wondering if you would come with me."

All three immediately agreed. I hadn't even told them where, why, or what had to be done, yet they trusted me. "Meet me at the base of Sol's temple in a few minutes?" I asked. When they each nodded, I rose and took up my son, hugging him to my chest. "Tonight, there will be a feast."

"Fees!" he parroted.

I grinned. "A feast *and* a dance. Do you like to dance, Reyan?" I dipped him backward as he laughed.

"Dance! Dance!"

Padren and Malia stood and when Padren held his hands out, Reyan demanded to dance with him as well. "We will await your return, Citali," Padren promised. Reyan's bubbling chatter trailed after them long after they'd disappeared down the hall.

The wolves filed out behind them, all saying their goodbyes. Chase prattled on about how he could lift one of the heavy cut stones by himself. Holt retorted that he'd like to see him try to lift it so his ego could finally stop exponentially growing. Red chortled at that and Amaris pushed the guys through the doorway, directing them like a herd of stubborn goats.

Beron strode over to stand beside me. Noor and Caelum joined us. "So," Caelum said, rubbing his palms together, "where are we going?"

"Let me show you what no one else alive has seen," I told him.

He froze at the words. "Does this mean…?" His question hung between us, unfinished and unspoken.

"I need to return to the Shadow Lands."

"Why?" Beron asked.

"To destroy something for the Sculptor."

Beron swallowed thickly. "Okay, then, we should probably get going. Do we need a ship?"

I shook my head. "I wasn't sure I could do it, but I tried this morning and I can."

"Do what?" Caelum asked, flicking a glance at Noor.

"Come and see," I told them, walking out the door to the base of Sol's temple where dark shadows were being cast over the sand. I slipped my hand into one and watched it disappear up to my elbow. "I can move through shadow the way Noor can make portals."

Noor grinned. "How did you figure out you could do this?"

"I started thinking… since I could speak to Beron through them, moving words and thoughts, why not something more substantial?"

Beron took hold of my hand before grabbing Caelum's, who lightly grasped Noor's fingers. I led them into the darkness and onto the dark sand beach I remembered. I had borrowed shadow from this place to defeat Anubis, but allowed them to return when I no longer needed them. Noor spun in circles, clutching her chest in pain.

"Are you okay?" I asked worriedly. "I didn't know how being this far away from Sol might affect you."

"I'm okay for now," she replied tightly.

I nodded my head decisively. "We won't linger."

Caelum and Noor fell into step behind me and Beron as we took the sandy path that led to the great obsidian pyramid. Beron almost missed a step when it finally came into view.

I announced, "This is the House Anubis built, the House of Mirages." I urged them on when I heard a faint hammering noise coming from within, telling me the Sculptor was near.

Beron asked, "Do you hear that? Someone else is here. They're hammering."

I glanced at my sister, whose lips parted. "Is it him?" she breathed.

"It is."

"He's *here*?"

"The remnant is here," I corrected. "The Sculptor is with the creation rock. The two are connected somehow, though."

We walked into the only door on the pyramid's immense side and I took them through the winding passages. Shadowfire still lit the corridors, its dark flames steadily burning the torches hanging on the wall but never devouring them.

"Something ancient is here. I feel its presence," Noor whispered.

Caelum quickly agreed. "As can I."

Beron gave my hand a squeeze.

We came to the room where the remnant pool lay. "Do not touch the remnant or drink from its water," I warned. "The Sculptor was very clear about what will happen to anyone who defies this order. I can speak more precisely on the matter if need be, but would prefer you all just agree not to go near it."

"And you?" Beron asked.

My lashes fluttered. "It can't alter me further than it already has."

Noor and Caelum stood transfixed, watching the mercurial water churn. "I can feel its power. This is what I felt," Noor told me, unable to tear her gaze from the remnant.

"It has a heartbeat," Caelum added, his voice filled with awe.

Beron watched me as I strode to the pool. His heart thundered when I stepped into the remnant and cupped a portion into my hand. "I'll be right back," I told him.

In a blink, I stood in the presence of the Sculptor once again. His skin shifted colors from ebony to bone, from sand to soil, then back again. Always shifting, never settling. It was beautiful to behold. He raked the dust from his pale, white hair, keeping his silvery eyes fastened on me.

"You were the right choice, Citali," he told me. "For me *and* for Lumos. Dark sun. Gift of the moon. Asena. Queen of Wolves."

His moved his tools to one weathered palm, then held out the other in invitation. I poured what I'd brought of the remnant pool into it. He crouched down, careful of his rusty, ragged gown, and touched the soil. Then he dragged the rest of the chromatic liquid from our world to this place, where it surrounded the creation rock.

One thing had bothered me since the moment I saw the remnant in the Shadow Lands. "Why did you give this to Anubis?"

"For you," he replied simply. "Though, he had it for quite some time."

"Did he ask anyone else to drink it?"

He shook his head. "He would have offered it to Elara, but it was not his to use as he pleased. I warned him against abusing the power given to him for protection and preservation when he began contemplating allowing her to partake of it and taste eternity."

"He said he often came here and spoke to you."

"When I allowed it, and only for as long as it took to push him toward you. You have been on my mind for a very long time, Citali."

I shook my head, perplexed. "Why wait? Why not make me long ago and stop this before it got out of hand?"

"Because it was not your time," the Sculptor chided. "*Now* is your time. You were born for the present and future, not for the past." He looked back to the creation rock. "I must get back to work. There is much to do."

"Can you help me with the spirits? I don't know how to shepherd them. I know nothing," I lamented.

He smiled. "I am always sculpting, Citali. My chisel will guide you."

Before I could thank him, I was back in the room, standing in the middle of a now-empty stone pool. "The remnant is gone," Caelum marveled.

"The Sculptor took it away," I told him. Beron offered a hand and I climbed from the pool that had changed me so completely.

For the briefest second, I wondered if I'd been changed at all. Anubis claimed he was simply awakening what was already inside me. Maybe the Sculptor simply allowed the remnant to unlock and unleash what had long lain dormant.

"What other secrets does the pyramid hold?" Noor asked.

"It's empty. Most rooms have nothing in them. It's..." I wrinkled my nose, "odd."

Beron swallowed. "Did he hurt you?"

"When he hurt you, yes," I answered truthfully. Anubis had injured Beron's soul, and by extension injured mine. I loved him so much it frightened me. The love I had for the Wolven was different than what I'd felt for Merik. This was all-consuming; as if the Sculptor had made us for one another.

I wondered if he had.

He'd chiseled Anubis away, only to leave a perfect sculpture of me, Reyan, and Beron. I could almost see it.

"He didn't try anything...?" Beron led.

I let out a long breath. "No. Even though he told me I was made for him more times than I can count, I think he did that, not to convince me, but to convince himself. Anubis was still in love with a girl who died long ago. He wanted to take her spirit away from Sol and bring it here."

Noor raked her lip through her teeth. "When will you reclaim the spirits?"

"Soon, but not tonight. Someone special prepared a fabulous feast and I don't want wayward spirits to show up unannounced," I punctuated with a wink.

Noor glanced at Caelum and they seemed to share a thought. "When you decide it's time, we will help any way we can."

I gave a wan smile. "I appreciate the offer, but this is a path you cannot walk with me. No one can."

# 33

Before we left the Shadow Lands, I absorbed the shade that blocked the sky. Sol did not tread here, but if she moved this way, she could see it now. Her heat and light could reach it, and the spirits who wanted to rest in this place would still see her cresting in the sky above them.

Sol glowed just below the horizon. Orange bled into the azure overhead.

No stars glittered in the sky here. It was solid and sadly empty.

Would Lumos alter his course to fill it? Would all the sky – the world – feel hollow without the stars shining above?

In addition to removing the shadow looming over the land Anubis had claimed for himself, I altered the sea, infusing it with brine. Beron watched as I waded to my waist to set it into motion, waves building and crashing upon the dark shore. He watched as my palms coaxed color from its inky hue, shifting it to the blue of the Wolven's eyes.

Caelum and Noor were quiet, holding onto one another on the shore. They were quiet, but their eyes were troubled.

Perhaps they'd been parted from Sol and Lumos too long and the dark somberness of this land had begun to bother them.

When the sea was changed, I took them home through the shadow.

Reyan was dressed in a pleated, golden kilt Noor had commissioned just for him. He loped around the room as my sister and I dressed for the feast. She was dressing for her role as Aten, also in pleated gold. "What will you wear?" she asked, fastening a fine strand of sun diamonds to her neck.

I was still in my dressing robe. Grinning, I caught her eye in the mirror she stood in front of. Her hands went still before she guided her last earring through her lobe. Noor smiled back. "What are you thinking?"

I whispered to the shadow and it formed a dark dress alight with shadowfire at its hem. Dark flames licked up the belled skirt to my hips.

Noor's lips parted in surprise and Reyan drew closer. "Will it hurt him?"

Shaking my head, I told her, "It's not true fire. It's not hot, and it's no more real than this…"

From the shade, I conjured a small, tawny cat. My son laughed and immediately began chasing it. I gave it translucent wings and a long, soft mane. "Pretty kitty!" he shrieked, chasing after my conjuring.

"The Sphinx would pin you to the ground if she knew you'd conjured a tiny version of her for Reyan to play with," Noor told me.

I grinned. "She could try."

She shook her head. "I worried for you when he took you from here. I worried he would make you see things, like this shadowfire, that looked so real you couldn't tell they were lies."

"If it weren't for the Sculptor, that's exactly what Anubis would've done. He certainly tried, but the Sculptor spoke to me. He wrote messages to me in the Book of the Dead and challenged me to keep thinking about those who grounded me in reality."

Noor smiled proudly. "I'm so glad you had his favor."

I had it still, but didn't say it.

My sister moved to her powders, dusting her face with a delicate sheen of gold. "Is it difficult?" she quietly asked, pausing to watch my reflection.

"Is what difficult?"

"Being changed."

I nodded once. "I didn't expect it to be. I guess I didn't have time to consider it and all the implications until now."

"Maybe you can speak to the Sculptor and ask him to take your immortality away?"

A sigh slid from my chest, caving it. "He won't. It's part of his design."

I didn't expound and Noor didn't push. We would have plenty of time to talk about everything. Later. When Reyan wasn't around to hear the details.

I bade the shadows to weave my hair into a series of braids that laid over its bulk, winding together like snakes in a den. Then I asked them to line my eyes and turn my lips to dark cherries.

When it was time, I told Reyan that the kitty had to leave for now because it was time to eat. He pouted for a moment, but then let me lift him into my arms. That lasted until he saw Beron in the hall waiting with his Lumin brother. "Up!" my son yelled, stretching toward the dashing Wolven.

Beron and Caelum wore similar black tunics. Caelum's was embroidered with Lumos; Beron's was the same, but with a wolf's profile cutting into Lumos's face.

The Wolven took Reyan and swung him onto his shoulders, dancing around to make him clap. Beron smiled, seemingly as delighted with the game as my son was. And in that moment, my heart settled a little, knowing they shared a crucial commonality: mortality. They would chase each moment of joy like it might be their last, because one day it would be. It would make the triumphs sweeter, the defeats temporary and surmountable. It would make their existence more meaningful and vital.

And I would be there to see it all and live it with them.

Anubis thought that the impatience of a mortal's heart was a flaw, but that wasn't true at all. It was a gift. It kept them pushing toward more moments where they lived instead of merely existed. It kept them busy instead of idle.

It was beautiful.

I smiled at them and Beron's eyes caught mine. The blue glittered. Into my mind he spoke: *Dance with me?*

*Now?* I laughed. *You look a little busy at the moment.*

He smirked, his dimple deliciously denting his cheek. *Not now. Later. I want to formally claim your first dance.*

*Holt will be heartbroken,* I teased.

*He'll survive it.*

*And you wouldn't?* I quirked a brow.

*No. I would not survive rejection from you, Citali. No matter how inconsequential it might seem.*

Caelum and Noor stood and waited patiently as if they knew we were having our own personal conversation. When I looked at my sister, she gestured toward the expansive room where the feast would take place. I heard musicians tuning their instruments, dragging horsehair across strings, plucking chords in rhythms they knew by heart. I could smell the delicious food Noor had asked to be prepared and hear the hands that placed the dishes on the tables. Then I felt Beron's hand slide into mine.

"Ready?"

I nodded. My heart thumped a beat – finally.

With him by my side, his thumb rubbing the back of my hand, it thumped another.

Beron's presence, with his steadfast love and loyalty, brought me to life, while Reyan made it worth living. He kicked against Beron's chest, urging him to go faster. Beron squeezed my hand once and took off, running with Reyan on his shoulders.

Caelum, Noor, and I laughed.

When we drew near the room, I hesitated just outside. Beron stepped inside first, taking Reyan on a trek around the room, introducing him to Luminan priests and his mother, finally meeting up with the pack who was gathered around a large table.

Noor bit the corner of her lip and looked at me curiously. I tried to wave off her concern. "You should go in. I just need a second," I told her.

She shared a look with Caelum, then swept into the room while he lingered beside me.

My chest suddenly constricted and my skin flushed. I didn't feel like I was going to shift, but the feeling was very similar. Like the skin I once wore was too tight again and I needed to burst from it before I died.

"Are you okay, Citali?" Caelum gently asked.

"No, I'm not," I answered honestly. "I feel worried and fearless all at the same time, settled and disturbed, happy and bereft. I feel too much all at once to sort it out and it's making me feel crazy." He looked at his feet, then up at me, the crown of moonlight glowing on his forehead. "Why?" I croaked. "Why show it to me at all? Why now?"

He nodded in understanding. "I felt that way at first, Citali. But given enough time and persistence from the water, silt settles to the river bottom. And right now, you are the river, flooded and spilling over."

"And clouded with silt." That was exactly what it felt like. "I don't want to ruin everyone's night, but I don't know how to step into that room."

He smiled. "Then it's a good thing you have your friend here to enter it with you. *And* to tell you that you don't have to worry beyond the next step. Tomorrow will be there when you reach it, as will next month, next year, and next century… All you need to focus on is right now. This step. This moment. This breath. This heartbeat. Just be present and enjoy it."

I shook my head. "You're so ridiculously nice, Caelum. Do you know that?"

He smiled. "I think that was a compliment."

I took a deep breath. "It definitely was. Thank you. I needed those words more than anything else right now."

He inclined his head and offered his arm. "Shall we?"

I wrapped my arm around his gratefully. "Thank you… friend."

The moment we entered the room, none other than my favorite priest walked by, causing me to forget the blinding silt and drowning emotions. I might have seen him watching my sister. I also might have moved my foot in front of his so that he stumbled most ungraciously before he reached Noor. My sister might have scowled at me and I might have smiled.

Caelum might have had a smile on his lips when he caught and steadied Kiran. Beron might have laughed from across the room, and the pack might have joined him.

Kiran dared to glare at me, though fear soon threaded his eyes. "You should be more careful, Priest, and watch where you're walking instead of gawking at other things…" I warned.

Why Sol did not scorch his infatuation with Noor from his mind, I wasn't sure. I wondered if the Sculptor would eventually regret carving me out, making me immortal, and giving me the great power he bestowed me with… because I didn't have nearly as much restraint as the gods of illumination.

Kiran smoothed his kilt and attempted to hide his embarrassment as he bowed to us and continued through the room – this time, watching his feet instead of my sister.

I glanced up at Caelum. His crown was again hidden, but I could almost see it glowing, a steady pulse beneath his pale skin. "I suppose you'll chastise me for tripping him and tell me it wasn't nice."

The Lumin chuckled. "It was nothing he didn't deserve."

My brow quirked. "Is the Lumin jealous?"

"Not at all," he defended, but not with a straight face.

I danced with Beron and Reyan first, the three of us swaying as Beron held my son. Holt demanded the next dance and Amaris let Reyan grasp her hands and lead her onto the floor, melting when he twisted and twirled.

Holt stepped on my feet at least a dozen times, apologizing twice over. Chase and Red took the formal Luminan waltzes… and that left the Helioan music. Padren and Malia danced with Reyan while I took the Wolven to the floor. Much to his mother's chagrin, a crowd formed around us.

As we moved as one, I could finally see that what Chase had described was true. Helioan dances were far more sensual than those from Lumina. They were choreographed for touch, for barely-there grazes, flirtatious looks, and Beron's smirks as he ate up the attention I paid him.

Speaking of Chase, he grinned like a wolf from his seat at the table and raised a glass when Beron and I caught our breath between dances.

That night, we feasted together, seated as a pack comprised of wolves and blood and friends. For a while, I forgot tomorrow and only allowed the next moment to matter, just as Caelum advised.

It was glorious.

At the end of the night, I carried Reyan to my rooms and laid him in bed while Beron pulled back the covers for my son.

Both of us were still giddy, unable to stop smiling, riding the high the evening had provided. He and I swept onto the balcony where Lumos cast his pale rays on us.

"Asena," Beron breathed, gently clasping my waist and reeling me in. *She-wolf.* My shadowfire gown flared and flickered in his eyes. "Dark sun. Gift of the moon. Fire of my heart," he rasped, kissing my lips tenderly. "Queen of Wolves."

He took something from his trouser pocket. It was a silver cuff inlaid with fangs and claws, and I couldn't help but smile. The Sphinx was right, after all. *Queen of Wolves*, she'd dubbed me. Queen of Claws and Teeth.

My immortal heart thumped, swelled in my chest, and struggled toward my Wolven. His brows furrowed as he fidgeted "I want the rest of my heartbeats to be yours."

I held my arm out for him to place his cuff before he could finish the words. "The rest of mine will be yours, too."

"But your heart will live forever," he argued. "You'll eventually forget me."

"I could never forget you, Beron. We are mated. That's not something I could ever forget. It's not inconsequential – to me."

"It's everything," he breathed. "It's everything to me, Citali."

I smiled. "Good. Then hold your arm out so I may place *my* cuff upon it, and thus, mark my territory…"

Beron grinned. "Such a wolfish thing to do."

I shrugged playfully as I drew a line around his bicep. Shadow slid into his skin and an undulating wave moved through his flesh, until I blew on it and it caught fire. "Shadowfire. A piece of me. Just as the cuff you placed on my arm is a piece of you."

He kissed me until I was drunk with the feel of his soft lips and confident hands, as the god of the moon moved to allow room for Sol, until he pulled himself away and promised we would have many full and busy nights together soon.

# 34

The Sculptor promised that Sol and Lumos would help when I asked for guidance and he was right. The gods of illumination answered my questions and patiently explained how things were before Anubis tried to throw off the balance.

The spirits walking the earth needed help staying grounded. In times past, the earth spun so fast that its force kept them from drifting away. When the earth spun, Sol and Lumos did not have to move about as they did now. They set themselves in the sky and the spinning world made it appear as if Sol rose and set, and as if Lumos traveled the night sky, his face changing nightly to form phases.

When the world went still, Sol and Lumos used their power to press the spirits wearing flesh tightly to the sand and soil, but only my power could set the world into motion again.

The moment they said it, I instinctively knew how it had to be done. The Sculptor guided me still.

Gathering the shadows came easily to me, as did guiding them to set the earth in motion. Lumos and Sol were glad for this change. They were powerful, but even gods grew tired.

And after fulfilling their purposes and Anubis's as well, the two needed a long, restorative rest.

Sol and Lumos eclipsed on the day the spirits were sent to me, descending from the sky like small wisps of clouds at first, then pouring like a torrential storm. There were so many I should have been overwhelmed, but the Sculptor chiseled the doubt and fear from me. I had embraced my power, accepted my shadows, and was ready to usher the souls toward the Shadow Lands.

That was to be their home, a calm place to rest, though the world was theirs to walk as well. They were free to roam, guide their descendants, and enjoy an eternity of peace.

At the base of the obsidian pyramid, I found Beron and Caelum's father among them. He introduced himself and told me to be patient with his wife before fading away.

Then I found Merik, who told me he was proud of all I'd done, and that all was finally well because of me. His optimism nearly choked me. He told me he loved me, and I told him I had loved him, too. When I told him stories about Reyan, it seemed to give him purpose. He left me then and set out walking in the direction of Helios to go see his son.

Finally, I found my mother. She knew me immediately and told me how she'd watched me grow and mature into the woman I was now. She saw me survive things no one should have had to, but she also saw me triumph. When she tried to hold me, I felt her cool touch for the briefest moment. That was when I understood the warmth she once had was gone. I'd never felt her arms around me, and I never would in the way I needed. A heavy weight settled on my chest with the realization.

I only trailed away from her when Zarina approached us.

Her spirit looked as she did when she was healthy, and I was beyond glad spirits didn't take the last form the flesh holding them had taken. Zarina was finally at peace. She told me as much, but I didn't need to hear the words when I could see it in the unhurried, easy way she walked, mirrored in her calm expression.

I promised them all I would be back soon and told them that the House of Mirages was theirs. The island was theirs. The sea, too. The world itself. I told them they were free to wander the earth as they pleased and urged the dead to once again guide the living.

The fact that the spirits were at peace chased away my apprehension. I wasn't afraid to leave them in the Shadow Lands, but I couldn't tarry among the spirits when my loved ones' hearts still beat. While they lived, my purpose lay with them. Once they were gone, I had an eternity to spend in the shade with the dead.

I returned to Helios and went to Reyan, finding him peering at the moonlit sky. Padren held him on their balcony, and even he was quiet. Gathering and shepherding the spirits, setting the world spinning – it had taken far less time than I imagined it might, though it had taken another day from my son. Another I would have to strive to make up for.

"What's wrong, Reyan?" I asked, holding my hands out to him. He stretched toward me and let me hold him on my hip.

"Stars gone," he said sadly. "All gone."

I looked up at the empty sky, surprised that it made me ache to see it devoid of the night diamonds I had come to love and appreciate.

"Reyan," I began, unsure of my words. "Do you know who you are to me? And who I am to you?" Reyan's lip began to quiver and his big eyes welled with tears. "Don't be sad," I whispered. "I am your mother, Reyan. And you are my son. And there is nothing in this world I would not do for you."

He hugged my neck. "Mother?"

I nodded against him, then held his head to my chest and confirmed it again. "You are my son and I am your mother. And I love you more than there are stars in the sky."

"Stars gone," he said again.

"Look again, baby. They aren't gone at all…" I said, offering a watery smile.

My shadows slid upward, then broke apart into a thousand dark pieces. They were nothing but wisps, barely visible against the blue, until I bade them to turn their forms into countless sparkling crystals.

I had set the world into motion today, and now, the world would glide by the stars I made and it would appear like they were moving, just as it would appear that Sol and Lumos still raced and arced over our heads, though they were still and finally able to rest and just be the light they were sculpted to be.

"I love you more than anything, Reyan," I told him.

Reyan's chin stopped wobbling. He wiped his tears away and beamed a smile at Padren, who returned the expression. My son pointed at the sparkling stars and yelled for Malia to come and see them. "Stars back!" he yelled. "Malia, stars back!"

Malia joined us on the balcony. "What's all the fuss out here, sweet Reyan?"

Padren laughed. "Nothing much. Just Citali returning the stars to the sky."

To them, it seemed like I'd done exactly that. In truth, my shadows had conjured them. They were no spirits set like jewels in the sky now; they were merely the product of a mirage. I had become the spinner of illusions, a thought that unsettled me as much as the mirage of stars made my family happy.

Noor and I watched the river slide past. The eddying currents churned and twisted, dipped and folded, but the strong water continued to flow southward. Never hesitating. Never unsure. Across the bank, a crocodile lazily slid from the sand into the water, keeping close to the reeds to disguise itself.

The earth moved so that Sol appeared to set, and the horizon glowed a beautiful gold, as close as nature could come to the glow that lay within my sister. The wind toyed with our matching dark hair as it caused the reeds to sway.

"You wanted to talk?" she prodded.

"I'm ready to go home, Noor."

Her brows met. "But… you *are* home."

I shook my head.

"Do you want to go to the Shadow Lands?"

I shook my head again. "I want to go to the House of Wolves. You are my family, Noor. My sister and my blood. But they are my pack and they're family, too. They miss their home, and so do I."

Her shoulders fell from their usual regal pose. "I understand."

"You and Caelum need time to do what you set out to do in the first place: unite the kingdoms and build a new House together. I expect grandeur from a home named the 'House of Eclipses', just so you know."

"Could anything be as grand as an obsidian pyramid?" she asked sincerely.

I smiled. "Truthfully, I prefer the House of Wolves' rugged timbers. I want to live there for a time. There will be plenty of time for the House of Mirages… later."

She nodded in understanding, then her eyes slid to my arm. "It's about time you exchanged cuffs," she said, a grin stretching over her lips.

I flexed my bicep to see it again. "With the mate bond, I didn't know if cuffs would matter to Beron."

"He was human for more years than he's been the Wolven, and you can't deny that he's a bit possessive of his mate." When she laughed, it was a foreign but welcome sound, one I still wasn't completely used to hearing but wanted to hear again and again.

"Not as bad as I expected, actually. I enjoy riling him."

Noor grinned. "You always have."

I clasped her hands. "I'll come and visit often. I will miss you, Noor."

She turned to me. "You're just a portal away from me, and I'm just a shadow away from you."

I hugged my sister to my side and held her there. She draped her arms over my shoulder and leaned her head on mine.

"I saw my mother and Zarina," I whispered. "I saw Merik."

Her arms tensed. "Are they okay?"

"They're perfectly at peace, completely content."

She relaxed again. "Good. I hope you can find peace one day, too, Citali."

I told Beron I was ready to go home – to the House of Wolves – and for a moment, he was quiet, as if he was waiting for me to laugh and tell him I was only kidding. Then he asked me if I was serious.

I was.

With a stunned, happy look on his face, he relayed the message to the pack. In my mind came four distinct voices, all exuberant. Chase whooped and said *It's about time!* Red offered a *Yesssssssss*. Holt gave a quiet grunt of acceptance and Amaris squealed.

Vada, who'd been staying at the House of the Sun since the evening of the feast, decided it was time for her to return to Lumina. That evening, she approached me and Beron in the courtyard. Reyan chased the tiny Sphinx across the stone as Padren and Malia laughed and urged him on. Vada spoke quietly to Beron, but I couldn't focus on her or what she was saying to him because my attention was fixed on the man standing just behind her. The man looked like he could be Caelum and Beron's older brother. Lumos had borrowed his likeness once, the first time he'd appeared to me, but this spirit belonged to Beron's father.

"What is it?" Vada asked, glancing behind her carefully.

"Your husband is here with you," I muttered to her.

"Father?" Beron choked, looking all around.

His father gave me a message, which I relayed. "He wanted to see you both. He just came from visiting Caelum."

"He said that?" Beron asked.

"Not in words. It's… I can somehow feel his thoughts. He doesn't need to speak."

Beron's emotions roared through me like the winds of an intense gale. Sadness, happiness, exhaustion… His father could feel them, too. He was sad to provoke such a heavy response. He would leave now and return when Beron was more settled. "He's going back to the Shadow Lands now, but he will return to see you again soon." Vada turned, searching for him behind her, but her husband had faded into the shadows. "He's gone."

A tear escaped her eye, but she gracefully brushed it away before clearing her throat. "Thank you, Citali." Her eyes flicked to the cuff on my arm, then to Beron's. She gave me a soft smile.

Beron left with her to find Caelum, who intended to travel to Lumina with his mother for a time. I knew it would be a short visit. He and Noor did not like to be apart. I knew the feeling; the absence of Beron stretched between us with each step he took.

"Oh, to be so in love that you miss him the moment he leaves," Malia mused, half-teasing. "I remember those days."

"You do not," Padren fussed.

"Don't tell me what I know!" she insisted, waving him off. "I'm happy for you, Noor."

I thanked her, unable to fight the smile Beron always left in his wake. He *did* make me happy.

Holding onto one another, we moved through shadow from the land of arid heat and sand to the land of mountains and trees that dripped green needles, to air so fresh it was almost too sharp to breathe sometimes, and water so blue as it crashed over the rocks, I wondered how it got its color.

The pack was relieved to be home, infused with newfound energy and excited to be on familiar ground. Reyan was happy to be back, too. He ran around the House hiding and surprising an unsurprised Padren who played his part well, pretending to be astounded every time Reyan popped his head up from behind a table, chair, or fireplace.

Beron chatted with Holt as Red cooked a meal worth gorging on, without burning a single piece of our food. He teased me, asking if I wanted to handle the baking in the morning. I declined for everyone's sake, and the pack, scattered throughout the House, shouted their relieved thanks that I'd turned down his offer.

*Traitors.*

After a delicious meal together, and after the laughter and comradery faded and the quiet night called, Malia and Padren put Reyan down to sleep. They would watch over him tonight.

I stepped onto the porch and joined the pack.

To release some steam and enjoy the night air, the wolves wanted to run together beneath Lumos. This would be my first outing with them in wolf form, and I thrummed with an untapped energy that could only be described as a frenetic buzzing in my bones and want in my gut.

Red and Chase playfully fought in the yard, Red faking a kick and Chase throwing an elbow. Amaris groaned at their antics. She stood with Holt and Beron, who grinned as I closed the door and joined them on the lawn.

Lumos shone brightly overhead. He seemed to move closer, and I felt that familiar tension building in my bones. He called me. He called all of us, his wolves.

Holt was first to shift. Beron quickly followed, then turned to face me. It was then that I saw the claw marks I'd marred him with the first and only time I'd shifted. I covered my mouth in shame. "I didn't know I scarred you," I told him.

*I look even better with the scars.*

I swore his wolf smirked, pleased with his new slashes. They glowed like Caelum's moonlight crown, a pale, whitish-blue gray, almost as if Lumos himself had made the gashes and left his essence emblazoned in Beron's skin.

Chase shifted. Amaris did, too.

Then Red.

I was the only one left standing on two legs. Their massive heads swiveled to me expectantly and I leaped from the porch, the pads of my wolfen feet meeting the rocky earth. I snarled. *Why are you all so much bigger than me?*

Chase cackled. *You're tiny. What did you expect?*

*Don't worry, Citali. It's not the size of the wolf, but the ferocity of the bite,* Red advised.

Amaris laughed. *Say the ones who feel the need to compensate for their tiny –*

*Enough.* Beron interrupted. *Are we running or what?*

I felt the breeze ruffle my warm fur. Felt my shadowfire ignite. Holt laughed and pawed at Chase. *Quit gawking at her.*

*Where are we racing to?* I asked my pack.

*Another race, Citali? Do you wish to lose to me as a wolf, too?* Chase goaded.

*To the river. First one there howls,* Beron challenged, cutting him off. *Go!*

We took off, our claws shredding the earth, propelling our massive bodies forward. My muscles burned, unfamiliar but right. Trees and boulders blurred as I pushed faster. And then… through the shadows Lumos's bright face cast from the trees, I disappeared, howling when my paws splashed into the cold mountain water.

Beron met me a full minute later. *How?*

My gums pulled back as I grinned. *I thought I told you once never to underestimate me, Wolven.*

A delicious chuckle filled my mind and something pleasant curled within my stomach.

Chase, Holt, Red, and Amaris caught up quickly, panting and confused. I didn't want them to know my secret just yet, so I kept it, fending off their questions and assumptions until Holt took off into the pines. We followed him, cutting paths through the woods, onto the snow caps and down into the warmer valleys again. We ran for hours.

In wolf form, I felt alive. Free. Invincible.

But I couldn't stay a wolf forever. Before dawn, Beron and I split from the pack and headed toward the hot spring.

He shifted back into human form, standing proudly on the side of the mountain, waiting for me to follow suit. I still wasn't completely used to changing from one form to the next at will, but with some effort, managed to become human again. Beron's eyes fell over me as if seeing me for the first time. And like a woman who let down her hair, allowing it to spill over her shoulders and cascade down her back, I let my shadows loose, asking them to swirl around me so he could see what I truly was now. What I'd become and always would be.

He came to me and placed his hands on either side of my face. Then he kissed me so softly, I almost cried.

"I choose you," Beron whispered.

I brushed his hair back from his face. "I choose you, Beron. And I'll be here… always."

# ACKNOWLEDGEMENTS

I'm ever thankful to God for his mercy and blessings in my life. I thank my family for their constant encouragement, my friends for their support, and fans for loving my characters and stories as much as I do.

A special thanks to Melissa Stevens for designing the perfect book cover, interior, trailer, tarot card and every other thing related to bringing this book to life visually. You are absolute magic and I adore you and am thankful for your friendship and presence in my life.

Thanks to Stacy Sanford for waving her magic red pen over my manuscript and polishing it until it is as fierce as Citali's shadowed flame.

Thanks to Steffani Christensen for illustrating the gorgeous night dune scene featuring Beron and Citali, along with our terrible, beautiful Sphinx and sly, handsome Wolven. I love your creativity and working with you is effortless.

Thanks to @NessiArts for illustrating a portrait of our favorite couple. You captured them beautifully and I'm so excited to finally share your work with the world.

Thanks to Cristie Alleman, Stephanie Christensen and Amber Garcia for reading this book before anyone else and helping me make the story better. I appreciate your time and keen eyes.

Lastly, thanks to you, the reader. Whether you're a member of the Bondtourage Reader Group, social media stalker – er, follower – or this is your first Bond book, I appreciate you reading the story that bled from my soul.

# ABOUT THE AUTHOR

Casey L. Bond lives on a rural farm in West Virginia with her husband and their two beautiful daughters. She writes phoenixes – gloriously flawed and morally gray characters that fiercely rise from the ashes of their circumstances. World building is one of her favorite hobbies, along with stamping metal jewelry, swimming, and enjoying the beauty of nature. She thinks thunderstorms are better than coffee and that watching a meteor shower is the closest thing to magic you might ever see. She's a firm believer that every amazing book needs a world you want to wrap yourself in, a character you want to win, and a love you would fight for.

Learn more about her work at www.authorcaseybond.com

www.ingramcontent.com/pod-product-compliance
Lightning Source LLC
Chambersburg PA
CBHW020342310726
48979CB00015B/2474/J

* 9 7 8 1 0 8 7 9 1 4 5 3 4 *